THE WAR NO ONE WANTED

WAR OF THE SUBMARINE: BOOK 2

R.G. ROBERTS

Copyright © 2023 by R.G. Roberts

All rights reserved.

No part of this publication may be reproduced, distributed, or transmitted in any form or by any means, including photocopying, recording, or other electronic or mechanical methods, without the prior written permission of the publisher, except as permitted by U.S. copyright law. For permission requests, contact R.G. Roberts at www.rgrobertswriter.com.

The story, all names, characters, and incidents portrayed in this production are fictitious. No identification with actual persons (living or deceased), places, buildings, and products is intended or should be inferred.

Originally published on Kindle Vella as season 2 of *War of the Submarine*.

Cover designed by MiblArt.

To every reader who waited a little too long for this one while it refused to be written in the right order.

Thank you.

Contents

	Prologue: Thornback	1
1.	Stepping Up	11
2.	Bad Tactics	21
3.	Moray	29
4.	Paying the Piper	39
5.	Personal Boogeymen	47
6.	Once Over Dust	55
7.	Twice Over Rust	65
8.	The Unexpected	75
9.	Mountains to Climb	87
10.	Pissing Contests	97
11.	Winds of Change	109
12.	Good Old Boys' Club	119
13.	If It Ain't Broke	133
14.	Homecoming	147
15.	Farewells	163
16.	Everything Old is New Again	175
17.	Problem Child	189
18.	Second Chances	201
19.	First Shot	211
20.	Sprint and Drift	227

21.	Blood in the Water	235
22.	So Others May Live	247
23.	Bull in the China Shop	261
24.	Laying Traps	275
25.	Someone Else's Mess	287
26.	Eternal Patrol	299
27.	Changing Tides	309
28.	Old School	321
29.	Old Friends	329
30.	Sacrificial Lambs	343
31.	Suicide Mission	361
32.	Old but Golden	373
33.	Bad Luck and Worse	385
34.	Declaring Victory Too Soon	399
Epilogue: Distinguished Gallantry and Valor		415
Also By		419
About R.G. Roberts		421

Prologue: Thornback

16 April 2038, the mid-Indian Ocean

Attack submarines spent much of their careers spying. USS *Thornback* (SSN-855) was better at it than most, but Lieutenant Commander Toni Platz missed talking to the outside world. A short and stocky woman who played lacrosse at the Academy, she missed clean air, friends, and sports.

As if to spite her love of the outdoors, *Thornback* had spent the last two months parked off the coast of Réunion, a tiny French island hosting a suspicious increase in ship and submarine activity. All of 970 square miles and with a population of under one million, Réunion didn't exist on the U.S. Navy's strategic map until three massive underwater stations cropped up in her vicinity. *Then* Naval Intelligence picked up rumors of a secret French submarine base located there. Sixty-nine days of watching, however, failed to reveal a proverbial smoking gun. Finally released from her watchdog duties, *Thornback* steamed east for thirty hours before heading up to periscope depth and streaming her communications wire.

As the submarine's executive officer, or second-in-command, Toni managed the boat's daily schedule. She also dealt with administrative minutia, which meant everything was her problem.

"I was thinking about a swim call." Commander Duane Elliot, *Thornback's* CO, leaned against the navigation table in the sub's control room, one ankle crossed in front of the other. He was tall—too tall for submarines—leggy, and one of the best-looking blondes Toni'd ever met. "We've been cooped up too long."

Toni grinned. "You mean you want to air out that peculiar smell of bacon and Vaseline."

Every sub had a scent. *Thornback,* although a brand-spanking new *Cero-*class on her first deployment, was already pungent. *Someone—*Toni never ferreted out who—packed away a case of Vaseline right next to a hot water heater in the chiefs' berthing. Within a week, the smell permeated the hull, and *Thornback* became known as the "Vaconator."

"Perish the thought." Elliot laughed. "I've grown fond of it."

Toni snorted. "Pull the other one, Captain."

Before she could say more, the radio watchstander approached, message tablet in hand and wide-eyed. "XO?"

"Something wrong, Wang?" Toni asked.

"Flash traffic." Wang gulped.

Toni grabbed the tablet, pulling up the first flash message. *Two?* The navy hadn't sent multiple flash messages since September 11, 2001, thirty-seven years earlier. Toni was *born* in 2001, so she'd never even seen a real flash message, just fake ones for drills. This one made her heart try to hammer out of her throat. *Flash* was the highest precedence for naval messages, meant to be used for enemy contact or national emergencies.

Her eyes swept over the message.

Enterprise Strike Group encountered Kilo-*class submarine in Strait of Malacca.* Kilo *assumed hostile and sunk. Indian Naval forces attacked without warning. Enterprise CSG engaged by two Indian carriers and escorts.*

USS Kidd *and USS* John Finn *sunk. USS* Belleau Wood *has* Enterprise *in tow...*

"Holy shit," she whispered. No nation dared fire on American warships since Vietnam. Engaging a carrier was suicide!

Two destroyers sunk. Toni's stomach churned and acid bubbled in her mouth; she swallowed it down. The XO couldn't look weak, not even when faced with news like this.

She'd known the world was creeping closer to war. Everyone had. But they'd expected war with *China,* only to have the Pacific behemoth explode into a four-way civil war after the communists threatened Taiwan one too many times. *Enterprise* had been on her way there, Toni remembered. How had they managed to sink an Indian submarine instead of engaging Chinese forces?

What kind of ever-loving cluster happened in the Strait of Malacca? Shaking herself, Toni opened the update to that message—and immediately wished she hadn't.

Enterprise sunk. *Kidd* and *John Finn* with her. *Belleau Wood* and *Fletcher* survived, just a single cruiser and destroyer, but they'd been pounded and were out of missiles. Two Indian frigates were reported sunk, but both of their carriers were combat effective. Now the *Indian* strike group patrolled the Strait of Malacca, closing it to American ships, while *Fletcher* and *Belleau Wood* limped away.

It was the navy's worst defeat since World War II.

Nausea churned in Toni's stomach, and she tasted acid as she almost threw up. How many were dead? How many were people she *knew*? And how in the world would the politicians explain this to the public? *Enterprise* alone had a crew of over two thousand... Were they all dead?

She rubbed her eyes with a shaking hand. This was unbelievable. What kind of idiot shot at the wrong nation's submarine? And what kind of trigger-happy moron on the Indian side started a *battle* instead of looking for a diplomatic solution? Sure, tensions were high. *Thornback* wasn't rolling around out here by accident. Everyone wanted territory out in the Indian Ocean, with underwater stations popping up on every corner ridge and valley. Resources were plentiful, and no one really policed who got what. But *shooting*?

Toni's eyes flicked back to the tablet, dread coiling in her chest. There was another, newer, message—one from just three hours earlier. Hands trembling, Toni clicked to open it.

FLASH FLASH FLASH

151900Z APR 2038

TO: ALL UNITS

FM: CINC

OPREP 3 PINNACLE

RMKS/1. UNITS OF INDIAN NAVY SANK 2 US-FLAGGED MERCHANT VESSELS WITHOUT WARNING. SURVIVORS RECOVERED BY HMAS HUNTER.

2. FRENCH FORCES CAPTURED ARMISTICE STATION, INDEPENDENT INTERNATIONAL UNDERWATER SETTLEMENT, SINKING USNS AMELIA EARHART T-AKE 6 AND EXPELLING ALL AMERICAN, BRITISH, AUSTRALIAN, AND CANADIAN NTATIONALS.

3. CONGRESS PASSED DECLARATION OF WAR AT 1600Z 15APR2038.

4. INDIA AND FRANCE DECLARED WAR ON UNITED STATES AT 1800Z 15APR2038.

5. ALL FRENCH AND INDIAN NAVAL ASSETS TO BE CONSIDERED HOSTILE. //

Toni felt like her voice came from a thousand years away. "The Indians attacked the *Enterprise* CSG, and Congress declared war."

"What?" Commander Elliot's head snapped up.

"They declared war," she repeated. "First time since World War II. We couldn't even make it a hundred years, could we?"

"Fuck me," Elliot whispered.

Everyone in the attack center, or "conn," stared. Elliot's eyes were wide and lost, and if her captain was lost, where was she? Could this be a prank? It couldn't be real. Tensions were high in the Indian Ocean; the French liked to flex their muscles, and the Indians bossed everyone around like they were the Queens of Sheba, but no one wanted war!

This was World War I all over again, with treaties crisscrossing the world, separating countries into alliances.

"At least it's just India and France," Elliot said. "The odds won't be in our favor, but we're better trained. Beats fighting with China."

"As long as they stay in that civil war they started." Toni grimaced. China invading Taiwan had been coming for years, and *that* was the war the U.S. Navy trained for. Except that fight had somehow become a four- or five-way civil war that no one else wanted a part of.

But now they were supposed to fight *India* and *France*? How had that happened?

In hindsight, Toni might remember that the pot had started boiling the moment humanity began exploiting underwater resources. The Indian Ocean was rich in oil, gold, manganese, copper, nickel, and other resources. Everyone wanted a piece of the pie.

Most countries didn't want to share.

At least the U.S. finally got on the naval buildup bus, albeit years later than their now-enemies. *Thornback* was the result of America's efforts, commissioned just last year and the last of the *Cero*-class nuclear attack submarines. Her newer sisters were Improved-*Ceroes*. Both classes were the successors of the *Virginia*-class submarines designed in the early 2000s and built over the next two decades. Like the *Virginias*, they were multi-mission attack submarines, able to spy, fight, and deploy special forces without reconfiguring.

Thornback was 389 feet of sleek fighting power, with four torpedo tubes, a vertical launch system for twelve missiles, and a crew of a bit over one hundred thirty. Her weapons room could store up to twenty-eight torpedoes or Harpoon missiles, three more than the *Virginias*. Thankfully, the sensitive nature of their mission meant ten of those torpedoes were war shots.

"We need to find somewhere to arm up." Toni bit her lip. "We need real torpedoes. A lot of them."

"We need orders, too." Elliot swallowed.

Toni did some quick mental math. "It's seven a.m. at home now. You think anyone's awake to send orders, or do we go deep and maintain stealth until we get to Diego Garcia?"

Diego Garcia was what the navy called the British Indian Ocean Territory. The U.S. partially leased it from the Brits, and it was the closest place that *might* have weapons for them.

Close being two days away.

"Let's head—"

"Conn, Sonar, new submerged contact bearing zero-zero-four," Chief Hale's voice blared out from the intercom to Toni's right. "Got it on the lateral array and the dome, recommend coming left to determine range."

"Sonar, Conn, any idea on classification?" Elliot asked.

"Conn, Sonar, negative. This puppy's super quiet. Holding him is touch and go."

"Standby," Elliot replied, staring at the intercom like it might bite him.

Toni blinked as her captain turned to look at her. Shouldn't they turn? She cleared her throat. "Coming left would head us in the right direction for Diego Garcia."

"And close the distance on this contact." Elliot fidgeted. "There's not supposed to be any other American subs in this area..."

"You think it could be an enemy?" A cold chill tore down her spine. They were at war. The rules were different, weren't they?

Why the hell hadn't anyone sent them updated orders? *All French and Indian naval assets to be considered hostile.* Those words were as useful as a hole in the head. Were they allowed to shoot?

What if the contact was some neutral third party?

Elliot gulped, his face pale. "I—I don't know."

"What do you want to do, Captain?" she asked gently. Decisions were his job; executing them was hers. But he just *stared*, stared like he didn't know where he was or what to do.

Oh, no. Was she watching her friend and captain fall apart?

Elliot stuttered wordlessly.

Toni took a deep breath. "Let's come around to identify this new contact. We'll stay slow until we're sure. Either way, he probably hasn't heard us, so we're safe."

Everyone knew American submarines were the quietest in the world. They had plenty of time to make decisions.

"Go ahead," Elliot whispered. Toni resisted the urge to shake him, instead passing the order to the Officer of the Deck.

Once that was done, she stepped up to whisper to Elliot: "You should probably get on the 1MC and tell the crew we're at war."

Huge green eyes met hers. Was Elliot sweating? "Right." He nodded once, twice, four times. "Right. I'll do that."

"We'll be fine, Captain." She forced a smile for him, but her heart pounded madly. Two days to Diego Garcia. It was the lone British/American base in these waters. Could she manage him for that long, or would he snap out of it?

Elliot nodded again. Then again. Finally, he stumbled over to the brackets holding the 1MC, or general announcing system, microphone. Elliot picked it up with the enthusiasm of a man announcing his own funeral.

"Conn, Sonar, high speed screws!" Chief Hale could be heard without the intercom. "Torpedo in the water, bearing three-five-three!"

Elliot froze.

"Captain?" Toni asked. He didn't move; she poked him in the arm. "*Captain?*"

"Conn, Sonar, torpedo is homing! Estimated range four thousand yards, speed five-zero knots!"

"Captain, *do something!*" Seconds ticked by; the torpedo raced forward at fifty knots. From that close, the torpedo needed less than two-and-a-half minutes to reach them. Elliot still stood in the middle of the compartment, pale, wide-eyed, and with his mouth hanging open. Toni ordered: "Ahead flank! Hard right rudder!"

"Ahead flank, aye!" The sailor at the helm seemed to be waiting for the order. "My rudder is right hard, no new course given."

Thornback rolled into the right turn, heading away from the incoming torpedo. She picked up speed slowly, the deck vibrating gently under Toni's feet. The sub's top speed was fifty-two knots if they didn't strain the reactor. She could outrun the torpedo—if she could pick up speed fast enough. Ignoring her frozen captain, Toni leaned into the intercom.

"Maneuvering, Conn, I need everything you have, and I need it now!" she said.

"Conn, Maneuvering, what the hell is going on up there?" the Engineering Officer of the Watch asked.

Toni gaped. They hadn't gone to battle stations. No one knew. Why wasn't Elliot doing *anything?*

"We've got a torpedo on our tail," she snapped into the intercom, then turned to the Chief of the Watch. "Sound battle stations!"

"Aye, ma'am!"

The donging of *Thornback's* general alarm filled the cramped space; Toni ignored it and looked at the navigation plot. A bright red icon represented the torpedo on their tail, and it looked close.

"Sonar, Conn, range to torpedo?" she asked.

"One thousand yards, still closing!" Chief Hale's voice was high, too high. "Computer identifies it as a French F21 Artemis torpedo."

"Very well." Her throat was tight.

The torpedo was almost directly on their heels. *Thornback* passed twenty knots. A thirty-knot speed difference bought them almost a minute. Could *Thornback* speed up fast enough? The engineers would have to take the reactor to full power and shift the reactor coolant pumps to fast speed. By the book, that took several minutes.

Nuclear engineers were not trained to cut corners. Nuclear engineers were trained to follow the checklist every time. Toni knew that because she was one of them, and nothing in training prepared her for this. How the *hell* had they let a French submarine get so close? The French weren't supposed to be this quiet!

"We need to contact someone." Elliot stumbled a step toward Toni. "Let them know what happened."

"Radio, is the comms wire still out?" Toni asked.

"Negative, XO. Snapped off when we turned and sped up."

"Very well." Toni swallowed. What would they say, anyway?

"Conn, Sonar, impact in thirty seconds!"

"Pass the word to brace for impact!" Elliot ordered. He was finally in the game. Too little, too late.

The Chief of the Watch made the announcement anyway. They were trained to, just like they were trained to escape a sinking submarine.

Instructors never mentioned the escape methods probably wouldn't work. Everyone knew that.

"Fifteen seconds!"

Toni moved left and braced against a bulkhead for balance, flexing her knees. *Lock your knees and break your legs*, the training group always said.

Elliot met her eyes. "I'm sorry, Toni."

She swallowed. "Me, too."

"Five seconds!"

The F21 Artemis' high-powered PBX B2211 warhead exploded just aft of *Thornback*, shredding the submarine's propulsor, ripping her rudder off, destroying both aft sonar arrays, and bending her stern planes. The shock wave pitched the boat forward as the explosion breached *Thornback's* HY80 steel hull. It punched into her ballast and trim tanks, continuing into her engine compartment. Water flooded in on the heels of the shockwave, bubbling through the engine room and into the maneuvering room, drowning any watchstander the explosion left alive.

The transverse bulkhead between Maneuvering and the reactor compartment crumbled, allowing the sea to meet *Thornback's* 150-megawatt S10G reactor. The reactor went into auto-shutdown immediately, but its energy wasn't needed to destroy the submarine.

The torpedo's shockwave was enough. Welds burst and metal bent; the last thing Toni Platz saw was water rushing into the control room while people screamed.

USS *Thornback's* SUBMISS/SUBSUNK buoy activated at 23:09 Greenwich Mean Time, just over seven hours after the United States declared war.

Before noon the next day, Russia declared war on the United States in solidarity with their allies. That evening, the United Kingdom, Australia, Japan, and Canada declared war on the belligerents.

Within days, a free-for-all brewed in the Indian Ocean. France, Russia, and India gobbled up the choicest underwater territory, snatching independently owned stations or those belonging to their enemies. Caught flat-footed, the U.S. struggled to respond, deploying forces half-armed and half-trained. *Thornback's* killer, the French attack submarine *Barracuda*, claimed three more victims in the first week: another two American nuclear subs and one Australian diesel submarine.

Within a month, the war had a name: World War III.

Chapter 1

Stepping Up

29 July 2038, Groton, Connecticut

War or no war, the Sub School looked the same. The same dilapidated brick buildings—the navy's budget never stretched to more beautification than "once over dust, twice over rust"—the same haphazard landscaping, and the same aged but nice portraits inside.

The simulators were high-tech, because the submarine community took training seriously, but they, too, had endured the wrath of penny-pinching bureaucrats. Now there was money aplenty, but what Chief of Naval Operations in their right mind threw it at a schoolhouse? The navy's rapid loss of submarines was a much more immediate problem.

Nearly every sub lost meant a crew lost, which wreaked havoc with the American submarine community's meticulous personnel detailing. The executive officer, or second-in-command, of a sunken boat, couldn't very well move on to become the commanding officer of another submarine, not if his or her new address was on the bottom of the Indian Ocean. The Bureau of Personnel scrambled to keep up, swapping people's jobs, moving this commander here and that commander there—generally playing ping pong with senior officers detailed to command a submarine.

An elbow jammed into his ribcage in greeting; Commander Teresa O'Canas grinned. She was slender and sharp in her khaki uniform, with dark, curly hair she kept short in lieu of battling it into an acceptable navy hairstyle. Teresa bounced up and down on her toes.

"You gonna paint a picture of Ballard Hall, or you just going to stare like an idiot?"

"Figured the idiot was more up my alley." Commander Alex Coleman chuckled and shoved his hands into his pockets. "I was starting to think you'd gotten cold feet."

"Me? Nah. I keep my butterflies firmly sealed inside my stomach, thank you very much." Teresa gestured at the double doors leading into the brick building. Ballard Hall had felt like their home away from home for months; Alex spent more time here than he did with his family, training, training, and more training. "Time to go find out our fates."

"I suppose it is." Alex tried not to chew his lower lip. Keeping his hands in his pockets, breach of military discipline or no, hid how his palms sweated, but keeping a good friend from noticing his nerves proved harder.

Alex Coleman was a depressingly normal fellow, with short blond hair kept as long as Navy regs allowed. If you asked Alex, his blue eyes were his best feature. That was only because you couldn't see his brain from the outside. He was of average height and skinny enough to eat an entire buffet and not notice a pound gained. There was a swimmer's muscle under the slim exterior, however; Alex might hate to run, but he loved to dive.

Not that it helped him right now.

Teresa shot him a curious look. "You look like you swallowed a lemon. Why so worried? Even if you bomb the test, you're at the top of the class. Navy'd be dumb to give you some trash hauler to command."

"The navy doesn't *have* trash-hauling submarines."

"Don't be so sure of that. They delayed *Jimmy Carter's* decommissioning." Together, they walked into Ballard Hall, crossing the quarterdeck into the heart of the Submarine Commander's Course. Teresa flashed her badge at the watch, snickering. "'Course, since none of us knows how to drive a *Seawolf*-class, they'll have to pull some grandpa off his retirement couch to command her."

Alex snorted. "Some Cold War relic can't do worse than the rest of us are doing."

"No shit."

Alex and Teresa were set to join the ranks of the elite. Everyone, every*where*, knew that the American submarine force was the best of the best. Years of training went into crafting each commanding officer into a combination of an astute warfighter and a top-notch engineer. Yet three months into the war, the United States already lost *half* the subs initially deployed.

The fact that most of those subs were lost due to bad decisions by their commanding officers was the worst-kept secret in the navy.

Up one set of stairs and two right turns brought them to the classroom housing SOAC Class 2038-2. It was a utilitarian room, painted a neutral blue. Dry Erase boards lined the walls on each side, covered in reminders and exam notes. To Alex's left, there was the *Wall of Honor*: the list of subs (and their COs, by default) with the most kills of the war. The subs on the bottom half of the list were all on the bottom of the ocean; Alex tried not to look at those. But the ones on the top drew his eye.

1. USS *Moray* SSN 853, CDR Jane Phelps—4 sub, 6 surface

2. USS *Idaho* SSN 799, CDR Kenji Walker—5 sub, 4 surface

3. USS *Skate* SSN 854, CDR Anabella Santiago—5 sub, 2 surface

4. USS *Guam* SSN 813, CDR Rico Sivers—1 sub, 6 surface

Any tendency to look at those totals and dream was dashed by the opposite board, *Those on Eternal Patrol*. One hundred six days into the war, and there were already six subs on that list. Six subs lost with all hands, more than seven hundred fifty sailors lost. *Thornback* could be discarded; they were sunk probably before they knew the war started. But the others... Alex swallowed. *New Hampshire, Colorado, New Jersey, Oregon,* and *Kentucky*. All *Virginia*-class submarines, just like the ones Alex spent his entire career aboard. He looked away from the wall and headed toward his seat.

The classroom held desks for a class of twenty-five, each decorated with one classified computer and dual monitors. The chairs were serviceable but not that comfortable—typical Navy wisdom said that *too* comfortable of a chair would be an invitation to go to sleep. Joke was on them; Alex could sleep *anywhere*, a skill learned due to some misbegotten escapades back in college. Being a submariner only polished that until it shone.

Most of their classmates were already seated, tension hanging over the room like a dark cloud of doom. Alex wasn't the only one worried; even Teresa went quiet. Normally, prospective commanding officers knew what sub they were assigned *months* before starting the training pipeline—but that training pipeline was also usually six months long, instead of the three-and-a-half months they were three days away from completing.

War changed a lot of things. Alex scraped his hands over his face and stared at his bland white desktop. It was surreal. Five months ago, his career was in the dumpster, torpedoed by USS *Kansas*' vindictive CO. Then the French tried to take the largest underwater station in the world and lit off a world war. Somehow, Alex got his people off that station, hijacked a cruise liner, and saved his least favorite admiral along the way. Here he was, inches away from his lifelong dream of submarine command, all because a bored, college-aged Alex Coleman once learned how to make bombs out of coffee creamer. Those bombs scared the hell out of French Marines sixteen years later, buying Alex's people time to get off Armistice Station...and buying Alex a second chance.

Captain Henry Forrester, their senior instructor, cleared his throat. He was a skinny man with wild hair just on the wrong side of the regs. But no one cared. Forrester made a name for himself sneaking USS *Challenger* right up to the Russians' front door in the Baltic in the years before the war and had enough spastic energy to wear a hummingbird out. Everyone liked him—except when he was grading tests. "Ladies and gents, put your hard hats on," he said. "It's time to find out your fates."

An invisible fist closed around Alex's throat. Lord, why was he so nervous? Teresa was right. He *was* at the top of their class; snuck in or not, he'd earned his place.

"Breathe, Alex," Teresa leaned over to whisper. "At least you're near the front of the alphabet—or on top if they go by rankings. Bet you're gonna get one of those shiny new Improved-*Ceroes*."

"I wouldn't know what the fuck to do with one." Alex swallowed before a nervous laugh could escape. "Never even been on a normal *Cero*."

"First time in command sounds like a great time to start."

"She's right. I'm betting on you to get something new," Commander Tommy Sandifer leaned in to say from Alex's other side.

"Betting?" Alex asked warily.

"Oh, no one told you about the class betting pool?" Tommy laughed. "That's because you're the favorite. No one tells the favorite."

Teresa elbowed him. "See? No need to be nervous. We're only expecting great—"

"I know you're naturally gregarious, Commander O'Canas, but I think even *you* might want to pay attention right now," Forrester cut in.

The class snickered, and Alex breathed a little easier.

"Now, on with the show. First up, Commander Adnan Aga—USS *Grunion*, SSN 849." He paused so the class could applaud, and Gianni Ferri could slap Adnan on the back. *Grunion* was a *Cero*, just three years old and an absolute catch for someone ranked sixth in their class. "Commander Gabrielle Allard—PCU *Bumper*, SSN 862."

Someone hissed; Gabrielle gasped. *Bumper* was newer still than *Darter*, so new that she wasn't even commissioned. *Bumper* was one of those Improved-*Ceroes* Teresa thought Alex might get, and Gabby was right behind him in class standings...

"Commander Alexander Coleman—USS *Jimmy Carter*, SSN 23."

Stunned silence greeted those words; Alex felt like someone punched him in the gut. Someone whispered, "What the fuck?" maybe Teresa; Alex wasn't listening. Someone else muttered something about *Jimmy Carter* being a death trap, and Alex ignored them, too. He just stared at Captain Forrester dumbly as three months of busting his ass went down the drain.

Forrester spoke hurriedly: "Commander Hugo Duncan—USS *New Mexico*, SSN 779."

Alex didn't pay attention to the rest. He vaguely remembered hearing Teresa receive USS *Douglass*, which wasn't a new and shiny *Cero*, but she was at least one of the last *Virginia*-class submarines built and only seven years old. *Douglass* was a good boat, one you could take the fight to the enemy in. Whereas *Jimmy Carter* was the oldest attack sub in active service at a ripe old age of thirty-three.

Toward the end of their class, Tommy Sandifer got USS *Georgia*, a Block V *Virginia*-class, and Alex tried to smile for his friends. Tommy had a boat that could wreck an entire fleet's day with surface-to-air missiles—or destroy a small country. That smile came hard. Alex's boat probably couldn't interface with the fleet's newest missiles.

"Your tests this afternoon will contain a class-specific section," Captain Forrester continued. "Use the next few hours to review anything you need about your future command."

Forrester left, leaving Alex to stare at the screensaver on his assigned computer, emptiness gnawing at his gut. He choked back a laugh and then, on second thought, let it out. Laughing was better than screaming in frustration. Alex scraped his hands over his face.

"Fuck me."

"This has got to be a mistake." Teresa's scowl deepened. "No *way* do they give the guy at the top of our class a boat that was a month out from being razorblades."

"That close?" Alex forced a wry smile. "Ain't that a delicious shit sandwich?"

"One you sure as fuck shouldn't have to eat," Teresa said.

"Maybe they think that they need the best to ride herd on such an old boat?" Tommy asked. But even he sounded dubious.

"Maybe it's some super-secret spy mission?" Gabby Allard suggested from the row in front of him. "That's what *Jimmy Carter* used to do."

Alex snorted. "Not likely."

Most of the class's eyes were on him; Alex wanted to sink into his chair and hide. Being the center of attention always made him want to do his best groundhog impression, even among people he considered friends. Or at least professional acquaintances, in a few cases. Alex sighed.

"I doubt it's a mistake," he said, eyes sliding back to his desk. "I got here…well, on a promise. And no one promised to give me a good boat at the end of it."

"What kind of promise?" Teresa asked.

"Doesn't matter. Let's just say I'm not surprised." Alex forced himself to look up, to meet her eyes. "Better *Jimmy Carter* than no command at all. Couple months ago, that's where I figured I was going."

"I'm sensing a big lot of something you're not saying here."

"No point in airing dirty laundry." Alex shrugged. "Guess I've got some studying to do. Got to learn about my old lady, you know."

He could feel Admiral Hamilton's hand in this, and trying to fight this assignment might end up with him back on the beach. The navy didn't advertise Alex's actions on *Kansas*, when he stopped his then-CO from sinking a civilian submarine, and for good reason. Doing the right thing mattered a lot less when you disobeyed orders to do it—particularly when said civilian sub got sunk by some mysterious third party but the blame still stuck to the U.S. like glue.

Yeah, going into that wasn't going to do him any favors. Cramming for three hours on the navy's sole *Seawolf*-class submarine probably wouldn't, either.

The Second Battle of Sunda Strait

If anyone had asked Lieutenant Commander Stephanie Gomez before the war if the Sunda Strait was a smart patch of water to fight over, she'd have called them crazy.

Unfortunately, the Sunda Strait was the sole path from the Indian Ocean to the Java Sea, cutting between the Indonesian islands of Java and Sumatra. Since it was located south of the Strait of Malacca—once the world's busiest waterway and now owned lock, stock, and barrel by the enemy—the Alliance was desperate to keep the Sunda Strait in business.

Missing the first few battles of the war *had* made Steph feel guilty. Not the first one, exactly—she was busy elsewhere when the navy got smacked in the Battle of the SOM—but the ones after that, where friends, classmates, and other surface warfare officers fought and died, those she felt guilty about. That lasted through her rushed time at the Prospective Executive Officers' course, a class she started less than a week after leaving Armistice Station when the war started.

Her original assignment, USS *Paul Ignatius*, sank at the Battle of Java Sea before she even finished class. That bounced her to USS *Jason Dunham* (DDG 109), another *Arleigh Burke*-class destroyer. Within a month of reporting aboard as the destroyer's executive officer, or second-in-command, Steph stopped feeling guilty.

Jason Dunham ran out of missiles during the Battle of the Sea of Japan six days earlier. Duking it out with two Russian frigates left her with only a handful of Evolved Sea Sparrow Missiles for point defense, and taking out a pair of Russian corvettes left her lower on ammunition for her 5 inch/62 gun than anyone in their right mind liked. A quick sprint into Yokosuka, Japan for rearming didn't help much, either; the U.S. Navy weapons depot there was drier than dirt and echoed like a cave.

If the crippled Japanese Naval Self Defense Force hadn't ponied up twenty SM-6 standard missiles and a few hundred rounds of high-explosive ammunition for *Dunham's* gun, the destroyer would've sailed naked into the Second Battle of Sunda Strait. As it was, having only twenty missiles in a Vertical Launch System made to carry ninety-six was like putting pennies in your quarter jar.

Steph Gomez liked having a jar full of quarters, thank you, but no one asked her when they sent her destroyer out to play without a full deck. Besides, she was only the XO, and the captain got to fight the ship—her job was navigation.

Steph was good at navigation. She was damned good at her job, really, and always had been. Armistice Station hadn't been exile for her; that shore duty turned out to be great for her career, particularly now that she had Admiral Hamilton's kiss of approval. She probably hadn't needed it, but it was sure nice to have. Even in wartime, admirals liking you was a quick ticket upward, and Steph knew she wanted command of her own ship.

She was what her last captain called a Hispanic bombshell of enthusiastic competence, born and bred in the South to love guns, hunting, and getting down and dirty. Steph thought about becoming a Marine, but the call of the sea was stronger than her love of shooting, so she took a NROTC scholarship to Norwich University, where she got to climb mountains with a rescue unit until the navy sent her out to the big blue.

Now she stood on *Jason Dunham's* bridge, looking out at suspiciously clear skies and seas as her crew fought for their lives for a stupid-but-critical patch of water.

"All stations, TAO, Winchester, I say again, we are Winchester," the ship's tactical action officer reported over the internal net.

"Shit." Steph clung to the arms of her chair as the Officer of the Deck sent *Dunham* into another turn. The destroyer strained at her seams, leaning hard to port—the outside of the turn—her screws churning up a rooster tail of water in her wake. "OOD, stand by for gunnery action!"

"OOD, aye!" Ensign Angelina Darnell held onto the navigation pelorus at the center of the bridge for balance. "Shift your rudder!"

"Shift my rudder, aye! My rudder is left thirty degrees, no new course given," the helmsman replied.

"Very well."

Steph's head snapped left, squinting to pick out ships on the horizon. Two Indian *Talwar*-class frigates bracketed a French frigate—but those *Aquitaine*-class FREMM frigates were practically destroyers, tough customers and damned hard to sink. Despite that, one burned off to port, hit by *Dunham's* last missiles. *Dunham* hadn't smacked her alone, though, and that *Aquitaine* got her revenge before she was done. *Jack H. Lucas*, *Dunham's* younger sister ship, broke in two as Steph watched. Worse yet, *Sterett* had gone to the bottom twenty minutes earlier, accompanied by an Indian destroyer.

But the cruiser was the big loss. *Monmouth* was a flaming wreck; Steph didn't know how she kept floating, but no way was she going to keep at that for long. She grimaced.

"This three-to-one loss ratio sucks ass," she muttered.

"You can say that again, ma'am." Ensign Darnell glanced her way and shrugged. Formality went out the window somewhere around her first battle. Darnell was a superstar; otherwise, she wouldn't be the general quarters officer of the deck as an ensign.

"Should I?" Steph grinned. "I think—"

The *booming* of *Dunham's* 5 Inch/62 Caliber gun cut her off as the watch down in the Combat Information Center targeted the French frigate. But it was just on the edge of their range and already increasing speed. Steph grimaced. Hits were unlikely.

Light flashed on the horizon.

"Vampire, vampire, vampire! Incoming missiles bearing two-two-zero!" the tactical action officer announced over the internal net. The words blared out of the speaker. "Brace for impact!"

"Brace for impact!" Steph echoed the shout out of habit, clinging to her chair for dear life. *Whatever smart soul forgot to put seatbelts on bridge chairs can go right to hell!*

Dunham shuddered as her forward Close In Weapons System went into full auto. Steph's straining eyes couldn't pick out the missiles, but she knew they were there. CIWS tracer rounds lit up the sky—

The explosion was close enough to shatter the glass of the bridge windows.

Chapter 2

Bad Tactics

Groton, Connecticut

His head still swimming with facts and figures, Alex wolfed down a mediocre ham sandwich in front of the computer in Ballard Hall. Most of his classmates went out for lunch, but he had a new boat to learn about and no time to do it in.

Alex might've been an introvert, but he usually liked to go out for lunch with a few friends like Teresa and Tommy. Groton was full of mom-and-pop restaurants, and even though he'd grown up around here, there was always a new hole-in-the-wall to discover. Not going with them today—one of their last days at the Sub School—made his heart ache. Once they left here, they'd all command submarines at war, and statistics said a lot of his classmates wouldn't be coming home.

Shaking himself, Alex turned back to the computer, drinking in all the information he could find.

Jimmy Carter was a hundred feet longer than her two decommissioned sisters, had eight torpedo tubes (twice that of the *Virginias* and *Ceroes*), a maximum speed of forty-three knots (a knot faster than a *Virginia* but fourteen knots slower than the lightning-fast *Ceroes*), and a gargantuan Multi-Mission Platform stuck in her middle designed for special operations.

Years ago, *Jimmy Carter* had been famous for splicing listening devices into cables, sneaking SEALs into places they weren't wanted, and spying on a variety of friends and allies. Unfortunately, the brand-new *Parche* had replaced her as the navy's go-to spec ops submarine; unless Big Navy wanted two such boats, that MMP would be a useless roll of fat, making Alex's command three thousand tons heavier.

Joy.

Captain Forrester returned to the classroom a few minutes before their lunch break ended, and Alex closed the capabilities and limitations file he was studying. Rising, he crossed the room to meet Forrester, who flinched. Alex pursed his lips, but he supposed it was nice to know that this wasn't Forrester's idea. Not that he had to ask which admiral he'd pissed off. Alex adopted as neutral an expression as he could manage.

"Captain, do you know if the *Seawolf* simulator is still operative?" Alex asked. "I'd like to request as many hours in there as I can get."

Forrester's flinch became a full-out cringe. "Sorry, Alex. They dismantled the *Seawolf* simulator last year."

No, that wasn't a giant's hand grabbing him around the throat; Alex just felt like it was. "Oh. Great."

"If it helps at all, you can use *Virginia* answers for your test," Forrester said, as if Alex hadn't spent three hours speed learning about his future boat. "No one can find the *Seawolf* answer key, anyway."

"That's, uh...nice to know. Thanks."

Great. That message was clear, wasn't it? He'd been railroaded twice over. No simulator, and no one gave a damn about how he did on this test, did they? Admiral Hamilton promised him a submarine after his actions on Armistice Station, but she was going to give him the oldest and shittiest boat she could.

His feet carried him back to his desk as Alex fought back the urge to make like a turtle and pull his head in. Forrester felt sorry for him, did he? Everyone did. Three-and-a-half months of busting his ass, of working to be the best of the best, and here he was.

After stopping a glory hound of a CO from shooting civilians, after outfoxing hundreds of French Marines and their wily commander to escape from Armistice Station with thousands of Allied civilians—yeah, this was what he got. America's oldest attack submarine and Captain Forrester's pity.

Fuck that shit.

Alex sat quietly as his classmates returned. He said nothing as Forrester initialized the test; after a moment, the blue *start* button appeared on the computer screen, blinking cheerfully. Despite sixteen years in the navy, and three other courses at the sub school, this was Alex's first electronic test. The navy needed decades to embrace not printing out already-computerized message traffic, but it looked like the Sub School had finally made it into the present.

Shit, *Jimmy Carter* commissioned when Alex was *five*. Given how far behind the power curve naval technology tended to be, would the boat be fully analog? God help him if the screens were all CRTs. Alex hadn't seen one of those since elementary school.

Zipping through the tactical section and the administration section, Alex reached the class-specific section and paused. Then he caught sight of the board on the left side of the room, where everyone's assignment was listed.

A. Coleman, *Jimmy Carter* SSN 23.

Oh, why the hell not? Alex turned back to the test and started selecting answers.

The Sunda Strait

The explosion shook *Jason Dunham* from bow to stern, and for a moment, it looked like the sun detonated on top of their bow.

The bridge windows shattered, glass blasting inward. Someone screamed, or was that several someones? Steph, who'd been looking right at the explosion, closed her eyes on instinct with a split second to spare. She hadn't had a lot of experience with close-in fireballs until her boss on Armistice Station proved you could make a mean blast out of coffee creamer and charcoal a year earlier. That taught her right quick not to look too closely at the bright and shiny things.

Unfortunately, Ensign Darnell had never learned that lesson. She was also closer to the glass, standing centerline by the pelorus. Darnell caught the blast straight in the face, convulsed, and then collapsed to the ground, howling in pain. *Bulletproof glass, my Southern ass!*

Darnell's face was covered in blood, and every window on the bridge was broken. That left three-quarters of the bridge open to the salt air, thick with smoke and burning metal. Coughing, Steph swung out of her chair.

"Boats, pass the word for medical emergency in the pilothouse!"

"Boats, aye!" The Boatswain's Mate of the Watch spun to the 1Mc, *Jason Dunham's* general announcing system. "Medical Emergency,

Medical Emergency, Medical Emergency in the pilothouse!"

Crouching by Darnell's side, Steph quickly checked her over for injuries. Aside from her right eye, the worst seemed to be a few cuts across her forehead. "Keep your eyes closed, Angelina," Steph said. "Help's on the way."

Darnell sucked in several panting breaths. "I'll be okay, ma'am."

"I bet you will." Steph squeezed Darnell's shoulder. "Don't touch the eye. I'll be back in a sec."

"Don't worry about me, XO. Take care of the ship." Darnell managed a pale, pained smile.

Part of Steph wanted to argue or wanted to mention that she was pretty sure that eye was toast. Six or so lifetimes ago, one of her high school friends took a BB shot to the eye when they were screwing around shooting cans. Tomás survived, but his eye didn't—but Steph had a destroyer to drive and a battle to fight.

Rising, she took Darnell's place at the center of the bridge. "This is the XO. I have the deck and the conn."

"Helmsman aye. Rudder is left thirty degrees, no course given."

"Steady as she goes."

"Steady as she goes, aye. Steady course one-niner-four."

"Very well." Steph squared her shoulders and glanced around the bridge. "Anyone else hurt?"

"We're good, ma'am," Boatswain's Mate First Class Devon Shorkey replied for everyone. "Nothing more than a couple of cuts."

Steph nodded, twisting to look out at the foc's'le, the front end of the destroyer where her five-inch gun sat. Fortunately, the gun—Mount 5-1 in Navy parlance—seemed intact. Shrapnel littered the deck, and there was a fire aft of the gun, but—

Boom!

Another round burst out of Mount 5-1, still aiming for the French FREMM frigate. With *Jack J. Lucas* heading to the bottom and *Monmouth* still burning, *Dunham* was now almost alone, with just *Nicholas* for company.

Puffs of smoke filled the air as the French and Indian frigates started firing their own guns.

"Weave me a zigzag, helm," Steph ordered. "Ten to twenty-five degrees off this base course."

"Helm, aye!" The young sailor at the helm was eighteen, wide-eyed, and with freckles so bright her face almost seemed to glow. But her hands on the wheel didn't shake one bit.

Steph leaned into the internal comms speaker. "Combat, XO, I have the deck. Looks like the enemy has also swapped to guns. Any chance *Nicholas* has missiles left?"

"XO, Captain, no go, she's Winchester," Commander Matt Tabor replied.

"Damn."

Luckily, Steph didn't press the button to swear under her breath; she'd hoped that *Nicholas,* one of the missile-heavy *O'Bannon*-class, would still have something left to reach out and touch the enemy with. Unfortunately, like *Dunham, Nicholas* had only one 5 inch/62 caliber gun. Not much to shoot with. Steph shook herself.

"Captain, XO, we're in a random zigzag up here to mess with their targeting as best we can."

"Captain, aye. *Nicholas* will be alongside shortly to commence a gun run at the enemy in tandem."

A peek out the starboard non-windows showed *Nicholas* roaring up from behind; the newer destroyers were faster and smaller than the *Arleigh Burkes* and carried a bigger missile punch—at the expense of having crap for anti-submarine warfare capabilities. But at least there were no subs in the force that came against them earlier, even if the three-to-two odds *Dunham* and *Nicholas* faced weren't great.

Boom. The five-inch fired again, rattling every loose fitting on the bridge now that there were no windows to dampen the sound. Their rate of fire was slow; was the team down in CIC conserving ammunition, or was there a mechanical problem? Steph wanted to ask, but it wasn't tactically relevant from her position on the bridge. Good tactics said the captain should be in CIC while the XO was on the bridge, but man, not knowing things up here *sucked*.

Boom. They were still ten miles away from the three enemy frigates; did that look like a hit? Steph squinted.

"They better sink those bastards before we get in OTO Melera range," Shorkey muttered as stretcher bearers burst onto the bridge to tend to Ensign Darnell.

Steph shot him a lopsided smile. "Those seventy-six millimeter shells are two inches smaller than ours, Boats. We'll be okay."

"Not if they make us look like Swiss cheese. Ain't no shooting those down like we can missiles, XO."

"I'm pretty sure the captain's smart enough to stay outside their effective range," Steph replied. God, she hoped Tabor was. He'd been a sound tactician so far, but this battle had been a shitshow from the onset. Bad intel got their forces split in half, rushing to save two supply ships the Indians supposedly captured—only to find them sinking and in flames before *Dunham* and her cohorts were even in missile range.

She leaned forward to talk into the speaker again. "Captain, XO, any chance of help or missiles from our friends down south?"

Bad planning meant the Second Battle of Sunda Strait ended up happening in two parts, with two American destroyers and a pair of frigates engaging French ships in the southern end of the strait while *Dunham* and her cohorts fought in the north. Steph wasn't sure whose brainchild it was to separate their forces, but she was knee deep in the shitshow it had caused.

Damn, she'd heard the war was a bit of a mess when she was at the prospective executive officers' course, but this was something else.

"Negative. We lost comms with *Badger* ten minutes ago. No joy raising them since."

"Bridge, aye."

In peacetime, no one worried about lost comms. In wartime...everyone knew what happened to American ships who dropped off the net without warning.

The Indian fleet was in better shape than USS *Jason Dunham*. Led by INS *Rajput*, they pursued the Americans through the darkening afternoon, resorting to guns now that they were out of missiles. This was not the first fight of the war that turned into a running gun battle, but it was the first where the Indians had the upper hand.

Vice Admiral Aadil Khare had no intention of relinquishing *any* advantages, either. He was a tall man, with a curved mustache and hard eyes that rarely creased, even when he smiled. Now he stood on the flag bridge of *Rajput*, resolutely ignoring how she was not the carrier he desired.

Still, she was growing on him.

A *Kolkata II*-class destroyer was the premier fighting flagship of his navy, but it was not where Khare wished to be. Bristling with vertical launch cells for sixty-four missiles and carrying two 76-millimeter OTO Melera super rapid gun systems with a rate of fire of over eighty rounds per minute, *Rajput* was a tough customer by any Navy's standards—except, perhaps, the United States Navy that was such a plague upon the Indian Ocean.

But they were learning, the arrogant Americans.

Pushing them out politely—through corporate alliances and spending cash earned in undersea stations and mining outposts—had not worked. Nor had humiliation; when Indian and France forcibly ousted America and her allies from Armistice Station on the eve of the war, a small group of U.S. Navy personnel hijacked the cruise ship meant to carry them away. And they'd done more.

Before the mess on Armistice Station, Admiral Khare was India's rising star, a likely candidate for the next Chief of the Naval Staff. He was a proud man whose love of golf was only outweighed by his ambition. Now he was relegated to the flag bridge of a destroyer instead of leading his navy, desperate to rebuild his reputation.

Khare sneered, looking at the burning ruins of USS *Badger* and *Shields*. Survivors in life rafts dotted the ocean surface, more from *Shields* than *Badger*. The latter was a frigate and went down far faster than her destroyer counterpart—and faster than the first two ships the Indians engaged early in the action. One of those, the other destroyer, was still burning, but Khare was sure it would sink soon.

Both American ships were newer than his own—*Rajput* commissioned in 2026, twelve years ago—but they were no match for his task force. Khare might not have his navy's newest ships, or even the fleet he wanted, but he knew how to use the ships he had. Three *Shivalik*-class frigates, two *Kolkata II*-class DDGs, and five *Kamorta*-class corvettes packed a bigger punch than two American destroyers and a pair of their frigates, particularly when Khare strapped mobile BrahMos missile launchers onto the *Kamortas* to augment their capabilities.

Small and hard to track on radar, he sent the *Kamortas* in first to saturate the American's much-vaunted missile defenses. Just like in previous battles, the legendary AEGIS system defended an American task group well—but it wasted two missiles on every one sent their way. The Americans shot down *most* of the BrahMos missiles Khare shot at them...but they couldn't get them all, and the BrahMos was the fastest shipkiller in the world.

The anti-ship missiles the Americans sent his way in response were almost insignificant. One *Kamorta* sank with all hands, but the others escaped unscathed, racing out of range after shooting their missiles and escaping the paltry response. Khare smiled to himself. America was good at air defense, but their offensive power on the seas suffered when they did not have an aircraft carrier to back them up.

With *Enterprise* on the bottom of the Strait of Malacca—not very far away in the nautical scheme of things—and *Gerald Ford* still waiting to see if China's civil war would deter an attack on Taiwan, the long arm of America's naval power was considerably shorter.

"Shall we close with the other group, Admiral?" Captain Kiara Naidu, his chief of staff, asked.

"After we pick up the survivors from *Kulish*." He turned to her with a smile. "*Trishul* reports there are only two American destroyers left. We will complete our victory by sinking them."

She grinned. "With pleasure."

Taking a deep breath, Khare sat back and let a sense of vicious pleasure roll through him. Yes, he could get his career back on track. A few more victories like this and he would be his navy's premier admiral.

Khare glanced at the ammunition readout to his right and frowned. Missiles killed ships, and all his ships were running low. Perhaps he would contact BrahMos Aerospace upon their return to port and talk about their production bottlenecks.

Chapter 3

Moray

The Sunda Strait

"I think this is the first running gun battle since World War II," Steph said to Commander Matt Tabor two hours later.

They stood together on *Jason Dunham's* now-windowless bridge as the destroyer weaved back and forth within the confines of the Sunda Strait, avoiding shallow water and trying to close range with the enemy frigates. The smell of smoke and burned metal wafted in through the broken windows, and glass still crunched under foot. With thirty on the crew injured and another ten dead so far, there were no spare hands to clean up the debris.

Nor was there time to mourn. Steph's chest went tight every time she thought about the sailors who'd died—and the handful in critical condition who were being treated in the destroyer's limited medical suite—but she had a job to do.

Was this war? She resisted the urge to hug herself. The fight on Armistice Station hadn't been quite like this; it had been so fast that she'd hardly had any chance to think...and she wasn't close to those who died. However, losing *her* sailors was different and left an empty feeling in her gut that was hard to shake.

But she was the XO. She had to keep her head in the game, particularly when she was new here.

Unfortunately, the French *Aquitaine*-class frigate and the two Indian *Talwars* they were chasing were both faster than *Dunham's* best speed of thirty-three knots. *Nicholas*, a newer *O'Bannon*-class, was a touch quicker, but going in alone against three frigates when she was out of missiles would be suicide.

"At least we've proven that a *Burke* can take a couple hits and survive." Tabor frowned. "Not that I really wanted that badge of honor."

"What, your life's ambition wasn't to take a few 76-millimeter rounds in the teeth?" Steph laughed.

Boom. They squeaked into good range, and the five-inch fired again. The first shot looked short, but damn, it was hard to tell at nine nautical miles. *Boom-boom-boom*. Those three bracketed *Trishul*, the Indian destroyer to starboard.

Boom-boom-boom-boom.

"Yes!" Steph almost jumped in celebration.

All four rounds hit *Trishul* head on. Glancing at the UAV—unmanned aerial vehicle, or military drone—video on the monitor to the far right—showed fires burning on the frigate's foc'sle.

"Combat, Captain, we got her gun! Well done—do it again on another one," Tabor ordered into the intercom.

"TAO, aye!"

Dunham's five-inch trained twenty degrees to starboard as the helm put her into another port turn, continuing their zigzag course. Steph was still driving—Darnell was below in medical, with HMC "Doc" Gillis doing emergency surgery to remove her eye—but right now that meant just watching the depth and making sure they didn't run aground while the helm executed the zigzag pattern.

Good water for the next mile. That gave them two minutes on this course. Why couldn't the navy pick fights in the middle of the big blue ocean? She could see Java from here.

Boom!

The ranging shot against the French frigate missed; Steph looked at the ammunition counter at the same time Tabor did.

"Just thirty rounds left." He grimaced. "*Nicholas* is down to a hundred high explosive."

"And nothing else is going to get through a frigate's hull, yeah." Steph sighed. She'd like to meet the hairbrained idiot back at Yorktown Naval Weapons Station who sent them out with ground bombardment rounds. That's what land attack missiles were for, and—

"Bridge, combat, new contacts bearing two-one-four, range forty nautical miles!" the tactical action officer's voice crackled out of the internal net's box. "Redeploying UAV for positive ID."

"Combat, Captain, any chance of them being our friends from the south?"

"Negative link tracks, Captain."

Tabor shot Steph a look, the unspoken thought darting between them at light speed. If this wasn't *Kelly's* group... "I'm on my way. You've got the bridge, XO. Try to sink these guys fast."

"You got it, boss."

Steph didn't watch as Tabor left the bridge; she heard the watertight door swing shut behind him and refocused her attention on *Dunham's* track. There was shoal water ahead.

"Right twenty degrees rudder," she ordered.

"Right twenty degrees rudder, aye. My rudder is—"

"Vampire, vampire, vampire! Vampire track 7088, bearing two-one-four, range three-nine nautical miles!" the TAO's voice erupted out of the speaker again.

"Hard right rudder!" Steph snapped. If she could get *Dunham's* head around fast enough, they could engage the incoming missiles with both CIWS mounts. Otherwise, only the aft one had a chance to kill it.

Taking two quick steps right, Steph pulled up the bridge tactical display. Her heart sank.

The incoming missiles were BrahMos-II anti-surface missiles. The newest version of the BrahMos was the fastest ship-launched attack missile in the world, capable of speeds up to Mach 7, or over 4,500 knots. With a 440-pound conventional warhead, the BrahMos packed a hell of a punch—one Steph saw used with devastating efficiency against the other ships in their task force.

And *Dunham* was out of missiles to defend against them.

Four BrahMos-II missiles needed thirty-two seconds to cross the range between the Indians and *Jason Dunham*. *Dunham's* sudden turn closed the distance between her and *Nicholas*, however, which made one missile lose lock on her and target the other destroyer instead.

CIWS mounts on both destroyers opened up within ten seconds at full auto. Both destroyers had recent upgrades to the Block 1C version, which could fire five thousand rounds per minute—eighty-three rounds per second—from their twenty-millimeter Gatling canons. Their independent radars fused AEGIS and SPY radar created tracks with their own, tracking the missiles' positions down to the inch.

The Block 1C CIWS had a bigger magazine than their predecessors. Two thousand five hundred rounds were enough for thirty seconds of continuous fire—but it wasn't enough to save *Nicholas*.

The newer destroyer shot down two of the three missiles targeting her, but the third smashed into her amidships, crashing into her aft stack and ripping through metal like paper. Two of her illumination radars tore off and flew into the air, turning into red-hot fireballs. One landed in the water just off *Dunham's* starboard side, boiling the seawater where it hit. The other crashed into the destroyer's superstructure two decks below the bridge, burning a hole through steel and igniting fires as it went.

One of those fires caught Commander Matt Tabor in a ladder well, burning him to a crisp.

30 July 2038, Groton, Connecticut

"Where the hell are the test scores?" Teresa asked the next morning, squinting at the wall where their scores were usually posted. She wasn't the only one in their class staring pointedly at the wall; test results were always posted first thing in the morning at the Sub School, sure as the sun would shine or it'd rain all spring in Groton.

How many tests had Alex taken in this place? Probably thousands. First, he'd come here for the Submarine Officers' Basic Course, prior to reporting to his first submarine, USS *Virginia*. Then he'd come back for the advanced course, SOAC, before his department head ride on USS *John Warner*. Then the prospective XO course before *Kansas*, and now PCO. The Sub School was the last stop before every important career milestone, with its same brick buildings and the same white walls covered in pictures of submarines visiting places around the world.

There would be no port visits to show the flag now. Now they were at war, and the reminders of that were on the walls, too. Alex's eyes drifted to the list of the subs on eternal patrol. Would *Jimmy Carter* end up on that list, with his name next to her?

"Alex? You okay?" Teresa asked.

"Maybe the computer broke." Alex forced a smile. Maybe his answers broke it. That would be nice. Or not so nice.

In the bright light of day, without anger egging him on, maybe putting those *Seawolf*-class answers in was a bad idea. He hadn't *quite* bombed the test on purpose...but he might as well have. Even with nothing to lose, he should respect the Sub School more than that, especially after all this time.

Except he was still mad.

He'd worked so damned hard to get to the top of this class, always with the disaster on *Kansas* in the back of his mind. Officers didn't survive going to Admiral's Mast, even if it was for a damned good reason. He had a second chance, and Alex wasn't going to waste it...until Admiral Hamilton's invisible hand directed him to the oldest boat in the fleet.

Yeah, she remembered.

"Don't be stupid. There's, like, five backups." Teresa cocked her head. "Isn't there?"

"Fuck if I know. Or care."

She punched him in the shoulder. "C'mon, I thought you were in a better mood after drinking your sorrows away."

"I was before the hangover kicked in." Alex shrugged, immediately regretting it. Damn, his left shoulder hurt. What *had* he walked into in his drunken stupor?

His wife, Nancy, had a problem on her own ship last night, so Alex went out with a few classmates so they could celebrate—and he could drink a few too many in his quest to forget where he was headed within the week. He stayed up too late and drank too much, but it was only graduation day, and who cared about looking spit-shined when he was going to the oldest submarine in the navy?

Besides, he could put his dress whites on in his sleep. Sixteen-and-a-half years in the navy and four years before that at Norwich University, the nation's oldest private military college, made him an old pro. Alex was smart enough to assemble the uniform *before* he started drinking.

Teresa laughed. "Wah, wah. You'll live, if half those Norwich drinking stories you told me are true."

"I take no responsibility for stories told while drunk."

"That's different from you sober how?" She grinned.

"More loquacious."

Finally, Captain Forrester walked in the room, suspiciously empty-handed. "Settle down, ladies and gentlemen. I know it's graduation day, but you've still got a few hurdles to overcome before you skip out of town. First, Admin wanted me to remind Commanders Maldonado and Dennis that you have some outstanding paperwork before you head to your new commands. Ms. Graves also wants to speak to Commander Coleman about flight reservations to Bangor."

Was it Alex's imagination, or did Forrester's voice get a touch frosty when he said his name? Nope, that glare confirmed it. Alex was on *someone's* shit list.

Well. That was nothing new.

"Additionally, we have a last-minute change in class standings after the final. Commander Allard, I hope you're ready to make the graduation speech, because you're this class's overall top scorer."

"I am?" Gabby Allard blinked, glancing at Alex. "I mean, yes, sir, I can come up with something."

"Good to hear." Forrester smiled. "You'll be making that speech in front of Rear Admiral Hamilton, whom I'm sure everyone remembers as the first female submariner to make flag rank. Certain...events have kept Rear Admiral McNally from joining us, so Rear Admiral Hamilton will be your graduation speaker."

Oh, fuck. Alex could feel the color flee from his face.

"Hey, what's that about?" Teresa whispered. "Were you already drunk by test time?"

"Nah, I just hate making speeches." Alex tried to swallow away the samba his heart was busy doing.

She twisted to look at him, eyebrows furrowed. "I know you're an introvert, but *geez*, that's a numb-nuts thing to do."

"I *really* hate making speeches."

"Bullshit. There's always more with you. I bet you're sneaky in your *sleep*." Teresa eyed him. "I'm going to ask Nancy about that next time we talk."

"Sure." Alex shrugged as casually as he could, trying not to think about—

"We have one more update before I go get your test results, this one less pleasant," Forrester continued. "We received word late last night that *Moray* sank with all hands."

A quiet chill settled over the class; Alex shivered, his gaze shifting to the leaderboard. *Moray* and Commander Phelps were there at the top—but now they'd *also* be on Eternal Patrol list.

God help them.

"Do we know what happened?" The words came out before Alex realized he was speaking; he gulped.

Forrester shook his head. "Not enough. However, the SUBMISS/SUBSUNK buoy triggered, and *Moray* is—*was*—one of NUWC's test beds for an automatic upload of Voice/Video Data Recorders." He sucked in a shuddering breath. "And while assessment of the sinking is still pending, I received permission to show the attack center video to you."

A murmur ran through the class. Alex couldn't tell if it was grief or anger. All he felt was a cold wall of dread washing through him, and he rubbed suddenly sweaty palms together.

The SUBMISS/SUBSUNK buoy was attached just aft of the sail on all U.S. Navy submarines. It had gone through several iterations and technical names over the years, but the function was the same: to launch if the boat was lost and mark the sinking location. Some COs welded them down to avoid the slight rattling of the buoy in its bracket; others disabled the emergency timer so the buoy couldn't be launched accidentally.

But nowadays, a buoy launch *plus* a VDR upload was like getting the black box off of a downed airplane. They knew the sub went down...and now they might know why.

"*Moray* was defending the *Abe Lincoln* Strike Group when this happened. An unknown submarine had already sunk a destroyer, *Ralph Johnson*, and *Moray* was sent after her killer," Forrester said. "Unfortunately, the VDR footage makes it plain that *Moray* was on the back foot from the beginning and spent almost thirty-eight hours trying to lose her killer."

Alex shivered. He only knew Commander Phelps in passing, yet this felt somehow...wrong. Like walking on someone's grave. But it was a learning opportunity, too. Never before had the navy possessed the ability to look directly into the attack center of a submarine only minutes before their demise. Previously, theories of what went wrong were only that: guesswork.

Swallowing back his unease, Alex focused on the display at the front of the classroom. It flickered from black to blue, with stark white words USS MORAY SSN 853 centered on the monitor. Then it flashed to a *Cero*-class sub's attack center, known to sub crews as "the conn."

Moray's *conn was a narrow space, with the helm consoles up forward and two lines of double-screened electronic consoles down each side. Watchstanders crammed into every seat and behind most of them; there was never room to spare on a submarine, particularly at battle stations.*

Ship control was to port, fire control to starboard, and the sonar, radio, and spec ops spaces were in a closet-size space Alex knew hid behind the fire control corner. Unlike older submarines—like the one Alex was about to inherit—there were no physical periscopes.

Cero-*class boats like* Moray *took after their older* Virginia-*class sisters with "always up" periscopes. Unfortunately, wartime experience proved those periscopes prone to battle damage. More than one boat returned to port with them bent and mangled beyond repair—but they made for a more spacious conn.*

Jane Phelps stood slightly off center, between the navigation table and the helm consoles. She was a tall woman, with blond hair pulled back in a messy bun. Her coveralls were rumpled and her eyes bloodshot, and she held a cup of coffee with stains on the rim. Her XO, or second in command, stood by the fire control consoles, leaning heavily on a chair back with his ball cap askew.

"Conn, Sonar, still nothing," said a voice coming from the speaker to Phelps' right.

"Conn, aye." Phelps sighed, meeting her XO's eyes. "What d'you think, Sam? Did we lose him?"

"I wish I knew." Scrubbing his hands over his face, the XO turned enough that Alex could read the nametape on his coveralls. Alex didn't know Lieutenant Commander Samuels, and now he never would.

"All right, people, I need your best guesses." Phelps' voice was gravely as she rubbed her eyes. "We've gone an hour without contact. Have we lost *Barracuda?*"

"Fuck," Alex whispered.

Teresa stopped wiggling in her seat to look at him. "What?"

"I've met that asshole." Looking at Commander Phelps and her team made Alex feel sick.

Barracuda and its captain, Jules Rochambeau, already crossed Alex's path twice. Once, in the murky waters around Armistice Station where *someone* sank a civilian submarine and blamed it on Americans. And then later, on Armistice Station itself, when France and India seized control of the world's largest underwater station at the start of the war.

Rumors said Rochambeau sank *Thornback*, too.

"They've got to be as tired as we are, boss," Samuels said. "We've been at this for thirty-seven hours."

"And five minutes," a lieutenant added from the fire control corner. "Don't forget those five minutes."

"Six," someone else said.

Tired laughter filled the space.

"You think they picked up Ralphie's *survivors* yet?" Samuels asked Phelps in an undertone. USS Ralph Johnson, *a destroyer, was reported sunk the day before* Moray, *defending the aircraft carrier USS* Abe Lincoln *from an enemy submarine attack.*

"God, I hope so." Phelps' eyes never left the tactical plot. "We can't afford to lose anyone else. Not after the Battle of the Sea of Japan."

Samuels grimaced. "Yeah, we're supposed to be the shooters in the 'submarine shooting galleries.'"

"Someone should tell the enemy that." Phelps straightened. "All right, people, we're not going to sit here all day with our tail between our legs. Let's move out a bit and see if we can't catch back up to the strike group." She turned to a dark-eyed lieutenant. "Officer of the Deck, come around and increase speed to sixteen knots."

"OOD, aye. Right standard rudder, steady course zero-seven-four. Ahead standard for sixteen knots."

"Right standard rudder, steady course zero-seven-four. Ahead standard for sixteen knots, aye," the helmsman replied, using the handwheel—hastily installed on most boats after the war proved touchscreens less resilient to shock damage than Pulsar Power LTD claimed—to bring the submarine about. "My rudder is right fifteen degrees, coming to course zero-seven-four."

"Very well." The officer of the deck's smile was wan; a tiny woman, she looked like a firm wind might blow her down. But *Moray's* deck didn't even vibrate as the boat came around.

"Passing course zero-zero-zero," the helm reported.

"Sonar, Conn, tell me if you hear a peep from our friend," Phelps said into the speaker most submariners fondly called the bitch box.

It looked so new on Moray, *nothing like the battered and scratched ones Alex was used to on older* Virginia-*class boats. Would* Jimmy Carter's *even have paint left?*

"Conn, ah, shit, torpedo in the water! Two torpedoes in the water, bearing zero-zero-niner, range approximately ten thousand yards!" The words rocketed into the space.

Phelps' head snapped around.

"Hard left rudder! All ahead flank!"

"Oh, shit." Alex bit his knuckle to stop from swearing more. Conventional wisdom said to turn away from the torpedoes, but turning to port meant *Moray* had to overcome all the momentum *already* taking her to the right. Phelps acted on instinct and yet—

Alex held his breath as *Moray's* watch team launched countermeasures, and then—finally!—a snapshot torpedo down the bearing of the two enemy torpedoes. He hated backseat driving, and Alex didn't have a whit of combat experience, but everything was out of order. *Speed then turn with momentum. Snapshot,* then *countermeasures. Depth, why isn't she changing depth?*

Too late, Phelps ordered *Moray to* dive, using their countermeasures—really just bubble-creating noisemakers—to coax the torpedoes away. She took *Moray* deep, too, right to fourteen hundred feet, a *Cero's* test depth. But why not deeper?

Or why not go shallow?

Moray corkscrewed once more, up to almost fifty knots and still increasing. Even the best torpedo the French had, the F21 Artemis, couldn't go faster than that, and Alex heard more than one of his classmates sigh in relief as Phelps' boat shook off the two fish on her tail.

Then two more torpedoes appeared out of nowhere, launched from just two thousand yards away...and right in *Moray's* path.

The VDR feed showed a giant lurch, water rushing in, and white-faced people screaming right before everything went black. In the last second, Jane Phelps turned to look straight at the camera, her lips moving silently:

I'm sorry.

Chapter 4

Paying the Piper

The fun couldn't end there. Silence greeted *Moray's* televised death; no one knew what to say or how to say it. Already knowing that Phelps and her crew were dead hardly lessened the blow. Watching it made the pain fresh, made the war *real*.

"I hope to hell they never release these to the public," Alex whispered to Teresa. "Just...*shit*."

"I hear you." Mistress of Fidgets though Teresa was, she sat perfectly still, her eyes wide, staring at the blank screen. "Holy fuck."

"Yeah."

Joy. His death could be caught on candid camera, too, couldn't it? Alex grimaced. Letting that idea roll around in his mind only resulted in dread gurgling in his stomach. Yeah. Awesome.

"She should've gone shallow when she couldn't outfox the torpedoes," Alex whispered before he could stop himself.

"You think that would work?" Tommy asked from his other side.

Alex shrugged. "If you go deep, you have two chances of survival: outrunning the torps or tricking the damn things into chasing something else. With the new torpedoes our enemies have, that choice becomes one, because we can't outrun them, now, can we?"

"That puts a new spin on sixteen years of training." Teresa's eyes narrowed. "But why go shallow? You lose the ability to hide in the layer."

"Yeah, someone might get off if you hit the roof as the torpedoes hit." Just saying those words made Alex grimace.

"You mean emergency blow when you know you're going to die," Tommy said.

"Better than a collision course with the bottom. Then no one gets off."

"Still might not work. Modern torpedoes pack a hell of a punch." Tommy scratched his chin. "Could just spray pieces of everyone everywhere."

"Oh, that's a grand image. Thanks for putting *that* in my head, Tommy." Teresa slapped him on the shoulder.

"Hey, it's Alex's idea."

Alex tried to shake off the memory of how *Moray* died, of how her sailors had no chance to get off the boat. Could he had done better? Hell, who was he to even *wonder* about that? It was arrogant thinking he could do better than the best submarine captain the U.S. Navy produced so far in the war.

He'd probably never find out, anyway, not commanding *Jimmy Carter*. No way would the navy give good jobs to its oldest attack submarine. He didn't want to imagine what his future boat looked like. Would she be seaworthy? How many sound-absorbing tiles had fallen off over the years? She probably had a tick or two that kept her from being as quiet as she once was, otherwise the navy never would've scheduled her for decommissioning.

Wasn't that a happy thought? Admiral Hamilton thought so little of him, even after he saved her life, that she sent him to a boat that would probably never see combat. Alex scraped his hands over his face. Talk about a less-than-fantastic silver lining.

That thought sat like a rock in his chest all through graduation preparations. The idea of dying for his country was one he accepted the day he graduated Norwich University and entered the navy. It was a possibility he looked right in the face back on Armistice Station, too. Yet somehow, the thought of others watching the video after the fact was...sickening. Worse than the thought of public speaking.

"You okay?" Teresa asked as they found their seats.

Graduation was in a big tent outside. It was off-white thanks to Groton weather and covered in ruffled bunting in red, white, and blue. The once-temporary tent was a permanent fixture at the Sub School these days; classes cycled in and out so fast that no one bothered to take it down. They just removed the decorations, chairs, and podiums so random New England storms didn't do them in.

Families were seated to the right, staff to the left, and the class in the middle. Everyone got uncomfortable folding metal chairs, because the government loved paying top dollar for cheap things. But at least they were clean. Nothing beat walking around with a big black smudge on the seat of your stark-white trousers.

"Alex?" Teresa poked him.

He shook himself. "Sorry. Yeah. I'm fine."

"Sure you are, 'cause you just managed not to notice your daughters waving at you."

"Thanks." Alex fought back a cringe and craned his head right.

His wife, Nancy, stood out in the crowd of civilian spouses. Her dress whites were sharp, with three perfect rows of ribbons and three-striped shoulder boards that matched Alex's own. She wore a command-at-sea pin, too, identical to the one Alex would wear after he assumed command.

Nancy was, as always, tall, dark-haired, and gorgeous. Alex had been with her long enough to stop wondering what she saw in him, but every now and then, he reverted to the awkward college freshman who ended up serenading her from the end of the Alpha Company hallway to convince her to go to the Regimental Ball with him. Fortunately, his roommate had backed up him, because running the gauntlet of Nancy's upperclassmen cadre hadn't been much fun.

They laughed about the "rookie dates" in the mess hall now, where Nancy's cadre hammered Alex with questions and tried their best to make him crawl back into a hole. But if there was one trait in Alex that overcame his shyness, it was stubbornness. He hung on, she grinned and went to the ball with him, and that was history.

They commissioned into the navy side by side, with their first daughter—as unexpected as she was loved—in the audience behind them. From there, their paths wandered apart: Alex into submarines and Nancy on surface ships, like the destroyer she now commanded: USS *Fletcher* (DDG 155). And *Fletcher* was a damned sight newer than *Jimmy Carter*, too. Not feeling bitter was hard, but hey, Nancy'd been on the fast track since college. Alex was proud of her.

Their daughters, Roberta—Bobbie to everyone except her grandmother, currently on a well-deserved vacation—and Emily, stood on either side of Nancy. They were miniatures of their mother in looks, a fact he was always relieved by, though Emily had inherited Alex's lighter hair. Both grinned and waved to him.

Fuck being a morose piece of flotsam; *they* were proud of him. That was worth more than the world. Alex smiled and waved back, which made Emily giggle. Bobbie, on the other hand, went right back to staring at the six-foot-long cutaway model of USS *Cero* the navy broke out for moments like this, her eyes narrowed in concentration. She'd studied it through the entire ceremony, either trying to memorize it or bored out of her mind.

Maybe both. He never knew with his sub-mad daughter. Alex,

seated in the front row despite his test shenanigans—sometimes, the alphabet wasn't his friend—tried not to nap through Captain Fitzpatrick's droning speech. Shannon Fitzpatrick was the first female CO at the sub school, well known for being damned good at her job—but she was dry as dirt. Talk about the honor of serving one's nation amid a war wore thin.

Then it was Admiral Hamilton's turn.

Hamilton was tall, with brown hair just going to gray and hard eyes that put her on everyone's *don't fuck with* list. She was the highest-ranking woman ever to serve on submarines. Rumor said she was on the short list to get her third star in a hell of a hurry. Thankfully, her hatred for one Alex Coleman wasn't well known—even if her fingerprints were all over his new assignment.

Hamilton was also the mentor of the same CO, Chris Kennedy, who chucked Alex under the bus the *first* time Alex visited Armistice Station. Hamilton and Alex worked together during the latter attack on that same station, but today proved that her promised resurrection of his career was riddled with mines.

Even noticing him in the front row made her eyes narrow. Alex flinched.

"Ladies and gentlemen, I will keep this short," Hamilton said after Captain Fitzpatrick finally introduced her. "In the upcoming few weeks, you will take command of attack submarines. There, you will be our nation's first line of defense in a war that has not gone as expected.

"We all know the stats. Seven boats sunk in one hundred and six days. Over eight hundred of our brothers and sisters are on eternal patrol, lost in a war that we thought would be an easy win. Our enemies, however, are losing boats at *half* the rate we are. And this morning, we lost contact with *New Hampshire* in the Sea of Japan. No SUBMISS/SUBSUNK buoy activated, but she's missed three check-ins. We all know what that means."

A little moan ran through the crowd.

"But the loses aren't the only issue. We must face that we have both a tactical problem *and* a captain problem.

"If you believe I'm lecturing you on World War *Two*, think again. This is the same game with new players. Peacetime and low-conflict operations gave little indication of how commanders would perform in combat, and submarine warfare uniquely depends on our COs.

"Many of those COs look great on paper. They perform well in exercises. They are top-notch administrators and excellent leaders. *But they lose.* And when submarines lose battles, we don't limp back into port like our skimmer counterparts. Surface sailors can jump overboard as the ship sinks. We, on the other hand, start underwater. And what happens? All too often, we die, and we take *one hundred plus* shipmates with us." Hamilton ground out every word like she was eating glass. "Every person lost is a highly trained submariner who will be harder to replace than the boat he or she sailed on. And we can't afford for this loss rate to continue.

"Something must be done. I'm not asking you to go out there and take no chances. Rather the opposite. We have to take chances if we are to put a stop to this 'March Across the Sea' our French, Indian, and Russian adversaries have begun. We must embrace a certain amount of risk, take sensible chances. And that begins with the captain, with the title you will all soon wear.

"Right or wrong, a captain makes a boat. Great crews *begin* with a great CO, and a terrible CO will nullify their good crew without even trying." Hamilton paused, and Alex tried not to think of Kennedy, who wanted glory without owning the guts to do the right thing. "A captain unworthy of the name may bring their crew home, but the sad fact is that survival is no longer enough.

"When you deploy and take your submarines to war, I want you to consider these facts. We are no longer at peace. We need warfighters in the tradition of Jane Phelps, and we need them to survive."

Christmas Island Naval Base (Australia)

Hours of hide and seek later, Steph got her damaged destroyer to the relative safety of Christmas Island. One of Australia's smaller territorial possessions, Christmas Island was of zero tactical importance before the war—which meant it was now hotly contested territory. The joint U.S.-Australian base under construction was just the tip of the iceberg. Soon, there would be supplies, missiles, and rumor said submarines. For now, there were always at least three "shooters" (destroyers, frigates, or cruisers) there to defend the island.

There were also dozens of good cell phone towers on the island, so Steph could call her boss' boss without interference after *Dunham* dropped anchor.

She didn't dare leave the bridge, no matter how tired she was.

Steph just curled up in her chair—the executive officer's chair, not the captain's; she wasn't that arrogant—and pulled out her phone.

Eyelids drooping, she pulled up the number from her contacts list. The direct one. Damn going through some staff weanie.

"Lieutenant Commander Gomez here, ma'am," she said. "*Jason Dunham* XO."

"I read your report on the battle, Commander," Commodore Denise Woodward, commander of Destroyer Squadron 28, replied. "You got sandwiched. Don't blame yourself."

"Captain Tabor's dead." Steph swallowed back grief and tiredness. She hadn't known her captain for long, but he'd been her *captain*...and they'd been through the fire in the last few months. They fought two winning battles, three losing ones—or four, she supposed. Damn, things were meant to be better than this.

"What happened?"

"Got caught in a ladder well when a piece of *Nicholas* hit us." Steph shut her eyes on the image of Tabor's broken body. "He survived the hit but not the burns. He died a few hours later."

There was a long pause on the other end. Finally, Woodward asked, "How many other casualties?"

"Just three." Steph forced her eyes open, watching blankly as the officer of the deck transitioned from an underway to an anchored watch. "We couldn't pick up *Nicholas'* survivors. Or any of the others."

"We'll send unarmed ships in to get them. The Indians and French have been very civilized about that."

"I hope they stay that way, ma'am."

"As do I." Woodward cleared her throat. "All right. A repair barge is on its way to you. We'll talk more after you've gotten some sleep."

"Aye, ma'am."

Steph hung up, letting the light breeze kiss her cheeks. *Jason Dunham* still didn't have bridge windows, but at least they'd survived. Not far away, two cruisers swung gently at anchor, along with two other destroyers—one of which looked half burned to the waterline. She squinted to spot the hull number beneath the scarring. *146.* Was that *Farley?*

Shit, *Farley* looked worse off than they did. Was she the only survivor from the southern group? No wonder they lost communications. *Farley* looked like she lost half her superstructure.

"You okay, XO?" Ensign Darnell approached, bandages hiding her mangled right eye. But the young woman could smile and insisted she wasn't out of the fight, her courage serving as an inspiration to a crew that just lost their captain.

"Just tired, Angie." Steph slid her phone into her pocket. "And hungry. You think that Suppo left us any sandwiches down in the wardroom?"

"I'm pretty sure he works for you, ma'am. That means you can have sandwiches whenever you want."

Steph chuckled. "Someone should tell him that."

"I could, but he outranks me by about a lightyear, so I think I'll delegate that one upward." Darnell grinned.

"I see how it is! You save your courage for simple situations like enemy action instead of facing off with supply officers." Steph wagged a finger at Darnell. "You'd make a terrible peacetime officer, young lady."

"Guess I'm lucky there's a war on, then."

Steph didn't look back as they headed down the ladder from the wardroom. There would be other battles to fight and repairs to do before then, but for now...she needed a break. The whole crew did.

Chapter 5

Personal Boogeymen

Once certificates were handed out and commands were officially announced, Alex joined his family for the post-graduation festivities. Like most things in wartime, they were plainer than those in peacetime. Today's features were three tables of appetizers—including a platter of cakes so dry Alex thought they were baked pre-war—two punch bowls, and nifty little cards proclaiming that SOAC Class 2038-2 was *Free and Ready*.

Reading the class motto made Alex cringe. Why in the world would anyone vote for that? His personal contribution had been *Shoot the Sunzabitches*, but apparently no one wanted to quote Mush Morton these days.

Or at least not where their little kids might read, he thought with a smile as Bobbie and Emily approached. His daughters were older than everyone else's kids—next oldest was Jonas O'Canas, who was two months younger than Emily.

"Congrats, Daddy." Emily bounced forward to hug him. "And you're so snazzy in your whites!"

Alex laughed. "Says the girl who spilled tomato sauce on these *same* whites when she was ten."

"Well, not the same ones." His fourteen-year-old daughter grinned. "I remember you throwing those out. With extra-special dramatic flair and *lots* of swearing."

Shaking his head, Alex wrapped an arm around his younger daughter and planted a kiss on the top of her head. Emily took after her mother in height and was growing fast. She'd end up taller than him before long. Her hair was Alex's, but her casual optimism always reminded him of his own mother, long dead.

Alex had barely been a teenager when his parents died in a car accident. He'd been lucky that his older brother, Sam, was just old enough to get a job and support them so that they didn't have to leave their childhood home. Money had been worse than tight, and he'd never have gone to college without a navy scholarship, but they'd made it work.

And his daughters would never have to worry like he had at their age. Emily could be optimistic and happy. Bobbie, on the other hand, was short, sassy, and married her father's contrary streak to her mother's brown hair and green eyes. Currently, she was glued to Twitter, which was a distinct drop in quality from her previous study of the *Cero* model.

Alex cleared his throat. "You keep reading stuff limited to two hundred eighty characters, kiddo, and you're going to forget how to talk in complete sentences."

"Very funny, Dad." She didn't look up. "Isn't *Jimmy Carter* old as dirt?"

"My boat's certainly more mature than you, but it's not a competition."

Bobbie stuck her tongue out.

"Sticking your tongue out is hardly the way a potential naval officer acts." Nancy walked up to arch her eyebrows at their eldest. "Unless your career goals have changed?"

"I'm sixteen, Mom. They change every five minutes." Bobbie rolled her eyes. "Besides, I'm reading tweets by some jackass French sub CO. Says he sank *Moray*, but that didn't happen, right?"

Alex froze. "Let me see that?"

"Sure." Shrugging, Bobbie handed the phone over.

Captain Jules Rochambeau @JulesRochambeau

Is @USNavy missing another submarine? Perhaps you should check on @USSMoray. She might not answer.

#Barracuda #moray #submarines #war

Fuck. Alex chewed his lip to stop himself from swearing aloud. "*Moray* sank last night. Or this morning, local. It hasn't made the news yet."

"And this guy tweeted about it?" Bobbie took her phone back. "What a dick."

"Bobbie." Nancy's voice was flat. She turned to Alex. "So, Bangor, huh?"

"I fly out in a week." The news wasn't as sobering as *Moray's* sinking, but a cold ball still settled in Alex's stomach. Going to war was bad enough, but flying across the country to do it and leaving his family behind felt like Admiral Hamilton just wanted to rub salt in his open wounds.

He'd expected a boat out of Groton. Nancy was stationed in Newport, Rhode Island, and their home in North Stonington, Connecticut, was as close to in the middle as you could get. The navy was usually good about trying to co-locate married couples, and since Nancy and Alex hadn't had the courtesy to pick the same specialty, that meant Newport and Groton.

He could see Nancy thinking the same thing but not saying it with the girls present. Her lips twitched. "That's quick."

Alex shrugged, forced himself to sound casual. "There's a war on."

"Do you know when you're going to deploy, Mom?" Bobbie asked, sounding very young.

"Not for a while yet." Nancy's smile looked as hollow as Alex felt. "*Fletcher* is still in the yards for her TACTAS install."

Bobbie and Emily exchanged silent looks. Alex wished to hell he could just hug them and make the fears go away, but his girls were too old—and too wise. Alex and Nancy were lucky that their deployments never overlapped before his assignment to Armistice Station and doubly fortunate that Nancy's mother lived with them to cover when other navy commitments took both away from home. But war changed everything.

"Come on," he said. "Let's get out of here and catch a late lunch somewhere. Girls' pick."

Bobbie scowled. "Don't you have to do some future captain-y things, still?"

"Nah."

Alex could check out of the Sub School in the morning, and he'd keep up with his friends and classmates online. Waving at Teresa and Tommy, he shepherded his family out of the tent and toward the parking lot.

"Commander Coleman." The ice-cold voice stopped Alex and Nancy both in their tracks, but Alex knew Admiral Hamilton wasn't interested in talking to his wife.

"You three go on. I'll be there in a sec."

Nancy shot him a questioning look, but Alex shook his head. So his wife saluted Hamilton and steered the girls away while Alex steeled himself for the inevitable ass-chewing.

"I expected better of you than intentionally failing a test, Commander," Hamilton said. At least she was decent enough to wait until his daughters were out of earshot.

"I assure you, ma'am, failing wasn't my intention." Now wasn't the time to point out that he only failed because no one could find the *Seawolf* answer key. Alex was damned sure his answers had been right, because his life depended on learning about his new boat.

Talk about motivation.

Hamilton's smile was razor thin. "I'm sure." She looked him up and down. "I wish you the greatest success on *Jimmy Carter*, Commander. I'm sure you'll do the navy proud."

"I'm so glad I've got your confidence, ma'am."

She snorted. "You're unconventional and uncontrollable. I don't like that, but maybe you'll prove me wrong and be what we need."

Alex swallowed. "I hope I'll get the chance."

If he didn't, it would be because *Hamilton* sent him to an ancient boat no one was going to put on the front lines. Was *Jimmy Carter* the death trap his classmates thought? He didn't want to ask.

"I'm sure you will." Nodding sharply, Hamilton turned on her heel and strode away.

Riding in a private plane from Groton, Connecticut, to Washington, D.C., seemed like either the height of luxury or a waste of gas. Even going back to the Academy, Winifred Hamilton heard stories about how well navy admirals were treated, but hopping on a plane to avoid a seven-hour drive boggled even her mind. Particularly when that plane had a full-on military communications suite.

Not that she needed it. Freddie's current title was Special Assistant, Submarine Warfare to the Chief of Naval Operations. Submarine warfare was quiet, lonely, and not something you talked about until it was too late to make a difference. But her boss was an aviator, and guys who drove jets knew jack about submarines. He probably hadn't set foot on one since he was a midshipman.

And suggesting he get *his* important butt up to Groton to tour a boat about to deploy would be shot down without consideration, too.

Freddie, on the other hand, lived and breathed submarines. Part of the first class of women assigned to submarines, she stood up to the Old Boys Club in the boats until they got over themselves and accepted her. And how had she done that? By completing every watch qualification ahead of her peers, studying harder, and doing better. Freddie always knew she wanted command, and she'd gotten it, first of a fast attack submarine, and later of a boomer, or ballistic missile submarine.

Admiral's stars came slowly, but when she put them on, she became the first female submariner to wear them. Technically, being shot at on Armistice Station made her the first female submariner to see combat, too, but Freddie wasn't going to wave that badge of honor around—she'd let that go to the gals on the boats who faced down the enemy every day now that they'd gone to war.

War.

Not long ago, her job had been to *avoid* war. The meeting on Armistice Station *had* been a peace summit before negotiations over Indian Ocean resources went in the crapper after Admiral Jeff McNally got jumpy and sank an Indian submarine. And then the unthinkable happened: instead of stopping to *talk*, the Indians went full bore and attacked with a fleet.

Sighing, Freddie leaned back in her too-comfortable seat. Rehashing the war's opening acts, even in the privacy of her own mind, would get her nowhere. Forty minutes until D.C., at which point she'd stop being a submariner and go back to being a politician. The idea didn't usually make her so angry; her ambitions always meant she'd aim high.

But encountering Alex Coleman always left her in a bad mood. The man was two for two on finding the *worst* trouble spot and sitting right smack in the middle of it. And the navy had enough problems without their personal problem magnet making things worse. Yes, he'd done a good job on Armistice Station—Freddie was honest enough to admit that she might be in a POW camp without him—but that didn't mean he was trustworthy.

The phone next to her right hand buzzed. Since Freddie believed in answering her own phones instead of hiding behind an aide, she picked it up.

"Admiral Hamilton."

"Freddie, it's Scrap," the CNO said, using his callsign as infernal aviators did. "I'm going before Congress in ten minutes and need gouge on the taking of Armistice Station. Give me all the information you've got, even the stuff that wasn't in your report."

"*Congress?*" Freddie slammed upright.

"The fucking media is still claiming cover up concerning the Battle of the Strait of Malacca, so the Senate's refused to confirm Jeff McNally as SUBLANT. Lord only knows what's going to happen when we tell them what happened in Sunda Strait."

Freddie bit off her feelings concerning Jeff McNally. He was a perfectly nice gentleman, not to mention a personal friend, but he'd *also* commanded the first American carrier strike group lost in combat since World War II. The man froze, plain and simple, but Big Navy didn't want anyone outside the lifelines knowing that.

"Sir, to be frank, we *are* covering things up," she said slowly.

"I know that. That's why I need some chaff. Talk to me about Armistice Station. What was the name of the young commander who saved everyone's bacon?"

"Commander Coleman." She gritted her teeth so hard they hurt.

"Is he available in the next few days? If I could have him testify before Congress—"

"I'm afraid he's in route to Kitsap-Bangor to take command of a submarine." Cutting a senior admiral off was rude, but the idea of *Alex Coleman* testifying before Congress was far worse. Lord only knew what the man would say. The navy needed *good* spokespeople, not a loose cannon.

Freddie regretted offering him a submarine. Pity the man hadn't taken the medal, instead. Caught up in the emotional high of surviving—and sneaking several thousand civilians away from the station before the French used them as hostages—she promised a future command to a reckless and unpredictable officer.

Shuffling him off to *Jimmy Carter* was the only way to mitigate the damage.

"Damn." Scrap—known to the public as Admiral David Chan—sighed. "Got any useful decoys I can throw in their faces to ram this confirmation through?"

"Sir, are you sure you *want* to? Jeff's a good man, but is he the man to lead the sub force through this war?" A shuddering breath rattled in her chest. "We're losing one out of every three boats we deploy, and Jeff didn't exactly do...well in the SOM."

"Which is why we have to rehabilitate him. I'm not letting some political or media shitstorm ruin a good officer," he replied.

"The current shitstorm will be a *lot* worse if we get caught in a lie." She didn't say *if you get caught in a lie*; one didn't call the CNO out like that. Freddie wanted to end her career with *four* stars. She still had two left to go.

"The media's got enough present battles and loses to distract them."

"I'm not sure the *Senate* does."

"I'll come up with something." Scrap was probably waving his hands on the other end. Freddie couldn't count how many times she watched him act out some imaginary air battle with nothing except his ego and ten fingers.

Of course, Scrap had the same amount of combat experience she did: zero. Less, if you counted Armistice Station in her corner.

"Good luck, Admiral," she said.

"Thanks, Freddie. Fly safe. We'll chat when you get back."

That *chat* turned into witnessing an hour-long ragefest where Scrap broke his favorite model plane *and* dented his farewell plaque from Strike Group Seven. Never the shrinking violet type, Freddie didn't shy away from that little display, but she *did* regret the time wasted.

The time would've been better spent on finding someone appropriate to fill the job as Commander, Submarine Forces Atlantic.

SUBLANT was supposed to be the senior submariner in the navy, and Congress had rejected Jeff McNally in ten minutes flat. Neither party wanted him. What *Freddie* wanted was to get someone competent in the job—but Scrap picked Admiral Long Trieu before she could make a coherent argument.

On the bright side, Long hadn't commanded the worst loss in U.S. naval history since World War II. On the *not*-so-bright side, he also hadn't seen the inside of a submarine since Freddie was a junior lieutenant.

Yes, the war of the submarine was a perfect time to have a F-35 pilot as Chief of Naval Operations.

Chapter 6

Once Over Dust

6 August 2038, Saint-Denis (France)

Some would say it made him a traitor to France, but Jules Rochambeau loved the tropical atmosphere of Saint-Denis. A soft wind wafted over the covered deck at the newly built officers' club, leaving the smell of the sea in its wake. Jules nibbled cheese while reading the news, a luxury he rarely had since the taking of Armistice Station—which, he was pleased to note, remained in French hands. Oh, the Indians had a detachment there, too, and were talking about using it as a submarine base, but *French* marines claimed the station, and French it would remain.

"Are current events to your liking?" Admiral Bernard asked as he approached, waving for Jules to remain seated. That was a rare honor—Jérémie Bernard was the chief of France's entire submarine force, and Jules Rochambeau was merely the commander of *Barracuda*.

"*Oui, mon amiral.*" Jules' handsome face creased with a smile. Pity there were no cameras, but his was a secretive service. "I particularly enjoy that the media calls us and our allies the Freedom Alliance—it is much less onerous to say than the Union for the Freedom and Prosperity of the Indian Ocean. And it sounds patriotic."

Bernard chuckled, accepting a drink from a uniformed server with a nod. The admiral was dressed casually, as was Jules. "*C'est bon.* As is the territory we have gained, thanks in large part to your contributions."

"I am a mere submariner, Admiral," Jules replied, leaning back in his seat. "With the exception of Armistice Station, I can neither take nor hold territory."

"No, but you have sunk those who would threaten our forces. As they do so. Port Louis fell three days ago, and India has nearly pacified the Maldives."

"I am glad to do my part." Jules cocked his head. "How much do you think they will let us keep when peace comes?"

"Island nations will have to be freed." Bernard gestured airily. "Our overeager Indian friends will never get to keep the Maldives. But smaller islands of shared culture and the underwater stations...we shall see."

Jules chuckled. "It is good that our friends are more ambitious. Our gains may go unnoticed in the end."

Bernard leaned forward, his brown eyes intent. "We are not colonizing fools. We French learned our lesson on that front. We do not take *nations*—we take equipment, sitting on the ocean floor. And we let those who once owned said equipment leave peacefully, as you did at Armistice Station."

Jules' fists tightened reflexively, thinking of how his perfect takeover of Armistice Station was ruined by Alexander Coleman. Had Coleman not intervened, war might have been avoided—

Yet Jules Rochambeau was a master of war, so perhaps he did not regret it. So far, France's quiet takeover of four additional stations in the Indian Ocean and five in the Southern Pacific had almost doubled his nation's GDP. In peacetime, France would have moved slower, gained fewer resources.

Perhaps war was for the best.

He met his admiral's eyes. "What is my next mission?"

"Lurk in the Gulf of Aden. Teach the Americans that they can no longer enter the Indian Ocean without consequences."

"I have already been there." Jules sank a destroyer and America's best submarine while he was at it, too. He sighed. "Should not our Indian friends defend the entrance to 'their' ocean?"

Bernard bared his teeth. "Do you not want to become the most successful submarine commander of all time? I hand you that opportunity."

"Am I not already?"

He let an edge creep into his voice. Bernard was his superior, but Jules knew his worth. Eight kills since April. No submariner in the world could match that. Even Britain's star, the much-vaunted Ursula North, only sank two ships—one a lumbering spy ship!—in that window. All *his* kills were warships.

Bernard laughed. "Oh, do as you're told, *Capitaine*. And tweet about it if you must."

Jules spread his hands. "Who am I to deny the world a little entertainment?"

5 August 2038, Naval Base Bremerton, Washington (the other side of the international date line)

Admiral Hamilton wasn't petty enough to keep someone from meeting him at the airport when he arrived in Bremerton, Washington...was she?

Alex sighed, glancing back at the rental car parked in the visitor spot for his new boat. Whatever the reason, no one had noticed his arrival at the end of Pier Five. In fact, no one seemed to notice much of anything. The dark-hulled submarine at the head of the pier was the sleepiest warship Alex could imagine.

Her younger cousin across the pier—whose brow skirt read "USS *Columbia* (SSBN 826)"—was busy. The ballistic missile submarine was in the middle of a stores onload, three sailors in a paint punt touched up paint on her outboard side, and a crane lowered equipment into her aft hatch while two officers watched.

Jimmy Carter had a measly three sailors on watch.

Pausing to shift his seabag to his left shoulder, Alex studied his new command. On the bright side, all of *Jimmy Carter*'s 453 feet looked well kept; the paint above the waterline even looked fresh. A second glance, however, showed her age. Rust peeked out from underneath the flat black paint and her sound-absorbing coating. Alex shook his head. *Once over dust, twice over rust.* Good to know navy traditions survived the war.

Jimmy Carter had been scheduled for decommissioning and dismantling before the war started five months ago. Extending submarines beyond their planned service lives was dicey, but war was war. They needed all the boats they could get, and this rusty lady now belonged to Alex.

Or she *would* be his once he took command from whichever

lucky soul was leaving. Well, time to pay the piper; Alex hefted his second bag and headed toward *Jimmy Carter's* brow. Much to his surprise, someone spotted him, and a flurry of activity on the boat's quarterdeck produced a short guy wearing coveralls from the submarine's forward hatch. After a quick conversation with the watchstanders, the newcomer headed down to meet Alex.

He was a gray-haired master chief petty officer who looked as crusty and unflappable as the rest of his breed. His faded coveralls bore the golden badge of *Jimmy Carter's* chief of the boat, and his sleeves were rolled up unevenly, revealing tattoos on both forearms. One was of a chicken chasing a shark and the other an anchor surrounded by roses. But his smile was cheerful and competent, which was more than Alex expected. Acid churned in his stomach.

The master chief was shorter than Alex's five foot eight. Skinnier, too, and his salute was casual. "Afternoon, sir. I'm Master Chief Bryan Morton, Chief of the Boat. We didn't expect you until tomorrow at the earliest."

Alex returned the salute with a smile. "Not a problem, Master Chief. I learned to drive, oh, a few years back. I did okay getting myself here from the airport."

"Glad to hear it, sir." Morton eyed Alex warily. Yeah, he expected to get his head ripped off.

I've had plenty of COs who would shit on you for this, Master Chief, but luckily for both of us, I'm not one of them. Alex refused to kick his first day off by being an asshole. So what if he'd gotten lost twice driving from the airport? Alex had never set foot in the state of Washington before today, but he found the base. Eventually.

"What can you tell me about her?" Alex asked, dropping his bags and stuffing his hands into the pockets of his khakis.

Nancy would've yelled at him, but she was back home and not there to gripe about uniform standards.

Morton barked out a laugh. "What'd they tell you up at the Sub School?"

"Jack shit and nothing."

A search of unclassified websites told Alex that contractors had been set to start dismantling *Jimmy Carter* last May. He assumed the navy retained custody of her since the unexpected explosion of war...but Alex remembered what they said about assumptions.

The master chief sighed. "We've got about half our allotted crew and most mission-essential gear back on board. They pulled the spec ops stuff over six months ago, but it doesn't look like we'll need that for straight-up wartime ops, anyway. We've kinda been the sump for everyone else here in Bangor, though; when someone has an emergency need before deployment, the squadron tells them to grab it from us if they can't order it in time."

"And they haven't quit even though we're technically in workups." Morton scowled. "Biggest personnel problem is that we're damn short on officers. We've got the majority of our divos, but most of 'em are greener than grass. We lost our last department head three days ago, too."

"Come again?" Alex blinked.

"The navigator got transferred to *Sole* when their nav got stolen by someone else. Weps and the engineer left a few months ago; both went to boats leaving on patrol. *Sole* got underway yesterday, so Lieutenant Chin ain't coming back. He was the OIC before he left. DCA is the senior gal now—that's Lieutenant J.G. Alvaro."

"No CO or XO?" Alex tried not to gape.

"Not other than you, sir. Commander Gordon left a month ago. Went to *Oregon*. Got sunk by some Russian not long after."

"Shit."

"You got an XO in your pocket, sir?"

"Not that I know of."

Alex scraped a hand over his face. U.S. subs were sinking like lead, but he hadn't expected his predecessor to be dead and gone. Normally, the navy gave incoming commanding officers at least a week of overlap with their predecessor, during which he or she learned about their submarine from the person who knew it best.

Not this time. USS *Oregon* sank with all hands defending American underwater stations near Alaska.

Sucking in a breath, Alex looked at the gargantuan submarine nestled alongside the pier. She was old, ungainly, and no one in their right mind would call *Jimmy Carter* beautiful. Even the boomer next to her looked better proportioned.

Morton eyed him.

"All right, COB," Alex said. "There's obviously a metric shit-ton of work to do. Bring the crew topside. I'll read my orders, and we'll get on with it."

Morton blinked. "You want me to rig up a microphone or something, Captain?"

"Nah." Alex shook his head. "I hate ceremonies, and the crew's not that big."

Even the thrill of being called "captain" for the first time couldn't suppress the flotilla of butterflies fluttering in his stomach. What was he thinking? He just signed himself up to talk in front of a group of people he didn't know.

Alex's hatred of public speaking started with his fourth-grade teacher deciding she could cure his shyness by forcing him to read books aloud in front of the class. Then she yelled at him for wanting to hide in a corner.

Public speaking. Definitely a reason he wasn't sorry for semi-bombing that last test.

"Give me five minutes, sir," Morton replied. "You want me to show you to your stateroom in the meantime?"

What he wanted to do was vomit.

Alex shook his head. "I'll just take a walk around topside."

Washington, D.C.

"You ready, Admiral?" Commander Maria Vasquez, promoted after their time on Armistice Station, asked Rear Admiral (Upper Half) Hamilton.

Freddie sighed. Her own promotion had been approved by the Senate in the early days of the war, but it didn't make her any fonder of that august body. Particularly not when her job was to hold the CNO's metaphorical hand during his testimony. Wearing two stars was nice, but being the CNO's security blanket was a drag.

"Admirals are born ready, Maria." She squared her shoulders, grateful for the small office one of Senator Angler's staffers provided to the navy team. *Probably without him knowing. The man is a menace.*

Maria stepped forward to twitch Freddie's tie tab into place. "You think the hearings will end this week?"

"Not if Senator Angler has anything to say about it. He wants this to be his ticket to the presidency." Freddie scowled. "Are my bat wings straight?"

"More or less. I'd rather wear an actual tie than this stupid tie tab," Maria replied, referring to the women's uniform version of a tie the armed services still wore, not-so-affectionately called bat wings. Maria looked her up and down. "You look good, ma'am."

"Thanks, Maria. Now here's hoping I don't have to *say* anything."

Two-star admiral or not, Freddie was still outranked by the CNO, so she ducked into the next room to fetch Admiral David Chan, the Chief of Naval Operations, with Maria following discretely on her heels. Chan was small, wry, and dark haired, as explosive in personality as he appeared physically. Normally the media's darling, he'd taken quite the beating during the first five days of the "Angler Hearings."

"You bring those facts and figures, Freddie?" Chan asked without turning away from the mirror he glared at himself in.

"Yes, sir." She managed not to grimace. "Eight subs since the war's start. One carrier, six cruisers, and nine destroyers. Also five frigates, seven littoral combat ships, and two oilers."

Being Special Assistant to the CNO meant Freddie did a lot of odd jobs, and the worst of them was tracking ship and submarine losses.

"And the media's *still* accusing us of covering up high-ranking incompetence." Chan, better known as his call sign, Scrap, spun to face her. "Fuck sticks."

Freddie sucked in a cautious breath. "They may have a point, sir. We've been notoriously bad about explaining losses—"

"I'm not firing someone for losing a battle!"

"Even if it's because of incompetence rather than bad luck or enemy action?"

"We're trying to fight a war." Chan rolled his eyes. "We don't have time to explain ourselves every time some captain or admiral stubs a toe."

Freddie resisted the urge to point out that stubbed toes meant lives lost. "I'm not sure Senator Angler will appreciate that perspective, sir."

"Screw him. He's a traitor. Spent six years in the navy, and now he's trying to nail us to the wall."

Freddie blanched. "You probably shouldn't throw accusations like that around with a war on—"

"Admirals, they're ready for you." Chan's aide stood in the doorway, trying to pretend he hadn't heard Chan ranting.

Freddie wished she had that luxury.

As promised, *Jimmy Carter's* crew assembled aft of the sail. This was the largest part of the submarine, the place the entire crew could gather—excluding those critical few on watch. The long, flat, and black deck of the submarine stretched aft from the sail, seeming interminably long to Alex before it vanished under the harbor's quiet waters to meet the propulsor. He was used to smaller submarines, to the compact Swiss Army Knife of the *Virginia*-class. This beast he was about to assume command of was like an alien creature.

Taking a deep breath, Alex headed their way, his eyes tracing over the sub as he went.

How a sub looked on the outside told him damn near everything he needed to know about the crew…and *Jimmy Carter* looked surprisingly good. Lines were faked out neatly. Everything was stowed in its place. What rust Alex could see was caused by saltwater mating with metal, not neglect. She was old, yeah, but maybe not decrepit.

On the surface, her lines were familiar, with a smooth edge leading up to the sail. Her planes, the vertical "fins" used to control a submarine's depth, were all underwater, so at least *Jimmy Carter* lacked the appearance of wings sticking out of her sail like some earlier classes of submarine. But she also lacked vertical launch cells forward; unlike the *Virginias* Alex was used to, his new boat couldn't launch missiles without using her torpedo tubes. That seemed like a little thing, but to an experienced submariner, it revealed an indisputable truth: *Jimmy Carter* was not designed to attack land targets. She was built to sink ships and submarines.

Of course, the *Seawolfs* had been designed during the Cold War, when America had a near-peer competitor in the Soviet Union. When the USSR died, the *Seawolf* funding did, too, which was why Alex's new boat was the last in a class of just three. She had been designed to fight an undersea war that never came. How would she do in the one that arrived now that she was thirty years past her prime?

Alex shivered. Old or not, *Jimmy Carter* was his. Independent command was the pinnacle of every naval officer's career. Back on Armistice Station, being chased out of his exile by French marines, could he imagine being here?

Hell, he still couldn't imagine he'd done the batshit-crazy things he did back then. Only in his nightmares did it feel real.

Focus, Alex. His mind liked to wander when faced with crowds. Alex wished he'd brought some note cards. Why was his chest so stinking tight?

"Attention on deck!" Morton's bellow sounded like it came from a much larger man. A dark-skinned lieutenant (junior grade) stood by the master chief, and Alex returned her salute. *Alvaro* said the nametape on her coveralls. Morton said she was the damage control assistant, hadn't he? *Damn, she looks young. If this kid's the senior officer, the navy's cupboard is stripped bare.*

"Welcome aboard, sir." Alvaro's voice was husky.

"Thanks, DCA." Alex forced a smile. No use scaring the kid or anyone else. The crew needed time to get comfortable with him. COs came in all shapes and sizes, and their personality quirks could make or break the climate on the boat.

Best not to think of the war or how if he failed these sailors none of them would come home. The sea of a hundred or so faces—wait, no, there weren't that many. Shit, how shorthanded was he?—watched Alex with a mix of apprehension and curiosity.

Most of them were young, too damned young. *Look confident, asshole.* Hatred of public speaking didn't fit with the tradition of a fearless and all-knowing commanding officer, but this crew needed to know he was competent. No one wanted to hear that he was the most nervous person present, no matter what kind of samba the butterflies in his stomach tapped out. Alex sucked in another deep breath. He'd never been a conventional leader, but if that's what his sailors needed, Alex would do his damnedest.

"At ease, folks." He waited for *Jimmy Carter's* sailors to relax. Curious eyes watched as he resisted the urge to stuff his hands back in his pockets, instead clasping them behind his back. "I know that this is far from the usual way to conduct a Change of Command, but I figured I'd save us all a lot of putting on dress uniforms and standing on ceremony. I also hate speeches, so I'll keep this short."

Breathe. Fucking breathe.

"Here's the obligatory professional biography. My name is Alex Coleman, and I'm coming to you from the Naval Detachment on Armistice Station." No need to mention what happened there—Alex was so glad that the Battle of the SOM got all the headlines! "Before that, I was XO on *Kansas* and Weps on *John Warner*. My divo tour was on *Virginia*, and I commissioned out of a tiny military college most of you have never heard of.

"My wife's also in the navy, currently commanding USS *Fletcher*, a destroyer. We've got two teenage daughters, which means my fuse is long and I'm good at detecting bullshit. I could stand up here and tell you my life story, but it's pretty damned ordinary. We've got years to get to know one another and plenty of work to get done in the meantime." *And if you haven't heard about that mess on* Kansas *or* Armistice Station, *so much the better.*

His eyes slid over to Morton. "Anything to add, Master Chief?"

"No, sir."

Did Morton think he was crazy? Normal? Incompetent? Alex

couldn't ask. Damn, he missed Master Chief Casey, but he was still on *Kansas* with Chris Kennedy, who Alex *didn't* miss.

"Then let's finish this thing." The butterflies were tapdancing now. Was Alex Coleman really going to take command of a submarine?

Kennedy would shit a brick.

"Attention to orders!" Morton barked. The crew snapped back to attention.

This is it. Fish or cut bait.

Alex unfolded his old-fashioned paper orders and read aloud: "To Commander Alexander G. Coleman, from Commander, Naval Personnel Command. Report not later than 5 August 2038 to SSN Two-Three, USS *Jimmy Carter*, homeport Naval Base Kitsap-Bangor, Washington, for duty as Commanding Officer."

Refolding his orders, Alex turned and popped a salute off to Lieutenant (junior grade) Alvaro. "I am ready to relieve you, Lieutenant."

"I am ready to be relieved, sir." Alvaro returned the salute.

"I relieve you."

"I stand relieved, Captain." The DCA waited for Alex to lower his salute first, and that was that. Alex Coleman was in command of USS *Jimmy Carter*.

There but for the grace of God go I. Alex turned back to face Morton, smiling to mask his nerves. It was over. He had command, and maybe he could skip out on future speeches. "They're all yours, COB."

The master chief's craggy face split into a smile. "Aye, aye, Captain."

Watching his COB send *Jimmy Carter's* crew back to work left Alex breathless. He'd burned for command of a nuclear-powered attack submarine since the age of eight, had learned he'd never get one at thirty-six, and now he was here. Sure, she was the oldest attack boat in the fleet, but Alex didn't care. *Jimmy Carter* was his.

And, hell, it wasn't like the navy was going to send them into the deepest reaches of combat, anyway. He'd be lucky to see *one* fight at *Jimmy Carter's* age.

Chapter 7

Twice Over Rust

The first spectacularly unpleasant surprise arrived the next morning.

Sure, Alex's first twenty-four hours aboard were full of bad news, including the number of crew missing (59 out of 141), the amount of equipment removed from the boat, and the shredding carpet in the captain's stateroom. The latter was a rude awakening when Alex's feet hit cold metal upon rolling out of his rack in the morning, but fortunately, no one was there to hear him swear.

That was a nice perk of being the boss, but it didn't make up for cold toes.

Still, his unhappy feet woke Alex up faster than usual. Most days, he stumbled around like a grumpy zombie before he got in a few cups of coffee, but now he could hear a voice much like his wife's laughing in his head while he danced away from the bare patches, muttering and whining. A quick shower warmed him up, though, and then he headed to the wardroom, or officer's mess.

Alex had just finished his second cup of coffee when Master Chief Morton knocked on the wardroom door.

"Come in!"

Alex was alone by then, shoveling down some scrambled eggs. They weren't great—they were made from powdered eggs rather than fresh ones, which told him a lot about either how good his supply officer wasn't or how little priority *Jimmy Carter* was for the sub squadron.

All the division officers had hurried out twenty minutes earlier, either getting to work or just fleeing from the captain. However, Alex found that an unexpected advantage of being the captain was that he set his own schedule. For the first time in his career, he wasn't at someone else's beck and call. It was a heady feeling, despite the substandard eggs.

Yet his sense of duty wouldn't let him sleep in. Captains shouldn't sleep while their crews worked, but it took two cups of coffee before he felt vaguely human.

"Morning, Captain." Morton leaned on the doorframe.

Being called "Captain" still made Alex's heart leap. At least until he saw Morton's grumpy frown and hunched shoulders.

Alex glanced at the stack of papers to his right and wondered how he'd overlooked some gem. "What's the problem, COB?"

"Fifteen of our new sailors arrived ten minutes ago." Morton scowled.

"Your expression says that's not a good thing."

Master chiefs were master chiefs, and there was probably a reason why his was cranky. Morton did seem surprisingly sharp for the type Alex expected the navy to assign to a worn-out boat like *Jimmy Carter*, though. He made a mental note to ask about that later.

"Ain't exactly a bad thing, Captain, 'cept they're fifteen new schmucks straight out of school. Got two third class petty officers in the bunch, but they made rank out of C School. The only second class is a yeoman, and he's never so much as seen a submarine, much less been on sea duty. Not a one of the kids has even toured anything that ain't been a museum for less than twenty years, either."

"That's...fantastic." Alex swallowed.

Morton laughed. "Isn't it just?"

Complaining wouldn't fix it, so Alex bit back a growl. "That leaves us still short, doesn't it?"

"Yes, sir, and way junior across the board. These guys aren't the only ones. Just about every sailor the squadron sent our way is new enough to squeak. An' the rest of them are problem children whose boats dumped them on the SUBRON before getting underway or medical cases still not cleared for sub duty."

Even better. Even the sailors Alex's boat had were young for their billets, inexperienced, and likely possessed little, if any, sea time. He'd known coming in that he wouldn't get sailors with combat experience—the war was only five months old—but Alex had hoped for more than newbies and problem children.

"You've been talking to the manning people at the squadron?" he asked.

"Yes, sir. They say they're 'working on the problem.'" Morton didn't have to say what he thought about that.

"I'll drop by and talk to the chief of staff today." Alex sighed. His to-do list kept growing, but he always could have said no when Admiral Hamilton offered him command. *Yeah, I could have some shiny medal and a desk job instead.*

Had Hamilton expected him to take that offer? His current assignment made a lot more sense if she had. *Bet she didn't expect me to do well at the sub school, either.* Alex tried to keep his feelings off his face. Morton didn't need to know he was saddled with a CO who hijacked a cruise ship a couple months after going to admiral's mast. Sure, he'd done the right thing. He'd saved a couple thousand civilians, too. But the navy didn't always care about that when you had a history of disobeying orders.

What would Morton think if he *did* tell him? Hell, he was better than Commander Chris Kennedy, who'd tried his best to sink a civilian submarine, but that was a shit standard of comparison.

Morton shook his head. "Not sure it'll do you much good. If you'll pardon me for saying so, the COS ain't gonna get much more done. She ain't payin' attention to any boat that isn't headed out on war patrol, that's for sure."

Alex smiled. "Master Chief, if you're anything but honest with me, then I'll worry. Be as blunt as you like."

Morton grinned the wicked expression of a sailor who'd been in the navy for twenty-plus years and offended many officers along the way.

"Now that you might not appreciate, sir."

"I'm sure I won't." Alex laughed.

His first command promised to be full of problems, but at least his chief of the boat was competent.

Christmas Island (Australia)

Eight days made a hell of a difference. Sure, the enormous sheet of metal welded over the hole on the O-3 level was ugly, but *Jason Dunham* could steam and fight.

Assuming she got the missiles to do it.

"What do you mean there aren't any SM-6s available?" Steph asked Lieutenant Audrey Yang, the DESRON 28 weapons officer, standing by the cubicle Yang called home.

Destroyer Squadron Twenty-Eight's offices weren't exactly shabby, but they weren't what Steph would call high-tech, either. Everyone was still working off laptops—two each, because classified and unclassified networks Shall Never Meet—and three different colors of desks dotted the office landscape. Given that the Christmas Island base was exactly two months old and this building three weeks newer than that, Steph supposed it wasn't bad. Just...rushed.

Kind of like everything in this war. We're making things up as we go.

"We've got nothing, ma'am. I'm sorry—I'm not holding back, either." Yang grimaced. "The only missiles we have are already in another ship's launch cells."

Steph stepped on the urge to swear. "What about SM-2s? They're antiques, but antiques still explode when they run into other missiles."

"The navy no longer has any SM-2s in inventory. They either all got shot off or..." Yang gestured helplessly.

"Or went to the bottom." Steph rubbed her arms, suddenly feeling cold. Taking a deep breath, she glanced around the sea of cubicles. Most of the furniture was plastic and hollow. It made for weird, echo-y noises and left her feeling like she was inside a demented egg carton.

"I was trying not to mention that."

"Sorry." Steph shook herself. "Can you at least tell me what priority we are for when ammo comes in?"

"First in line." Yang smiled wryly. "Unless a cruiser trumps you."

"Rank has its privileges, yeah." It went without saying that Steph was just a lieutenant commander. She was the *acting* commanding officer for her ship, and maybe, just maybe—

"Commander Gomez, a word?"

Steph spun, finding herself face to face with Commodore Woodward. "Yes, ma'am?"

"Step into my palatial office, please."

Steph followed Woodward silently, eyeing the taller woman's back. Woodward was a straight shooter, a good commodore who didn't pull punches and always told the truth. Commander Tabor had liked her, she remembered. XOs didn't socialize much with squadron commanders, particularly now that war turned commodores (previously a title used only by courtesy when they had the actual rank of captain) into one-star flag officers.

The door clicked shut behind Steph with a weird little shimmy noise; yeah, it was plastic, too, wasn't it? Woodward's office was just as cheap looking as everywhere else, empty of the usual "love me" wall covered in mementos of a senior officer's various tours. Had she left them back home in Mayport, Florida?

Probably doesn't want to lose all the pictures and plaques if a missile gets dropped on this place. Not that anyone on the other side had started bombing bases yet. They were probably short on missiles, too.

How had the pre-war planners not seen these missile shortages coming?

Right. Everyone thought the U.S. Navy would roll in, spank the enemy, and that would be that. It would be a short, victorious war, and they'd all be home for Christmas. Steph almost laughed aloud at the thought until she remembered where she was.

"I wanted to tell you in person that I've requested a new CO for *Jason Dunham*. Commander Tabor's replacement should be here within two weeks," Woodward said.

Steph tried not to twitch. "That's good news, ma'am."

"Your record so far is stellar, Commander, but I have to be honest—you're a very new XO, and while you've handled things well, I'm not sure you're ready to take the seat just yet. Not with a war on."

"I never thought I would, ma'am." *Just hoped.*

"I'm glad to hear it. You've got a brilliant future, Steph. Keep up what you're doing, and you'll be in the chair in no time." Woodward's face creased with a rare smile. "Admiral Hamilton tells me you did well on Armistice Station, too."

"I'm glad she remembers me fondly." Steph wanted to squirm, both from disappointment and delight. Admiral Hamilton was a submariner, so unlikely to ever be in Steph's chain of command, but she was *the* up-and-coming female admiral in the service. Everyone knew she'd be CNO someday—and Steph *had* done well on Armistice Station.

Even though it had been an absolute clusterfuck.

Washington, D.C.

"I can't believe they're hanging me out to dry." Rear Admiral (Upper

Half) Jeff McNally paced from one end of his small Norfolk, Virginia, office to the other.

McNally was the picture-perfect naval officer: slender, well-built, and with the classic "look of eagles." He looked nothing like the admiral who froze up in the Battle of the Strait of Malacca and doomed three ships in the war's opening hours.

Captain John Dalton remained seated, watching his boss grow redder in the face. He was plumper than his admiral and with a small bald spot on the back of his head that he'd stopped bothering to hide when he got promoted to captain. "You don't know that they are, sir."

"The hell I don't." McNally twisted to glare at him. "Don't look at me like that. No one's gunning for *your* head."

"No, sir, they aren't." John didn't need to mention that was because *he* hadn't frozen. John wasn't exactly the hero of the Battle of the SOM—in his opinion, that was Captain Julia Rosario of USS *Bella Wood*—but he'd done his duty.

The silver star Admiral Rodriquez pinned on him even said he'd done it well. It was one of the war's first two silver stars, as a matter of fact—and it all but guaranteed John would get admiral's stars someday. *And I won't dishonor them the way McNally has*, he promised himself. The award was made even sweeter since it was pinned on him while standing next to his longtime friend Nancy Coleman. Nancy was his wife's college roommate and her destroyer, *Fletcher*, had been one of the few survivors of that hellacious battle.

"With Congress chewing on the CNO's ass every day in those 'Angler Hearings,' you know he's going to pony up a scapegoat. And I'm the most convenient one." McNally flounced into a high-back chair. "As if there was any goddamned way to know the Indians would *dare* attack a carrier strike group!"

It might have helped if you didn't sink one of their submarines in a fit of paranoia, John didn't say. Unfortunately, he was still this man's chief of staff. "At least we aren't also at war with China?"

"No, just this damned Union for—what the hell is it?"

"Union for the Freedom and Prosperity of the Indian Ocean," John replied. "Don't ask me for the French version. I took Latin at the Academy."

McNally's scowl was fierce enough to make his nose shrink by a factor of two. "India, Russia, and France. We knew they were sharing technology, but now they're gobbling up every bit of choice real estate in the Indian Ocean—and under it! Who the hell let them think they had any right to do that?"

"Might makes right. It's colonization all over again, just without any natives on the ocean floor to make things awkward." John shrugged, but he was glad to be off the topic of McNally's fading career. "Russia needs warm-water stations—and ports—so they come down from the north. And France is busy dividing up the IO with India, conquering every island nation that doesn't willingly ally with them."

"Most of the cowards jumped face first into that damned Freedom Union."

John shrugged again. McNally wasn't wrong; nearly every nation bordering the Strait of Malacca jumped in with the Freedom Union, as did Madagascar and every former French colony in the Indian Ocean—except Mauritius, which France took with barely a shot fired three days into the war. India nabbed the Maldives almost as quickly and was in the middle of looming over Sri Lanka like a hungry shark.

Then Russia all but destroyed the Japanese Naval Self-Defense Force...along with a good chunk of the U.S. Navy's Seventh Fleet.

No one was sure how many hundreds of sailors died since the war started. The Red Cross still hadn't gotten POW reporting procedures in place; everything was chaos. *Some* Americans must have been picked up by the enemy...but even if they had, there were probably close to seven thousand Americans dead.

In just five months.

While John Dalton sat in a small office, babysitting an even smaller man.

Naval Base Bremerton, Washington State

Ninety minutes after breakfast, Alex's second unpleasant surprise presented itself.

"September tenth." Alex tried not to let his jaw drop. Instead, he concentrated on sitting back in the surprisingly plush chair at SUBRON Five's headquarters. "You want me to get underway in thirty-four days?"

Commander Alicia Melendez, Submarine Squadron Five's Chief of Staff, rolled her eyes. "That's what I said."

The sub community was small, but they'd never met. Alex knew Melendez's reputation, however, and two minutes in her presence confirmed its accuracy: *arrogant, narrowminded, and not as competent as she thinks.*

Melendez looked down her long nose like he stank and treated him like dirt from the moment he walked into her office. She was a handsome woman, with stylishly arranged dark hair and an immaculate uniform, one she probably had tailored, despite that being against regs. But the smugness in her expression robbed Melendez of actual beauty. He bet her permanent sneer did nothing for her working relationship with any of the COs in the squadron, either.

Melendez wasn't his superior. She was the commodore's chief of staff, or principal deputy, but the commodore was Alex's boss. Melendez was only a hair senior to Alex, too; she made rank just a month before him. They were both O-5s, he was *Jimmy Carter's* commanding officer, and she was an idiot.

He bit back the impulse to tell her to pound sand. "That's going to be a problem."

"We put you in the job to solve problems, Captain, not complain." Melendez made a show of crossing her hands on her desk. "You might not have noticed, but the war isn't going well for the navy. We need every boat in theater, including *Jimmy Carter*."

Alex gritted his teeth. Melendez clearly knew about how Chris Kennedy nailed him to the wall on *Kansas*, sticking him with a coward's reputation and winding him up in a career-ending admiral's mast. That explained a lot. Maybe they were even friends; Kennedy liked meticulous assholes like her. But reputation or not, Alex had no intention of sitting on his hands while his country fought for its life.

In the first five months of the war, the navy had lost nine submarines. That was three times the number built per year during peacetime and thirty percent of the total deployed. Combat in the Indian Ocean kept heating up, and the world's "premier" navy had yet to rise to the challenge. Even the surface side struggled, and rumors of missile shortages indicated that submarines would be even more important in the future—maybe even old ones like his boat.

The U.S. wasn't the only nation under pressure. Faced with the Indian-French-Russian juggernaut, America made allies of her own out of the usual customers. Britain and Australia signed on out of necessity; the Freedom Union wanted them out of the Indian Ocean, too, so it behooved Britain and Australia to join up. Japan needed help resisting Russian territorial ambitions but soon regretted their entry into the "Grand Alliance" when the Battle of the Sea of Japan decimated their navy.

It was ugly all around, and not just because of Melendez's expression. The prewar U.S. Navy expected to outclass their opponents...and didn't. Worse yet, the three big navies of the Grand Alliance were severely outnumbered.

Odds in the Atlantic had the potential to grow worse if a second front opened against the Russians, too. That led to an unhappy compromise that sent half the boats stationed on the East Coast north to help the Brits prepare against the Russians, while the rest and the West Coast submarines teamed up with the Australians against the French and Indian navies.

"Lecturing me won't get *Jimmy Carter* underway any faster, Commander," Alex snapped. "I'm at sixty percent enlisted manning, and that's only because fifteen puppies straight out of prototype arrived this morning. I'm missing half my wardroom, including an XO and all three senior department heads. Your manning people have been stonewalling my COB ever since he reported on board. While I would love to get underway in accordance with your *precious* schedule, we might need a bit of help from the squadron."

Melendez flushed. "I had no idea *Jimmy Carter's* manning issues were so severe."

"Then you might just want to investigate why your people haven't passed that information up the chain of command." Alex set his jaw and resisted the urge to call her a liar. It wouldn't get him the crew he needed, no matter how true.

"I'll see what I can't do." Melendez's lips curled. "But you'll have to wait your turn. Unless you suddenly have a sea daddy in your corner willing to help?"

"I appreciate anything you can do." Alex's pleasant smile bordered on insolent, but what could she to do to him? No, he didn't have a senior officer willing to pull strings for him. Admirals hadn't liked him since *Kansas* got within twelve nautical miles of Armistice Station.

Master Chief Morton was right; Melendez was an incompetent tyrant. How the hell was Alex going to get a crew to go to war with?

He had thirty-four days to figure that out.

Chapter 8

The Unexpected

7 August 2038, 100 nautical miles out of the Gulf of Aden

"Range nineteen thousand yards to track 7011 and twenty-four thousand yards to track 7012," the sonar watch aboard USS *Razorback* (SSN 857) reported, grinning.

Razorback was just the second Improved-*Cero* class attack submarine and the newest American submarine sent into combat. She was a lean, mean, fighting machine: 396 feet of HY-80 steel and with four torpedo tubes full of Mark 48 CBASS variant torpedoes. They were all war shots, and her torpedo tube doors were open. She was ready.

All her younger sisters remained in workups, but *Razorback's* crew of 121 busted tail to get her out the door in record time, barely nine months after her commissioning. Lieutenant Commander Patricia Abercrombie was proud of them. They trained hard, played hard, and they were about to prove how well they fought.

Damn, what a way to get in the game. Excitement hummed through her control room, expressed in small smiles and quick glances. *Razorback* even still smelled new, with the tang of metal welds in the air. She hadn't been at sea long enough for most anything major to break, which left her crew a little paranoid, but here they were—about to make history.

"Solutions set," Weps announced.

"Solutions checked," Patricia confirmed, her eyes sweeping over the readouts. Pat Abercrombie was career navy, going all the way back to diapers. Her mother had retired as a master chief petty officer, and Pat won her way into the Academy despite two younger brothers both enlisting. One was a submariner, stationed on a ballistic missile submarine and far from the action. The other was an aviation mechanic, serving on a carrier much like the two in *Razorback's* sights.

She swallowed a grin, but not laughing out loud was hard when you had India's *only* two aircraft carriers in your sights.

Of course, they had others under construction. Intel even said one would commission next month. But that wouldn't make up for the loss of *Vikrant* and *Vishal*. This was a blow from which India might never recover—one to balance the scales in a war rapidly not going America's way.

A chill ran down her spine. Glancing around control told her that everyone else felt the same; *Razorback* was about to make history with her first kills. More importantly, their navy *needed* this, needed a morale boost and a tactical advantage. And *Razorback* was about to deliver both. The atmosphere was electric.

Belatedly, she realized something was missing and turned to stare at her commanding officer.

Commander David Harney was tall enough that he had to stoop almost everywhere in the submarine; only by standing close to the ladder leading up to the sail could he stand up straight. His powerful jaw and long nose almost looked like a beak, and busy eyebrows accented his angular face. He wasn't handsome, but he was striking. Not a face you forgot easily.

Harney was competent, charismatic, and generally great to work for. Unlike Patricia, he wasn't an Academy grad, but he was so damned good that she didn't even jokingly hold that against him. He led *Razorback* through her workups with an eye on the eventual goal of getting to grips with the enemy who had so far inflicted a three-to-one loss ratio on the U.S. Navy.

Yet now Harney stood rigid, wide-eyed, and silent.

"Captain?" Patricia stepped forward and then hesitated. "We're ready to fire."

"Target speed three-zero knots," sonar said, as if to add emphasis to Patricia's point. "Range now twenty-two thousand and twenty-seven thousand yards."

"We...we should get closer." Harney blinked. "Closer."

Patricia blinked. "Captain, we have solid firing solutions."

"Closer would be better." Harney shook his head. "Can't risk shooting the wrong ship."

Weps snorted. "There's only Indians out here. No one'll mind, sir."

"Don't say that!" Harney spun to face the weapons officer, finger pointing like a gun. "I will *not* be another Jeff McNally!" All remaining color drained out of his face. "We have to get closer."

The reference to the man who lost the *Enterprise* Strike Group made everyone in control flinch.

Harney started shaking. Four quick steps took Patricia across control to be by his side, her stomach rolling in fear and confusion. Every eye in the space was on them; *Razorback's* attack center was a cramped area, full of consoles, monitors, and sailors at battle stations. She reached out to squeeze Harney's arm, but he yanked away, stumbling back a step and hitting his head on overhead cables.

He didn't even swear; he just kept shaking.

"Sonar, what's the likelihood of detection if we sprint and close the range to twelve thousand yards?" Patricia asked.

"High. They've got two destroyers lagging behind as they turn into the wind to launch."

"Thank you." She turned back to Harney, speaking in an undertone. "Sir, this is the best shot we're going to get, and every minute we wait increases the range by another thousand yards."

"We can't shoot the wrong *ship*, XO. Not again."

Patricia swallowed. "Captain, this isn't the SOM, and you're not Admiral McNally."

"Do you know what'll happen to the navy if we do something like that again? From this far out, there's no knowing what our torpedoes will do!"

Then why did you set up for a long-range firing solution? Patricia wanted to scream. But that wouldn't help things. "The CBASS has a maximum effective range of twenty-one nautical miles. We're still around half that. There's no historical data suggesting that a CBASS will wander off, and even if they *do*, the only people around us are hostile."

"Can't miss. We can't afford to." Harney started shaking his head, now, over and over and over again.

"Targets increasing speed to three-five knots. Range up to twenty-five thousand yards and opening."

"Captain, we need to fire," Patricia hissed.

"No. No, I'm not. I won't."

Patricia's chest felt tight. "Would you like me to take care of things, sir?" she asked, swallowing. Maybe that was the way out. She could shoot these carriers, Harney could gather himself, and then things could go back to—

"No!" Harney wheeled to glare at her, eyes wide and wild. "Don't you dare! I won't tolerate mutiny on my boat!"

"*Mutiny?*" Patricia's jaw dropped.

"You heard me!" Harney's response was almost a scream. "Left full rudder!" No one moved. "Open the range, OOD."

"Open the range, OOD, aye," the navigator said slowly, glancing at Patricia.

Sighing, she nodded. Harney didn't notice, bouncing on his toes while the helm responded to the order and put the submarine into a slow left turn.

Without warning, Harney spun on his heel and fled control, hitting his head again on the way out. Patricia did not follow him.

Groton, Connecticut, U.S. Naval Submarine School

"And...I'm no longer in limbo." Lieutenant Maggie Bennett dropped into her seat, cracking open a Coke.

Much to her surprise, she wasn't the first back in the blue-walled classroom full of classified computers. Wartime meant a shorter lunch period than peacetime. This wasn't the relaxed learning environment it had been when Maggie was a young, aspiring submariner at the basic course. Now the instructors were driven and focused, and extra time was time to study. No nice, long workouts with leftover time to eat at the Submarine Officers' Advanced Course now!

Located at the Sub School in Groton, Connecticut—like everything else important in submarines, much to Maggie's displeasure, since she hated New England weather—SOAC polished up future department heads before sending them out to the fleet. In her case, it was SOAC Class 38030, full of forty-two fellow officers on the fast track to war.

Most of them were on shore duty when the war started. Some, like Maggie, were still division officers. She'd even been at sea aboard the navy's spy sub, USS *Parche*, albeit in the wrong place for all the fireworks. Maggie *thought* she had a lateral transfer to the intelligence community all lined up after that...but the Powers That Be had other ideas.

Maggie Bennett was a slender woman in her late twenties, with frizzy black hair that pretended to have curls. She tried harder to control it at the Sub School than she did when sticklers weren't watching, but otherwise, she was by-the-book. Most submariners were; training as a nuclear engineer reminded her why the book *mattered*. One wrong step with a nuclear reactor could lead to worse than disaster. Checklists existed for a reason, and procedural compliance was a religion.

So she rolled with the orders without complaint. Maggie had signed up to be a naval *officer*, not some movie star who got special treatment. Sure, staying in boats wasn't her dream job, but she was good at it, so there were worse ways to fight a war. And she couldn't imagine sitting on the sidelines while her friends went to sea, anyway. Still, the speed of it all was a little dizzying.

Two weeks after Congress declared war for the first time since 1941, Maggie was ripped out of *Parche* and on a plane to Groton, one of her least favorite places in the universe.

At least the lobster was good, and it wasn't winter.

"Get a call from the detailer?" Lieutenant Martin Sterling asked without looking up from his engineering manual.

Marty probably hadn't even left for lunch. Dry as dirt and just as boring, Marty rarely joined his classmates at a local restaurant and never even drank. Maggie'd never even seen Marty work out, which accounted for the beer belly he'd grown since their arrival at the Sub School.

Not that the navy cares if we meet physical standards these days, she thought, tearing open a brownie from the vending machine. *We're losing too many submariners at sea to kick people out for being overweight, especially when they're as experienced as Marty.*

One of the few things she and Marty had in common was that they both had assignments yanked out from under them. Neither knew where they were going, not even with graduation in twelve days.

In Maggie's case, *Moray* sank last month and clearly no longer needed a navigator. Marty, on the other hand, was originally slated to be engineer on *Sailfish*, but a medical emergency on another sub ignited a string of second-order effects that ended in Marty losing his orders, too. They weren't the only ones in Class 38030 who'd been jerked around—almost a third of their class got the Submarine Roulette treatment—but together with Benji Angler, they were the only ones left on ice.

Maggie shot him a sideways look. "You've got orders, too."

Leave it to Marty to sit there without saying a word. Sometimes, she thought he enjoyed watching the rest of them run around like headless chickens. He was the only one in the class who refused to lose sleep over losing his orders. Marty didn't care what boat he went to, as long as it had a reactor and a screw that went roundy-round.

Marty was what they called a "prior," or someone who'd been an enlisted sailor before commissioning. In his case, he'd been a nuclear machinist's mate, which meant getting him for engineering officer was any captain's wet dream. He *looked* like a slovenly nerd, with glasses that rode down his nose and a bald head that shined, but Marty was smart and could draw a nuclear reactor from memory on a napkin while drunk.

"I can't imagine what gave you that idea." Marty's tone was dry, but Maggie thought she saw a twinkle in his eyes.

"You gonna share with me or what?" Maggie liked gossip and hated not knowing everything. She knew that'd make her a good intelligence officer, but somehow the navy kept missing that memo.

"Well, the rumors are true, Ms. Know-It-All. They aren't decommissioning *Jimmy Carter*."

Her jaw dropped. "You're *also* going to *Jimmy Carter*?"

"Don't look so surprised. I heard they've got no department heads." He shrugged. "I'm guessing Angler is coming with us."

"All three of us?" Maggie frowned. "I guess that makes sense. The next class doesn't graduate for another two months. We're it, aren't we?"

"Nice of you to be so cheerful about it. You're not the one heading out to own the oldest nuclear power plant in the fleet."

She rolled her eyes, counting reasons off on her fingers. "Oh, crap. First off, there's still a couple of *Ohios* around, so *Jimmy Carter* isn't quite the oldest. Second off, you'll love the challenge. Lastly, I hear they're going to re-commission some *Los Angeles*-class boats. *Those* are really ancient."

Marty shrugged. "My luck, I'll get sent to one of those after *Jimmy Carter*."

Maggie bit her lip, trying to hide her butterflies. This was far from a challenge *she'd* appreciate. She loved being on the cutting edge of both tactics and technology, and *Jimmy Carter* was everything but that. Even worse, her new assignment was a sad echo of her last one. *Parche* was the first *Cero*-class to be modified for spy work...built from the keel out to be *Jimmy Carter's* replacement.

It was a double blow for a woman who wanted to transfer to

intelligence. Maggie's original assignment had been to *Moray*, an even newer *Cero* commanded by none other than Jane Phelps. Disappointment gurgled bitterly in her gut.

No one would have refused her request for a transfer to the intelligence community if the war hadn't given the navy an insatiable appetite for submariners. *Needs of the navy*, her detailer said. No surprise there.

Angry, she shoved a loose curl out of the way, too annoyed to wonder how it escaped her bun.

"I doubt Angler gives a damn, but you look like someone stole your puppy," Marty said.

Maggie grimaced. "They call them orders for a reason, right?"

"Yep."

"*Jimmy Carter* commissioned in 2005. She's five years older than me!"

"Bet your skin's better, too." Marty looked back down at his manual. Old fashioned as he was, it was a hard copy—and was that a *Seawolf*-class manual? Where the hell did he get that?

Maggie's frown deepened. "I just hope we don't wind up with some old geezer who commissioned back when the boat was new or some no-load idiot of a CO to balance out *our* high scores."

That would be her luck. It really would. Marty groaned.

"I hate it when you make sense."

This is not *how I wanted to spend the war.*

Jason Dunham might not be officially hers, but Lieutenant Commander Stephanie Gomez still had a job to do. So, on the morning of August 7th, she organized a memorial service for the sailors they lost.

Most of the bodies had already been sent back to their families. This wasn't the 1940s; they didn't need to bury their dead at sea, and families didn't have to wait weeks or months for notifications. Modern communications were quick, and casualty notification officers were deployed within twenty-four hours of Steph's initial report...but that didn't make things easier on board.

A crew was a family. A dysfunctional and weird family, to be sure, but a family. *Dunham's* crew was particularly tight-knit, and losing four of their own—particularly their captain—burned.

Peacetime navies weren't used to losing people, and despite the burn scars running down *Dunham's* port side, Steph knew the U.S. Navy hadn't quite grown out of its peacetime habits.

So she assembled the crew on the fantail, stole a chaplain from one of the cruisers, and put together an impromptu service. Then she strong-armed her supply officer, Lieutenant Nguy, into putting together a Steel Beach Picnic on the missile deck afterward, complete with music, beach towels, and a barbeque. Anything to keep the crew's mind off the loss.

Laughter started slowly, but by lunchtime, the music was louder and the crew happier. Steph stayed off to the side—the XO wasn't supposed to be anyone's friend—but smiled to herself. She'd have to thank the command master chief later; this was a good idea. Even if she couldn't hear herself think over whichever boy band blared out of the speakers.

"Commander Gomez, I presume?" a voice said from behind her.

Steph turned, eyes going wide when she spotted a short, Hispanic man wearing two admiral's stars. He wore coveralls and a submariner's dolphins, but how did an *admiral* get on her destroyer without anyone telling her? His nametape read *Rodriquez*, which told her nothing helpful.

"Yes, sir." She gulped. "Can I, uh, help you?"

"I'd apologize for being an asshole who crept up on you, but I'm afraid it's my nature." Rear Admiral (upper half) Rodriquez grinned. "Being an asshole, that is. Your quarterdeck watch tried to call you on the radio, but they didn't get an answer, so I came hunting."

Feeling like an idiot, Steph looked down at her radio, only to find its battery dead. "I'm sorry about that, sir, I—"

"No need to apologize, XO. I've been around long enough that I can find my way around most destroyers, so long as no one makes me go inside the skin of the fucking ship if it's a class other than *Evans*." He snickered. "We submariners get uneasy with all this sunlight."

"Would you like to go inside? I know it's loud out here." Steph didn't like being caught flat-footed, particularly by strange admirals.

"Nah, I don't burn that damned easily. I dropped by to pay my respects, but I understand I'm a bit late." He grimaced. "Good of a time as any to tell you that *Dunham* is chopping over to my surface action group as soon as you get a CO and some weapons."

"We'll be glad to get back in the fight, sir." Steph wasn't sure about fighting a surface ship under a submariner, but at least last submariner she worked for had guts. That was more than she could say about Admiral Allen.

"I bet you will. Commodore Woodward says you've got a good

ship and a better crew—I'm going to need both. I'm not really a big believer in sitting by watching the fucking paint dry, if you know what I mean."

Steph grinned. "You'll have our best."

"I'm counting on it, Commander."

The Western Pacific Ocean

"And *that* is how you do that," Commander Chris Kennedy said with a grin, gesturing at the periscope display screen on board USS *Kansas* (SSN 810).

Punching his captain in the face would have made Master Chief Chinedu Casey's day, but chiefs of the boat did not do such things. Even when rearranging Kennedy's arrogant, narrow features was so richly deserved.

I fucking hate this man. "It is good to get some of our own back, sir," he said instead of redecorating the bulkhead with Kennedy's nose.

Control on *Kansas* was oddly quiet for a boat that just sank one of the enemy. Kennedy stood dead center, his eyes gleaming. At least he'd been too busy tactically to strike a pose.

This time.

Kennedy wasn't as good looking as he thought he was; like most everyone on a boat with great cooks—which *Kansas* had—he had gained weight on deployment. There wasn't much room to run on a boat, and Kennedy hated to shave, so he let the morale and welfare team sell "no shave" chits to the crew. That left Kennedy with a weird, scraggly goatee of blond fuzz going gray that did nothing to make him look as dashing as he thought.

Casey, on the other hand, was short, dark-skinned, and barrel chested. He knew he could take Kennedy out with one punch if he dared, but it would end his career and wouldn't do the navy a bit of good. So Casey restrained himself to fantasizing.

It was a nice fantasy, though. Casey might've hated his captain less if he hadn't had to watch the asshole try to shoot a civilian submarine before the war even started and then nail the XO to the wall for *failing to follow orders* when he tried to stop him. That tanked the career of one of the best officers Casey ever worked for. Alone, it would've been enough to make Casey unwilling to piss on Kennedy were he on fire, but then the asshole went and sank a French frigate before the formal declaration of war.

Only the fact that the U.S. *did* go to war with France saved Kennedy's ass, along with his fairy godmother, Admiral Hamilton, who seemed to see *something* in the jerkwad. She always had Kennedy's back, which meant the bastard kept on the golden path and *Kansas* just had to endure him.

It was a pity the man combined being a good tactician with being a shit leader.

"We've lost almost a dozen subs in the war so far, Master Chief," Kennedy said as if Casey didn't already know. "*Moray* was the worst loss, but even they didn't make enough of a difference. We'll make more."

"We've got the best crew in the navy, Captain." *They damn well have to be, to put up with you.* "We'll do whatever it takes."

Kennedy preened; Casey snuck a look at the XO, who looked a little bit hunted, like she'd been run over by a particularly enthusiastic truck. Lieutenant Commander Alison Hunt was a good sort, too good for Chris Kennedy. Like a turtle, she retreated into her shell if you kicked her often enough.

And Kennedy sure as fuck loved to kick people.

Still, he had to give the man credit. They were all still breathing, and the poor bastards in that Indian boat breaking up weren't. Casey resisted the urge to take a listen over at sonar. Judging from the expression on Senior Chief Salli's face, it wasn't pretty.

"Might be the first *Akula* II sunk by an American boat in the war so far, sir," he said, because Kennedy was *their* asshole, and *Kansas* damned well deserved the credit.

"*Akulas* aren't anything to write home about, not even the newer ones India bought from Russia." Kennedy scowled for a moment. "Still, you're right. It's better than most people manage, and we also got that *Scorpene* earlier. They're newer and quieter. We're on a roll. Has anyone else managed two in one day?"

"*Moray* did, Captain," Hunt said quietly.

Kennedy didn't *quite* roll his eyes, but his scoff was audible. "They won't remain the gold standard for long. We'll overtake them."

Casey's eyes flicked over to meet Hunt's; neither pointed out that *Moray* couldn't overtake anyone from the bottom of the Indian Ocean. But Kennedy being crass was no surprise.

When no one answered, Kennedy frowned, eyes narrowing as he

glanced around the space. "XO, we should celebrate. Surf and turf tonight!"

Hunt's smile was wan. "I'll let Suppo know."

"C'mon, XO, you can't still be down about that hit on *Belleau Wood*." Kennedy wrapped an arm around Hunt's shoulders and ignored the way she tensed. "We're making history here! *Kansas* is going to be the *Wahoo* of this war—just you wait!"

"I'll go talk to Suppo, sir." Hunt ducked out from under Kennedy's arm and fled. Not wanting to give the captain a chance to follow her, Casey stepped forward.

"Want me to secure from battle stations, sir? Crew could use some rest after a long and successful chase."

"Damn straight, COB. See to it. I'll be writing my patrol report."

"COB, aye." Casey managed to smile, despite the fact that he worked for a prick who just insinuated his XO shouldn't be upset over her little sister's death on board USS *Belleau Wood*.

The cruiser had survived the Battle of Cocos Islands—barely—but a full third of her crew hadn't, including Lieutenant (junior grade) Lily Hunt. Kennedy was of the opinion that losing her sister back in May meant the XO should be fine by now. Casey just added that to the list of reasons why rearranging his captain's face would be a great swan song on the way out of the navy.

Not that he'd do it. Someone had to protect the crew from this sadly competent asshole.

Chapter 9

Mountains to Climb

9 August 2038, the Pentagon, Washington, D. C.

Vice Admiral Long Trieu was a decent sort, but he was having a terrible day.

"That's three boats in three days, Freddie." The new Commander, Submarine Forces Atlantic, slumped in his chair, looking tiny and pale against the shiny black leather.

His cavernous office was empty except for the two of them, and there was no need for Trieu to keep his public, confident, face up. And Freddie could see the exhaustion etched into his features.

Since none of the sunken subs had sunk in the Atlantic Ocean, one could be pardoned for assuming Long might not be responsible for them. However, he was *also* SUBFOR, or Commander, Submarine Forces, the senior submariner in the entire U.S. Navy. Which meant every sub was his.

Including *Missouri, Washington,* and *Balao*.

"I know, sir. Freddie didn't sigh. She was tired of being the ball bounced between the CNO and SUBLANT. The CNO didn't know jack about submarines, and the man he picked to be the senior submariner in the entire navy was...lacking.

Not for want of effort. Just temperament.

Trieu didn't even fidget. He just stared blankly at the tablet displaying the electronic SUBMISS/SUBSUNK message announcing *Balao's* demise. The silence stretched on so long that Freddie didn't know how to break it; she tried to sit back in her own chair and wait, but she burned to pick up a phone and *do* something.

Then her phone beeped, and for a moment, she hoped she'd get her wish. But it was just a text from Maria, with a link to a tweet—

Captain Jules Rochambeau

@JulesRochambeau

It is a pity @USNavy isn't what it used to be. I admit I was expecting more of a challenge. May our brothers and sisters on USS Balao rest on eternal patrol.

#BarracudaStrikesAgain #war #submarine

"*What* the hell?" Her jaw dropped.

Trieu jumped. "Freddie?"

"This—this is..." Shaking her head, she extended her phone, waiting for the explosion.

Trieu read the tweet, read it again, and then slumped in his chair, seeming to shrink by at least fifty pounds. "Isn't Captain Rochambeau that French hotshot?" he whispered.

"Yes, and now he's *gloating* about sinking *Balao*." Freddie tasted blood. Had she bitten her tongue too hard?

"God, could this get any worse?" Trieu sighed, and then a knock came on the door.

His aide, a bright young woman named Commander Wongchai, stuck her head in. "Sir, we have a problem on *Razorback*. The XO just flew a P4 message to their Commodore... Apparently, Commander Harney's lost it."

"What? How?"

"Message is on your tablet, sir."

Trieu pulled it up, and Freddie pretended she didn't see his hands shaking while Wongchai handed her an identical tablet. Her eyes raced over the message.

...lined up shots on two Indian CVs, but CO was unable or unwilling to take the shot. All he would say was that we couldn't afford to shoot the wrong ship. CDR Harney locked himself in his stateroom yesterday and refuses to emerge. Am heading for Pearl; request instructions immediately.

"Sweet lord," Freddie whispered. Trieu said nothing.

And then more nothing. Finally, she sighed.

"Sir, we need to replace him. We can't have COs melting down in combat and *not* sinking the enemy. We lose enough boats as it is without giving the Indians freebies."

"There had to be a reason, right?" Trieu finally said.

"There certainly is." Taking a deep breath, Freddie sat back in her chair, willing herself not to look back down at the tablet. "You read up much on World War II submariners?"

"Everyone knows about Mush Morton and Dick O'Kane, sure." Trieu cocked his head. "Where are you going with this?"

"I'm talking about their early problems with COs who were 'insufficiently offensive minded' and struggled to shoot the enemy."

"Submarine warfare was new then. We've been the best in the world at this *since* World War II. It has to be something else."

"I'm sure some big-brained think tank will figure out the root cause in four or five years, but the problem is the same. We have at least one CO who can't—or won't—shoot. There will be more."

"Then what the hell am I supposed to do? Line up a firing squad and shoot Harney at dawn for cowardice before the enemy?"

Freddie wished she could be sure he was joking. "We replace them. Starting with Harney—stick someone in the seat who we know won't go to pieces when the shooting starts."

Trieu dropped his head into his hands. "Because we have so many of those. Jane Phelps is dead, remember? Unless we pull Chris Kennedy out of *Kansas*—he seems to be doing okay, and an Improved-*Cero* is a step up from a *Virginia*."

"Not him." Freddie kept a straight face with an effort. She remembered Kennedy, remembered taking him at his word for what happened when *Kansas* first tried to protect Armistice Station. Now...she wasn't so sure. Kennedy might be the brilliant straight shooter she once took him for, but maybe he was a braggart and a fool. The U.S. Navy needed a sure thing. "I was thinking of John Dalton."

"Dalton? He's still Jeff McNally's chief of staff."

"A position where he's wasted. He made some good calls at the SOM. Let's give him *Razorback* and see if he can make some more."

"He's an O-6. Full captains don't take O-5 level commands."

"With a war on? I bet he'll jump at the chance." Freddie allowed herself a small smile. *I bet he'd command* Razorback *from a handstand if it got him away from Jeff McNally's falling star*, she thought.

Freddie wasn't blind to John Dalton's ambition, but she didn't mind ambition—not if it was married to capability and good common sense. Dalton seemed to have both. She had no idea if those skills translated over to an ability to kill the enemy, but his conduct in the Battle of the Strait of Malacca at least indicated he wouldn't go hide in his stateroom.

"Probably." Trieu sighed. "All right. I don't have a better idea, so Dalton it is. Now, what do I do about *Albacore's* screw issue? What if...it wasn't accidental?"

"I can investigate that if you want," she replied and watched relief make his features sag.

"I'd appreciate it, Freddie. Very much."

"I'm here to help, sir."

Making a mental note to talk to her real boss, the chief of naval operations, Freddie settled in to help SUBLANT solve problems he shouldn't need help with.

"Captain, the mascot's missing."

"Shit." Alex turned away from studying the helm consoles in control; they were practically antiques, and without a simulator to familiarize himself with his submarine, all he could do was poke around the space and try to learn things. He'd *thought* the worst news of the day was the fact that exactly zero of his officers had ever been underway on the boat, but this was something else.

"Yep. An' we can't exactly replace the fucking thing, either. It's been discontinued for decades."

"Dare I ask what it is?"

Sub mascots were funny things. *Seawolf*—the previous one, not the current one, though it might've been passed down for all Alex knew—had a giant ceramic frog named Hank that was a legend at the Sub School. *Kansas'* had been a real live beta fish named Seaman Swimmy Pants. *John Warner* sported an ugly taxidermized eagle. A boat's original crew picked their mascot, and the sub kept it through their entire lifespan, which, in *Jimmy Carter's* case, was thirty-three years.

"A stuffed rabbit with Big Pointy Teeth," Morton said with a straight face. "From *Monty Python and the Holy Grail.*"

Alex blinked. "Either you're pulling my leg, or I'm not seeing the reference."

"You're too young to remember when President Carter got attacked by a rabbit. Hell, even *I'm* not that ancient, but this isn't my first tour on Smiley, so I already know why our call sign is 'Killer Rabbit' and the murderous rabbit is our mascot. You can find the video online if you want."

Alex's laugh came out with so much force that it snorted out his nose. "God, I love the sub force."

"Me, too, sir, but fact is that someone yoinked the Murder Machine, and now everyone thinks we'll have bad luck for the whole goddamned war."

"Murder Machine?"

"Yep."

"Can't we find a new one on eBay or something?" Alex wasn't going to try telling his crew that they *shouldn't* have their mascot. First, that would make them hate him, and second, it was bad luck.

Morton shrugged. "If you want to spend like two hundred bucks, sure. You're the one making fancy command pay."

He sighed. "And no one knows where Murder Machine went?"

"Some people suspect that the old nav stole it when he left. No one liked Lieutenant Chin."

"And *Sole's* out on a war patrol, so it's not like we can just fucking ask." Alex scraped a hand over his face. "Okay, fine, I'll go surf eBay. I'm sure it won't be the strangest thing I do while in command." He turned to squint at Morton. "This isn't some haze-the-new-captain test, is it?"

Morton grinned. "I wish it was. But nobody wants to hide Murder Machine. It takes it personally. It always gets revenge."

"Jesus."

"Are you fucking *kidding* me?" Commander Chris Kennedy flung his clipboard as Master Chief Casey rushed into control. It bounced off a junior fire control tech, who squeaked and dove behind her chair. Then it ricocheted off an angle iron and crashed to the floor with a metallic clank.

Why did all the drama have to happen in control? Casey wished Kennedy could explode in his stateroom like a responsible CO. Control was cramped, full of critical equipment, and even more importantly always manned with a watch team.

"There's nothing here, Captain," Lieutenant Commander Hunt said. "Either the intel is bad, or we missed them."

"I can't *believe* we goddamned missed an entire shipment of AIP submarines heading to India. Eight of them, XO. Eight!"

Kennedy spun away from his second-in-command, stomping a few disgruntled steps. Every sailor in the space suddenly became fascinated by his or her console; no one wanted to meet the captain's eyes.

"I know, sir." Hunt didn't even cringe; she was getting used to this, wasn't she?

Then Kennedy's eyes zeroed in on his least favorite person. "This is *your* bailiwick, Nav," he snarled at Lieutenant Sue Grippo, *Kansas'* navigator. "Did your people fuck this up?"

"No, sir. No way to." Sue met Kennedy's eyes, but Casey could see how she wanted to flinch away. "The coordinates were provided to us. We're at them."

"No way to screw it up." Kennedy's upper lip curled into a sneer. "Did you account for their proposed course and speed?"

"Yes, Captain, we did."

"Do you know what a blow sinking cargo ships carrying *eight* advanced *Scorpene*-class boats would be to the Indians? And to the French? I bet the Indians wouldn't pay for them if they were on the bottom of the ocean, and they can't build a good submarine worth a damn without French help." Kennedy strode over to the navigation table, zooming in on the electronic chart and glaring at it. "We had a chance to cripple them, and *some* people let it pass us by!"

Sue flushed red; Casey stepped up next to the captain. Next career, Casey was going to run a daycare. It had to be less stressful.

"Shit happens in war, Captain," he said quietly. "Looks like luck wasn't with us today. Next time will be different."

"It had better be, Master Chief." Kennedy turned a narrowed-eyed, dark glare on him. "I'm not here to fail. *Kansas* will damned well make her mark on this war."

Casey forced a smile. "Of course she will—"

Kennedy stomped out of the space, not even slamming the hatch shut behind him.

"Sir," Casey finished belatedly, exchanging a look at the XO.

She shrugged helplessly and then gestured for Sue—who was still red with fury—to follow her out of the space before Sue exploded.

Maybe he'd be an air traffic controller. It had to be easier than this.

12 August 2038, Bremerton, Washington

By the end of Alex's first week in command, he wanted to strangle someone. Subs didn't really have yardarms, at least not in the old school way, but damn, someone should be swinging. *Jimmy Carter* still lacked thirty percent of her crew, yet they were less than a month out from leaving for war.

Then, to add insult to ever-loving injury, his boat had an executive officer assigned for thirty whole hours before the squadron yanked her away, too. Alex's splendidly pleasant call from Commander Melendez announced that Sandra Carrasco was out and George Kirkland was in.

Sometimes, the whirlwind was too hard to keep up with. Feeling too weak for the damned job, Alex retreated to his stateroom and called his best friend, John Dalton. They'd been close since meeting when Alex was a lieutenant (junior grade), with Alex serving as John's best man at his wedding and John becoming godfather to Emily, Alex's youngest daughter.

John was a few years ahead of Alex, and he was always willing to offer advice—or just be a safe person to bitch to about submarine-specific things that Nancy's expertise didn't quite extend to.

"...Kirkland? You sure that's his last name?" the voice on the other end of the phone asked.

And yeah, that phone was probably older than Alex, with a cord that kept tangling no matter how hard he tried to keep it straight.

"I did. Why?" Alex kicked his feet up on his tiny desk and tried not to groan, glaring at the holes in the carpet. Lieutenant (j.g.) Alvaro offered to have someone patch it, but with the litany of problems aboard *Jimmy Carter,* Alex ranked that one too far down the list to bother with.

"Just...um. Wait one sec." Papers shuffled, and something hit the floor with a crash. "Oops. Sorry, my predecessor's inability to remain organized was only surpassed by his tactical ineptitude."

"You're such a charmer, John." Alex laughed.

John Dalton wasn't precisely a neatnik himself; on *Virginia*, Alex's fellow junior officers called Dalton the most disorganized navigator in the history of the navy. Alex wouldn't *quite* accuse his friend of being a slob...to his face.

"Nice, hell! I was Admiral McNally's chief of staff two days ago, not replacing an idiot who couldn't figure out which pot to piss in when the damn thing was labeled."

"Was it really that bad?" News was slow to reach the navy's armpit of Bangor; rumors that a submarine commander lost his mind out in the Indian Ocean arrived just the day before. Until John called *Jimmy Carter*, Alex had no clue his best friend was the brand-new captain of USS *Razorback*.

"That bad and worse," John said. "Harney had a meltdown in control, let *two* Indian aircraft carriers sail by as he babbled. When the XO tried to interfere, he accused her of mutiny. The Indians got away, and then *Razorback* damn near got sunk when Harney tried to sprint right through their ASW screen. He locked himself in his stateroom for the rest of the patrol while the XO got the boat home to Pearl. So here I am. Trying to unfuck this disaster and get the boat back to war."

"Ouch." Alex knew the navy had problems finding commanding officers who didn't melt down in combat, but that was bad. "Why you?"

"I was available, I guess. At least I've commanded a submarine before, and I've been in combat, so I guess they figured I wouldn't cry *right* away," John replied. "Hell, *Razorback* is the second newest *Cero* in the fleet, so I can't really complain."

"Except for the fact that Harney was supposedly a superstar, and now you're cleaning up his mess?"

John snorted. "Yeah. But how many oh-sixes get to *command* a submarine these days and not have it be a boring missile boat or sub tender?"

"You're excited, aren't you?"

Alex tried not to glance around his threadbare stateroom. Shoving down envy took an effort. John was an honest-to-God *captain*, not merely called that by courtesy. *Razorback* was John's second command, but his first boat had been a *Cero*, too. And he came out of the Battle of the SOM with a silver star. John was on the fast track toward admiral's stars, had been for years.

Not that Alex wanted to be an admiral. He just wanted one chance to matter.

"Of course I am. Do I sound like I wanted to sit on the sidelines with a war on?"

"And here I thought you might've gotten your fill in the SOM."

"Of surface ships, sure," John said. "Missile and air combat are for the birds. Give me torpedoes any day."

"Yeah, I'm not too fond of the ground-pounding shit, either." Alex grimaced.

John was one of the few people he told about the mess on Armistice Station, from being chased by French marines and setting off fireballs made from coffee creamer to hijacking a cruise ship.

"You'd think after that they'd put you in something other than *Jimmy Carter*," John said. "Keeping cool under fire counts for a lot."

"So I've heard." Alex forced himself not to lash out at Admiral Hamilton. *Pay your dues and do your job*. No one made him steal that firing key on *Kansas*; it was the right thing to do, and he'd do it again. Better to focus on the present. "You were saying something about knowing my incoming XO?"

"Right. Sorry. It's not much, but he was the Weps here on *Razorback* a couple months back. I sent his fitness reports onto the Bureau since Harney's meltdown left me a stack of paperwork three miles high. They were...well, let's just say that they weren't the flowery things I'm used to reading."

"No, let's not leave it at that. What the hell aren't you saying, John?"

"Easy, I'm not the enemy here."

Alex sucked in a deep breath. Another email pinged into his inbox, and he clicked it open out of habit. Just his luck. The Bureau of Personnel regretted to inform *Jimmy Carter's* CO that they could not possibly detail any more chief petty officers to his command. Alex would just have to make do. His lips twisted into a silent snarl.

"You still there?" John asked.

"Yeah, sorry. More good news from the detailers, that's all." Alex ground his teeth.

"You inherited a barrel of monkeys, didn't you?"

"Let's just say I think no one told the Bureau that *Jimmy Carter* wasn't decommissioning, because they sure as hell didn't plan for our manning."

"Ouch."

"Tell me about it. In fact, I'm not sure how the hell I got a decent

COB out of this, because—"

Knock, knock.

"Hold on," Alex said and then raised his voice. "Yeah?"

"Sorry to bother you, Captain." Master Chief Morton opened the door and stuck his head in. "A Lieutenant Commander Kirkland is on the quarterdeck. Says he's our new XO."

"Bingo. Send him on down, COB."

Morton nodded. "Aye, sir."

"Time for me to go, John. Duty calls and all that jazz," Alex said as the door clicked shut.

His friend laughed. "Have fun. Hopefully, I'll see you soon. We're heading to Australia, chopping out to SUBRON Twenty-Nine."

"Have fun with that. I hear Commodore Banks has a sense of humor on par with my crusty underwear's."

"Oh, that's a delightful image. I'll be going now."

A few minutes ticked by after Alex hung up, leaving him wondering how anyone could need so long to walk the hundred feet from the topside quarterdeck to the captain's stateroom. At least talking to John improved his mood. Alex hadn't seen his friend since before the war started—hell, not since before *Kansas* left on deployment. Their wives, former college roommates, talked more often, but Alex had a feeling he and John wouldn't be in the same circles any time soon.

Finally, the knock came.

"It's open!"

Later, he remembered his first impression of George Kirkland was that he looked skittish. George's eyes darted around Alex's stateroom before finally focusing on his captain, and his hands twitched like he wanted something to hold. The XO was taller than Alex by a few inches, and heavier. Since Alex could eat an entire cow and still be skinny as a rail, however, that didn't say much.

Alex bounced to his feet, holding out a hand. Only once he smiled did George meet his eyes.

"Welcome aboard, XO."

George's handshake was deceptively firm. "Thank you, sir."

"Pull up a battered chair, take a seat, and tell me about yourself." Alex gestured toward the other chair, which looked like someone pulled it out of a dumpster. George didn't seem to notice.

Only later would Alex wonder what John was about to say concerning George Kirkland.

Chapter 10

Pissing Contests

23 August 2038, Washington, D.C.

Rear Admiral Freddie Hamilton's quiet morning started with twisting her ankle and ended with a phone call. Tripping over the cat on her way to grab her phone only made her snarl a swear.

Her apartment was empty except for her and Tinkerbell, the temperamental tomcat she adopted from a rescue three years earlier. Freddie liked it that way; ambition made sharing life hard, and no one else moving her things around kept her happy. As long as everything was *just so* at home, she could concentrate at work.

Her twice-a-week cleaning service were the only people allowed to move things, and Johnny knew where everything belonged.

"Hamilton." Sucking back a groan, she leaned against the bar and stared longingly at the scotch. It was far too early to drink, but the toxic war-politics cocktail made her want to.

"Freddie, it's Long Trieu," said the Commander, Naval Submarine Forces Atlantic. He wasn't her boss, but Freddie sometimes felt like he was—she spent as much time in his office as she did in the Pentagon, which was damned inconvenient. SUBLANT was based in Norfolk, Virginia, which was four hours away from her normal office in D.C.

And this was her day off.

"What can I do for you, sir?" she asked, giving her favorite scotch another longing look.

No, the Glenmorangie could wait until dinner.

"I need...a favor," Vice Admiral Trieu said. "If you don't mind."

Instinct told Freddie that she should make up plans. Call her mother, schedule lunch, *anything*. But duty won out; there was a war on, and admirals like her fought administrative battles.

She took a deep breath. "Of course."

"I'm, well, I'm scheduled to testify in front of Congress today. Concerning sub losses." His ragged breath was audible. "I...don't think I can make it."

"Is everything all right?"

"Of course it is." Trieu's voice turned brisker. "I just have other commitments."

Freddie glanced at the clock. The hearings were due to start in two hours—just enough time for her to throw on a uniform and get downtown. Great.

"I'll take care of everything, sir," she promised.

Nineteen days away from leaving for war, Alex still lacked a full crew. The navy's manning system wasn't equipped to deal with the first naval war since WWII, and *Jimmy Carter* remained two dozen sailors short. Peacetime practices got chucked out the window right away, yet nothing concrete replaced them. Getting a submarine ready for war turned into a cluster of rushed tests and preparations, thrown together with no rhyme or reason and conducted with little supervision.

On the morning of August 23rd, Alex stood on the pier, running his eyes over his submarine. This was part of his daily routine, one moment he could steal for himself in a hurricane of activity. Morning colors were over, and his crew hauled stores on board, preparing for *Jimmy Carter's* first underway in over a year. Outwardly, they looked good. There were fewer chief petty officers than Alex liked, but at least his mismatched crew seemed to be bonding.

Alex smiled as the wind carried a few jokes his way.

"Check this shit out, Trebing," ET2 Margarita Velasquez said, waving some obscene drawing and wearing an infectious grin. "Your artwork is improving!"

"Better than your singing, sure," FT3 Joe Trebing shot back as the sailors surrounding them laughed.

"You just don't fucking appreciate my skills, sweet cheeks." Velasquez pirouetted messily before passing a box of bread to another sailor. "You've got no goddamned taste."

"You wouldn't know taste if it bit you in the ass." Trebing tossed cereal up the brow.

"You only get to bite my ass in your dreams, darlin'."

Alex chuckled to himself before turning away. Some captains disliked "unprofessional" behavior like swearing, but saltiness didn't bother Alex when it was just a wrapper around a competent package.

"My confidence level in *Jimmy Carter* is *not* increasing, Captain. Or in you."

The acid voice from behind him made Alex swing around, snapping off a salute. Nothing chapped his ass as heavily as rendering honors to incompetent officers who outranked him by about two seconds, but Melendez was the asinine sort who insisted on formalities.

Salute the rank, not the asshole wearing it, his drill sergeant told Alex a lifetime ago at Norwich University. It was good advice then. It was better now.

"I'm terribly sorry to hear that, Commander." He smiled blandly and stuffed his hands back into his pockets. Melendez never got command, did she? If the rapidly expanding U.S. Navy gave Alex Coleman a submarine—even after the antics that sent him to Admiral's Mast—that said a hell of a lot about her. *It's got to grate on her that she's spending her time annoying a guy whose good traits are being ornery and unorthodox.*

The chief of staff scowled. "This is hardly amusing, Commander Coleman."

Did she have to tack his rank onto everything? Thankfully, Melendez was on the growing list of problems, which would vanish as soon as he left Bangor. Alex shrugged.

"I think we'll do all right, COS."

"You'd *better.*"

Rolling his eyes would be a bad idea right now. Really, it would.

"You get us what we need, and we'll get underway on time," Alex replied. He wasn't sure if Melendez dragged her feet on purpose, but working with the squadron was as productive as grilling underwater. War had to be easier than this.

"Your department heads arrive today," Melendez said, glaring at the working party loading stores.

Alex blinked. He knew *Jimmy Carter* was due three lieutenants from the next SOAC class, but the bureau was slow to provide names and arrival dates. "That's news to me."

"I told your XO." She crossed her arms.

"I'm sure you did." *This morning, probably.* George was an administrative monster. Paperwork didn't last an hour in Lieutenant Commander Kirkland's inbox, and he shared news like a high school gossip. George would sooner die than neglect to pass along something important.

He wasn't the dynamic or engaging XO Alex wanted, and he was absurdly hesitant to talk to their enlisted sailors, but Kirkland got the job done. Finding him now was easy; there George was, clucking like a mother hen over the supply officer's shoulder as Lieutenant (junior grade) Kasuga checked the inventory list.

"Perhaps *they'll* help you get this rust bucket on track." The unexpected insult threw Alex for a loop, and he twisted to stare at Melendez, gaping. She sneered. "God only knows how you'd get *Jimmy Carter* underway in time otherwise. A boat this old should be razorblades. She creates more work than she's worth."

Alex's eyes narrowed. "I'd appreciate you not saying that in front of my crew, *Commander*."

So much for his newfound ability to deal with stupid people.

Her smile was sickeningly sweet. "My apologies. I'm sure *Jimmy Carter* will do well escorting convoys and guarding TRANSPLATS."

"We'll do whatever mission we're given." The words came out flat.

She was probably right. Odds were that *Jimmy Carter* would never get the chance to mix it up with enemy submarines, but his crew didn't deserve the second-class citizen treatment.

"I'm sure." Melendez's smile turned acidic, and Alex fought down the urge to forcibly remove it by smashing her face into a bollard. She continued: "I have work to do at the squadron. Don't hesitate to call if you need anything."

"Thanks." *I'm sure you'll get right on it. Sometime in 2045.*

Melendez strolled away, leaving uneasy butterflies doing laps in Alex's stomach.

Day twelve of the Angler Hearings—because heaven forbid politicians work every day, even with a war on—concentrated on sub losses. Eleven boats lost in just four months.

Congress was packed for the hearings, with both parties ready to fire on all cylinders at a navy that wasn't living up to expectations. With sixty-seven attack subs in active service—now fifty-six, four of which were in the shipyard for repairs—that represented a loss of over sixteen percent of the total American offensive arm in an underwater war. Congress found those numbers frightening, and while she wasn't going to show it, Freddie agreed.

Freddie handled herself well—you didn't get to wear stars if you knew how not to put your foot in it—but she didn't enjoy justifying someone else's policies. Nor did she like Senator Angler's pointed questions concerning Vice Admiral Trieu's absence. However, seven hours of grueling questions later, she and Maria Vasquez escaped and headed down the Capitol steps.

Normally, she liked the view out at the city of D.C. It wowed her in ways that Freddie couldn't define, reminding her of what there was to fight for. Sure, their government was messy, but America was worth fighting for. Today, she believed that no less...but damn, she was exhausted. It would be really nice if Trieu were there to do his job like he promised, but here Freddie was, still covering for him.

"Well, that was a barrel of laughs," Freddie said, managing not to grimace. There was no knowing who was watching here, and politicians enjoyed believing that naval officers *liked* them.

"It went better than it could have, ma'am."

"You only saw four hours of it." Freddie softened the words with a smile. Admiral's aides rarely got a day off, which meant Maria took leave when Freddie did—and Freddie cancelling her leave meant Maria had to, too.

In Maria's case, that meant driving back to D.C. from the beach, which left no one happy.

"I would have been back faster if you sent a helicopter for me, ma'am." Maria blinked innocently. "But for some reason, you said no."

Freddie snorted out a laugh. "Can you hear me explaining that one to Senator Angler?"

"I'd like to see you try." Maria grinned.

"I bet you would."

Mood improving, Freddie turned to walk toward her car—only to find a well-dressed man in her path. He was short, dark-skinned, and his intelligent eyes screamed *reporter*.

"Admiral Hamilton!" At least he had the grace not to smile like he was her friend. "Mind if I ask a few questions?"

Freddie forced a smile. "Of course not. You are?"

"Mark Easley, *Washington Post*." He offered a hand; Freddie took it. Playing nice with the media was required at her level.

"A pleasure."

"I was hoping you'd comment on the navy's habit of whitewashing how leadership failures lead to tactical losses," Easley said, still wearing that same damned smile.

Freddie tensed. "That sounds like a thesis, Mister Easley, not a question."

He didn't even blink. "*Is* the navy intentionally covering up failures by senior leaders? The Battle of the Strait of Malacca saw the loss of USS *Enterprise*—the first American aircraft carrier sunk since 1945—and two destroyers. The Battle of the Sea of Japan saw us lose six ships, and the Second Battle of Sunda Strait lost seven more.

"Rumors say Admiral McNally froze up at the Strait of Malacca, but he's still in a cushy job in the Pentagon. Admiral Allen died at Sunda Strait, but stories from sailors who were there say she shouted contradictory orders and berated her own officers as *Monmouth* sunk. Yet the navy releases nothing. When *will* the public hear about these actions from the navy brass?"

"I'm not in a position to comment about surface battles." Freddie felt her smile go strained. "You may not be aware that I am a special assistant to the CNO for submarine warfare, so my visibility on what happens above the surface is limited."

"Then what about the rumors of sub captains losing it in action?"

Where the hell did you hear that? Freddie took a deep breath in lieu of screaming. "I can't possibly comment on that. Submarine operations are always classified."

"Come on, Admiral. Give me *something* to prove that the navy isn't intentionally hiding criminal levels of incompetence from the public."

"Mister Easley, I don't have all the details you're looking for." *Just some of them,* she didn't say. "But I can say that this is the first major naval war we have fought since World War II. No matter how much you train, the real thing is very different. And humans are fallible. There will be mistakes, and...unfortunately, deaths."

Easley's eyes narrowed. "Is the U.S. Navy no longer the powerhouse we have been lead to believe?"

"Recent loses have not diminished our strengths," Freddie said, wishing she could believe herself. "American industrial capacity is unparalleled, and even now, new ships and submarines are rolling out of the yards and getting ready to fight. Recruitment is up *without* a draft, and even battles we lose provide precious lessons learned."

"As well as sacrificing precious lives."

"I'm not sure what you want to me to say about that, Mister Easley." She met his eyes, not liking how he glared. Did he hate the military or just her?

"Perhaps express regret for the men and women you send into

harm's way, some of whom never return again?"

"I regret every death, both civilian and those in uniform." Lieutenant Jesse Lin's face flashed through her mind unexpectedly; Freddie fought the need to cringe. The loss of Armistice Station was four months in the past, but she'd never forget the sound of bullets winging by her head or the smell of coffee creamer fireballs. Or forget Jesse Lin, who she'd barely known but had seemed like a nice kid.

The French celebrated Captain Jules Rochambeau for that takeover. If Freddie ever got to command a strike group, she planned to hunt him down.

"I'm sure you do." Easley's smile wasn't quite a sneer.

Maria, to her left, shifted, making a show of checking her smartwatch. "Admiral, you'll be late for your meeting if we stay longer."

"Thank you, Maria." That smile felt more natural. "Good day, Mister Easley."

"Thank you for your time, Admiral."

Freddie walked away as normally as she could, keeping her expression neutral and pace steady. Only once she and Maria got in the car did she allow herself to scowl.

"What a bastard." Freddie hissed from behind clenched teeth. "Thanks for the save."

"I live to serve, ma'am."

Freddie chuckled. "Someone has to."

The Northern Indian Ocean

Jules Rochambeau was France's reigning king of submarines, but Annette Garnier was a close second. Commanding *Amazone*, a fast attack sub a few years older than Rochambeau's *Barracuda*, she didn't have quite as many bells and whistles to play with as her rival. But she did have guts, patience, and a good eye for targets.

Capitaine Garnier started the war further south, sinking ships closer to Australia with little fanfare. Grandstanding wasn't her style—at least not until she could outclass her famous, womanizing counterpart.

"Rochambeau refused this mission, you know," she told her first officer in the quiet of her stateroom. They were alone, planning for the future the way a good team did.

Commander Louis Martin arched an eyebrow, his dark face unreadable. "What for?"

"Not glorious enough." She rolled her eyes.

"Typical." Louis shrugged. "If our Indian friends are being honest about their intentions, we should see some British or American ships or submarines coming this way to help Sri Lanka before long."

Garnier smiled. "And then we sink them."

Rochambeau thought flashy victories would bring him glory. Perhaps he was right. But they would also make him a target. Patience would win the war for France, and Annette Garnier intended to be alive to see that day.

Let the enemy target Rochambeau. She would still be here when they were finished with him.

Bremerton, Washington

"I still can't believe you didn't get your orders changed." Scowling, Lieutenant Maggie Bennett hauled her sea bag out of the SUBRON Five duty van. The van was more gray than white, and in desperate need of a wash, but hey, it wasn't meant to win a beauty contest.

Thank goodness she wasn't, either. Maggie's hair was more out than in her bun, and she thought she had a crease down one side of her face from sleeping on the plane. The air smelled better than she did, probably by a lot—salty with the smell of the sea and not too fouled by navy engine fumes.

"What'd you expect me to do, call my dad?" Benji Angler yawned.

Lieutenant Benjamin Winthrop Angler IV—Benji to his friends—was possibly the most photogenic naval officer Maggie ever met. Even after long hours in a plane and the dingy van, Benji looked great. He was tall, but not too tall, red-haired, and green-eyed, with a grin most women went stupid over. He was also way more down to earth than his pretentious name suggested.

Jimmy Carter's three prospective department heads flew into Washington State from Connecticut the night before, crammed into coach alongside a family of nine with twin screaming toddlers.

Courtesy of the twin terrors, two delayed flights, and a highway accident, not one of them managed four hours of sleep.

Maggie shrugged. "Might've worked."

Benji, soon to be their weapons officer, laughed. "Probably not. I'm not sure Dad *didn't* call an admiral or two to make sure I got something 'less dangerous' than *Pacu*. He wasn't happy when I stayed in after the war started."

"If I had an all-expense-paid trip into politics waiting for me, I'd bail." Marty Sterling sounded bored. "You're stark-raving mad."

"That's what my mother said. *She* wanted me to marry some rich girl and get busy making Benjamin Winthrop Angler the Fifth."

Maggie snickered. "I'll take a sugar daddy if you can find me one. But not you. Just so's we're clear."

"Oh, yeah, that's my dream job. Hooking up nosy fellow department heads with my dad's friends. Come to think of it—no, there's a reason I'm still in the navy." Benji rolled his eyes.

"On second thought, it's a good thing you stuck around," Marty said. "If you die out there, we won't have to worry about future Benjamin whatever the hell your name is the fifths running around."

"Oh, thank—" Benji cut off as an angry-looking commander stalked by them, and all three lieutenants saluted. "Good morning, ma'am."

She grunted something and left them in her dust.

Maggie swallowed. "God, I hope that's not our new CO."

Marty shook his head. "No command-at-sea pin."

"Let's go," Angler said, hefting his bags again.

The squadron's duty driver had already disappeared. Help lugging their gear to the boat *might* have been nice, but the lieutenants didn't really expect it. They were reporting to a warship, not a cruise ship with room service and mints on their pillows.

Still, Maggie wished she'd packed a little less stuff. She'd tried to keep her gear down to a minimum—they *were* going to war—but she'd wound up with an overstuffed sea bag, a big duffel, and her uniform bag. Not to mention her carryon from the plane. Fortunately, the walk wasn't too long.

"At least they look busy." Maggie looked the boat up and down as they trudged up the pier.

She'd sort of expected *Jimmy Carter* to be rusting away. The submarine looked surprisingly good, and sailors carrying stores swarmed all over her. Even the paint seemed fresh.

"She's a big bitch." Marty grinned.

"Biggest attack submarine in the world."

Maggie thought back on the information she'd memorized over the last two weeks. She'd never seen a *Seawolf*-class submarine in person. *Seawolf* herself was a museum ship in Houston nowadays, but there hadn't been a long weekend to fly down and explore her since Maggie got this assignment. However, she knew *Jimmy Carter* was modified from the original design. She was one hundred feet longer than her sisters, which amounted to ninety feet longer than the *Cero*-class boats Maggie knew best. Even with over two-thirds of her bulk hidden underwater, *Jimmy Carter* looked humongous.

"I bet she drives like a bloated cow," Benji said, and Maggie snickered.

They approached the submarine from astern, and Maggie finally spotted what looked like another officer or a chief petty officer standing on the pier. It was a slender guy wearing coveralls; all Maggie could see from behind was the khaki-colored belt only officers and chiefs wore. Enlisted sailors wore blue belts with their coveralls, which meant that this guy was senior enough to answer some questions.

The other two glanced her way, nominating Maggie as their spokesperson. She scowled but stepped forward. If someone had to look like an idiot, she'd rather do it instead of suffering secondhand embarrassment.

"Excuse me. Can you tell me where to—" She gulped when he turned toward her, and Maggie caught sight of the scrambled eggs on the brim of his *Jimmy Carter* ball cap. There was also a command at sea pin on the right breast of his uniform, just above the nametape. Maggie saluted. "Sir."

"Lieutenant." He returned the salute and those of her fellows. While the boys made polite, Maggie snuck a look at the man she assumed was their new commanding officer.

He was a little taller than Maggie's own five foot four. His hair was light and cropped short; it looked blond and didn't seem to be going to gray. He was skinny as a post, and the blue eyes in his angular face seemed full of good humor.

"Are you the three amigos, or am I safe in assuming you're my wayward department heads?" He smiled.

"Uh, yes, sir. I'm Margaret Bennett, your navigator. This is Benjamin Angler and Martin Sterling, Weps and the engineer, respectively."

"Alex Coleman," the captain replied easily, shaking each of their hands. "Welcome aboard."

"Thank you, sir," she replied for the trio, noticing for the first time how nervous Benji looked. *Weird. Doesn't his dad being a senator mean he meets important people all the time?*

"I'm sure the XO will smother you with the details later, but suffice it to say that I'm glad to see you three. We've got a lot of work to do and nineteen days until we get underway. You'll be busy," Coleman promised. "I know *Jimmy Carter* probably isn't your dream job, but she's a good boat. Even if she is older than...probably all of you."

Maggie blinked.

Benji put on one of his winning smiles. "We're glad to be here, sir."

"Bullshit you are." The response was cheerful. "Gentlemen—and lady—I won't lie to you if you don't lie to me. I'm a believer in brutal honesty. Stick with the truth and we'll all be just fine."

What could they say to that? "Yes, sir," the department heads chorused.

At least he didn't look like a screamer. Maggie glanced at the giant submarine, sucking in a deep breath. And least *Jimmy Carter* didn't look ready to sink at the pier.

Yet.

Chapter 11

Winds of Change

War changed surprisingly few things about civilian life in the U.S.

The economy—caught flat-footed when other nations beat America in the race to the ocean floor—roared back to life when the war started. Jobs were plentiful, and if one ignored the deaths fighting overseas, which the American public was shockingly good at, everything seemed normal.

Including online auction sites.

Sighing, Alex rubbed his eyes and wished he could sic one of his daughters on this task. He knew how to use eBay—anyone not living under a rock in 2038 should—but he was pretty sure that a warship's commanding officer had better things to do with his time. Particularly since eBay was a blocked site on navy networks, which meant he had to do it from his phone.

And, since no cell phone ever made got good service while inside a metal tube, that meant he got to do it standing on the ass end of his submarine. While the five sailors on the quarterdeck watched curiously, undoubtedly wondering what weird thing the old man was up to now.

Damn, these Rabbits With Big Pointy Teeth were *expensive.* Why the hell did his boat have to have a collector's item as its mascot?

Because the whole fucking boat *is a collector's item, that's why.* Alex scowled at his phone. At least he could be relatively certain that his boat cost more than—

"Do you have a minute, Captain?"

The voice came from behind him; Alex jumped.

"Jesus, George. Try not to sneak up on people, will you?"

"Sorry, Captain." His XO went red. "I was just wondering if you'd heard anything from the squadron about our video data recorder install. Or the last chart system upgrade. I'm concerned that going to war with the newest system is just waiting for something to go wrong—and this combat systems upgrade makes me nervous, too."

Alex took a deep breath before speaking, trying to ignore the literal hand wringing from Lieutenant Commander George Kirkland. "I agree that it's a lot of changes in a short period. However, they're done, and we're getting underway in seventeen days."

"The VDR isn't upgraded yet. I don't understand why we *need* to install it at all."

The way George fidgeted and scuffed his feet against the black upper hull made Alex wonder if there was something else at work here. Two weeks of getting to know George Kirkland taught Alex that he was a rule-following, exacting sort of fellow.

Alex cocked his head. "Tell me you're not worried about a video recorder catching you doing something naughty."

"No, sir!" George reared back. "Never."

"Then...?"

"Some of the crew...well, they seem uneasy about the idea." George shrugged. "I overheard some of them talking about it."

"George, I guarantee you that Big Navy isn't going to care if they talk about girls, boys, porn, or their grandmas' underwear. Hell, I'm pretty sure no one's going to give a good goddamn if they streak across control on the midwatch—at least no one that's not you and me, anyway. The VDR is there to help assess lessons learned. And sub losses. Not to spy on the crew."

George gulped. "I just...just wanted to bring up their concerns, Captain."

"Has anyone voiced them to you?" Alex asked.

"Well, no. But I'm the XO, so I guess they wouldn't." George gestured toward the quarterdeck watch. "No one's supposed to like the XO, right? I'm the designated bad guy."

"When you have to be, sure," Alex replied. "They don't have to like you, but the crew needs to *trust* you. And there's no sign they don't," he added when George flushed again. "So, for now, let's just assume that this is the time-honored tradition of sailors bitching because they're sailors, all right?"

"If you say so, Captain."

Man, Alex wished he could pull that invisible nervous rod out of George's ass. If the XO relaxed a little, the crew would probably be less nervous around him. *But that would require George being less nervous around* them, *and I think that's the real problem here.* He managed not to grimace where it could make George feel worse.

George would get better with time. Most XOs did.

"C'mon, let's go check on the VDR install," Alex said, instead of harping on George's nervousness.

It seemed to do the trick of reassuring his XO; George bounced into action, leading Alex eagerly toward the aft hatch. Meanwhile, Alex glanced at his phone one more time, grimaced, and clicked buy on a two hundred buck Rabbit With Big Pointy Teeth.

Washington, D.C.

Walking through the halls of the Pentagon was always humbling. It was the one place in America where admirals were a dime a dozen, and Freddie's two stars sometimes felt inadequate. Silly her, she'd assumed that some of the high-ranking admirals would go to sea once war started; instead, their number seemed to double overnight. The generals from the other services were just as bad, even though the bulk of the fighting was so far at sea.

Rear Admiral Freddie Hamilton exchanged a greeting with a marine three-star as she passed. They were the only other service knee-deep in this mess, which was probably why there were fewer marines than everyone else here in the Pentagon. Marines could take and hold territory—even underwater stations—and they were the navy's brothers and sisters with rifles. But why the army and the air force kept fighting for larger budgets, she didn't know.

At least the coast guard was getting into the sub-hunting game and fitting depth charges on their cutters! Freddie was all for their brown-water brethren joining the fight. The easy rivalry between the navy and the "coasties" vanished the moment a war was on. The triumvirate of seagoing services were in this together. What good the ground and air types thought they could do was a mystery.

She reached the outer security guards to the CNO's office, and they waved her by after checking her badge. From there, it was a few steps to the half-open door.

"Freddie, you see Admiral Trieu this morning?" Scrap, otherwise known as Admiral David Chan, asked instead of greeting her.

"No, but I'm not technically his keeper," she replied. "I've been buried in that report concerning sub losses you asked for. The one for the Angler Hearings."

Scrap grimaced. "Yeah, I know. Helps a bundle that *Drum's* gone and got themselves sunk yesterday."

"At least some of the crew got off, including the CO." Freddie already had them on a plane to Honolulu; from there, the sixty-nine survivors would fly to D.C. where she could personally debrief them.

Technically, *Drum's* survivors were the responsibility of COM-SUB*PAC*, or Commander Submarine Forces Pacific. But Vice Admiral Brown was even less on the ball than Trieu, which meant he just babbled gratefully when Freddie promised the CNO's office would take care of things.

"We got the VDR footage yesterday." Scrap crossed his arms and glared. "It looks like Commander Lamm hesitated too long and got her ass shot off."

"I saw that footage. She followed procedure, going to periscope depth to confirm her contact's ID before shooting."

"Yeah, and in doing so, she lost the chance to sink a French frigate and instead got *herself* sunk. That procedure's stupid. It meant we've now lost *ten* submarines in five months. *Five months*, Freddie. The media's going to eviscerate me. Particularly that Easley asshole."

She felt her lips twitch into a sneer. "I've had the pleasure of meeting him."

"Then you know that he's going to make a huge fucking deal out of the fact that *Drum*—the first Improved-*Cero*!—got sunk by old-fashioned depth charges. Like this is 1938." Scrap kicked his desk. "Century-old technology takes out one of our newest boats. Best news ever."

Now wasn't the time to point out that *rocket*-propelled depth charges were a different beast than the old, roll 'em off the deck type of the last world war. These were at least Cold War vintage, which was about two percent better.

Freddie sat on her temper, taking a deep breath. "It might be time to look into that reliable old technology ourselves, sir," she said. "At least for our surface ships."

"Are you kidding?"

"Well, if I read the surface ship loses right, they're not doing much better than the subs are," she said without blinking. "Though at least you get more survivors of missile engagements."

It was easier to live when your boat wasn't *already* underwater, of course. Sinking happened faster when you were already partway to the bottom.

"Don't get me started on those idiots." Scrap glanced down at his phone. "Where the hell is Trieu? He was supposed to be here an hour ago."

"Do you want me to call him, sir?"

"I already tried. Twice." Scrap checked his phone again. "Texted, too. No answer."

A weird feeling settled in Freddie's stomach. "That's not like him."

"You owe me one, Master Chief." Finding Master Chief Morton in control, Alex stepped up next to him, angling his phone so the COB could see it. "Murder Machine II, coming right up."

Morton laughed. "I'll buy you a beer, sir."

"You see the price on that sucker? You owe me at least two."

"Sounds like abuse of power to me, but okay." Morton's shit-eating grin faded when George whirled around from where he was hovering over the navigation table.

"COB! Even joking about that is detrimental to good order and discipline, particularly when there's a war on," George hissed, his voice far too loud.

Control was a small space, already cramped with three electronics technicians, two contractors, Lieutenant Maggie Bennett, and the command triad of Alex, George, and Morton. Every head turned to stare.

Morton raised his voice. "Carry on, folks. XO's just pulling my leg. Old folks like me need that sometimes, keeps us young."

George flushed; Alex stepped between him and everyone else in the space, speaking in an undertone. "A little joking never hurt anyone, XO. We'll be all right."

"Yes, sir." George's face closed off in a miserable pout.

Alex hunted for words to reassure him but came up empty. After several pointless seconds, he resorted to doing his job.

"How's the install going, Nav?" he asked.

"Pretty good, sir. If you don't count the fact that their program doesn't support Windows 10, and well...Smiley is a few years behind on her operating system." Maggie shrugged. "Looks like the contractors will have to patch the software and come back tomorrow."

"You're telling me that our shiny new combat systems suite is built on top of a twenty-year-old operating system?"

"Hey, sir, it's the navy. We're lucky it's not Windows 98 or something older than *all* of us, not just the newest kids out of sub school."

Alex sighed. "Ain't that the truth?" He glanced over to where ET2 Velasquez had just crawled out from under a console. "Everything solid under there, ET2?"

"For some definition of solid, sir," the young sailor replied. "Pretty sure this wiring's older than I am."

"I'm not sure some of it isn't approaching my age." Alex felt his smile go crooked. *Jimmy Carter* commissioned in 2005, but her keel was laid in 1998—two years before Alex's birth.

Velasquez's eyes went wide. "Shit, sir, that's old."

"Petty Officer Velasquez!" George spun around like a top, looking ready to do a tea kettle and explode.

"Sorry, XO. Jus' saying." Velasquez shrugged, but her apology was ruined by the amused glance she exchanged with the other electronics technician.

George missed that; Alex chose not to comment.

"Now, children, there's no need to make fun of the captain for bein' old when *I* reported on board this boat when he was still in diapers," Master Chief Morton cut in, leaning casually against the helmsmen's chair. "This here's my third tour on board good ol' Smiley, so you just bring it."

Perth, Australia

On the other side of the world, another CO stared at his ship in dismay. She was sleek and gray, painted in the lighter blue-gray color favored by Australia and Canada. She was destined to become HMAS *Warrego*, the third ship in Australia's brand-new class of guided missile destroyers, but in her case, destiny was delayed: *Warrego* was up on the blocks of a dry dock, with contractors crawling all over her hull.

The *Torrens*-class DDGs were the most powerful ships the Australian Navy had built in generations—but France's foremost submariner sank the lead ship four months ago.

Most navies would accept that Captain Jules Rochambeau of the

French attack submarine *Barracuda* sent many warships to the bottom since the start of the war, and *Torrens* was simply one of many. The Royal Australian Navy, however, refused to excuse *Torrens'* loss lying down. Instead, they returned to the drawing board and reworked the new class into lethal anti-submarine warfare assets.

Commander Fletch Goddard agreed with the idea...in principle. In practice, it delayed construction of his destroyer by over five months...and that delay promised to grow still longer.

June 19, 2039. That was the new projected completion date, almost a year away. Two days earlier, yard workers discovered a bug in the destroyer's number two generator while testing *Warrego's* combat systems suite. A *non*-repairable bug.

That lovely surprise required ripping out the entire generator, which meant dismantling a main engine room. The shipyard was working double shifts around the clock, but between repairs to active ships and upgrades to old ones, *Warrego* dropped to the back of the pack. She got to stay up on the blocks in Australia's newest naval shipyard: Naval Shipyard Perth.

The shipyard was huge—four times the size it had been a year ago and growing exponentially as Australia laid down one warship after another. And there was only one hard and fast rule: active ships came first.

The aged frigate up on the blocks next to his beautiful destroyer proved that point. *Parramatta* was thirty-five years old, and any sensible navy would've turned her into scrap by now. But Australia was fighting for her life, desperate for ships after the disastrous Battle of Cocos Islands.

Technically a victory, in that the French and Indian forces withdrew without capturing the island, it was the worst "win" in Australian naval history. Fletch lost a lot of friends that day, and he'd never forgive himself for sitting on the beach while they died. Australia lost *nine* warships—four frigates, three submarines, and two patrol craft—in the Battle of Cocos Islands, leaving his navy pitifully small.

That led *Parramatta* to the yards for another upgrade cycle. *She* was due to leave the shipyard in just a few months, despite eating three French-fired Exocet missiles during the battle. The strikes killed almost half of *Parramatta's* crew by the time the fires were under control, and the Royal Australian Navy was still scrambling to find officers to man her.

Yet *Parramatta* would make it into the war long before Fletch. He grimaced. His navy's future lay with state-of-the-art ships like

Warrego, but they needed shooters now. *Parramatta*, old as she was, could still shoot.

"Did you hear about *Adelaide* and *Yarra*, sir?" Lieutenant Commander Charlene Markey, his executive officer, asked quietly from his side.

Fletch stood on the shipyard side of the dock, amid the wartime bustle of navy technicians, civilian contractors, and every other expert Australia could squeeze into their newly expanded shipbuilding business. The yard was loud, busy, and smelled like someone or three someones were welding nearby. Fletch was squeezed between one crane-swing area and two cargo-loading area, but it was the only place he could get a good look at the ship the Royal Australian Navy had promised him.

Lieutenant Commander Markey, fortunately, was small enough to fit in the alcove with him.

In a land full of people who outsiders believed were tall, tan, and light-haired, Markey stood out. She squeaked past five feet tall wearing boots, was as pale as a ghost, with dark hair and dark eyes she claimed to have inherited from some Indian ancestor.

Experience told Fletch that Charlene—she preferred Charlie—burned like an over-fried fish when she spent too long in the sun. They hit it off about a year ago at the war college, and Fletch never regretted asking for Charlie when he headed to command.

Fletch's grimaced deepened. "I did."

Yarra was the second *Torrens*-class DDG, and *Adelaide* one of Australia's only two helicopter carriers. *Now we're down to one.* That same damn French hotshot, Rochambeau, sank both, but that wasn't what caused the sick feeling in the pit of his stomach.

Fletch had been friends with *Yarra's* captain for thirteen years, and he'd gone to primary school with the *Adelaide's* CO. Fletch's ex-wife was even one of his old friend's many cousins. They spoke before *Adelaide* got underway…and now they would never speak again. The helicopter carrier went down so fast that less than thirty percent of her crew escaped, her captain not among them.

"I heard we lost a sub out there with the *Adelaide* group," Markey added, but Fletch shook his head.

"The sub was American. So were the two frigates."

"Lovely," his XO breathed. "Makes us feel blazing useless sitting here, doesn't it? A French submarine attacks one of *our* undersea platforms, and more Americans die defending it because we don't have enough ships."

Fletch sighed. The Australian and American navies had spilled too much blood together in the last five months. "Neither do they. We're up shit creek together, Charlie. Particularly given the recent surge in Indian shipbuilding. They commissioned *six* new destroyers last month, and Lord only knows how many submarines."

"And here we sit, awaiting our *one* destroyer."

"Indeed." Ten months was too long to sit on the beach. Fletch's eyes narrowed. "For the moment."

Washington, D.C.

Admirals were generally considered self-sufficient people, but when Long Trieu failed to show up for work a second day in a row, people paid attention. No one was about to mark SUBLANT as an unauthorized absence—he was an admiral, for crying out loud—but the CNO got worried enough to send Freddie out to his house when Trieu continued not answering his phone.

Banging on his front door only made two neighbors come out and stare, so Freddie called a locksmith.

"I feel like a goddamned burglar," she muttered to Maria. Standing there in her working uniform while being glared at by residents of a suburban Herndon, Virginia, neighborhood was *not* on her to-do list today.

Thank goodness the neighbors weren't staring at her. Yet.

"I think burglars come at night, ma'am."

"It would certainly be cooler." Why did August in Virginia have to be so hot? She missed Groton, the mecca of submarine warfare. At least it was less humid.

"Just a few more minutes and I'll have it, ladies. The new electronic locks require me to talk to the security company," the locksmith said, glancing over his shoulder at them. "You *did* say you have permission to do this, right?"

"It's a health and welfare check for a fellow naval officer," Freddie replied. "Or a matter of national security, if that makes you feel better."

The locksmith frowned. "Um, shouldn't it be one or the other?"

"When it's an admiral, it can be both."

"Right. I'll just do my job and blame the government, then." He turned back to the lock and continued fiddling.

Thirty seconds later, the door popped open. Ducking inside, the locksmith silenced the alarm with the manufacturer's code. Freddie followed him in, the hairs on the back of her neck rising. The house felt too still, not lived in. Like something was...off.

"Admiral Trieu?" she called. No answer. "Long?"

Silence greeted her. Freddie was vaguely aware of Maria thanking the locksmith behind her, but she ignored the pair and headed deeper into the house. Nothing in the foyer; no lights on, even. The front hall was equally empty, as was the dining room. She peeked up the stairs on her way by, but there seemed to be no lights on up there, and Freddie decided to head up there last.

"Hello?" she said. "Anyone home?"

Finally, Freddie came around the corner and into the living room. And froze.

Vice Admiral Long Trieu sat on the couch, pale and chalky white. He was perfectly upright, his eyes closed like he was sleeping—but Freddie knew he wasn't.

Beside him, the bottle of sleeping pills laid open...and empty.

Chapter 12

Good Old Boys' Club

Less than twelve hours after arriving on board *Jimmy Carter*, Murder Machine II was already up to no good.

Alex woke up to a crew-wide email—sent from an anonymous external email account that no one ever owned up to—featuring pictures of Murder Machine "sleeping" in the XO's rack while George sang in the shower. He was even dressed in a cute little bow.

George sputtered denials and fled breakfast when confronted about his off-key singing while Alex almost choked on his coffee. He *always* heard George's singing through the door to their shared head every morning...and it really was as bad as the email claimed. He just never commented, because making fun of the XO was mean when George was such an easy target and Alex was the captain.

But if he wasn't guilty, that meant someone else crept into the XO's stateroom to stage the Rabbit With Big Pointy Teeth while Alex was in his underwear next door.

At least morale was good.

NAVY CAUGHT IN ANOTHER COVERUP

Mark Easley, Washington Post

Five months deep into this new world war, the U.S. Navy is—once again!—on the receiving end of too many questions.

Multiple sub loses—eight confirmed as of this writing on August 29, 2038, and perhaps as many as fifteen—remain shrouded in mystery. Surface ship losses, including one aircraft carrier, occur at a rate higher than that in World War II. Admirals die in secrecy (two of them now, can you believe it?), and the navy insists that everything is *just fine*.

And what's the navy's newest plan? Replace the late Vice Admiral Trieu with Rear Admiral Winifred Hamilton, the highest-ranking female submariner in history. If confirmed by Congress, she'll be promoted to Vice Admiral and become the navy's senior submarine officer.

This is great news. It's long overdue for the navy's biggest boys' club.

It's also flack thrown in the public's face to distract us.

The navy has real problems. Sailors are dying because

of incompetent—dare I say criminal?—mismanagement. Captains and admirals freeze up in combat, hide in their cabins, or find that their old paperwork ninja skills fail to intimidate the enemy. And then what happens?

American sailors die.

The navy deserves better.

The nation deserves answers.

Perhaps Vice Admiral (select) Hamilton will give them to us.

INDIAN DIPLOMATS EJECTED FROM SRI LANKA AFTER SECURITY BREACH

Carra Garlock, New York Times

Financially flush for the first time in history after the 2027 Rush to the Ocean Floor, it finally looked like the small island nation of Sri Lanka might move mountains. After a longtime alliance with Norway led to the development of three major underwater habitats, Sri Lanka's GDP quadrupled, the government could finally pay off a lingering 2016 bailout from the International Monetary Fund—and begin turning a profit. Tourism was up, trade with India on the rise, and China was a good neighbor.

Now China remains in flames, deep in the grip of a four-way civil war for control of Asia's greatest empire. Meanwhile, India extended a hand of friendship—full of riches—to their small neighbor to the south, requesting access to Sri Lankan oil terminals in exchange for "neutrality" in favor of India and the ULP.

Sri Lanka seemed poised with a counteroffer. Already a member of the Non-Aligned Movement, or NAM, Sri Lanka was excellently positioned to be a mediator between the various nations now at war in the Indian Ocean. Preliminary talks suggested that President Rajapaksa would propose a cease fire to the U.N., offering to host a peace conference in Sri Lanka's capital, Sri Jayawardenepura Kotte.

Now everything has changed.

Negotiations slammed to a halt yesterday when Indian hackers were caught red-handed inside the Sri Lankan defense mainframe. Indian Defense Ministry representatives claim innocence, but the Sri Lankan Chief of the Defense Staff, General Correa, confirmed that there is hard evidence linking the Indian government to the hackers.

As a result, Indian diplomats have been ejected from their neighboring nation, including the entire embassy staff. Boarded up and not even under guard, the Indian Embassy stands empty—but for how long?

The government of Sri Lanka, however, has not been idle. President Rajapaksa has reaffirmed her nation's neutrality but has also entered into talks with the "Grand Alliance" (the U.S., U.K., Australia, Canada, and several smaller allied nations) concerning mutual defense should any of the Union for the Freedom and Prosperity of the Indian Ocean act against them.

The Indian Foreign Ministry provided no comment when asked about further negotiations with Sri Lanka.

Time will tell if Sri Lanka remains neutral or if the Grand Alliance gains a foothold right on India's doorstep.

The XO was on a manhunt to find who snuck into his stateroom, and Alex wasn't going to help.

XO-hazing was one of the sub navy's oldest and finest traditions. Executive officers responded in one of three ways: laughter, anger, or stilted tolerance. Frankly, Alex expected the latter out of George Kirkland.

Unfortunately, he got dogged determination to find the culprits. Alex didn't have the heart to tell George he was pretty sure the entire crew was in on this. He sure as hell didn't mention *he* was pleased by the shenanigans. *Jimmy Carter's* crew was young, untried, and tossed together like odd vegetables in a blender. Alex still didn't know what flavor smoothie they'd make, but pranking the XO was a good sign.

Lunch that day included clam chowder. It wasn't the best choice—navy soup came from a can—and with the meal slammed in between torpedo loading and battle drills, it made for a slow lunch. But it also gave the junior officers in *Jimmy Carter's* wardroom another opportunity.

Running late after a marathon spot check forward in sonar—which Alex would've blamed on George if their young sonar officer, Ensign Edwardo Vincentelli, wasn't smirking so hard—George rushed to the chair to Alex's right and plopped down.

Several junior officers exchanged barely smothered grins, which Alex pretended to ignore.

George, ever oblivious, turned to Maggie. "Is the VDR install complete, Nav? And have you heard any other complaints? I don't want the crew forgetting to do their duty because they're nervous about being on video."

Alex suppressed the urge to groan. George's last boat's VDR was installed before the crew even reported aboard—*Razorback* was one of the newest subs in the fleet—yet he remained wrapped around this particular axle.

Maggie smiled easily. "The contractor finished this morning, sir, OPTEST sat. And everyone seems to be getting used to the idea. Pretty sure they'll be competing for who can say the worst thing on video."

"They had best not!" George reared back as if slapped. "If I catch people being inappropriate, I will hammer them!"

Alex sipped his water to hide a grimace. "Oh, I think we'll find a happy medium on that one, XO," he said. "We'll have worse things to worry about during wartime than a few dick jokes."

George flushed. Maggie giggled. A sailor slipped between Alex and George to put a bowl of soup in front of the XO, and Alex did a double take when he realized it wasn't the normal mess attendant—it was Lieutenant (j.g.) Yoko Kasuba, *Jimmy Carter's* supply officer.

Here it comes. Hot sauce or asinine amounts of pepper? Alex couldn't see around Kasuba without giving the game away.

Vincentelli's lurking smile became giggles until Kasuba kicked him on his way by. To Vincentelli's credit, he didn't yelp—but the kid still had a terrible poker face.

"Captain, I think we can do better than that," George said as he lifted his soup spoon. "In fact—"

The spoon bounced off the soup.

Frowning, George looked down and tried again.

Bounce.

"What in the *world* is this?" George's voice squeaked too much to sound threatening.

Vincentelli dissolved into giggles. Maggie, mid-sip of red "bug" juice, almost snorted it up. Kasuba, cackling, vanished back into the galley. The other officers at the table looked back and forth between Alex and George and, when they saw their captain trying not to laugh, gave up and joined in.

When no one answered, George poked at his soup again, almost hard enough to break the saran wrap covering the bowl. Bright red, the XO put his spoon down on the table with extreme care before looking up at Vincentelli.

"Was this your idea, Ensign?"

Vincentelli gulped. "No, sir." He squared his shoulders. "But I did help. A little."

"Clearly, Mr. Kasuba has too much free time on his hands." George's frown deepened; he didn't bother to remove the saran wrap, and Alex couldn't blame him. A clever junior officer might *also* go for hot sauce in the chowder.

Then again, maybe George liked his chowder that way. Some people did. That was always a risk with pranks. *Jimmy Carter's* wardroom table had a rack holding seventeen different brands of hot sauce, from Texas Pete to Old Red, and running out of hot sauce was a boat-wide emergency.

"I'm sure your vengeance will be a sight to behold," Alex said when no one else dared answer. "However, as the impartial scorekeeper—as all captains must be in the time-honored war of Junior Officers v. XO—I award points to the JOs today."

Maggie's eyebrows waggled. "Do department heads get to play, sir?"

"Only if you want to get caught in the crossfire. Do you *really* want to give your division officers an excuse to prank you?"

"Nav's talking crazy, Captain," Benji Angler spoke up from Maggie's right. "Is it too late to sign on as junior scorekeepers? Impartial, of course."

Alex chuckled. "Wise choice."

"Please excuse me, Captain." George rose. "I find I've lost my appetite."

"Of course."

Alex wouldn't call his XO a poor sport in front of the other officers...but he remembered getting pranked by the kids back on *Kansas*. Alex gave as good as he got—including rigging the lights in their staterooms to change color on his command—until Commander Rothberg brokered a peace treaty that included the division officers returning all three sets of coveralls they stole from Alex.

Pranking the XO was all in good fun. It was half hazing ritual for a new XO, half test for the division officers. Were they creative enough to get away with it? Would they avoid pissing the captain off in the process? Good officers found ways around problems instead of avoiding them.

Alex watched George leave the wardroom with a sinking feeling that George *wasn't* retreating to plan revenge.

31 August 2038, off the coast of Sri Lanka

This was a waste of missiles.

Vice Admiral Aadil Khare, Indian Navy, frowned. The view from the bridge of INS *Rajput* was without a doubt spectacular. Another pair of Brahmos-NG missiles burned into the early morning sky, turning the light blue and pink colors bright orange with fire. Their boosters lifted them well clear of his flagship destroyer, and then both missiles turned north, toward Trincomalee. The port city was home to SLNS Tissa, one of Sri Lanka's larger naval bases.

SLNS Tissa wasn't Sri Lanka's naval headquarters, however, a choice Khare made consciously. Targeting Columbo, the largest city on the island, would inflame public opinion and kill far too many civilians. Annoyed through India was with Sri Lanka, killing civilians was not the goal—and there was no quicker way to turn public opinion against the ULP.

Everyone knew reckless killing of civilians was off the table. You had to at least make a visible *effort* not to kill them. This was not the twentieth century. Anyone who endorsed tactics like firebombing would surely hang for it.

"Are you certain this is...the best plan, Admiral?" Captain Kiara Naidu, his chief of staff, asked from his right.

Khare sighed. "I am not. However, we have our orders."

So did the task force around him. *His* ships, thankfully. He was not entirely under a rock for the incomplete victory at Armistice Station. He had a good little group of ships, one he intended to grow with time. And then fleet staff would notice his service. And his skills.

"I find the reports of missile shortages back home...concerning." Naidu frowned. Like any good chief of staff, she was on the same page as her admiral. "Momentum is on our side. But if we slacken the pace of our victories..."

"I know." Khare swallowed the desire to swear. "But the Americans are suffering worse than we are, and the Australian Navy is all but finished."

"As is Japan, but it would be nice if our Russian friends kept their promises to provide more missiles," she replied.

"That it would." Khare flinched as another two missiles burst into the dark sky and hated himself for it. He should be used to this by now.

"Do you think Sri Lanka will give in, sir, or are we wasting our time?" Naidu asked quietly.

Khare shook his head. "A few missiles thrown at patrol boats will only make them more stubborn. I am not sure what our leadership wants to do...unless they *wish* to push Sri Lanka right into America's lap."

"I don't see the sense in that."

"Nor do I." Khare crossed his arms and glared at the horizon.

But his country's leadership was not made of fools. They had *something* in mind, of that he was certain. But what?

So far, the war was almost ridiculously slanted in the ULP's favor. With Russian gains in the north against Japan—and the utter decimation of the Japanese Naval Self-Defense Force—and France's resurgence in the southern Indian Ocean, India had solid allies at her back. Allies of convenience, to be sure, but allies with common interests.

Nearly five months into the war, they'd destroyed three times as much "Alliance" tonnage as that belonging to the union. In *warships*. And while battles distracted foreign decision makers, the ULP claimed fourteen major underwater stations, plus another seventeen minor ones.

About two-thirds of those stations had been independent prior to the war, the rest majority owned by nations arrayed against the Union. Those stations were the true targets of the war, not military victories, and Khare found it ludicrous that the "Grand Alliance" hadn't caught on.

India needed space, money, and resources to continue building her future. Influence, too, free of American interference. *That* was what they hoped to gain.

Eventually—probably soon—the war would end in a negotiated settlement. India would give up some of her gains, as civilized nations must.

But not all.

Victors got to keep *some* spoils in every contest. Khare was a student of history and strategy. The Union's advantages grew more overwhelming by the day, and when they offered the Grand Alliance a way out with honor, the Alliance would take it.

Khare bared his teeth as two more missiles launched toward Sri Lanka. Not yet. First, they would bleed.

The Eastern Indian Ocean

"Damn it, I can't believe you let them slip by us!"

Master Chief Casey ducked into control just in time to catch the tail end of Commander Kennedy's tirade. As usual, Lieutenant Sue Grippo was his target; she stood red-faced in front of the captain, glaring mulishly but trying not to take the bait and scream back.

Eventually, the navigator was going to snap, Casey decided. She was a good officer, had potential to be one of the best, but getting beaten down by Kennedy for the last nine months left her a shell of her former self. Once a dynamic and cheerful leader, Sue was now quiet and withdrawn.

Casey still wasn't sure why Kennedy hated her. Was it because Sue sided with Commander Coleman back during that idiocy when Kennedy tried to kill a civilian submarine? They'd both been right, but the fact that Kennedy only got to punish Coleman probably pissed him off. Sue came out of it unscathed—except for Kennedy's irrational loathing.

"They were outside our patrol sector, Captain," Sue replied quietly. "And out of range. The Link track from *Stockdale* is three hours old, and—"

"Shut up, Nav. If I wanted stupid excuses, I would've asked for them." Kennedy paced across the space as watchstanders busied themselves looking anywhere but at their captain.

"Yes, sir."

"Sometimes I wonder if you even *want* to be in the navy." Kennedy huffed. "Or if you *deserve* to be."

Casey tried not to sigh. Working for Kennedy was like riding a rollercoaster; the highs were high, but damn were the hills steep. Worse yet, *Kansas* was doing okay in the war, which meant they were mid-pack when it came to counting ships they'd sunk—and that wasn't good enough for Commander Christopher Atticus Kennedy.

Sue visibly bit her lip before turning back to the navigational plot.

"Ready to hit port and get some R&R, Captain?" Casey asked to fill the silence, strolling up as casually as he could. No need to tell Kennedy that the boys at fire control had called the chief of the boat when the captain got frisky.

And where was the XO? Avoiding conflict, probably. Maybe still grieving for her little sister. Lieutenant Commander Hunt hadn't been the same since her sister died when *Belleau Wood* got hammered in the Battle of Cocos Islands.

Kennedy scowled. "I'd like it better if we could've killed another *Scorpene* before pulling back in."

"Hey, we still got one this patrol, plus the *Akula*. Add that French frigate we got last week, and we're sitting pretty, sir," Casey said.

"Not as good as I'd like. They gave John Dalton command of *Razorback*."

"So?"

"So he's already got a silver star. *And* he's had command before." Kennedy crossed his arms. "They're going to roll the red carpet out for Dalton. I can see it coming. Give him the best assignments, clear his path straight to flag rank. Going to be impossible to compete with."

Casey thought he heard someone snort. He couldn't disagree; what did Kennedy think this was, a video game?

"I wouldn't worry none about that, Captain. You do your job, and you'll get noticed. War means there'll be plenty of promotions to go 'round, right?"

"Only if—"

Boom!

Kansas shook like a giant hand reached out to use her as a saltshaker, rattling Casey's teeth so hard he thought he might lose a few.

"What the fuck was that?" Kennedy whirled to face Sue. "What did you do?"

"Splashes! Splashes bearing zero-zero-niner at less than one thousand yards!" one of the sonar operators shouted.

Kennedy staggered, leaning on the periscope display for balance as he shook his head drunkenly. "Splashes?"

"They're using goddamned depth charges, Captain," Casey growled, a sinking feeling coiling in his stomach. "I recommend diving, fast."

"Depth charges?" Kennedy looked at Casey like he was crazy, but thankfully, their prideful captain was no fool. "Crash dive!" he ordered. "Make your depth eight hundred feet."

"Full down on the planes, make my depth eight hundred feet, aye," the planes operator replied. "My planes are at thirty degrees down."

"Very well." Kennedy was sheet white; for once, Casey couldn't blame him.

Boom!

Another blast shook the submarine, this one from further away. Casey's teeth still hurt, still—

Boom—boom!

"How the hell did we end up in World War II?" Kennedy asked no one in particular. "This depth-charge bullshit belongs in last century! And where the fuck is it coming from?"

"It's got to be an aircraft, sir. Otherwise, we'd have heard whoever's dropping these things," Casey said.

Sue cleared her throat. "Captain, do you want to set battle stations?"

"Of course I fucking do! Do your job, Nav. Don't just stand there and stare at me."

"Officer of the Deck, aye." Sue turned to the chief of the watch, her face almost expressionless. "Set battle stations torpedo."

"Chief of the Watch, aye!"

Casey ignored the donging of the general alarm, watching Kennedy glare at Sue's back again. He wasn't sure how the hell he was supposed to continue refereeing the captain's hatred for the navigator, particularly when the XO avoided conflict like a sexually transmitted disease.

Fortunately, their attacker was an aircraft, which meant that when *Kansas* dove deep under the layer, the P-3 Orion—an airframe that

Lockheed Martin sold India decades earlier, because the assholes had once been their allies, and that was such a happy thought—lost their track and eventually stopped chucking small bombs at the submarine.

Which was good. Kennedy's pontificating about dodging depth charges like Mush Morton was less fun, but still something Casey could live with.

The Pentagon, Washington, D.C.

"Feel different, Freddie?" Admiral "Scrap" Chan asked as the newly minted Commander, Naval Submarine Forces Atlantic, walked into his office.

"A bit charbroiled." Freddie grimaced, resisting the urge to look at the new stripe on the sleeve of her dress blues.

She was a vice admiral, now; earning a third star was nice. Few women ever attained that rank in the U.S. Navy, and she was the first female submariner to do so. It should have felt like an accomplishment.

Instead, all she could think of was Long Trieu's rushed funeral and the newspaper articles calling her own appointment chaff used to distract the public from a losing war.

"Ignore the assholes," Scrap said. "And sit down already. You're the senior submariner in the navy now, Freddie. No need to pop to."

Smiling, Freddie lowered herself into the sinfully plush chair across from the chief of naval operations' desk. She eyed that polished wood desk for a moment; yes, she still wanted it. Someday.

But not today. Today, she faced rising sub loses and needed to find a way to turn things around.

"We need to make some changes," she said. "Starting with how we screen commanding officers."

"Don't tell me you're buying into that media crap about 'the captain problem.'"

"I'm not buying into anything." Freddie folded her hands. "However, I *am* looking at the available data, and *that* tells me we have a problem. Between Harney breaking down on *Razorback* and our plethora of sub losses...it all comes down to the men and women in command. And too many of them aren't up to the task."

Scrap frowned. "What do you propose?"

"More stringent tactical training, to start. We have to stress captains *before* they get to command. If we can do it enough, we might weed out some of those who will get their crews killed."

"Some?"

"We won't save them all. We're at war." Freddie took a deep breath. "But if we don't stop the bleeding, we're going to die a death of a thousand cuts."

Scrap was silent for a long moment. "I can't pretend to be an expert on subs, Freddie," he finally said. "It's your sandbox. I'll stay out of your way—just turn this war around."

The CNO didn't have to say Freddie's career was on the line. If she couldn't stop the rash of sub losses—now up to one out of every three subs deployed against the enemy—Freddie didn't deserve to earn a fourth star.

Chapter 13

If It Ain't Broke

2 September 2038, Newport, Rhode Island

Newport was one of the nicest places to be stationed in the navy, hands down. Particularly if you didn't like California. The weather was as nice as you could find in New England—today was a touch crisp, but still sunny and clear—the food was great, and traffic wasn't bad. Once a sleepy navy base, the navy's pre-war expansion reawakened the base with a snap. A base previously full of schoolhouses and not much else, now it was homeport to twelve destroyers, with four more destined for Newport but still in the pipeline at shipyards up north.

Commander Nancy Coleman crossed her arms and tried not to scowl. USS *Fletcher* (DDG 155) was about to leave the local shipyard in record time—yet an eerie feeling of doom gnawed at the pit of Nancy's stomach.

It wasn't fear of combat. She'd faced that beast already, and unlike far too many of her friends, classmates, and colleagues, Nancy had both survived and thrived. She wore a silver star—America's third-highest award for valor in combat—on her uniform to prove her mettle. No, it was the creeping thought of going into combat unprepared.

Again.

"You see that email about our weapons on load, ma'am?" Commander Ying Mai, her executive officer, approached to ask.

They stood on the edge of the dry dock together, watching as it filled with water. *Slower than watching paint dry.* Nancy's lips twitched. *Fletcher* was the first ship to use this brand-new dry dock in the newly christened Newport Naval Shipyard—not to be confused with Newport *News* Naval Shipyard down in Virginia—and it seemed like the new shipyard was operating at half speed.

She wasn't sure she could blame them. Ten years ago, the naval base in Newport, Rhode Island, was home to several sleepy schoolhouses and always in danger of closing. Today, Newport was home to seven destroyers and the repair yard that *Fletcher* currently called home.

But at least *Fletcher* was soon to be wet again.

And when her destroyer reentered the water, it would be complete with a towed sonar array that might've saved so much trouble back in the Battle of the Strait of the Malacca. If they'd known that sub was there, they might have realized it was Indian before Admiral McNally took a shot and—

"Captain?" Ying touched her shoulder.

Shivering, Nancy shook herself. "Yeah, I saw it. We get to deploy with a quarter-size missile loadout because of shortages. Joy."

"You can say that again." Ying sighed. "Makes me nervous. Not that I'll say it in front of the crew."

"Same. We can talk a good game about 'making do,' but it's hard to put warheads on foreheads without the warheads." Nancy grimaced. "Not that I'm sure what foreheads they'd aim us at. We seem to be pulling back."

"No one's said anything about a strategic retreat."

"No one's said anything about *strategy*, you mean." Nancy continued to watch her ship; *Fletcher* listed a little to port, and if the yard workers didn't correct that in a hurry, the destroyer would flop on her side and ruin Nancy's entire war. "We're still reacting to the Union's attacks...and losing when we do."

"I saw that *Farrell* and *Basilone* got hammered yesterday. My roommate from Annapolis is *Farrell's* XO. Or was. I think she's dead."

"I'm so sorry, Ying." Nancy wished there were words, but commiserating over friends' deaths was far too common these days.

She didn't want to count the number of friends she'd lost. Not now. Maybe not ever.

It was easier watching the yard workers scramble to right *Fletcher*. Her destroyer crept back onto an even keel with agonizing slowness.

Ying sucked in a ragged breath. "Me, too."

The silence dragged on a few beats too long; faces of lost friends danced in front of Nancy's eyes. There was Tyler Marshall, a friend of a decade who died commanding *John Finn* in the SOM. And Anka Walczak, dead on *Kidd* in the same battle. Nancy could list others. Some she knew well, like RJ Cousteau on *Ralph Johnson*, her classmate at the Surface Warfare Officer's School. Others were more Alex's friends than hers, but still faces she knew, professional acquaintances who she knew and liked.

And for what? To lose?

To retreat?

Nancy signed on to fight, if need be to die, for her country. But not for no point.

This war started because an incompetent, trigger-happy admiral sank the wrong submarine. The Indians retaliated, ships were sunk, and suddenly, the world was at war.

No one thought it would last this long, particularly not if they were American. Nancy and her fellows always assumed that the U.S. Navy would take their licks—because *no way* would they take the first shot, not with their politicians—and then come back and win with a vengeance.

So much for that.

Sighing, Nancy turned back to her battle-scarred destroyer. The burns on *Fletcher's* port side were still visible aft; they'd replaced the missing CIWS gun mount, but painting over the scorch mark proved challenging. There was a haze gray paint shortage. Who would've thought?

"Let's get back to work," she said.

Ying nodded gratefully. "Yes, ma'am."

031823Z SEP 2038

TO: ALL SUBMARINES

FM: COMSUBLANT

SUBJ: P4 COMMANDERS UPDATE SEP-001

RMKS/1. USE OF DEPTH CHARGES (BOTH ROCKET-PROPELLED LAUNCHED FROM SURFACE SHIPS AND AIRCRAFT-DROPPED) HAS BEEN REPORTED BY FRENCH AND INDIAN NAVAL UNITS.

2. ALL SUBMARINE COMMANDERS, BE ADVISED THAT ENEMY SURFACE AND AIR UNITS MAY DEPLOY DEPTH CHARGES TO DEPTHS OF UP TO 800 FEET.

3. NO USE OF NUCLEAR DEPTH BOMBS REPORTED. ALL WARHEADS USED SO FAR HAVE BEEN CONVENTIONAL.

4. COMBSUBFOR ADVISES ALL UNITS TO REMAIN IN STEALTH WHENEVER POSSIBLE AND BE MINDFUL OF AIRCRAFT PRESENCE. STEALTH IS AN ATTACK SUBMARINE'S STRONGEST LIFELINE. WHEN YOU MUST ATTACK, DO SO DECISIVELY AND THEN RETURN TO STEALTH IMMEDIATELY. //

Alex handed the message tablet to George without a word. They'd already been in the in the wardroom together, reviewing the results of *Jimmy Carter's* latest torpedo loading drill, when the message from the new head of all U.S. Navy submarines came in.

Just my luck that our new lady and master is an admiral who hates me. Alex suppressed a smile. At least Hamilton sent him to *Jimmy*

Carter. It wasn't like she'd take the boat she promised him away.

"Depth charges?" George squeaked. "This—this is unbelievable."

"Not as much as it should be." Alex sat back in his chair, pinching the bridge of his nose to wish a headache away. "Navies never throw anything away. It's not surprising that France and India—and Russia, I have no doubt—have a bunch of Cold War–era depth charges gathering dust in storage."

"Don't they have expiration dates?" George asked. "Torpedoes and missiles do."

"Probably. But even if half the spread you chuck overboard fails to explode, you've still got a bunch of underwater explosions." Alex shrugged. "Math says that's decent odds if you're trying to screw with a sub the cheap way."

"Cheaper than a torpedo, you mean." George remained stark white.

"Most things are. Except missiles. And unlike torpedoes and missiles, you're not worried about an expired depth charge cooking off in the tube when its motor starts—those things don't explode until after they're clear of your ship or aircraft. If I was some surface ship driver, I'd be happy to throw some of them overboard if a sub was hunting me."

George shuddered. "That sounds terrible."

"From the sub perspective, sure."

"You think we're going to use them, too?" George looked down at the message again, eyes wide, like he was afraid it might bite him. "The surface pukes, I mean."

"I can ask my wife." Alex grinned. "She's a surface puke."

"She—oh, crap, Captain, I'm sorry. I didn't know. I shouldn't—"

"It's fine, George." Even needling his XO wasn't much fun when George started shuddering like that. *Nancy* would find being called a surface puke funny; she had plenty of derogatory nicknames in her pocket to use in revenge. But George sucked the life out of a lot of things.

Even watching the kids prank him wasn't as amusing as it should've been. George just grumbled and fled instead of taking revenge like a proper XO. Alex kept hoping he'd pull his head out and have some fun...but if George didn't figure that out, Alex would have to stop the games.

Gently, though. He didn't want to hurt morale just because the XO didn't know how to play along. Going to war was no joke, so anything that kept the crew happy and not focused on the possibility of imminent death was a good thing.

Particularly when they were about to join that war in a thirty-three-year-old submarine.

Naval Station Pearl Harbor, Oahu, Hawaii

Commander Teresa O'Canas made a point of trying to mentor fellow officers, particularly women. The sub force was still mostly a boys' club, even if the ranking submariner in the navy was (for the first time ever!) a woman. So she tried to take promising female officers under her wing, which led to meeting Rose Lange.

"So how's life on *Douglass* treating you?"

Teresa grinned. "Wonderful. I've got a fantastic crew, and we've completed repairs ahead of schedule, so we're leaving on patrol the day after tomorrow."

"South Pacific?" Rose asked around a french fry. Teresa's most brilliant protégé was deliberately uncouth; Rose disregarded her manners just to prove she belonged in the boys' club.

"Seems like." She couldn't say more, not even in a McDonald's on the naval base in Pearl Harbor. Hawaii wasn't the best place to deploy from to hit up the many French-owned territories in the Pacific, but it was the best America had until old bases were dusted off and re-opened. "What about *Bluefish*? See any action?"

Rose snorted. "Not likely. We're the bluest boat in the fleet."

Teresa cocked her head. "That sounds like an in-joke I'm missing."

"Several." The young lieutenant sighed. "Let's just say I wish *you* were my CO."

Ah. It was time for a casual lunch to turn into a mentoring session. Teresa tried to remember if she'd heard anything significant about *Bluefish*. She knew the other boat was a *Cero*-class, unlike like her own *Douglass*, but the navy gossips had zilch to say about *Bluefish* or her crew. *At least that means her CO isn't a raging drunk.*

"If I was, we wouldn't be having this superbly serious conversation," she replied.

"I could live with that." Rose's scowl deepened.

Teresa cocked her head. "How bad is it?"

Rose hesitated. "Not bad enough for me to air all of our dirty laundry, I guess." She slumped in her seat. "But not great."

"I'm sorry to hear that." There wasn't much Teresa could say; they weren't civilians who could quit and go home. Orders were orders. An officer stayed on a submarine until their tour was over or the boat sank. Maybe it was time to change the subject. "Speaking of shitty situations, you hear about the massive one the Brits pulled?"

"No." Rose's green eyes lit up.

"It started when they thought they'd lost *Gallant*," Teresa said. "So the surface action group *Gallant* was working with goes bonkers—they're sitting in the Bering Sea, the weather's gone to crap, and they're trying to keep Russian subs from heading around the top of Siberia to finish off the Japanese Navy."

"Isn't *Gallant* Ursula North's boat?"

"Yep. The best the Brits have." Teresa didn't like admitting that Ursula North might be the best in the world. She led all Alliance submarine commanders for both total tonnage and number of warships sunk. *Take that, you good ol' boys!*

North was a legend for the run she made through Russian-held waters to help stave off the destruction of the Japanese Navy after the Second Battle of the Sea of Okhotsk; she ran out of torpedoes and had to reload *twice* before pulling into port because she sank so many enemy ships. Everyone in the sub community knew her name.

France's Jules Rochambeau was the only one in North's league, but Teresa heard he was a first-rate asshole. He'd sent several of her friends to the bottom, too.

"So what happened?" Rose asked.

"Well, the Brits think they've lost her, and sonar conditions for the SAG just keep getting worse. They detect a submarine and assume it's Russian, so they start flinging out depth charges as the weather goes to pot. They launch a couple hundred of the things before *Gallant* finally struggles to the surface, bleeding air, and with North threatening to sink every one of the bastards if they don't stop dropping depth charges on her head."

"Good for her." Rose's grin was fierce.

North's temper was legendary enough that even *American* submariners heard of it. She was supposedly an aristocrat, heir to some title or another, but North knew how to be a crass bitch.

"Oh, yeah. You can imagine." Teresa laughed. "They deserved it. Depth charges are bad enough. Having them dropped on you by your *own* navy has to chafe."

"I take it that the Brits caught on?"

"Took them a bit, but eventually *Gallant* limped back into Sasebo. What the British surface guys didn't manage, a storm almost did.

From what I understand, she'll be months in the yards getting repaired."

"Fucking awesome. That's *really* what we need."

"Well, maybe *Douglass* and *Bluefish* can fill the gap." Teresa grinned again, mostly for show.

Losing one submarine commander shouldn't have the potential to change the course of the war, but Ursula North wasn't just any submariner. Taking her and *Gallant* out of the picture weakened the Alliance. Rumors said the Russians were hot to open a second front in the Pacific, and *Gallant* helped keep them back.

So far, the bulk of the war was in the Indian Ocean and the Southern Pacific around Australia, with the Russian fleet confined mostly to the northern approaches of the Pacific leading toward Japan. The Alliance was already stretched thin, too thin. The Freedom Union, on the other hand, had boats and money to burn, and without someone like Ursula North there to whittle down their numbers, it would get ugly.

Teresa swallowed. That gap was going to be hard to fill, and her boat was next up to try.

One of the nice things about being in port was that Alex got to talk to Nancy every night. They had to schedule the call—fifteen hundred his time was nineteen hundred in Newport—around trying to get their respective commands ready for war, but it was nice to hear his wife's voice.

One of the better perks of being the captain was that he had a direct outside phone line in his stateroom, which sure as hell beat trying to have a private conversation topside on his cell phone. Liking his crew didn't mean he wanted to share his soul with them. So Alex could flop on the narrow bed in his stateroom and talk to the woman he loved, content that no one could hear him trying not to freak out.

"Six more days," Nancy said. "Fastest I've ever known a ship to go from dry dock to deployment."

"They confirmed your departure date?" Alex swallowed back the need to fret. He was damned proud of Nancy, who'd earned one of the first two silver stars of the war—not the only ones, now, but still the first—but the idea of her going back into combat scared him more than going himself.

"September ninth. A week to the day after we came out of dry dock. We'll test systems and complete our pre-deployment certifications as we cross the pond." He could hear her grimace.

Alex inserted as much fake cheer into his voice as he could muster. "And if you don't pass, combat readiness is only a waiver away?"

"I thought you sub guys were supposed to be better about this stuff." Nancy laughed. "Or so you've always claimed."

"Yeah, that was before I came to the thirty-three-year-old boat." Alex resolutely ignored the holes in his stateroom carpet. Again.

"You still leaving the day after us?" she asked.

"Yep. But the commodore cleared me coming out to see you off, even if he didn't quite call me stupid for it. Said it's the least he can do for the navy's first pair of married COs heading to war in the same week."

"And isn't *that* a distinction I love having?" Nancy groaned. "I'd rather make history in some other way, if that's good with you."

"Babe, I'd rather not make history at all." Alex swallowed. "This is going to be so hard on the girls."

"I know," she whispered. "I'm so glad my mom will be there, but...I can't say no. And neither can you. It's the job."

"As long as you don't use the 'it's not a job, it's an adventure' line on them, I think they'll forgive us," Alex said. "Mostly."

"Just try to stay alive, okay? This war's turning rougher on submariners than it is on us surface ship drivers. I am *not* explaining your death to Bobbie and Emily. You got that?"

"Hey, no need to worry about me. In this old lady of mine, I'm sure I'll be furthest from where the fire is hottest. Particularly if Admiral Hamilton has anything to say about it."

"I still think you should have gotten *some* recognition for what you did on Armistice Station," Nancy grumbled. "And don't tell me about your lovely old boat. Even I know submarines aren't supposed to get past thirty."

"I'm okay with you keeping the limelight, remember? Introvert. No spotlight for me." Just thinking about being a crowd's center of attention made Alex shudder.

"Sometimes, I wonder how I fell so hard for you. Must have been that ornery streak a mile wide." Nancy laughed again. "But speaking of history, I got that message you forwarded on about depth charges. No one in the surface navy's talking much about them, though I gather the Brits pulled theirs out of storage last month."

"Yeah, just in time to depth charge the shit out of one of their own boats." Alex snorted. "Great call on their part."

Nancy sniffed. "Dear, I know everything seems simple when you're crawling around in the dark, but all subs *do* look alike on active sonar. And the best sub near *my* formation is a *dead* sub."

Now wasn't the time to mention how much trouble that attitude got Admiral McNally in; Nancy remembered the Battle of the SOM better than anyone. Besides, Alex didn't believe for a moment that his wife would be reckless enough to shoot at—or depth charge!—a sub without positive identification.

"It's a pity we're on opposite coasts and we can't set up a friendly match so I can show you how hard we are to kill, babe."

"You just keep telling yourself that."

Two officers stood on *Jimmy Carter's* aft deck as their captain talked on the phone, enjoying the sunset...and the quiet.

"You know, I thought you'd be out enjoying the smashing Bremerton night life instead of hanging out with yours truly on my duty night." Maggie grinned.

September evenings in Washington State were muggy and not much to write home about; Maggie wasn't particularly upset to be on duty, though she was bone tired. Getting an old submarine ready to go to war wasn't like she expected. Something was *always* broken, and spare parts were no longer in the navy's inventory. Oh, no, that would be too easy. After all, the *Seawolf*-class boats were all supposed to be decommissioned—including the one whose deck she stood on.

The lack of parts meant scouring every shoreside warehouse to see if this needed gauge or that needed relief valve had been forgotten under someone's desk, and sometimes—far too often—purchasing an equivalent part off of eBay. Maggie's sailors had already replaced two monitors in control with internet-sourced parts, an absolute no-no in peacetime. But the rules changed when you were about to go to war, and *just like that* the boat had a credit card for said purchases.

Honestly, she wasn't sure the captain even asked for permission, but no one came around to smack him for it after the fact. At least *Jimmy Carter's* navigation system was up and running, which was more than she could say for last week.

Her companion on *Jimmy Carter's* deck laughed. "Yeah, it's really hot and fast here. Just like I always dreamed of." Benji Angler shook his head. "I'd rather be on the boat. At least then I can use bad cell service as an excuse to ignore my mom when she calls with another inevitable lecture."

"What's with your mom, anyway? Isn't she proud to have a kid wearing navy blue and gold in the biggest naval war in a century?"

Maggie's own parents were torn between worry and pride. Support for the military remained at an all-time high; the war combined with undersea resource exploitation to create a boom in the American economy like never before. Sure, America's sailors were out there dying—but not in numbers like those from the previous world wars, so it was easier for the public to go on with their normal lives. Screaming support for those in uniform probably made them feel better about it, too.

Benji snorted. "My mom? Hell, no. She expected me to get out after the five years the Academy requires were done, just like Dad did. They planned for me to go into politics."

"Aren't you going to?" she asked as she inspected the submarine's lines. As command duty officer, or CDO, Maggie's job included checking all the lines before bed.

"Maybe someday." Benji shrugged. "I'm not really that excited about the idea, but Mom wants me to be a third-generation senator. Great-Grandpa Stevenson was in the House and Great-Grandpa Angler was *just* Governor of Maryland, but Dad and Grandpa both got in the Senate. And Mom thinks it'd be amazing if I could win Dad's seat when he goes for the presidency."

"Wow. That's...a lot." Maggie liked to study people—she wouldn't like intelligence if she didn't—but naval intelligence didn't have much to do with politics, and holy cow, Benji's family plan was ambitious. Funny, because Benji was a pretty normal guy.

Way more normal than Marty Sterling, who Maggie was pretty sure only left engineering to eat and sleep, and sometimes not even that. He even needed reminders to shower.

"Tell me about it. I'm kinda thinking about staying in for at least twenty, just to mess with her plans."

"My mom's an orthopedist, so I can't really relate." She smiled crookedly as they wandered toward *Jimmy Carter's* outboard side. "Did help every time I bummed some limb or another in gymnastics, though."

"Sounds useful. My mom always says a plan is like— What the *hell* is that?"

The greenish tint to the water caught her eye just as Benji slammed to a stop. Carefully, Maggie peered over the side—the sloping, round side of the boat was slippery, and the sound-absorbent tiles made for bad traction—only to see florescent-green liquid gooping up near *Jimmy Carter's* starboard side forward.

It looked almost like the innards of...a lava lamp?

Maggie blinked.

"God, something's leaking," Benji said. "But what looks like this? It's too far forward to be the reactor—and that wouldn't be green, no matter what idiots think—and oil doesn't exactly glow. Fuel sheens kind of purple, and—"

Maggie giggled.

Benji twisted to look at her. "What?"

"I've seen this before." She bit her lip to keep more laughter back. "I guarantee you it's chem lights. Some numb nuts busted a bunch of them open, then threw them over the side. We just better hope no one's called the local news and told them there's a 'radioactive' leak in the harbor."

"Shit day to be CDO, huh?" Benji winked.

"Oh, stuff it." Maggie punched him lightly in the shoulder. "When it happened on USS *Firstboat*, it was a disgruntled sailor who'd just gone to Captain's Mast. I'm hoping this one's just another junior officer prank."

"Still, we'd better call the captain."

"Nah, I'll call the XO." Maggie grabbed her radio off her belt. Handheld radios were still the best way to communicate within the submarine, because physical wires to transmit the signals could be laid inside the hull when it was built. Wireless signals bounced around all whackadoodle.

"Not the captain?"

"He's on his nightly call with his wife. I'd hate to interrupt that for a prank."

Maggie grinned like she was joking, but she really wasn't. Everyone on *Jimmy Carter* respected Commander Coleman. No one was sure how the oldest attack sub in the fleet got such a *good* CO, but they were determined to keep him.

Having a captain who worked just as hard as everyone else was rare, so no way was Maggie going to bother him with stupid stuff. The navy paid her to make decisions—she was the third ranking officer on the boat, right after the XO—and she was just fine with this one.

Victorie Station, 300 feet underwater, 90 nautical miles south of Tromelin Island

Victorie Station was one of the oldest undersea oil drillers in the world. Founded in 2034 as the Rush to the Ocean Floor swung into high gear, it was the brainchild of American investors and French ingenuity. Add in a few Australian engineers, and Victorie Station became the world's biggest underwater oil exporter by mid-2035.

Unlike Armistice Station, Victorie never dove into the tourism business, instead concentrating on drilling for oil. The sea near Tromelin Island (itself off the coast of Madagascar) was surprisingly dense with oil deposits, so the families that moved out to the station got rich quick—and then got richer.

Soon, Victorie became a sprawling hub of seven smaller stations, each producing twice as much oil than an older semi-submersible platform could manage in a year. Despite the headache of transporting oil to the surface, straight underwater drilling proved safer than using semi-submersible platforms with surface crews. The inconvenience of working underwater was outweighed by safety considerations; water pressure and, well, *water* helped prevent explosions.

And where there were workers, there were businesses. Families made their homes on Victorie Station, and families had needs. International corporations—like WAAS, or Worldwide Acquisition And Services—opened up shop to meet most of the demand, but mom-and-pop stores cropped up, too.

Jennifer Kudalis started out with one restaurant on Victorie Deux in 2035. Three years later, she owned a chain of six, one on each of the drilling stations (except Un, which was still just a worker platform; no one lived there, and with how dirty it was, *no one* wanted to eat there).

She'd become a staple of Victorie Station early on, invested her profits back into the place and turned that into a small fortune. Jenn was only a medium-size fish in an ever-growing pond, but she *liked* her pond.

Until French Marines arrived to chase her out.

"You can't *do* this," she said when her landlord, Andre Payet, came to evict her while she was working on the weekly payroll for her hundred-plus employees. Jenn looked up from her books to find Andre backed by French Marines who were busy scaring all of her paying customers away. "I pay my rent every month for every restaurant. I never cause trouble. Christ, I own a thirty-five percent interest in Victorie Trois!"

"I am sorry, Jennifer," Andre whispered. He was a small man, both in stature and speech, with dark skin and sad eyes. "They say it is the law."

Jenn crossed her arms, tossing her graying blond ponytail over one shoulder with a jerk of her head. "There is no law out there. That's the point of coming out into international waters where there are no taxes."

"Please go quietly. The other investors will reimburse you. They have promised." Andre reached out to put a comforting on her arm; Jenn shook it off.

"*What?*"

One marine twitched like he wanted to walk forward; Andre shook his head. "*Non, je l'ai.*"

The marine glared and fingered his weapon; a chill ran down Jenn's spine.

"This is horseshit, Andre." She swallowed, still watching the marines. None of them looked sympathetic. "My life is here."

"Perhaps they will let you come back someday." Andre's smile was weak. "After the war?"

"What does the war mean to me? This is just business."

"You are American." Andre shrugged. "I think they care about that."

Jenn had nothing to say. Still under the watchful eyes of the marines, she gathered two bags of personal belongings—all she was permitted to take from *two years* of a life!—and watched Andre sign a receipt for the rest.

She doubted she'd see any of it again.

Chapter 14

Homecoming

7 September 2038, Washington, D.C.

"Smile, ma'am, it's our last day in the Five-Sided No-Fun Factory," Maria Vasquez said as she put the last picture into a box.

That one was of Freddie's last seagoing command, USS *Columbia* (SSBN-826). It was a gorgeous picture of *Columbia* on the surface, silhouetted against a brilliant sunset sky full of reds, oranges, and purple. Freddie remembered that underway—they test-fired two ballistic missiles and four LSRAM anti-ship cruise missiles. It was still one of the highlights of her career. The matting around the picture was signed by all of *Columbia's* officers, as was the tradition when an officer departed.

Thinking of that boat, a ballistic missile submarine, made a bittersweet feeling twist in Freddie's gut. She'd always hoped for another command at sea—a strike group, or even a fleet, someday—but her new fate was to be chained to a desk.

Not that it wasn't a nice desk. It was *the* nicest desk for a submariner, in fact, that of the chief submariner in the entire navy. COMSUBLANT was also COMSUBFOR, Commander, Submarine Forces. This was the pinnacle of her career, unless she got to command a regional fleet or became CNO. She didn't even mind that her prestigious new job was in the mecca of surface warfare: Norfolk, Virginia.

Maria was right. Anywhere was better than the Pentagon.

"I won't miss this place," she said. *Or trying to coach the CNO through understanding submarine warfare.* But she couldn't say that out loud. Not even with three stars on her collar.

"Me, neither," Maria replied. "Norfolk's not my favorite place, but even Norfolk traffic is better than D.C."

"Not by much." Another reason to hate the world's largest navy base—the pre-war buildup only made its legendary bad traffic into a nightmare. Freddie grimaced. Thank goodness she'd have a house on base. "Speaking of traffic, did you hear what happened out in the IO?"

"You mean those stations near Madagascar?"

"Right in one." Her smile felt thin. "Having a competent aide is so nice. Remind me to never, *ever* let them promote you away."

Maria grinned before turning serious. "I heard that Alliance minority interests were forced out of both Reunion Floor and Victorie Station. The other investors paid them off after using French Marines to escort every American, British, and Australian citizen off their stations."

"Sounds familiar, doesn't it?"

"Too familiar." The way Maria looked away said she was thinking of Lieutenant Jesse Lin, lost on Armistice Station during the "peaceful" removal of everyone France deemed undesirable.

The memory still made Freddie's blood boil, but Maria had been *right* there when Jessie got shot. How must she feel? Maria never said, and Freddie was afraid to ask. She swallowed. Thank God the navy paid for therapy these days. She'd made sure Maria went, too, after that mess.

Maybe she should've signed Alex Coleman up. It hadn't occurred to Freddie since he didn't report to her, but should it have?

"So, did Captain Fatell share the re-commissioning plans with you?" Freddie asked, mostly to change the subject. "I asked him to get your opinion."

"He did, and I have to admit I feel kind of funky about it."

Freddie cocked her head. "Is funky a technical term? I'm an old fogie admiral, and I can never tell."

That won her a smile, and Maria shrugged. "Honestly, ma'am, I'm nervous about extending *Jimmy Carter's* service to thirty-three years. Recommissioning five *Los Angeles*-class boats that all originally entered service in the nineties? Are we sure their hulls are still good?"

"NAVSEA says they are."

Maria shuddered. "I'm not sure I'd want to go to sea in one. They've been sitting pier side for ten years."

They both knew that ships and subs in layup—known in the fleet as in "mothballs"—were theoretically maintained so they could be reactivated within a few months. But a submarine's hull had a limited lifespan, and it wasn't just like you could replace the entire hull. You had to keep the water out of the people space, and a sub that couldn't dive was useless in war. Particularly this one.

"I know. But Electric Boat says they can't make more than six *Ceroes* next year, even working double shifts. The only way to close the gap is to reach into the cupboard and recommission something."

"It's still an enormous risk, ma'am. Even if it's necessary."

Freddie sighed. "Let's get to work. You'd better tell my public affairs guys to write something pretty up about it, too—best to get ahead of the media on this one or they'll rip me apart. Again."

"I'll get right on it if you swear to never recommend me for command of one of those things. I'd rather command a trash hauler." Maria shuddered.

"Deal."

The first car Alex noticed when walking out of Bradley International Airport in Hartford, Connecticut, was the silver police car parked right by the Delta Airlines entrance. Its passenger side window was open, and a waving hand caught Alex's attention before a familiar voice calling his name registered.

He stuck his head in the window. "What are you doing here, Sam?"

"I'm here to pick you up, dummy." His older brother popped the door open, allowing Alex to slide in.

Frowning, he sat back as the police car weaved its way into the evening airport traffic. The seat was uncomfortable, but that was no surprise; Sam probably dumped heavy stuff in it all the time. Still, at least the changing leaves outside looked like home; that was something, even if it wouldn't last long.

Anxiety gripped Alex's gut. Nancy was leaving for war, and he wasn't far behind her. Jesus, how would the girls cope? He swallowed and tried to make his voice sound normal.

"Where's Nancy? When I talked to her on the phone last night, she said she and Emily were going to pick me up."

Sam grimaced. "She got called into some sort of emergency on the ship, so she asked me to come get you." His expression shifted into a wicked grin. "It was me or her mother, an' she figured you'd prefer your big brother, even if I showed up dressed like a state trooper."

Sam was a lot like Alex, only bigger—and, they joked, a lot meaner. Broad where Alex was narrow, Sam shared Alex's light hair and blue eyes, although he kept his hair buzzed short to hide where it was graying. Alex, as a submariner, had no use for a military high-and-tight haircut and always laughed that his brother looked better in uniform than he did.

"As long as you don't arrest me." Alex chuckled. His brother had been a Connecticut state trooper for almost twenty years now, and he *had* pulled Nancy over for speeding.

Twice.

"Nah, I'll let you off today."

"Well, that's a relief." He grinned. "I know Bobbie's at soccer practice, but last I checked, I had two daughters. What'd you do with Emily? Stuff her in the trunk? I thought police officers weren't supposed to do things like that these days."

"Very funny. She's grounded. Your mother-in-law said something about a party."

Alex blinked. *"Emily?"*

His younger daughter was the responsible one of the pair. Bobbie, named Roberta after her grandmother in a semi-failed attempt at conciliation after Nancy got pregnant in college, was the wild child. Roberta Perretti proved harder to win over than Alex and his wife hoped, but her namesake's attitude was exactly as expected.

Unfortunately, Bobbie inherited her father's defiant streak along with her mother's outgoing nature. Emily, on the other hand, was the level-headed, straight-A student. Alex could count the number of times she got into serious trouble on one hand with fingers left over.

"Apparently, she was late getting home last night. Personally, I think Roberta is overreaching, but she's not my kid. I'm just Uncle Sam, and I'm an innocent bystander here. I've got my own kids to discipline."

Alex shook his head. Truth be told, he and Nancy had a good pair of girls, particularly since both Bobbie and Emily grew up with two military parents. They were remarkably well adjusted, particularly given the way their parents' deployment cycles usually alternated, with one home while the other was gone for six months.

War only made that worse. Flying across the country four days before deploying on a war patrol was deep in someone's definition of stupid, but Alex needed to be here for his family.

The coming months would be hard enough on his daughters without Alex skipping out on Nancy's departure. His mother-in-law had lived with the Colemans for over fifteen years, but both parents had never deployed at the same time. The navy avoided things like that during peacetime, but war changed everything. The girls needed his support now, particularly since his own departure would come so close on Nancy's heels.

They were going into harm's way, leaving behind daughters who were plenty old enough to understand that either—or both—might not come back.

Not for the first time, Alex was glad that they'd made their home in North Stonington, Connecticut. North Stonington wasn't quite halfway between the subbase in Groton and the surface base in Newport, Rhode Island, but it *was* close to where Sam and his family still lived in his and Alex's childhood home. At least Emily and Bobbie would have more family to turn to.

"Ouch!"

Lost in his thoughts, Alex didn't hear Sam talking to him until his brother punched him in the shoulder.

"Wake up, little brother. I asked how that submarine of yours is doing."

"Um." Instinctively, Alex bit back the urge to vent about some of *Jimmy Carter's* ongoing problems, particularly his humorless XO. "Okay. Mostly."

"This from the guy who's been burning to command a submarine from the age of what, eight?"

"This from the guy who the navy gave its oldest attack boat to. Getting underway might be...ugly." Alex slumped in his seat. "My list of broken toys is longer than your arm."

Sam's eyebrows shot up. "They're not going to send you to war in a leaky sub, are they?"

"No." Not *leaky*, anyway. That didn't appear to be one of *Jimmy Carter's* issues. On second thought, his insanely overprotective older brother probably wasn't the one to vent to. "We'll be ready, Sam. It's just not going to be pretty."

And wasn't that the story of his life?

USS *Razorback* (SSN 857) got underway for war after two weeks of drills and a short training underway to get John familiar with his new crew. If the training cycle seemed rushed, that's because it was—John didn't even get time to stop by the simulators in Groton to blow the rust off before taking command in Pearl Harbor.

Command. He was back in the seat, back in a *Cero*-class boat. Sure, *Razorback* was the first of the Improved-*Ceroes,* which was a step up from his last boat, the original *Cero* herself. There were minor differences, but only a handful: *Razorback* was seven feet longer, a hundred tons heavier, carried eleven fewer sailors, and was six knots faster.

Those extra six knots made *Razorback* and her younger sisters the second-fastest submarines in the world, right behind the *Yasen*-class the Russians had been building in fits and starts since 2018. But the *Yasens* were supposedly louder than John's new lady. *Razorback* was quiet, deadly, and had the best crew John could ask for. She even smelled new.

He just wished he'd joined the boat under better circumstances.

"What's up, Patricia?" John asked, walking into control.

The space was eerily quiet; too many sailors *weren't* looking at him, which said sad things about his predecessor's final meltdown. Fortunately, his XO, Lieutenant Commander Patricia Abercrombie, seemed immune to everyone else's unease.

Patricia was a tall woman, dark-skinned and green-eyed, and every move she made demonstrated the kind of effortless charisma John always *wished* he had. He knew he was a good CO, but he got by on subject-matter expertise and a decent sense of humor. Patricia Abercrombie had that special *something* that made people want to follow her, with a smile politicians would envy and that made sailors want to do their best. She was easily the most confident person in control—which, sadly, wasn't a high bar at the moment.

That was probably because she was the one to turn Harney's ass in, John thought. But at least he could commiserate with her about having a boss who went to pieces in combat? What a thing to have in common. The thought made a bitter smile twist his lips. At least Harney avoided shooting. John hadn't stopped Admiral McNally from starting the damned war.

"Sonar picked up a bottom-bounce contact at long range, sir. Someone's creeping toward Pearl from the north, and not in any of the approach lanes."

"That sounds fishy." John walked over to the electronic chart, frowning.

Approach lanes toward U.S. and Alliance ports changed frequently, but they were always sent out to every sub. Using them was the best way to announce yourself as friendly without making extra noise—and noise was death for a submarine.

But this fellow was well outside the lane. John flicked up an overlay, his frown deepening. "He's not even in last week's lane."

"No, sir." Patricia's face turned carefully expressionless.

"You think we've got someone sneaking in on us." It wasn't a question.

She hesitated. "If they're lost, Captain, they're a long way off track."

"And they don't pay us to make assumptions." John smiled. "I agree. Let's investigate this fellow—maybe he'll be our first customer. Anyone want to take a bet on if he's French or Russian?"

Blank faces greeted the question until his chief of the boat, Master Chief Cary Uffington, spoke up. "I'm betting French, sir. We're not far off French Polynesia."

"If by not far you mean a couple thousand nautical miles." Patricia snorted. "I'll take Russian, sir, just to prove that COB can't do math."

Uffington scoffed. "Ma'am, I was a corpsman before I came to the dark side, not a bean counter. *Or* a navigator."

"Hey, I resemble that remark." John grinned, glad the ice was finally broken. "They used to call me the most disorganized navigator in the history of the navy back on *John Warner.*"

That particular nickname had been coined by a young and brash Alex Coleman, before they'd become close friends. But once their then-captain, Commander Loare, got wind of it, the nickname stuck like grease on a bearing. John hadn't shaken it until he left command of *Cero*, and here he was, advertising it to his new crew.

But laughing at him meant they weren't afraid he'd freak out. That was worth something. He knew the investigators had a hell of a time figuring out what happened; this crew loved Harney and wanted to protect him from himself, even when he turned against their best interests and had a mental break with the idea of combat. They'd hoped it was temporary...but it wasn't, and Patricia was forced to take command from a captain she idolized.

Come hell or high water, John was going to put this crew at ease with him...and the idea of going into combat together.

"Should I be worried about that, Captain?" Patricia asked, but John thought he caught a gleam in her eye.

"Not so long as you don't trust me with too much paperwork. Provided it shows up in small doses, I probably won't lose things." John glanced back down at the potential enemy on the navigational plot. "Let's go to battle stations and go greet this fellow. Give him a good old American welcome."

Several people chuckled.

John settled in to wait as *Razorback* closed the distance with an enemy, glad this was one he probably was *supposed* to shoot.

A few hours after returning to the Coleman home in North Stonington, Connecticut, Alex sprawled on his own couch with his fifteen-year-old daughter dozing off beside him. Usually, Emily was too "old" to fall asleep on the couch watching old movies with her dad, but tonight was different. Tonight, everyone wanted to be together. Even Bobbie, sitting sideways in a recliner, flipped through a magazine on her tablet and pretended not to watch the movie.

Alex wasn't tired, since his internal clock remained on Pacific Standard Time, but five hours on a plane still left him feeling like he'd been through a blender. But there was no way he was going anywhere near bed before Nancy came home. Not when she was caught out on her ship dealing with stupid pre-deployment crap that he understood all too well.

He felt a little guilty sitting on his own couch while his wife worked, but it wasn't like he could go help her. Alex would just be in the way if he tried. And he'd given his own crew as much liberty as he could, because somehow or another *Jimmy Carter* was slightly ahead in their pre-deployment preps.

That left him on the smooth leather of their worn couch. The Colemans had plenty of money to replace it, but they both loved the stupid thing. It was almost fifteen years old, one of the first pieces of "nice" furniture Alex and Nancy bought after they were making enough money to start furnishing their house properly instead of running around like crazy people with a baby—which quickly became two—and all of those necessities. That couch had survived two moves and two teenagers, and Alex figured it could wait until he retired.

Whenever that would be. Less than a year ago, he'd been marking time until twenty years in the navy. But now there was a war on, and even officers who'd gone to Admiral's Mast got second chances. Hell, he might not even retire as a commander. Could he make captain? Eventually?

What a crazy thought.

Shaking himself, Alex returned his attention to the old movie about navy pilots taking to the skies in World War II and smiled when Emily muttered about how much simpler things were back then. Slightly before ten, his wife slammed through the front door, still talking on her cell phone.

"No, I really don't care how many times her boyfriend has threatened to call his congressman. No one drafted Ensign Blumenthal into the navy. In fact, the navy paid for her damned engineering degree! This is a scheduled deployment. Blumenthal has known it was coming for two months. We're leaving Thursday morning. Tell her that she's not on the ship by zero-nine-hundred, I'm going to report her as a deserter."

There was a pause, and Alex watched, head cocked, as Nancy snarled silently at whichever of her subordinates was on the other end. Finally, she continued:

"Do you need me to call her, Davad, or can you put the fear of God into the girl?"

Another pause.

Emily stirred. "Mom, do you have to be so loud?"

"Of course she does." Bobbie sighed a long-suffering sigh. "Mom's only got one volume setting."

Alex tried unsuccessfully not to snicker, which turned Nancy's head his way. She shot him a smile before turning her attention back to the phone, switching her "professional" mode back on.

"Good. Then I'll see you Thursday morning. Between now and then, I'm going to try very hard just to be a normal person, but don't hesitate to call me if there's an emergency."

A moment later, Nancy hung up the phone and dumped it, her car keys, and her uniform's cover on the counter.

"*Hi* to you, too, Mom," Bobbie said, earning herself a tired eyeroll.

"Evening yourself, sunshine. And you, too, Emily, unless you're still ignoring me. Shouldn't you two be in bed?"

"We have the day off from school tomorrow, Mom." Emily sat up, heaving a sigh. "Besides, Dad said we didn't have to."

"That's because your father is soft and squishy and has no sense of discipline," Nancy retorted, but she was smiling at Alex as he crossed the room to greet her.

"You've always been the better naval officer out of the pair of us," he replied, wrapping his arms around her. And it was true. Their professional attitudes reflected in their home life, too; Alex enjoyed being the nice parent as much Nancy preferred to play the disciplinarian.

Nancy leaned into his embrace, and Alex closed his eyes. Thirty-two days passed since Alex left Groton for Washington State and *Jimmy Carter*, but it felt like forever. Coming home made Alex really wish he'd gotten a boat out of Groton like he expected—then he could have spent this last month at home with his family instead of the width of a country away.

"You'd better believe it." Nancy kissed him lightly.

Emily gagged theatrically. "Eww, Mom. Isn't there some reg against public displays of affection or something?"

"There is." Bobbie didn't even look up from her tablet. "But she's gonna ignore you, anyway. They both are. They always do."

"This isn't public, kiddo." Alex laughed.

His daughter scowled. "Don't call me kiddo. I'm fifteen, Dad."

He arched an eyebrow. "Act like an adult, and I'll treat you like one."

"Sure you will. You'll *still* let Grandma ground me and complain when I don't go to bed on time. Or Mom will, anyway."

"Keep talking like that and I won't suggest ice cream," Nancy said before Bobbie could join in on the complaining.

"Ice cream? At this time of night?" Bobbie scoffed. "Never."

Nancy grinned. "Cosimo's is still open. Let's go."

Razorback crept along silently in the path of the mystery submarine approaching Pearl Harbor, her course almost a direct reciprocal to the potential enemy's. It had taken the American sub three long hours to get in position, during which John felt his crew's eyes staring at him.

He knew they were wondering when he was going to crack. On his way back from a quick trip to the head, he overheard one fire control tech asking another when their new captain was going to "pull a Harney" and lose it. John waited a few extra seconds outside of control so they couldn't guess he heard them, but he couldn't get the words out of his head.

He'd faced combat before. John was pretty sure that he was okay, but he supposed Harney hadn't known he was going to go to pieces until it was too late, either. Still, John had done his best to reassure his crew. He wasn't a charismatic leader like Pat Abercrombie or his friend Alex Coleman. Time would just have to prove to them that he was smart, competent, and knew his business.

"Conn, Sonar, tonals match that of a Russian *Yasen*-class fast attack. System reports eighty percent chance that it's K-566, *Ulyanovsk*," *Razorback's* sonar chief reported through the intercom box at the center of control five minutes after John took his nature break.

"Conn, aye." John licked his lips to mask the thrill running down his spine. "Range?"

"Twenty-seven thousand yards, sir."

The tension in control ratcheted up; John wished he knew a way to defuse it, but he couldn't find one. Instead, he centered on doing his job: "Conn, aye."

Glancing at the plot, John did some math.

Organization wasn't his strong suit, but math he could do, just like any proper nuclear-trained submariner. The U.S. Navy's torpedo of choice remained the tried-and-true Mark 48 ADCAP mod 7 CBASS, the newest version of a torpedo first deployed when John was three years old. Rumor said there was something new in the pipeline, but until the guys and gals at Lazark farted that out, John was stuck with a torpedo whose *official* range was twenty-one nautical miles...but whose recommended effective range was more like half that.

Rumors of torpedoes missing targets when fired at longer ranges—and resulting in dead subs—had already done several laps around the fleet. John had no intention of adding *Razorback* to that list.

"Any indication he's heard us?" he asked.

"No, sir, he's carrying on fat, dumb, and happy," Patricia replied. "Only one course change since we detected him, and that was obviously to clear his baffles. He's worried about someone sneaking up behind him, not someone coming out from Pearl."

"Then aren't we the lucky ones today?" John grinned. "Let's stay calm and let him walk right through the door, then. No need to take three or four shots when two torps will do—let's let him close to fourteen thousand yards."

"XO, aye."

Did he see Patricia twitch? Sure, fourteen thousand yards—seven nautical miles—felt close, but it was a big ocean. John couldn't afford to miss, not with an enemy rolling right up on Pearl Harbor's doorstep.

"Firing point procedures, tubes one and two, track"—he leaned over to check—"7011. Make both tubes ready in all respects, including opening the outer doors."

"Firing point procedures, tubes one and two for track 7011, make both tubes ready in all respects, including opening the outer doors,

Weps, aye!"

The excitement in *Razorback's* control room was contagious; John could feel the worry bleeding out of his crew as they worked together to target the incoming Russian sub. Did they trust him not to babble and run away yet? He hoped so.

Now time to wait.

Razorback continued forward at five knots while her enemy closed at ten; that meant it took twenty-six minutes to close to John's preferred firing range. Theoretically, John *could* have kicked up his boat's speed to close the range—*Razorback's* best silent speed was supposed to be twenty-nine knots—but he wasn't about to risk detection. Not with the stakes so high.

Minutes ticked by. John wanted to pace, but control was too cramped for that, and it might make his crew nervous. Instead, he spoke quietly with Patricia Abercrombie, discovering a mutual love of craft beer. Finally, the intercom crackled.

"Conn, Sonar, range fourteen thousand yards. Target course and speed constant."

"Captain, aye!" John turned to the fire control team. "Your solutions up to date, Weps?"

"Yes, sir!"

John shivered. This wasn't like combat on *Enterprise* with the strike group; back then, he was a passenger, giving minimal direction and hoping that the cruiser and destroyer captains could protect the carrier. They'd done their best, but Admiral McNally's foolishness hamstrung them, resulting in *Enterprise's* loss—along with two destroyers and thousands of sailors. Not to mention getting blown off a sinking aircraft carrier and into the water, an experience John wouldn't forget and didn't want to repeat.

Today, however, John was in command.

"Tubes one and two—*fire!*"

Weps' hand slapped down on the buttons. "Tubes one and two fired electrically. Weapons away."

Moments later, sonar added through the intercom: "Two fish running hot, straight, and normal."

"Very well." John's heart beat faster. If the Russians were going to hear them, now was the time—

"Conn, Sonar, aspect change! Target is turning—target has launched noisemakers!"

"Conn, aye," Patricia answered; John was too busy.

"Ahead full for forty knots," John ordered, watching *Ulyanovsk* turn on his plot. "Left standard rudder, steady course three-three-zero."

"Ahead full for forty knots, aye," Master Chief Uffington replied. The COB was the diving officer at battle stations, and like all of his breed, Uffington knew his job. He stood over the helmsmen and planesmen, watching every move they made. "My rudder is right standard, coming to course three-three-zero."

"Very well."

John swallowed, trying to hide his nerves. Would the Russian fire, or was he too focused on running? *Razorback*'s torpedoes needed about nine minutes to cross the fourteen thousand yards between the two subs at their maximum speed of fifty-five knots; the more the Russian sped up, the longer that would take.

"Intel says the *Yasens* are faster than we are, sir," Patricia whispered. "What if we gave them too much of a head start?"

"I never thought I'd see the day where our torpedoes were too slow, but you're not wrong." John shook his head. "We're going to have to get in a lot closer next time...or buy a lot faster torpedoes."

Patricia laughed. "I'll go search eBay for them after this, sir."

"That'll definitely be quicker than the navy stock system." John smiled to hide the tightness in his chest.

Ulyanovsk continued turning, picking up speed and dropping another set of noisemakers. But *Razorback* had the jump on her, and John's course change put his sub directly in the Russian boat's wake—right where *Ulyanovsk* couldn't shoot back.

"Conn, Sonar, aspect change—he's coming right!"

"Right ten degrees rudder," John ordered, his heart pounding.

"Right ten degrees rudder, aye," Uffington replied. "My rudder is right ten degrees, no new course given."

"Very well." John swallowed.

Following in another sub's footprints was almost impossible when you couldn't see what they were doing; sonar was *Razorback*'s "eyes," but there was always a delay between what her sonar operators could hear and what actually happened. If the Russian turned quickly enough, he might be able to clear his torpedo tubes and shoot back.

"Range?" John asked.

"Fourteen thousand yards and holding steady."

"All ahead flank." John never looked up from the plot, but he felt his boat quiver as *Razorback* reached for her top speed of sixty-three knots. He tuned out Uffington's repeat back.

"Torpedo range five thousand yards. Target speed...thirty knots and increasing," Weps reported.

"Sonar, Conn, any sign of him shooting?" John asked, wiping sweaty hands on the legs of his coveralls.

Five thousand yards with a fifteen-knot rate of closure. Six more minutes until their torpedoes hit—if *Ulyanovsk* didn't speed up more. Which he would.

Did shooting take this long in exercises? John couldn't remember.

"I think we caught him napping, sir," Patricia said. Her eyes were wide, too, which made John feel better. At least he wasn't the only one with his heart in his throat.

"And if we can stay behind him, he can't get a shot off without letting our torp smack him broadside." John nodded, glancing at the clock on the bulkhead over the helm stations.

Four more minutes.

Ulyanovsk banked left; *Razorback* copied, remaining in the Russian sub's wake like an annoying dingy. John's sub had the jump on their enemy and was still gaining ground, even as *Ulyanovsk* increased speed. But the Russians *did* seem slow off the mark—after their first turn, their reactions seemed...delayed.

"Ahead flank for fifty-five knots," John ordered, still watching the Russian sub. He couldn't afford to overrun his own torpedoes, even if it meant staying further from *Ulyanovsk*.

"Ahead flank for fifty-five knots, aye. My engines are ahead flank for fifty-five knots."

"Very well." John scratched his chin. "Maybe we're not the only ones this war caught by surprise."

"Sir?" Patricia asked.

"This guy doesn't feel like the Russian varsity." He shrugged. "It's nice to know we weren't the only one caught with the proverbial pants down when war started."

"Two minutes to impact," Weps said.

John glanced at the clock and then at the plot as *Ulyanovsk* started weaving. And then he smiled. "Take a look at this. He's following standard tactics instead of common sense—junking and turning, trying to spoof our torps off his tail."

Patricia moved to stand next to him, studying the Russian sub's track as it corkscrewed left, right, and then right again. "It might work."

"All it's doing is slowing him down. Our torps are wire-guided, which means that while he's making noise, we can see him"—John twisted right—"and Weps has him dialed in straight to hell, don't you, Weps?"

"You bet your ass I do, sir." Weps grinned.

"So he's not losing our torps. His only chance is to outrun them, but all these turns are making him lose speed. If intel is right, any given *Yasen* is faster than us—and faster than a Mark 48—but he's squandering that speed on maneuvering."

"You're saying that we've gotten lucky, and he's gotten dumb."

"Right in one." John's smile faded. "But what I plan on saying *after* we take care of our friend here is: what happens when we find a smart enemy who we can't shoot from too close for them to dodge?"

Patricia paled. "I...hadn't thought about that. Their boats are faster than the newest Mark 48s."

"That they are."

One minute later, two Mark 48 CBASS torpedoes—still too slow, in John's opinion—slammed into *Ulyanovsk* and sent her to the bottom. *Razorback* was close enough to catch the eerie string of implosions on sonar, and John was foolish enough to have his sonar watch put it in speaker.

That was not a mistake he'd make again. No, they weren't close enough to hear screams—assuming anyone died slowly enough to *scream*—but listening to another submarine die still filled his gut with a strange, rolling emptiness. If *Ulyanovsk's* captain was a little better, or John a little less lucky, that could be *Razorback* on the bottom.

The navy needed better torpedoes.

Yesterday.

Chapter 15

Farewells

The Coleman family spent their last day together. They went fishing in the morning on Alex's boat, spending several hours out in their favorite cove. Nancy and Bobbie stayed on the boat while Alex and Emily jumped in the water for a short snorkeling expedition, which ended when Emily dragged her older sister over the side into the water. Bobbie came up sputtering and dunked her sister in turn, which turned into a splash fight that Alex wanted no part in.

After prying the girls out of the water, they drove out to their favorite restaurant in Newport. They tried to avoid talking about the navy or about either upcoming deployment, but both hung over them like a doom cloud.

Their family had said goodbyes before many deployments over the years—four for Alex, five for Nancy—and they knew which routines worked. A quiet dinner at home and then evening came too early. Alex burned to hold Nancy and never let go, but he knew his duty...and so did she.

Morning dawned, and both Commanders Coleman donned their service dress blue uniforms. The family—complete with Nancy's mother, Roberta, piled into Nancy's Tahoe and headed up to Newport.

Alex took the family to breakfast while Nancy headed out to *Fletcher*, trying to ignore the butterflies dancing in his stomach. Worrying more about Nancy's deployment more than his own probably made him a hypocrite, but well, it wasn't like *Jimmy Carter* would stand into danger any time soon.

Fletcher, however, had already proven herself in battle. Nancy's silver star told that story, as did the scars running along the sides of the ship. That meant Nancy would be on the forefront of whatever battles came. Thinking about that made Alex both proud and vaguely nauseous, but he pushed both aside for the drive out to the base after breakfast.

One glance at Roberta told him his mother-in-law felt the same. She was the family's rock; Roberta was there when Nancy and Alex couldn't be, taking care of their daughters when the navy took them away. He didn't know what they'd do without her, and as much as he performatively bickered with Roberta, he adored her. She'd never fill the gap that losing his own mom at a young age had, but Roberta never tried. She was the second mother he'd never expected to have, and she meant the world to him.

Her green eyes—the one trait she and Nancy shared, since Nancy had been adopted as a baby—creased as she smiled what he knew was a forced smile. "We'll be all right, Alex," Roberta said.

"I know you will," he said as the girls forged ahead into the crowd. "And we'll do our best to stay the same."

"I never thought I'd say you have more sense than that damned girl of mine, but she seems to be looking for where the fire is hottest." Roberta's voice was husky with emotion. "I wish you were going out together."

"Me, too." Alex's throat was tight. "I'd give anything to be able to watch her back out there."

"Well," she said briskly, and her expression was so much like Nancy's that Alex wanted to scream or hug her, "wishes are for stories. We live in reality, so you'll both do your best, and we'll see you on the other side."

"That we will."

Hundreds of friends and family stood on the pier to see *Fletcher* off; wartime deployments were still new for the navy, and Alex could feel the electricity in the air. His uniform got him a lot of funny looks and some questions he couldn't answer. Several people assumed he was in charge of something or another, which Alex laughed off, pointing at his submariner's dolphins and playing stupid.

Laughing beat swearing, and besides, the girls thought it was funny.

He ran his eyes over his wife's destroyer. *Fletcher* looked good, despite the burn scars on her sides. Alex couldn't spot rust on the topside equipment, and every line was made up precisely. *Fletcher* was lean and ready.

After what felt like a lifetime, Nancy came down the brow, with the announcement of *"Fletcher, departing!"* ringing her off.

"Hey," she said, hugging the girls and then her mother tightly.

Alex could read stress in the tightness around her eyes. "I'm going to guess you don't have long?" he asked.

Nancy shook her head. "Our underway time was moved up an hour. Looks like *Lexington* needs an escort across the pond, and we've been nominated."

"Wish I could be there to watch your undersides." Alex tried not to grimace. The shortage of surface-to-air missiles meant the navy was returning to the old queens of the seas: aircraft carriers. Losing *Enterprise* meant they needed another carrier in theater quickly, and *Lexington*, like *Fletcher*, was newly out of the yards.

"You'd be welcome." Nancy squeezed his arm. "It sounds like *Narwhal* will join us partway across the pond, so we won't be alone."

Alex whistled. "Damn, they're so new they squeak."

"As long as they don't literally squeak, we'll be okay." Nancy chuckled and turned to say farewell to her mother...and then their daughters.

Both girls managed not to cry, though Alex could see Emily fighting back tears. Bobbie looked mulish, but Alex knew that meant she was upset. Both parents pretended not to notice when Bobbie's lower lip trembled. They knew she wanted to be strong.

When Nancy turned to him, Alex fought down the urge to tell her not to go. "Time to make history, babe," he said.

"Yeah, I know how you feel about that." Her smile was soft. "We'll talk every chance we can...provided you aren't too deep underwater."

"You know me. I like sitting on the bottom. It's quiet."

Nancy's cheek twitched. "Be careful out there, all right?"

"Same to you." Alex swallowed. "Let's just not make history in a bad way, all right?"

"Deal." Leaning in, Alex gave her a quick kiss. Doing more in uniform—even as a farewell—was a bit much, particularly between two senior officers. "Love you."

"Love you, too."

One last hug for the girls, and Nancy headed back up the brow to the ringing of the ship's bell. *Ding ding, ding ding!* "*Fletcher,* arriving!" *Ding!*

Emily's hand slipped into his. "This isn't like the other times, is it, Daddy?"

"No, honey. It isn't." Swallowing, Alex watched a group of young sailors trying not to cry while they said goodbye to their parents.

Alex shifted to wrap his arm around his younger daughter, and Emily leaned into his embrace. Guilt welled up in him as he held her close. Tonight, he'd get on a plane and leave the girls alone with their grandmother, probably for months.

Don't think about that now.

They watched in silence as *Fletcher's* crew streamed on board the destroyer, bidding farewell to their families and friends. Sailors manned the rails as *Fletcher* prepared to get underway, looking smart in their dress blues. Alex spotted a lot of pale faces among those young sailors, however. They knew they were going to war.

A soft sniffle came from Bobbie, and he turned to see her biting her lip. Wordlessly, Alex wrapped an arm around her, too. Yeah, Bobbie was a tough girl, but neither of the girls expected war to take both their parents away, possibly permanently. Roberta, on Bobbie's other side, kept a hand on her shoulder.

"I'm okay," Bobbie said. She didn't pull away.

"I know you are, honey."

Apparently, his tone wasn't bland enough, because Bobbie twisted to glare at him. "I'm fine."

"I didn't say you weren't," Alex replied. "But you don't have to be."

That made her scowl, and Emily rolled her eyes. "Just shut up and be miserable, Bobbie."

They had almost twelve hours until his red-eye flight boarded for Washington, and he'd make the best of them. Alex had never regretted his career choice, and still didn't, but sometimes he hated himself for—

"Excuse me, Commander Coleman?" An unfamiliar voice made Alex turn.

Immediately, he tensed. The woman before him wore a business suit that was far too expensive for her to be someone's dependent, and the badge hanging from her neck lanyard read **PRESS**. He suppressed the urge to step back.

"Can I help you?" Alex asked.

"Carra Garlock, *New York Times*." Her smile was stunning. "I was hoping to speak to you and your wife about your upcoming deployments. You're making history as the first spouses to deploy in command of warships during wartime."

Alex tried to smile. "We're aware, yeah. Hard to miss."

"Dad," Emily hissed. "That's not nice."

Now really wasn't the time to say he didn't care about being nice to reporters, was it? Particularly not with the girls here. Fortunately, Garlock continued, unabashed:

"Is your wife available? I'd love to interview you together."

"I'm afraid that you're too late." Alex gestured over his shoulder at the gleaming destroyer. "*Fletcher* is about to get underway."

"Surely your wife could—"

"*Fletcher's* captain is a bit busy right now," Alex cut her off.

"Then perhaps you might be willing." She smiled again.

Roberta Peretti stepped forward, her eyes narrowed. "Now is a terrible time, don't you think, young lady?"

Garlock blinked. "I beg your pardon?"

"This is a moment for families. Not for you." Roberta was a tiny woman, but she loomed forward like a lioness. "So feel free to get lost."

"I have the navy's permission to be here." Garlock flushed. "You can't make me leave."

"You might have permission to be on this pier, but I'm sure no one gave you permission to be a bitch." Roberta's smile was deadlier than any weapon *Fletcher* carried. "I'm sure your paper would appreciate a call about how you were harassing navy families on the eve of deployment."

"I'd be happy to tweet about it, too." Bobbie blinked innocently, looking so much like her grandmother's granddaughter.

Alex cleared his throat. "Why don't you excuse us, Ms. Garlock? We could use some family time."

"Of course." Garlock glowered but retreated, and Alex breathed a little easier.

The peace couldn't last for long, however; moments after *Fletcher* pulled away from the pier, Alex's command cell phone rang. He swore, earning himself a dirty look from his mother-in-law.

Detaching himself from Bobbie, Alex thumbed the phone on. "Captain."

"Good morning, sir, it's the XO. I'm sorry to bother you when you're on leave, but we just got a very strange email." George spoke quickly, too quickly, like he was bouncing up and down with nerves. "It's a welcome-aboard email from SUBRON Twenty-Nine in Perth."

Alex blinked. "We're not scheduled to reach Australia for at least a month, but that's nice of them."

"It's what's in the letter that I find strange, sir," George replied. "They're asking for our manning status, a list of all our spare parts, a timeline of how long it would take to decommission the boat, and what skeleton crew we would need to keep during that evolution."

"Say again *what*?" Alex shook himself. "We just finished *re*-manning the boat and dragging her back to life."

"That's what it says." George's confusion was palatable. "I quote: 'In the likely event of ineffective operational execution by SSN 23, prepare decommissioning plans IAW ref A. and ref B.' Reference A is the standard decommissioning instruction. Ref B seems to be a squadron-specific memo for re-allocation of personnel."

A cold chill washed over Alex as his wife's destroyer pivoted and left the basin. The submarine squadron his boat was heading out to join expected *Jimmy Carter* to fail. They were *preparing* for it, preparing to rip his people out of his boat and send them to the other eight or ten boats in the squadron, all like he wasn't building a top-notch team out of the dregs the navy had handed him.

Why would they do this? Why put *Jimmy Carter* back in the game only to send her all the way to Australia and *then* decommission her? It made no sense.

In the likely event of ineffective operational execution by SSN 23...

That meant he couldn't afford to fail.

Alex swallowed and put his captain face back on.

"Thank you for the update, George. We'll talk more about this when I get back."

Late that night, it was his turn to say farewell, although there were thankfully no reporters to dog them at the airport. Tears were shed, promises made, and Alex found his seat on the plane with a lump the size and taste of a rotting apple in his throat.

He tried to sleep on the plane—*Jimmy Carter* deployed in the morning, and as the captain, he needed to be at his best. But he kept thinking about his daughters' faces as both parents left for war.

It was a long flight.

Submarine Squadron 29 Headquarters, Perth, Australia

The captain was up to something, and when assigned to USS *Kansas*, that was never good.

Master Chief Chindeu Casey felt like the world's most unfortunate babysitter. *Kansas* wasn't a bad boat. She even had a better-than-average crew that tried *really* hard to make their more-arrogant-than-usual captain feel good about himself.

Unfortunately, trying wasn't always enough for Commander Kennedy, which was why Casey found himself kicking his heels in the outer offices of Submarine Squadron Twenty-Nine. There wasn't much to do here; it looked pretty much like every submarine squadron HQ back home, and Casey'd lost track of how many of those he'd been in. There weren't even magazines to read while he waited, which made him resort to stupid phone games. The only unique thing about SUBRON 29 was that it was one of two American squadrons currently stationed at the Aussie naval base in Perth.

Both squadrons in Perth were brand new, with ten attack boats apiece, re-created out of their World War II ghosts specifically for this *new* world war. No one denied that was what this was, not now, not with the Russians driving south and the world on fucking fire. At last count, the Freedom Union owned sixty-three percent of operable underwater stations in the Indian Ocean.

Now they were expanding into the South Pacific, too. And that didn't count how Russia had already won the Sea of Okhotsk and claimed the Bering Sea. American forces were holding them out of the Sea of Japan for now—after the destruction of most of the Japanese Navy—but lord only knew how long that would last. The Brits promised help, but they had a long way to go, either battling through the Arctic or coming through the Mediterranean to the Red Sea, and then all the way across the entire Indian Ocean into the Pacific.

Kansas and her Perth-based sisters were uniquely positioned to fight in either the Indian or Pacific theaters. Rumor said a third squadron would either be transferred to Perth from San Diego, but for now, the subs out of Perth and Hawaii were the best frontline forces America had...particularly with the way missile shortages restricted surface ship actions.

Besides, hiding near an undersea outpost you suspected the enemy of wanting was much easier in a submarine.

But no one from *Kansas* was hiding right now. The boat was one week into a two-week maintenance standdown, which gave the crew some liberty and the captain time to plot and plan. Hence their strange evening visit to SUBRON 29 headquarters, where the furniture was oddly *nice* for an office area slapped together mid-war.

There were a bunch of drinks out there with Casey's name on them, and he'd really rather be working on them right now than sitting here, thank you very much.

Finally, Kennedy emerged from Commodore Banks' office, all smiles and polite farewells to the boss. Not that Casey was surprised by a bit of ass-kissing; that was the navy way. Commodores wore stars on their collars these days, which meant someone ambitious—like Kennedy—would always brown nose a bit. Nothing big.

"Ready to go, Master Chief?" Kennedy's grin stretched from ear to ear, and he was practically prancing.

"Sure think I've warmed this chair up sufficiently, sir," Casey replied. "What d'you need me to do?"

"Ah, turns out I brought you down here for nothing. Turns out the commodore was more than willing to take me at my word." Kennedy puffed his chest out. "Sorry about that."

The man didn't sound terribly sorry, but Casey hadn't become a chief of the boat without learning how to bullshit a bullshitter. "No problem, sir. You know I'm always available to back you up."

Especially when that means saving you from yourself, he didn't add. Good master chiefs knew that even the best officers stuck their foot in sometimes.

Kennedy wasn't one of the best.

"We should be getting a new XO in the next week or so," Kennedy said, leading the way toward the door. "Commodore Banks concurred that Lieutenant Commander Hunt would be better suited to a desk job. She hasn't been right since *Belleau Wood* took that hit."

Casey stopped cold, right in front of the squadron's operations officer, who jumped. "Come again, sir?"

"You've seen it, too, COB. Hunt's a good person"—he shrugged—"maybe too good for our line of work. But we need someone with some real get up and go if *Kansas* is going to make a mark in this war. I plan on taking us to where the fire is hottest, and I need an XO who has my back."

"Does Commander Hunt know about her upcoming transfer, sir?" Casey asked slowly.

"Nah, you can tell her when we get back to the boat."

Great. His CO wasn't just a jerk; he was also a coward who left the dirty work to the chief of the boat.

But at least Casey knew he'd be more compassionate about it than this ambitiously cold fish.

Bremerton, Washington

An efficient hum of activity filled *Jimmy Carter's* control room the way it never had during drills, and for perhaps the first time, Alex really felt like he commanded an honest-to-God ship of war.

Then George went and ruined it. "Is every watch station manned and ready?" he asked the officer of the deck...for the third time.

Alex tried not to make a face. He was four cups of coffee into the morning and not at his best, but did George really have to fret like a mother hen? Now, George paced around the control room as the crew settled into their stations.

In his own days as an XO, Alex believed in letting the watchstanders do their jobs. A gentle nudge here and there was more than enough to get top performance out of people who already knew what to do. Unfortunately, George missed the existence of that playbook.

"Yes, sir. All stations report manned and ready." Maggie sounded like she was one repeated question away from breaking someone's neck, but George missed her glare by a mile.

Jesus. He was more nervous than Alex, and Alex was the one who got fired if they gooned this up!

Then again, it wasn't peacetime. Alex would have to do something *monumentally* stupid to get the axe. With the U.S. Navy desperate for commanding officers, administrative-type firings of the prewar era were over. Even drunk driving wasn't a surefire way to lose command.

Hell, a frigate CO a few piers down demonstrated that when she crashed her car into the base's front gate last week. Alex figured that as long as he didn't T-bone the pier while pulling away, he was probably safe.

But was *Jimmy Carter* safe? Fear that he'd lose his first command right after gaining her made the coffee sit like acid in his stomach. The specter of that email from SUBRON 29 hung over his head like an executioner's axe, just waiting to drop. Alex forced himself to focus; he couldn't afford to lose himself in worry right now.

Oh, joy. George had moved on to asking random questions.

Alex cleared his throat; George remained oblivious. "XO."

George paused midway between the electronic chart table and the helm. Standing next to George's intended destination, Maggie sighed loudly in relief. Alex needed to have a word with her about this, didn't he?

ET2 Vasquez stuck her tongue out at the XO's back. Even better. His hodgepodge crew still had a lot of rough edges.

"Yes, sir?" George bounced over to where Alex leaned on the bulkhead near the sonar room.

"Let's talk a walk topside." Alex headed aft for the hatch out of control.

"Are you sure, Captain? Now?"

"Yup." Alex didn't speak again until they'd climbed the amidships ladder and emerged on the exterior deck of the submarine, near *Jimmy Carter's* line handlers.

Alex glanced their way, checking for protective equipment and wondering if this was where their inexperience would bite him in the ass. Everything seemed fine, and the two junior officers supervising appeared engaged. He couldn't go crazy. He had to trust his people.

The tiny crowd on the pier was relatively quiet as *Jimmy Carter* made preparations to leave for deployment. The navy's personnel system had manned Smiley out of sailors formerly assigned here, there, and everywhere, which meant most of his sailors hadn't brought their families out to Washington State. Like Alex, they said their farewells back home. It was an eerily *normal* beginning to their first war patrol, particularly compared to *Fletcher's* departure just twenty-four hours earlier. There wasn't even any press on the pier—though he was glad not to see that Garlock lady here.

Still, being ignored stung. A funny feeling of grief and insignificance swirled in his gut, but he pushed it aside. Continuing aft, he waited until they had a little privacy. Here, the watchstanders on the quarterdeck could see them but not hear; this was the best Alex was going to get when he was within an hour of getting underway. Then he stopped and swung to face his XO. "George, we need to talk about how you're managing the crew."

"Captain?"

God, he wished the man would do more than stare at him like a lost blowfish. Alex buried his hands in his pockets and took a deep breath. George wasn't going to like this conversation, but that was the breaks.

"Look, I'm not the type to dictate leadership style to someone else, but something's got to give. You're making the crew nervous."

"I'm only—"

Alex held up a hand, and George finally looked offended. But he shut up because Alex was the captain. "Your nerves are freaking people out. Everyone knows *Jimmy Carter* hasn't been underway in over a year, and the more you triple and quadruple check *everything*, the more they think something's got to go wrong."

"Captain, it's my *job* to make sure that this evolution goes smoothly, and that means that every single step is verified." George crossed his arms, sticking his chin out.

"No. It's the officer of the deck's job to run the checklist and report to me." Alex managed not to sigh. "Look, I understand you were a department head a couple months ago, but now you aren't. You've got to take a step back and supervise. When you step in and get involved in a routine evolution, it should be to keep something from going wrong."

"Yes, sir." His XO deflated like someone had stolen his favorite toy.

What the hell was Alex supposed to say to that? "All right. Let's get back to work."

George saluted and headed forwards toward the hatch, leaving Alex alone on the aft deck. Several weeks ago, George confessed that he went back to sea for a second department head tour, spending an additional three years as a navigator on board *Razorback*. He hoped more sea time would help him screen for XO. He was still on that extra tour when the war started…and hadn't expected to make the next career milestone until orders to *Jimmy Carter* came along.

He never even attended the Prospective Executive Officers course. Didn't that explain a lot?

Alex shook his head. At least George *meant* well. Beating him upside the head with his own failings wouldn't get anywhere. Hopefully, time and experience would teach George what he needed to know. That was a problem for another day.

Today, Alex's reactor was hot, and his crew was ready. It was time to go to war.

Chapter 16

Everything Old is New Again

11 September 2038, Pearl Harbor, Hawaii

It was only seven thirty in the morning Pearl Harbor, Hawaii. Sunlight reflected off the crystal-clear water onto the hull of a *Cero*-class attack submarine where a crew was just getting to work; sleeping in didn't happen, not on USS *Bluefish* (SSN 843). Oh, no. Not even on a Saturday. Sure, some sailors had liberty, but not many. There was a war on, and Commander Peterson was a hard captain to please.

Still, no one was really surprised when Shore Patrol showed up on the quarterdeck for a courtesy turnover. Rowdy sailors led to incidents with the locals, which led to arrests. The Honolulu PD didn't have the manpower or time to prosecute all the idiots, so they handed them back to the navy. Generally, everyone considered that a win.

Not on *Bluefish*.

Lieutenant Bobby O'Kane trudged up to the quarterdeck, resisting the urge to throw his radio overboard. He was in his late twenties, and good looking if you liked guys who used to be football players and joked they'd been hit in the head one too many times playing for Navy while at the Academy. His hair was brown and his eyes browner; Bobby thought he might've been boring if not for a strong jaw and a great smile. But looks didn't help much in the business of being a submariner, which was why Bobby had worked his ass off to graduate near the head of his SOAC class.

That gave him his first choice of job—navigator—and class of boat—*Cero*. Unfortunately, he didn't get to pick *which* boat he landed on, and even then, no one had warned him about *Bluefish* before he arrived three months earlier. No, that was an adventure he got to discover for himself.

At least the officer of the deck called him—he was the command duty officer—instead of notifying the captain or the XO. Charlie Maguire was pretty bright for a brand-new ensign. It hadn't taken him long on *Bluefish* to figure out that liberty incidents were Bad News.

Yeah. Bad news. If Shore Patrol was just *now* bringing their miscreant back, that meant he or she did something stupid enough to wind up in the brig overnight, and then *forgot* to notify the boat. Bobby contemplated throwing himself overboard. There was nothing that turned the Old Man into a cranky witch faster than one of their sailors getting into trouble.

Heading up the final ladder from Officers' Country to the quarterdeck, Bobby suppressed another grimace. Commander Peterson had a point, sort of. They were at war. The drunken antics sailors got up to frequently ended in injuries and property damage, not to mention pissed-off locals. Still, the crew needed to let off steam *somehow*, and it wasn't like *Bluefish* was a barrel of laughs. Not that Commander Peterson cared. He would go ape when he heard—

Oh, fantastic. Bobby spotted their newest delinquent as soon as his head popped out of the hatch. The stocky sailor standing between the two MPs was one of the most recognizable members of the crew, hands down. After all, how many half-Japanese ex-hockey players could you stuff on a submarine?

Groaning, Bobby made a beeline for the phone, barely returning the officer of the deck's salute. This was *not* something he was going to put on a radio channel half the crew could hear.

Not that they wouldn't get the news in two nanoseconds. There were no secrets on a submarine.

"Weps," a voice answered on the second ring. Rose Lange was *Bluefish's* weapons officer and was a classmate of Bobby's at the Naval Academy until a severe case of mononucleosis set her back a semester. They were still close, not to mention glad that the Powers That Be stumbled into assigning them to the same submarine.

"Hey Weps, it's Nav." Bobby forced cheer into his voice. "As you know, I'm CDO today, and I've got a lovely little courtesy turnover here on the quarterdeck."

"Do I *want* to know why you're calling me?" she asked.

"It's one of yours." He paused, allowing her to finish swearing. "One guess who."

"Wilson." Rose sighed. "Again. I'm on my way."

Hanging up the phone, Bobby turned to Ensign Maguire. "Whatcha got, Charlie?"

"Shore Patrol picked up STS1 Wilson last night, sir. They said that he was too drunk to tell them what boat he came from. But he was energetic enough to tear Choi's Lounge apart." The officer of the deck shot a dark at Wilson, but the sailor just stood between the two military policemen, trying to look innocent.

That effort failed. Big time.

"Okay, then. Guess they pay me the big bucks to handle this, huh?"

Charlie grinned; like any new officer, he was happy to have someone senior show up to deal with a sticky situation. "Yes, sir!"

Taking a breath, Bobby turned to face the senior MP. "Hit me with the bad news, Chief."

"It's pretty much what your OOD said, Lieutenant," the burly black chief petty pfficer responded. "This...*sailor* of yours got in a fight with a pair of local girls after he was already roaring drunk and proceeded to break off part of the bar. With his bare hands. He also stuffed a barstool into a ceiling fan with enough force that the damn thing came out of the overhead. We picked him up after the bartender at Choi's called. By then, he was bruised and stumbling. This morning, he sobered up enough to tell us he was from *Bluefish*."

The litany of destruction made Bobby blink.

"STS1?" He swung to face the sonar technician.

"Well, sir, I can't say I *remember* much of that." Wilson shrugged. "I mean, I do recall the thing with the barstool. Both times, really. I think one of the girls stopped me the second time, or maybe that was the bouncer." He finally grimaced. "And I offered to pay for the damages. The MPs let me call over to Choi's this morning, and I'll make good on it, Nav. I really will."

If Bobby had a dollar for every time he'd heard a sailor promise that, he'd be rich. Wilson, however, *always* paid for the damage. The problem was that he never stopped drinking. *And he's so damn casual about it afterward. Why isn't he ever sorry?*

At a loss for what else to say to Wilson, Bobby turned back to the MPs. "Any special requirements before you hand him over, Chief, or do I just sign on the dotted line?"

"None, sir, assuming he goes through with paying for the damages. If Choi's Lounge sues, that'll be base legal's problem." The chief extended an electronic chit to Bobby. "Just sign here, Lieutenant."

Sighing again, Bobby scrawled his signature, counting the moments until Rose arrived to corral her special idiot.

Almost on cue, Lieutenant Lange arrived, her pretty face taut with fury. Like Bobby, Rose knew the captain would go nuclear. Wilson's division officer knew that, too, and trailed her glumly. Ensign Harriet Ainsworth was the lucky sonar division officer, and STS1 Wilson was more trouble than the rest of her sailors combined.

Normally, Bobby would diffuse a tense situation with a ridiculous joke, but he couldn't scrape one up. He also wasn't going to let Wilson get off that easy—the sonar man was a *first* class petty officer, and he was in his late twenties. Wilson knew better.

Bobby wanted to strangle him.

So did Rose, judging from the tongue-lashing she subjected Wilson to. It wasn't long, but it was to the point—and far less vulgar than Bobby expected. He'd known Rose for twelve years. In terms of razor-sharp sarcasm and pointed fury, chewing Wilson out today definitely was in the top three reamings-out he'd witnessed.

"She's great at this, isn't she, Harri?" Bobby leaned over to speak quietly to Ensign Ainsworth.

The dark-skinned ensign snorted quietly. "Makes me glad I'm not on the receiving end, Nav."

"Tell me about it. You should hear her go off when I call her 'Rosie.'"

"I *have*, sir," Harri replied.

"Go below and put a uniform on, STS1," Rose snapped. "And don't you even *think* about leaving this boat before I'm through with you."

"Yes, ma'am," Wilson replied. He didn't quite saunter to the nearest ladder.

"Sometime before the war ends, Wilson!"

Wilson scurried down the hatch. Rose turned back to face Bobby and Harri.

Rose and Bobby became fast friends after meeting at the Naval Academy's Summer Seminar, which meant he was used to her all-in attitude. Rose was blond-haired, green eyed, and pretty enough to turn almost any head, but her personality was abrasive enough to chase even the bravest away. Bobby O'Kane wasn't foolish enough to touch her with a ten-foot pole. Rose would probably just chew him to pieces, spit him out again, and then ask for seconds.

Now her shoulders slumped. "There'll be hell to pay for this."

Bobby groaned. "Tell me about it."

They both knew where this would end. If there was one thing that Commander Peterson wasn't known for, it was tailoring punishment to fit the crime. *Bluefish's* entire crew would suffer, and there wasn't a damn thing Bobby could do about it.

Jimmy Carter transited Puget Sound without difficulty and then sprinted down the West Coast until they were roughly parallel with San Francisco. After that, Alex angled his boat straight into the Pacific. The transit was only five days, not long to shake down a submarine for war, particularly when the first twelve hours were spent testing and evaluating the boat.

Alex's joy of being captain of an honest-to-God underway submarine died when his green-as-grass sailors bombed their first drill on day two. And then the second. Gritting his teeth, Alex pulled his command triad together—wrenching George away from micromanaging the department heads, who were among the most competent people on board—and built a robust training and drill schedule. By day four, his crew stopped fumbling core operations like surfacing, silent running, and torpedo loading. They still had a long way to go, but confidence gleamed in every smile. *Jimmy Carter's* crew of rejects and miscreants were starting to come together.

Even lunch in the wardroom was livelier.

The wardroom itself was probably Alex's favorite place on board. Even if the table and chairs were covered in standard navy blue vinyl, the walls were decorated with plaques, pictures, and mementos of places *Jimmy Carter* had visited. A few of them were marked *For Official Use Only*, which meant they were from places the boat never could never admit having been...even years later.

He wasn't envious of *Jimmy Carter's* previous captains. Not even when Murder Machine II was invited to lunch and stole the XO's chair. Alex just wanted to be worthy of having his name on the sign with all of Smiley's other COs, all the way back to the beginning.

"He's got to burn out," Benji Angler said, making a mess of slurping chili. "History says that sub COs who do best early in wars either get eclipsed or get sunk. Usually by the end of the first year."

"That's a pretty crappy statistic to bank on." Maggie Bennett was bleary-eyed and clutched a cup of coffee like it was made of precious gems. She'd had the night watch and rolled right into the morning drill set; Alex made a note to send her to bed if she didn't see herself there. Maggie continued: "Rochambeau has sunk six submarines we *know* of already. The asshole's on fire."

"Someone's going to get him," Benji replied.

"It better be soon," Elena Alvaro, the damage control assistant, said. She'd come out of her shell more slowly than the department heads, but so far, it seemed like Master Chief Morton was right about her. Elena was a rockstar. "We can't afford to lose more top boats to him."

"I hope so, too," Alex said. "I met him before the war, and Maggie's right...he's an asshole."

Maggie stared. "How'd you meet a French—"

The phone at Alex's side rang, cutting her off. Heart racing, he yanked it out of the cradle. Was this what it felt like to command a submarine at war? "Captain."

Marty Sterling's calm drawl gave nothing away. His engineer had the watch in control as officer of the deck, and as always, nothing seemed to shake him. "Sorry to interrupt your lunch, sir, but we just got a BSOD on the helm console."

"Come again?"

"Blue screen of death. I popped it over to hand electric so we don't smash into an underwater mountain or something. No need to man emergency steering, but all the computer-assisted modes are toast."

"Can you reset it?" Alex asked.

"Do you have a copy of Windows XP handy?" Marty sounded more amused than offended. "I tried a restart already, but it looks like Windows ate itself. And the damn computer is so old it needs a *compact disc*. If it took a thumb drive, I might try to slap an upgrade on it, but there's no USB ports. And it's not networked, even if we could download a copy on our underway bandwidth."

"Well, shit." Alex hadn't been certain what kind of engineer Marty was when he first met him, but a string of mechanical problems—each weirder than the last—was starting to teach him that Marty's droll exterior hid a brilliant brain. "What are our options?"

"Go back to Washington or stay in manual until Pearl," Marty replied. "Or, I mean, we could surface and scream for help, but I think that's a bad thing to do during wartime."

"Tell me about it. What are the restrictions in manual?" Alex wished to hell he knew this boat better—or didn't have a sneaking feeling that this would be all it might take for his next boss to deem the boat unusable.

"It won't auto update our course changes to the new system, so

Maggie's team will have to manual plot."

"That sounds like an *excellent* training opportunity. Let's make it work."

"Aye, sir. I'll buy a copy of Win XP off eBay next time we're shallow and have it delivered to Pearl."

Joy. When would his boat break next...and what might it cost him?

15 September 2038, the Mid-Atlantic

USS *Fletcher* (DDG 155) was on point again. After her experiences in the Battle of the SOM, that was hardly Nancy's favorite place to be—but today, they had P-8 Poseidon coverage, which meant the aircraft were on sub-hunting duty and Nancy's destroyer was free to do what she did best: defend the carrier against air and surface threats. *Narwhal* was with them, too, far out on the northern flank and keeping an ear out for Russian threats.

Not that there were a lot of those out here. Six days into their transatlantic transit, Nancy's crew was bored with drills and back in tip-top shape.

"I think we're ready to roll, ma'am," Lieutenant Commander Ying Mai said, leaning back in her comfortable blue chair in *Fletcher's* CO's cabin. "I just wish we had a full missile load-out."

"You, me, and every other destroyer in the fleet." Nancy Coleman smiled crookedly from the other side of the table. It was round, blue, and like almost everything on board decorated with *Fletcher's* unit crest in the center. A cliché, perhaps, but one Nancy unashamedly loved. "But I agree that we're ready. Five hard days of drills—plus all that training in the yards—puts us in a good place."

"Any idea where we're going?"

Nancy shook her head. "Not yet. We're supposed to stick with *Lexington* for a bit. Then rumor says we'll end up in a surface action group *somewhere* in the Indian Ocean, but your guess is as good as mine."

"I could do with a little less carrier escort duty." Ying shuddered.

"Me, too." It went without saying that their last carrier hadn't done so well, despite *Fletcher's* best efforts.

Being under Jeff McNally's command for the first battle of the war was hardly a good memory—even if surviving it had earned *Fletcher* a Navy Unit Commendation and Nancy a Silver Star. Out of the five ships that entered the Strait of Malacca on April 12, 2038, only two survived: *Fletcher* and a cruiser, *Belleau Wood*. And it had been damned close.

Nancy's phone rang; her hand snaked out to snatch it up without conscious thought. "Captain."

"Good afternoon, Captain, it's the Officer of the Deck," Lieutenant (junior grade) Matt Holloway said with an edge in his voice. "We've received a distress call from a merchant vessel bearing two-one-niner at twenty-two nautical miles. Combat is informing the carrier now."

"Make best speed to intercept. I'm on my way."

Much of the surface navy viewed *Fletcher* and her *O'Bannon*-class sisters as a cheap knockoff of the older (and more expensive) *Arleigh Burkes*. Smaller, missile-heavy, and designed for a smaller crew, the *O'Bannons* were fast, lean...and the result of a few compromises that left no one happy, like the weird placement of their Combat Information Center aft of the wardroom, a magnetic helicopter retrieval system that rarely worked, and no towed sonar array.

Fletcher's yard period fixed the last problem, but only a complete redesign (which was already done with the *Ernest E. Evans*-class) could change the others. Despite that, Nancy loved her mean little destroyer. *Fletcher* proved herself tough in combat, and as a bonus, the captain's palatial cabin was only two decks below the bridge.

She and Ying reached the bridge in less than a minute. By then, *Fletcher's* decks were trembling as she heeled to port and came up to speed. The sharp smell of salt drifted in through the open bridge wing doors; normally, Nancy loved that smell. Today, she ignored it.

"Coming to full power now, Captain," Holloway said. He was a skinny young man, a swimmer like Nancy's husband, with dark eyes and red hair crowning a face full of freckles shadowed by his yellow *Fletcher* ball cap. "Motor Vessel *Maersk Crown* reports carrying iron ore out of South Africa, bound for Jersey. She bears two-two-zero, range twenty-one nautical miles."

"Has she requested assistance?" Nancy headed to the surface search radar to look at *Maersk Crown's* track; she was too far out for a visual, but there were no other ships within five miles of the presumably big merchant on the plot.

"Yes, ma'am. She claims she was in company with another ship, *Ever Fortune*, and that ship was torpedoed."

Nancy's head snapped around. *"What?"*

Holloway shrugged. "That's what she said."

"XO, get on the horn with the carrier and pass that info to the strike group ASAP," Nancy ordered as a chill ripped down her spine. "Officer of the Deck, set flight quarters. I want a helo over *Maersk Crown* yesterday."

"OOD, aye!"

Nancy ignored Ying heading to the Combat Information Center to call the carrier on a secure line and picked up the bridge-to-bridge radio herself. "*Maersk Crown, Maersk Crown,* this is U.S. Navy Warship One-Five-Five, calling you on channel one-six, over."

"Go for *Maersk Crown,* Captain."

"*Maersk Crown,* this is One-Five-Five Actual, I understand you report a ship you were in company with was torpedoed, over?" The words felt surreal to say. The war was five months old, and no one—*no one*—had gone after civilian shipping.

This was the modern world. They were fighting *civilized* navies. No one targeted civilians.

Acid churned in Nancy's gut.

"That's affirmative, Captain. *Fortune* went down like a rock. I've put on all the turns I've got and am weaving like a drunk man." The voice on the other end was male but high with panic, slurring a few words in the rush to get them out. "Are you coming to help us?"

"We're in route now, Captain." Nancy didn't have the heart to tell him that zigzagging wasn't much defense against modern torpedoes, and at twenty-six knots, *Maersk Crown* couldn't outrun any of the torpedoes in the Freedom Union's arsenal. "ETA twenty-three minutes, over."

"Roger."

There was an ominous silence from the other end; Nancy hoisted herself into her bridge chair, thinking through the problem. She turned to Lieutenant Holloway. "Time to launch?"

"Five mikes, Captain."

"Very well. Set General Quarters."

"Set General Quarters, aye." Holloway turned to the Boatswain's Mate of the Watch. "Boats!"

"Boats, aye!" Boatswain's Mate Second Class Omerovic lifted the microphone for the 1MC, or ship's general announcing system, activating the general alarm with her other hand. "General quarters, general quarters, all hands man your battle stations. Traffic for general quarters is up and forward to starboard; aft and down to port. Set material condition Zebra throughout the ship. Reason for general quarters: potential enemy submarine contact."

Nancy picked up the handset for the intra-ship net between the bridge and CIC. "TAO, Captain, stream the tail."

"Stream TACTAS, TAO, aye," the tactical action officer replied.

Peacetime procedure required slowing down before streaming their Tactical Towed Array Sonar, lest they damage the hydrophones. Damaging new toys just a few weeks after the taxpayers gave them to her was frowned upon, but Nancy figured the government would hate her more if she lost the whole damned destroyer.

Within moments, *Fletcher's* TACTAS began deploying. The towed sonar array was basically a long string of hydrophones following in the destroyer's wake, extending out to one mile. This extended her passive—listening—sonar reach outside the bubble of her own ship's noise and gave *Fletcher* a better chance of detecting enemy submarines than ever before...and certainly a better one than she had back in the Battle of the Strait of Malacca.

Today, too, *Fletcher* could use her top speed of forty knots. Her design might've been a lower-cost compromise, but her swiftness was no accident. *Fletcher* and her sisters were faster than any American destroyer since World War II.

Nancy didn't want to think on how apropos *that* was five months into the Third World War.

"Time to intercept?" she asked.

"Eighteen minutes," Holloway replied. "Steady on Foxtrot Corpen. Winds are in the envelope. Request Amber Deck."

"Granted."

Nancy didn't listen to the 1MC announcement; instead, she shifted her eyes to the video screen to her left, watching as the rotors started turning on one of *Fletcher's* MH-60R LAMPS helicopters. She lifted the internal comms handset again. "XO, Captain, what's the strike group say?"

"*Lexington* can have two -60s off deck in fifteen minutes to help with ASW," Ying replied.

"Captain, aye." Nancy suppressed a frown. Would that be fast enough? Racing into a situation with a potential enemy sub lurking was halfway to insane, but what choice did she have? She swapped to the bridge-to-bridge radio. "*Maersk Crown*, this is One-Five-Five, over."

"Go ahead."

"Do you have visual on the submarine, over?" Nancy asked. It wasn't likely, but it was worth a chance.

"No way. I didn't stay to watch when they got *Fortune*. I just put on as many turns as I could."

"One-Five-Five, roger." Nancy let out a breath, watching *Maersk Crown's* track on the radar screen. Seventeen nautical miles to go. "Do you have a position where *Fortune* went down?"

"Standby."

"Captain, Striker Nine-Zero-Niner reports ready to launch. Request green deck," Holloway said before the civilian could come back with an answer.

Nancy nodded. "Green deck."

"Green deck!" BM2 Omerovic announced on the 1MC, and seconds later, Striker 909 lifted off *Fletcher's* deck, turning immediately into the wind.

With a top speed of 180 knots, Striker 909 could reach *Maersk Crown* in about five minutes, accounting for the twenty-six knots the merchant ship was cranking out straight toward them. *Fletcher* would need another ten to get there, but the MH-60R had dipping sonar and two lightweight torpedoes.

More importantly, the helo could transmit a contact back to *Fletcher*, so if the helo found an enemy submarine, Nancy could drop a rocket-launched torpedo right on their head faster than any French or Russian bastard could say *fire*.

The idea of staying outside a sub's torpedo range was nicer than racing in and getting her destroyer shot out from under her, too. Nancy had watched two other destroyers sink up close and personal. She was not about to join them.

Nancy turned back to the radar screen and blinked.

"*Maersk Crown*, this is Warship One-Five-Five, over."

Nothing.

A cold wave washed over Nancy, and she grabbed the inter-ship comms handset. "Combat, bridge, tell the helo to get me a visual of *Maersk Crown* now!" She swapped back to the bridge-to-bridge radio: "*Maersk Crown*, this is Warship One-Five-Five, over."

Silence.

Pearl Harbor, Hawaii

Before the war, submarines avoided mooring side by side like the plague. Captains liked to say that it was a good way to damage their sound-absorbent tiles, but the real answer was that it was *hard* to maneuver a submarine on the surface. Bringing one alongside the pier was difficult enough; why risk bonking another boat?

Wartime, however, was another matter. Now there wasn't enough pier space to go around near the war zone, which meant subs nested two and sometimes three deep alongside the pier. Alex wasn't a fan, but at least the assignment he received upon arriving in Pearl wasn't next to someone he didn't like. *Bluefish* seemed a decent boat; their line handlers were quick and efficient, even if the CO wasn't around when Alex popped over to say high.

Two hours after lines went over, the ringing of bells echoed over *Jimmy Carter's* 1MC, or general announcing system.

Ding ding, ding ding.

"*Razorback*, arriving," the petty officer of the watch announced over. The words were a near-perfect echo of "*Razorback*, crossing" passed by the submarine moored inboard of *Jimmy Carter*. The tradition of bonging senior officers aboard ships and submarines dated back to the Royal Navy's early days, and the commanding officer of a ship or submarine was always announced using the name of that vessel.

Alex was already topside. It only took a moment for his old friend to salute the officer of the deck and request permission to come aboard, and then John headed aft toward Alex. Alex saluted him, too, although it wasn't the sarcastically precise one that he offered superiors like Commander Melendez—this was the far more casual salute between officers who'd served together for many years.

"Welcome aboard, John." Alex offered a handshake with a smile.

"Thanks, I think." Captain John Dalton laughed. "This boat of yours is a monster, isn't she?"

John's easy smile made him look more like a naughty urchin than a naval officer. Alex's old friend had always been on the heavy side and fought constantly to stay within the Navy's weight standards, but you wouldn't guess that from his cheerful demeanor, and you couldn't see his bald spot when he was wearing a *Razorback* ball cap.

"You can say that again."

Jimmy Carter dwarfed the *Cero*-class boat moored between her and the pier. The sailors on board *Bluefish* seemed downright terrified when Alex maneuvered his boat alongside without help from any tugs an hour earlier, but they made it without incident. His gargantuan boat was surprisingly easy to drive.

Thank goodness for that. Swapping paint might've put them on someone's list to decommission the submarine, a thought never far from Alex's mind.

"You cut it close, you know," John said.

He knew that tone of voice. Alex smiled wryly. "How long do you have before you get underway?"

"About twenty-two hours."

"Ouch. Where to?" At least Alex could ask; standing on *Jimmy Carter's* aft deck, there was no one around them without at least a Secret clearance.

"Certainly not somewhere as climate as Pearl Harbor." John rolled his eyes.

"That's super helpful."

John laughed. "You just described *exactly* how I feel. I don't know where we're going. Somewhere in the Indian Ocean, probably. All I've got is a waypoint to go to, and they'll give me orders once I'm there."

"How the hell can we be this disorganized five months into the war?" Alex groaned, glancing out at the beehive of activity out on the pier.

Well, shit. *Bluefish* was busy loading stores and supplies, which meant the other submarine expected to get underway soon. But Alex didn't have orders, and *Jimmy Carter* had just arrived.

What a great example of poor planning. Shifting one submarine out of another's path wasn't like swapping parking spots in a car; while pier side and away from the war's front lines, *Jimmy Carter's* reactor was shut down. They'd need hours to get propulsion online or tugs to haul her out of the way. These pier assignments were a bad call on someone's part.

John shrugged. "Hell if I know. I just pulled in two days ago, and we've been spun 'round like a top to head back out again."

"You're the real captain here. You're supposed to know these things."

John just shook his head.

16 September 2038, the North Atlantic

"There's nothing here, ma'am."

Nancy could hear the frustration in Ying Mai's voice, and shoving down the desire to throw things and swear took a gargantuan effort. She sat back in her chair in *Fletcher's* CIC, closing her eyes briefly. "That's two in two days."

"Yes, Captain, it is."

"Very well. Thank you, XO." Nancy opened her eyes and stepped on the foot microphone for the tactical net. God, she was tired. "Lima Bravo, this is *Fletcher*, negative indications of M/V *Tower* at the provided coordinates. Oil slick and debris evident. No survivors, over."

It was *Maersk Crown* all over again. No survivors and just a little debris. Nothing left of a merchant ship that had been en route to the United States with material critical to the war effort.

And before *Maersk Crown*, there had been *Ever Fortune*. Three civilian ships gone in less than two days. None were U.S.-flagged, but what merchant ships were these days? American taxes were too high and inspections too onerous. Flags of convenience were the name of the game, and everyone assumed flying the flag of a neutral country would keep you safe in wartime.

Until this week, it had.

Or so they thought.

"This is Lima Bravo, roger. Discontinue your search and rejoin the formation, over."

"*Fletcher*, roger, out." Nancy bit back a snarl. She wanted to *sink* someone, not fruitlessly race to save merchants who died before her destroyer—or her helicopter!—were even in visual range.

But the damned sub already disappeared.

Chapter 17

Problem Child

The crew was on restricted liberty...again. News of Petty Officer Wilson's drunken antics reached Commander Peterson's ears within an hour. Details only made the captain's rage go from boiling to incandescent.

He didn't shout. Oh, no. Peterson wasn't the screaming type. Instead, he quietly cut the legs out from under everyone, decreeing that *Bluefish* sailors weren't allowed to spend the night anywhere other than on the boat and required everyone to file "liberty plans" before going anywhere. In *Pearl Harbor*. Last Bobby checked, Hawaii was part of the United States, and treating Americans like they were children *on American soil* was a big freaking hit.

Two days after Wilson's courtesy turnover, morale was beneath the earth's crust and digging deeper.

Yep, war was everything he'd imagined. Lieutenant Bobby O'Kane was the navigator on a miserable submarine whose main claim to fame was a search and rescue off the coast of Midway...and a captain who took his anger out on his crew. Bobby scraped a hand over his face, staring blankly at the report chit on his stateroom computer screen. One of his sailors was the newest violator of the liberty policy, and now Bobby got to write Electronics Technician First Class Van Haven up.

Get a hold of yourself, O'Kane, Bobby told himself firmly, fighting back a yawn. This wasn't the first sailor he'd punished, and it wasn't like Van Haven didn't *choose* to go to that bar, despite knowing the captain's policies.

Maybe he'd finish the darn thing in the morning. He didn't *have* to do it now, but Bobby did paperwork in spurts, like sprints at football practice at the Academy.

A knock on the door made him jump. He lived alone since his last roommate, *Bluefish's* former engineering officer, got fired for gross incompetence. They still didn't have a relief for Lieutenant Crocker, which meant Bobby could stay up as late as he wanted to without disturbing anyone.

Rubbing his eyes, he glanced at the time. Yes, it *was* almost midnight. Why was someone at his door? The boat wasn't underway, and he didn't have the duty. That meant he should've been able to enjoy a late-night admin session in peace.

Unless someone other than Van Haven disregarded the captain's new liberty policy. Bobby sighed. Everyone was bitter about the asinine new restrictions, but there was nothing Bobby or anyone else could do once the captain made up his mind. The XO tried to talk him out of it, but Peterson ignored him, too. *I really love my job.*

Knock, knock!

He'd forgotten about the door.

"Come on in, the water's fine!" Bobby twisted in his chair to face the music. Much to his surprise, Master Chief Machinist's Mate Ginger Baker stood in the opening.

"Sorry to bother you, Nav, but I saw your light on." Unlike Bobby, Baker still wore her uniform. *His* attire featured a blue Mickey Mouse T-shirt that his sister Mary gave him last Christmas, along with a bright orange pair of board shorts. Even Peterson wasn't anal retentive enough to care what his offers wore during their time off. Yet.

"It's no problem, COB." Bobby smiled. He wasn't a night owl, but if he couldn't sleep, he might as well not be cranky about it. "What's on your mind?"

"Actually, your broken outboard is." *Bluefish's* senior enlisted sailor leaned tiredly against the doorframe. On second glance, Bobby noticed that her normally immaculate appearance was frayed around the edges. A few of the tight braids in her black hair had even escaped their normally neat prison. Something was wrong.

There went his resolve to be cheerful. "What'd it do this time, explode?"

He was only half joking. *Bluefish's* "outboard," or retractable bow thruster, had been on the fritz since before Bobby reported on board. No matter how many times Bobby's sailors fixed the thing, it always broke again. A working outboard would have allowed *Bluefish* to maneuver in tight areas on the surface without the use of tugs. One that didn't might as well have been scrap metal. That thruster assembly was one of glaring weaknesses of the *Cero*-class design, which had been put into service more quickly than average. Bobby remembered his first boat having problems with their outboard, but *Bluefish's* was possessed.

The damn thing broke weekly.

Baker chuckled. "Not yet, sir. Though given what Welsh tried earlier, I wouldn't be surprised."

"Do I want to know?"

"Probably not. Forget I said anything." The COB grinned. Baker was one of the best master chiefs he'd ever met. He knew she would tell him if he needed to know. She was an old school chief of the boat and generally protected officers from their own curiosity.

"You said something?" he quipped, making her laugh.

"Actually, I was going to say that I probably have *good* news for you, for once. I was next door earlier, talking to *Jimmy Carter's* COB, and it turns out that they have a spare of that back-ordered pump you've been desperate for."

"What's it gonna cost us?"

Officially, the navy prohibited swapping out parts and supplies willy-nilly, but it happened all the time. The navy supply system hadn't caught up to the war's needs, and the horse trading inside the fleet kept boats ready to fight. Without it, *Bluefish* would never be combat capable. Back in July, a timely trade with *Gato* allowed her engineers to repair one of their main steam turbines. Now, it was Bobby's turn to wheel and deal.

He would've cheerfully handed over his right leg if it kept the captain from asking him about the outboard three times a day, every day. And six times on Sunday.

"That's where it gets interesting, sir, and we'll have to talk to Weps when she wakes up."

"That sounds ominous." Rose was notoriously stingy about giving up parts, particularly when she didn't get something directly in return.

"They don't want equipment, Nav. They're looking for a sonar tech. I thought we could send them Wilson."

"Wilson?" Bobby gaped.

"He'll go to Captain's Mast if he stays here. After this latest incident, the captain just wants him gone. It'll take longer to kick him out of the navy than to send him somewhere else."

Bobby'd never heard of trading a *sailor* for a piece of equipment. "The captain will go for this *why?*"

"Let me worry about that."

"Has anyone told *Jimmy Carter* what kind of sailor we're offering?" Bobby asked. A nasty inner voice told Bobby that he shouldn't care, but he wasn't that bitter yet.

"I'm not that shady. I told Master Chief Morton all about him." Baker smiled. "I get the impression that he doesn't care what kind of sailor he gets, so long as it's a warm body. They're about twenty sailors short over there and are scrounging them from anywhere and everywhere."

"It still seems kind of...low to send our biggest troublemaker over."

Baker snorted. "It's *Jimmy Carter*, sir. They're not going to need the best."

By the time *Fletcher* reached her first port visit in Naples—Italy was scrupulously neutral, despite France's diplomatic arm twisting—thirteen merchant ships on their way to the U.S. had been reported missing or overdue. Even more disappeared on their way to Australia. Britain, no stranger to enemies trying to strangle their economy by way of commerce raiding, estimated at least six ships lost in the channel and four in the Atlantic.

Alex saw the writing on the wall before most of his colleagues. That was the perks of having a destroyer CO for a wife, he supposed. But it still wasn't pleasant.

"It's got to be subs," Nancy said from the other end of their phone call. Alex walked over to the PACFLEET building by himself today; stealing a few minutes for a private conversation with his wife got harder and harder as the war grew in scope.

Pearl Harbor and Naples were exactly twelve hours apart, so while Nancy got ready to turn in for the night, Alex was on his way to a briefing.

"Sounds like. Otherwise, you'd have seen *someone* sailing away." Alex chewed his lip, dodging a car full of laughing sailors. "I'm kind of surprised they didn't stick around to sink you."

"Hey, I'd like to think we're a hard target."

"But you're still a target, babe. That's just how we think." Alex didn't enjoy calling his wife's ship a target, not these days. Even thinking about all the jokes he made about that in peacetime now left him a little nauseous. "Submariners don't really look at surface ships as threats."

Nancy scoffed. "You remember that this war *started* when a surface ship sank a sub it shouldn't have."

"Yeah, but the rules are different now that the shooting's started." Alex stopped outside the PACFLEET Operations building and watched a pair of sailors trying to wrestle an enormous stack of pizzas into the tiny back seat of a ship's utility truck.

"So why's this sub hiding, then?" Nancy asked. "If you're right and *I* didn't scare them off, why run from my little old destroyer?"

"Plausible deniability, maybe?" Alex frowned; that didn't feel right. "Unless no one wants to 'fess up to killing civilians just yet. If they don't shoot *you*, they can try to pretend the ships are disappearing by accident."

"That's a fuckton of accidents, Alex."

"I know. Thirty-eight at last count." He sighed. "I'm headed into a briefing about this shit. I'll email you on the secret side if there's anything worth sharing."

"Watch your back out there, okay?" Nancy's voice went soft.

"You're one to talk, babe. I'm still sitting pier side while you're chasing bad guys." Alex half-hoped he'd find some enemies on the trip from Washington State to Hawaii, but no such luck. His worst enemy had been Windows XP, thanks to John Dalton and *Razorback* clearing everyone out.

"Do it anyway. This war's getting weird, and no one knows what the hell's going on," Nancy said. "And call the girls when you get the chance."

"Yes, ma'am." Alex chuckled. "Love you. Get some sleep."

"Love you, too. Good night."

Alex hung up his cell, trying to banish the unease curling in his gut. Nancy was right. They were six months into World War III. Logic said they should know what they were fighting for by now, that things should be predictable or at least *logical*. Yet everyone—enemy and ally alike—was still scrambling for purchase.

Yeah, the Freedom Union kept gobbling up territory. And now they seemed to be commerce raiding, too. Was unrestricted submarine warfare a thing again? Everyone assumed that went out the door with World War II.

Shaking his head, Alex headed into the Pacific Fleet Operations Center. Hopefully, someone inside had some answers.

Toulon, France

Being back in Toulon was nice if you wanted rest and relaxation, but Captain Jules Rochambeau was not in this business to relax.

"We will regret this little holiday if Britain succeeds in convincing Egypt to close the Suez Canal to our shipping," Jules said in an undertone, ignoring the bright lights to his left.

"They will not do so." Admiral Bernard shrugged from his comfortable chair outside the recording studio of France's largest news channel. "Did you not hear? Egypt has declared neutrality."

"*Et alors?*" Jules rolled his eyes. "Neutrality means nothing and less with the United Nations neutered. No one will enforce it."

A few news crew members turned to stare at him, but Jules met their gazes one by one, and they all turned away. Perhaps being a growing legend was useful, though intimidating his own countrymen was less entertaining than killing the enemy.

"It is not in our best interests to breach neutrality. Nor is it in our enemies'." Bernard shook his head. "Not everyone is as...pessimistic as you are, Capitaine. *Oui*, the U.N. Security Council is split. Russia obviously stands with us and the rest of the Freedom Union, while Britain and America stand together. China remains busy tearing itself apart in civil war. This keeps the United Nations out of the war, as we all prefer."

"I did not say that was a bad thing." Jules sighed and resisted the urge to touch his perfectly styled hair. It would not do to ruin things before his interview. "Being unfettered by international opinion helps our national interests, particularly when both India and Russia greedily gobble up every bit of territory they can conquer, and we are more...selective." The last word made him smile. "But sooner or later, most nations will have to take a side, and despite the lucky happenstance of America firing the first shot, we do appear to be more belligerent since *we* are conquering territory."

"We will overcome that when the time comes. For now, we will concentrate on internal public relations, which is why you are here." Bernard smiled. "Did you not tell me you wished to be remembered as France's greatest submariner?"

"The competition is not stiff."

Bernard arched an eyebrow. "I can always call Commander Garnier in to do this interview instead."

Jules' eyes narrowed. "I did not say I would not do it. Just that I prefer to remain in theater next time. Traveling all the way to Toulon is a risk I do not deem worthy of the reward."

"And the upgrades to your submarine are not also worth it?"

"*Mon amiral*, we are building a subbase on Île Amsterdam. Can we not do upgrades there?" Jules leaned forward. "I am sure the public would love a glimpse into the war for French superiority as well."

Bernard laughed. "And you wonder why I want you in the interviews! Continue with this attitude, Capitaine, and you will eventually have my job."

"Perhaps someday." Jules did not blush. "I prefer to make my history first."

"*Très bien.* Go impress the media and build French prestige." Bernard waved him through the door as one of the television company's interns opened it. "And then we will get you back in the water to end this month-long drought of no kills you have been complaining about."

Rising, Jules put on his best smile. He already was the most successful submarine captain in French history, with seven enemy submarines and four enemy surface combatants sunk. There was no contesting that. Commander Annette Garnier, their second best, had only sunk *half* as many combatants…most of them surface ships.

Jules knew he was the best in the world at what he did. He just needed to get back out there and be *better*. But if his country wanted to turn him into a celebrity first, who was he to say no?

Eventually, Alex would learn not to get his hopes up. A computer could have provided a brief with more emotion than this lieutenant.

Lieutenant Goldsmith was blond, pretty, and obviously bored with this briefing. She stood in front of a group of assembled captains and commanders—all of whom were in command of their own ships or submarines or chiefs of staff to higher-ranking officers—like they were children in a kindergarten class. And she used a laser pointer, which Alex hated.

"As you can see," she continued, "merchant losses are steadily creeping upward. Intelligence indicates that since both sides are identifying war materials through hacking into AIS automatic updates, civilian ships aren't reporting what they're carrying. Instead, they claim cargos of mulch or other inane items.

"Yesterday, the U.N. attempted to pass a resolution prohibiting belligerents from sinking merchant vessels flying flags of neutral nations. It was vetoed by China."

"China?" a captain on the right side of the room asked. "What do they care? They're in the middle of their own bloodbath."

"There's some evidence that they were bribed to veto by another party." The lieutenant barely even twitched. "The follow-on resolution, proposed by Germany, however, passed. This calls for all merchants to accurately declare their cargoes in the Automated Information System *and* for belligerents to avoid sink ships not carrying materials that provide direct support to the war effort."

"Does anyone care?" someone asked.

"Are *we* going to obey that?" another captain said at the same time.

The lieutenant blinked, looking back and forth between the two blankly. After an awkward moment of silence, she continued with her prepared remarks:

"COMPACFLT has determined that the navy will provide escorts for all Alliance-flagged merchants transiting the war zone, as well as for any neutral nations trading with us. At least two surface combatants and one submarine will protect each convoy. Any convoy accompanied by civilian transport or cargo submarines will have at least two attack subs for protection..."

Alex slumped in his seat and tried to tune out the rest. Reading the slides up on the screen was more productive than listening to Lieutenant Goldsmith.

Finally, she clicked on her last slide. "Convoy numbers are chosen at random. Convoy assignments are not." Goldsmith pointed at the screen. "Here, you will see your convoy escort assignments. Please see the escort commanders if you have questions."

Alex squinted. Oh, there he was. Right at the bottom.

USS *Jimmy Carter* (SSN 23). Convoy 3211.

Joy.

Alex skimmed the rest of the group. Convoy 3211 was cobbled together out of odds and ends, because yep, no squadron commander wanted to send their best units off for convoy duty.

That was especially true if rumors were right and the Alliance wanted to push for Armistice Station again. Two miles of prime underwater territory, Armistice Station was independent until the French Navy rolled in during the opening acts of the war. Alex remembered *those* days far too well, even if he wished he couldn't.

Now the Alliance was torn between freeing Armistice Station and retaking the Strait of Malacca. The best of three navies were split between those tasks...which explained why *Jimmy Carter* was assigned to a convoy going nowhere near either. Alex suppressed a sharp stab of disappointment. He didn't really *want* to go back to his least favorite place under the ocean—two of his worst career experiences took place on or near Armistice Station—but he wanted to make a difference.

But subs over thirty just weren't in prime demand.

At least no one had started poaching his officers and crew and talking about decommissioning. A convoy escort assignment was still an assignment. That had to be worth something.

Shaking himself, Alex forced a smile as the officers split into small groups, one each dedicated to each of six convoys departing in the next few days. Just Alex's luck, Lieutenant Goldsmith provided the details for Convoy 3211, droning on about their projected route, the ships' cargos, and all kinds of useless mundane details.

Alex cleared his throat.

"Do we have any intel on what kind of threats might be in the area?" he asked.

Goldsmith looked at him like he'd gone mad. *Did I sleep through the answer? Or are we that overconfident?*

"Intelligence assessments indicate enemy forces won't attack a protected convoy." She tossed her head.

None of the other COs seemed willing to back him up, so Alex forced himself to shrug. "I see. Thank you, Lieutenant."

Her smile was superior, and Alex was glad he wasn't her boss. He'd have tried to wipe that expression off her face a long time ago and probably would have made a jerk out of himself doing it. "Of course, sir." She squared her shoulders. "Are there any other questions?"

Inevitably, there were. Every gathering of senior officers included twenty or thirty minutes of questions designed to let their askers could sound smarter than the average bear. Not a one of their questions seemed tactically relevant, however, and *that* worried him.

God, we're such a peacetime navy. Alex wanted to scream. *The shooting was fun, but now we're tired of it and want to go home. We're not really interested in seeing this through now that it looks like it'll take a lot of work.*

Perhaps he shouldn't be so critical. He was new at this business; maybe he was missing something. Still, he expected war to be more focused than this clusterfuck. Alex was a student of warfare. He didn't expect an organized war—the phrase "the fog of war" existed for a reason—but he'd hoped for more direction. He'd always been good at flying by the seat of his pants, but it wasn't a talent that the U.S. Navy had ever institutionalized or encouraged its officers to practice.

Something had to give. But what?

"*Jimmy Carter*, arriving!"

Master Chief Morton was waiting topside when Alex returned to the boat two hours later, his stomach rumbling. The walk *to* the briefing had been nice, but heading back on a Hawaiian afternoon was less pleasant. Alex made a note to self: September in Hawaii wasn't as climate as he thought it should be.

After returning the COB's salute, Alex shot him a wry smile. "Should I be worried with you for a welcoming party?"

"Depends on if you want the bad news or the good news first, Captain," Morton replied, scowling at a pair of sailors who were lollygagging on deck back aft.

Alex sighed. "Hit me with the worst stuff first."

"Well, sir, you can't say I didn't offer. Orders from COMSUBPAC's office came down while you were at the briefing, telling us to send a sonar chief over to *Kansas*, since they lost theirs to triple bypass surgery. They're getting underway"—he glanced to the left, where a pair of tugs were easing a *Virginia*-class submarine away from the pier—"right now."

"'A' sonar chief?" Alex swallowed worry—he knew Senior Chief Salli, assuming she remained on *Kansas*. She was a good chief, smart, reliable, and one of those he remembered fondly. "I trust you told them we only have the one."

"Yes, sir. The XO tried to call the local commodore's chief of staff, but no one would give him the time of day," Morton confirmed. "So, now Chief Escalante is getting underway. On *Kansas*."

"Outstanding." *It* had *to be* Kansas, *didn't it?* "Please tell me that's the bad news."

"It is. The *good* news—and a fuckton better, now—was that I swung a deal with *Bluefish*'s COB to acquire their extra STS1. So we'll have a first class petty officer as sonar supervisor with the chief gone." Morton shrugged. "He's supposedly a drunk, but I figure that's the least of our worries."

"Those sound like famous last words, Master Chief."

Morton only grinned. "Leave Petty Officer Wilson to me, Captain. I'll kick him into shape, one way or another."

Alex felt one eyebrow go up. "I'll hold you to that one, COB."

Chapter 18

Second Chances

22 September 2038, Pearl Harbor, Hawaii

"I'm going to kill him," Benji said. "He's been here three days, and I already want to murder him."

"Who did what?" Maggie asked, flipping through the underway check-off list while standing in the center of *Jimmy Carter's* control room.

The boat was due to get underway again in less than an hour. This was her second underway as navigator, and Maggie still felt nervous, both about her job and about the equipment she owned on the ancient submarine. They'd completed a lot of testing en route from Bangor, but there were still so many things they didn't know about *Jimmy Carter*...and so many things to break. Like the stupid helm console. What would go next?

Benji's face was red. "Wilson. STS-Fucking-One Wilson. My new leading sonar tech. Turd Burgler of the Year."

Maggie frowned. Benji was usually the levelheaded one; it was her job to freak out over small stuff. "What'd he do?"

"He's not here."

"What do you mean, 'he's not here'? Is he not at his station?" They'd set the Maneuvering Watch fifteen minutes ago, and everyone had an assigned station. Getting a submariner underway was an all-hands evolution, even if you were new.

Suddenly suspicious, Maggie glanced around control, but all of *her* sailors were present. The navigation ETs were checking charts, and the helm was manned, too. Her other sailors were topside, ready to serve as line handlers, before they came back inside the boat for their other underway jobs.

"I mean he's not on the boat. At all." Benji crossed his arms.

Maggie blinked. "Do you know where he is?"

"Do you think I'd be sitting here if I did? COB's been calling his cell for two hours, and he's not answering."

"Anyone tell the captain?" she asked. Maggie didn't even want to ask if the XO knew. It was the kind of thing Kirkland would latch onto. The XO was already pacing around the control room like a wild animal, trying to look at everything at once.

If he kept this up, the man was going to seriously damage his neck muscles.

"I have no idea, and I'm not looking forward to—"

"Has anybody told the captain what?" a new voice intruded, making both department heads jump. Guiltily, they turned to face their commanding officer, who was leaning against a bulkhead not far away, his hands stuffed in his pockets.

Maggie hated the idea of disappointing their captain, and she could tell by the look on Angler's face that he felt the same way.

"Uh...well, Captain, it seems like I'm missing a sailor from my department." Benji swallowed. "STS1 Wilson."

"The new sonar tech." The captain chuckled and shook his head. "Well, I suppose he *did* come with a warning label."

Maggie clapped a hand over her mouth to choke off a giggle. A missing sailor really wasn't a laughing matter, even if Wilson had a long and colorful history. Maggie burned to know what heinous thing Wilson did to get himself kicked off *Bluefish*, but unfortunately, no one felt the need to give her that novel.

"Yes, sir. I guess he did." Benji sighed. "Do you want me to write him up for missing ship's movement, Captain?"

Coleman shook his head. "Nah. Let's drop Shore Patrol a line to see if they picked him up. A little birdie told me he's got a longstanding relationship with them."

"I'll do that, sir."

Maggie tried not to cringe. Poor Benji looked like he wanted to sink through the deck plates and drown, but she had her own problems—and thankfully, STS1 Wilson wasn't one of them.

Fletcher left Naples within three days—two nights—of arriving. *Lex-*

ington and the rest of the strike group stayed in port, but Nancy's ship received an urgent reassignment and tore out of the Mediterranean as soon as supplies and fuel were loaded.

Nancy didn't mind being freed from carrier escort duty, though screaming across the sea with only her helicopters for company was a bit nerve-racking. So far, the Med wasn't an active war zone, but that changed the moment *Fletcher* exited the Suez Canal and entered the Red Sea.

Mindful of the little voice in the back of her head—one that sounded a lot like her husband—Nancy kept submarine threats on the forefront of her mind when she sat down with her senior officers to update their transit plan.

Fletcher had steamed into the Red Sea two hours earlier. Nancy could be reasonably certain no submarine would throw torpedoes around here, at least because they might hit ships from their own side. So she gathered her top tacticians in the destroyer's wardroom for a brain trust while *Fletcher* turned and burned south toward the Indian Ocean.

"Pulsar Power swears the dampers will blank out own ship noises up to thirty-five knots," Lieutenant Commander David Attar, *Fletcher's* combat systems officer, said.

He was a dark-skinned man whose Indian ancestry was carefully *not* remarked upon by most of the crew; Attar's family immigrated to the U.S. decades ago, but he was still sensitive about having distant relatives on the other side of a world war. Nancy kept an eye on him, not because she didn't trust him, but because she *did* and wanted to make sure he was okay. "Supposedly, we can hear whatever's out there no matter how fast we're going."

Lieutenant Viola Hawkins, her operations officer, snorted. "Yeah, but we all saw how well that worked out in the SOM."

Viola was David's physical opposite, pale and barrel shaped where he was dark and thin. Yet they were close friends, even though David was measured and cool while Viola was brash and loud.

"The tail *should* counter that." David shrugged. "We haven't had it long enough to know for sure, though."

"And I'm not exactly a fan of trusting pre-war guesses at the rate those houses of cards are falling down, either." Nancy smiled thinly. "I'd like options, folks. Short of playing it like a submarine and sprinting and drifting to open up our contact picture, I'm out of ideas how not to T-bone ourselves on a torpedo we never saw coming."

Ying Mai grimaced. "I'm with you there, Captain. I'd rather not be this war's *Indianapolis*."

"You had to go and bring up sharks?" Viola shuddered.

"I think the only other option is to go active, ma'am," David said. "Of course, any subs will hear us coming, but if we're racing around at thirty-five knots, they'll hear us, anyway."

"But will active sonar do us any good?" Ying rubbed her face. "At speed, we're likely to get garbled results."

"Why not sprint and drift? Maybe the sub guys are onto something." Viola cocked her head. "But don't tell any of them I said that."

"I'll try to keep it out of my next email to my husband." Nancy tapped her fingers on the wardroom table, thinking. "I know it's not a standard surface tactic, because we have *eyes,* and radar's a thing, but since our primary threat is subs..."

David cocked his head. "I think it would work. Depending on passive sonar conditions, we could sprint at top speed for three hours, drift for fifteen minutes to get a good picture, and then sprint for several hours more. Our average speed would still be almost thirty-seven knots."

"Why drift?" Viola asked. "Why not steam at five knots or so?"

Nancy shook her head. "Screws turning get us heard. But coasting down from forty knots will keep our speed through the water up and the tail extended without creating own ship's noise."

"And it gives us a chance at detecting any enemy without them hearing us." Ying grinned.

"All right. It's time to use submariners' tricks against them."

When Benji stubbornly stayed in submarines after the war started, he never expected to be assigned to a boat like *Jimmy Carter*. His initial reaction to the assignment was the same disappointment Maggie was unable, or maybe unwilling, to conceal. Contrary to what he told his fellow department heads, Benji *did* make that angry phone call home—but not to his father.

No, he called his mother, whose favorite uncle was the secretary of the navy. While she didn't quite admit to asking Uncle Gerald to transfer "her darling boy" someplace safe, she didn't deny it, either. Nor would she change her mind. By the time Benjamin Senior got involved, Benji had been on board *Jimmy Carter* long enough that he didn't want to leave.

Jimmy Carter was old, but he knew they'd make a difference.

His political-minded and ambitious father wasn't comfortable with the appearance of keeping his only son out of the line of fire, but Benji was sick of *anyone* pulling strings. He was assigned to *Jimmy Carter*; on *Jimmy Carter* he'd stay.

Besides, even if the XO was an overly enthusiastic administrator, Commander Coleman was a *leader*. Lord only knew who he'd pissed off to get assigned to *Jimmy Carter*—Benji knew politics well enough to know the captain was in someone's doghouse—but only eight days into deployment, Benji couldn't imagine going to war under anyone else.

"I knew this guy was a problem child when we got him from *Bluefish*, Captain, but I never imagined he'd get to work so damn quickly," Master Chief Morton said as the three of them climbed into *Jimmy Carter's* duty van after a long walk down the pier.

Technically, the van was only theirs for another hour or so—then it reverted to the squadron and would go to the next boat that rolled through Pearl on their way to somewhere else. But the keys were still in the ignition, and the van was in better shape than the interior of their boat. The sleek, white Ford van even *smelled* new, but then, who kept a thirty-plus-year-old car if it wasn't a collector's item?

That was a great spin. Benji was going to war in a collector's item. Maybe he could sell it to his dad that way. Benji had to hide his smile; laughing while chasing down his miscreant sailor was *not* a good move. Not if he didn't want his captain to hate him.

Coleman slouched in the passenger seat. "I don't think I can hold this against you, Master Chief. The kid's been on board less than seventy-two hours." He glanced over his shoulder to where Angler sat in the back. "Same goes for you, Weps. Wilson might be your problem now, but I think we can leave most of the blame with *Bluefish* today."

"Thanks, Captain." Benji tried to hide his knees went numb with relief. "I still can't believe he tried to fingerpaint with wine. *Expensive* wine, too! Like, stuff my mother wouldn't turn her nose up at, and that's saying something."

"At least he paid for the wine." The captain shrugged, making Morton laugh. "Even if he smashed five bottles of it against the wall in the name of making art."

Wilson was hardly *Jimmy Carter's* first liberty incident in Pearl, but so far, Commander Coleman had taken the crew's shenanigans in stride. Benji knew some COs struggled to keep their people in check, but *Jimmy Carter's* captain was a realist.

There was a war on. Pearl was the last friendly port of call most subs hit before going into the war zone. Stressed young sailors needed to drain tension off somehow. As long as they didn't hurt anyone or destroy property without paying for it, Commander Coleman didn't seem inclined to hammer anyone for getting rowdy out in town.

Wilson's antics might just change that. For everyone.

Benji tried not to groan.

Getting to the base brig didn't take long, although finding a parking spot was a challenge. The building was in typical Pearl Harbor beige with a slanted blue roof; under normal circumstances, Benji would've said it was too pretty to be the brig. But the sign up front made it clear that this was where the masters-at-arms hung out—and he got to look at that sign twice more while Master Chief Morton circled, looking for parking.

"They're busy today," Coleman said as Master Chief Morton gave up and dropped the two officers off by the front door.

"Have you been here before, sir?" Benji had no frame of comparison. For all he knew, the brig looked like this all the time.

"Nope." Coleman smiled before his expression darkened. "I'm not real familiar with navy brigs, though Wilson's not the first sailor I've bailed out."

"That sounds like a story." Benji was relieved that Commander Coleman wasn't the type to rip his head off, but Wilson was still *his* sailor, his problem. His captain coming along for the ride only made things more humiliating.

Coleman frowned. "Maybe another time."

There was a line. Once Benji and his captain were inside, they had to join the queue behind several chiefs and a handful of masters-at-arms. Off to the right, he could see where Shore Patrol hung out between patrols; there was a group there on break, paying no attention to the growing line for the brig.

Several minutes passed. By the time they reached the front of the line, Master Chief Morton still hadn't returned from his parking search. Benji wanted to laugh. Wasn't that the story of navy life? There was a war on, and they were still worried about sailors parking outside their assigned spots. Finally, they reached the front desk. Its gray metal top looked like it had seen better days, with several dents that the computer monitor and keyboard were artfully arrayed around.

A very bored-looking yeoman second class sat behind the monitor, her eyes on the screen in the perpetual blank fuzz of someone who spent too long staring at names. Her nametape read "Bright."

"Can I help you?" she drawled, not bothering to look up.

He glanced Coleman's way, but the captain seemed absorbed in checking an email on his phone. "Lieutenant Angler, Weps on *Jimmy Carter*," he said. "I'm here for STS1 Wilson. We're kind of in a hurry, so..."

She still looked bored. "First name?"

"Uh..." *Shit.* He flushed. Unlike his father, Benji was terrible with names. Although he worked hard to get to know every sailor in his department, Wilson was brand new.

"Nathan. Goes by Bud," Coleman said, putting his phone away.

Bright typed the name into her computer. She made a face but still didn't look up.

"This is the second time STS1 has been here this *week*. We sent him back in a courtesy turnover the *first* time—for second offenses, we require a detailed plan from the sailor's command, describing liberty policies, punishment, and—"

"Excuse me," Commander Coleman cut in mildly.

Bright continued right over his interruption, rolling her eyes. "*Our* command policies require a memorandum of understanding signifying that the sailor's command is responsible for ensuring the sailor pays for all damages. Additionally, we need a custody agreement signed by your CO, which will undoubtedly take several hours."

"Fine," Coleman said when she paused for breath. "Where do I sign?"

"Excuse me?" Her head finally came up.

"Alex Coleman, *Jimmy Carter.*" The captain flashed a smile that wasn't friendly at all.

Bright jerked upright in her chair like someone had slapped her. "How can I help you, sir?"

She knows that word after all. What a surprise. Benji suppressed a smile as his captain replied:

"Give me whatever you need signed, and I'll sign it. Petty Officer Wilson is my responsibility, but I'm not going to stand here detailing my command's policies for your amusement. If your OIC has a problem with that, he's free to call me."

"Yes, sir." Suddenly, Bright sounded meek. The officer in charge of the brig was a lieutenant commander, and no way was he going to call the CO of a submarine to argue.

"Now hand me the paperwork, YN2, and fetch my miscreant sailor. You're all that's between my boat and getting underway, and I'm sure you have better things to do than add additional paperwork to my day."

"Yes, sir," she repeated, gesturing desperately to one of the masters-at-arms as she handed the electronic "papers" over. Benji just watched with interest.

Coleman's annoyance was obvious as he scrawled his signature in the six required places, which probably explained why the masters-at-arms returned so quickly with Wilson in tow. Unfortunately, Wilson looked right at home between them, and he smiled cheerfully at the yeoman behind the desk.

"Mornin', Bright Light. Long time no see." His cheeky chirp earned a scowl in return, but Benji didn't feel sorry for Bright. Nicer people than her had to deal with Wilson every day. Then Bright glared meaningfully toward the pair of officers, making Wilson follow her gaze.

The misbehaving sonar tech had the grace to look abashed, particularly once he spotted the captain. Then his gaze flickered over to Angler nervously. Damn, the kid looked young. Benji did a check-in interview with Wilson the day he arrived, but now Wilson's age really sank in. He must have been one of the rare enlisted sailors who made each rank on the first try—and some of them twice, given what Benji remembered about his disciplinary record.

Wilson had been "busted" down a rank at least once. Benji figured today would make twice; he'd be a petty officer second class before sunset. Particularly given how annoyed the captain seemed.

Master Chief Morton arrived just as the captain signed the last piece of paperwork. He and Coleman exchanged an unreadable look while Wilson shifted anxiously, but neither seemed concerned with how nervous they made the young petty officer. Finally, the COB filled the silence.

"You and me are gonna be spending some good quality time together, boy-o." Morton stepped forward to take Wilson by the arm.

"I'll, um, uh, look forward to that, Master Chief."

"Save me the sarcasm, STS1," Morton retorted. "You're in so deep that you're gonna need a lifeguard to pull you out this time."

Under other circumstances, Wilson's panache would impress Benji. Wilson even kept his smile in place. "Good thing I can swim."

Damn, the kid had balls. Benji could see why *Bluefish* traded him away.

Morton scowled. "Shut your trap, Wilson, unless you want me to shove my boot so far up your ass that you're tastin' leather and using boot black for toothpaste."

Wilson chewed his lip, shoulders rolled, but his embarrassment didn't last long. Would it ever? He did keep his mouth shut while Morton led the small group into the bright Hawaii sunshine. It was a hell of an innocent-looking day to go to war. It was also way too nice out to nail Wilson to the wall, but the sonar tech had brought it down upon himself.

"Should I go grab the car, Captain?" Benji asked, figuring that Morton had his hands full with Wilson.

"No, I think Master Chief can handle that," Coleman replied, checking his phone once more. "The boat's setting the Maneuvering Watch again, so we've got a few minutes. You have anything you want to say to your miscreant sailor, Weps?"

Benji blinked, but Morton headed out to the car without protest. What *should* a department head say in a situation like this? This was his first major disciplinary incident. He swallowed. "Nothing that can't wait for Captain's Mast."

Coleman shook his head. "Oh, I'm not taking STS1 Wilson to Mast."

Benji watched Wilson's head snap around in shock.

"You want to leave him with the SUBRON, sir?" Benji asked, trying to think about how they'd convince the squadron to accept a troublesome sailor on such short notice. And how would his department manage with one less sonar watchstander when they were already undermanned?

"Nope."

Another moment of silence passed; Wilson's eyes grew to the size of monster truck hubcaps. Coleman, however, shoved his hands in his pockets and smiled.

"Captain?" Wilson finally squeaked.

"I'm a big believer in second chances, STS1," Coleman said. "I've been the recipient of a few myself. But I *don't* put much stock into third chances. You understand what I'm saying?"

"Yes, sir." Wilson's eyes gleamed. He knew he'd gotten off easy, and—

"I'm not dismissing your case, STS1." Coleman's voice was suddenly hard. "And if you think I won't hammer the ever-living shit out of you at Mast, you need to pull your head out of your fourth point of contact in a big hurry. *But* I'll give you a chance to unfuck yourself and sit on this until you've been on board for longer than thirty-five seconds. You've got one hell of an uphill climb ahead of you, though, and you'd better be the best sonar tech in the entire goddamned navy if you don't want to go shopping for a new profession.

"I get the sneaking suspicion that you stayed in the navy with a war on because you might actually give a damn beneath that cool kid, troublemaker persona. So here's your chance. Fish or cut bait."

Wilson swallowed. Fidgeted. Stayed quiet. And he still hadn't answered when Morton pulled the car up.

"You're on the Maneuvering Watch, Wilson," Coleman added as he slid into the front seat. "So I hope you're not too hung over. I'd hate to run into another submarine because your head is pounding louder than the ambient noise level outside the boat."

Wilson blanched.

Chapter 19

First Shot

22 September 2038, the Pacific Ocean, outbound Pearl Harbor

Jimmy Carter hooked up with Convoy 3211 shortly after four that afternoon. The excitement of being in the open ocean during wartime wore off a few hours after that.

As the only sub assigned to a twelve-ship convoy, *Jimmy Carter* spent most of her time racing back and forth to sterilize different areas ahead of the rest of the ships…and checking out every visual contact a civilian could imagine was a periscope. Most of them turned out to be waves, but one was an abandoned, half sunken, small boat bobbing like a child's toy in the ocean. Alex marked that one as a hazard to navigation on the chart and moved on with life.

Like many other convoys *Jimmy Carter* would escort over the following months, these giant merchants were stuffed with medical supplies, foodstuffs, and military equipment destined for Alliance forces based in Perth, Australia. Most came from the U.S., where industry was ramping up to meet wartime demands, but a few came from the U.K. All flew flags of convenience; unlike the previous world war, when the United States had a huge and proud merchant fleet of her own, now American-flagged merchant ships were few and far between.

Common sense said flying flags of neutral countries *should* protect those ships. Experience now said it wouldn't, not an enemy could positively identify what they carried and where it was going.

The aggregate value of the cargo was about sixty-five million dollars. When you added in the replacement value of the ships, it skyrocketed to over eight *hundred* million. And then the total value of the entire convoy jumped up to almost five-point-three *billion* dollars if the original cost of the escort ships were included. *Jimmy Carter* accounted for three billion dollars of that price tag by herself, but Alex doubted his boat was still worth half that. After all, if the war hadn't cropped up, she'd be in pieces.

Even the highest-quality razorblades didn't cost that much.

At least Alex felt like a real sub commander out on patrol rather than a glorified museum keeper. Unfortunately, *real* submarine COs seemed to spend a lot of time being bored.

The rush to get his boat ready for sea left Alex expecting something exciting. The walls of *Jimmy Carter's* common areas were full of mementoes from places her previous sailors couldn't admit they'd been, keepsakes of missions that "never" happened. His boat had a history of excellence, and he ached to add to that legacy. The navy, however, seemed to have other plans.

None of them fit in with Alex's desire to make a difference.

"Have a moment, Captain?" George stuck his head in Alex's stateroom through the open door on the second day of the convoy escort.

"I've always got time for you, XO." Alex hoped George would calm down, but being underway seemed to make him *more* nervous rather than less. Rumor said the XO had a habit of popping up in control at odd hours, just to watch the team at work, and while Alex admired the dedication, he also wanted George to sleep.

The circles under his XO's eyes told him that George was already trying to juggle too much and watch everything.

"I sent the requested information to SUBRON Two-Nine. The chief of staff requested a copy of our watch team replacement plan, so I sent him that, too." George's smile was finally natural. "He told me there's a lot of boats light on crew, so if they do decommission us, everyone will have a spot."

"That's a big *if*, George." Alex's throat went tight with fear, but he forced the words out. "The navy needs every boat we can get."

"Sure, but we both know how old *Jimmy Carter* is. Half the operating systems are on versions of Windows no longer supported by anyone, and the other half have been upgraded so they're no longer compatible. It took hours to get the nav table working when it went down yesterday."

Alex's eyes narrowed. "You sound a touch eager to see this boat become razorblades, XO."

"I just wonder if it might not be a good idea. Safer." George shrugged. "Smarter use of resources."

"Don't say that to the crew," Alex said. "We're building a team here, and if they know you want to rip them apart, the whole thing will go to pieces."

"Sir, it's not that I *want* to. I just think Commodore Banks' idea has merit."

"Don't say that, either." He hated that he had to tell his XO this, but Alex could see the gleam in George's eyes. Decommissioning *Jimmy Carter* would be an administrative problem.

George knew what to do with administrative problems.

This war stuff, on the other hand... Alex shook himself.

"A crew is only as strong as its weakest link. You're the XO. You've got to be one of the strong ones," he said. "They have to trust you to *lead* them."

George licked his lips. "I know that."

"Good. Then you won't bring up the decomm idea again, and let me know if the chief of staff wants more information."

"Yes, sir." George's frown said he was unhappy, but sometimes, captains had to put down ultimatums.

29 September 2038, Washington, D.C.

Yet another day dawned in D.C., and politics came with it.

The capital was the one place that had changed the least, Freddie Hamilton mused as she sat in front of the senatorial panel for the Angler Hearings yet again. Or had it? Only half the politicians were grandstanding for the cameras. The other half seemed either terrified into silence—sometimes a bonus—or determined to actually *help*.

Granted, their idea of help was...skewed.

There had been a time when she dreamed of standing in front of Congress in her glittering uniform, of representing the naval service and talking them around to the things that the submarine community needed. In her daydreams, the Senate chamber had looked just like this, with the blue carpets and redwood desks and the viewing area above the chamber full of curious people. Reality turned out to be surprisingly close to her fantasies, with the chamber almost full.

But that was where the similarities stopped. As a naive young officer, Freddie hadn't understood how things worked in the halls of power. Change didn't happen on the Congress floor. It happened in back rooms, where deals were struck and alliances made.

Unfortunately, Freddie Hamilton was not important enough to strike deals with. She was here as either the subject matter expert or the scapegoat for the submarine community's failures. She had yet to figure out which.

"Admiral, what do you have to say to the fact that USS *North Dakota* was sunk just three days ago? That makes *sixteen* American submarines sunk since the onset of the war." Senator Angler spoke as much for the cameras as he did for her, with his hands folded in front of himself and his handsome face in profile.

Freddie wanted to punch him.

"Senator, every submarine lost is a tragedy, but we are at war." Vice Admiral Winifred Hamilton squared her shoulders and refused to be intimidated by the panel of sixteen senators glaring at her. "*North Dakota* was torpedoed defending Americans and American allies on Salt Station. Her crew performed admirably."

"But her captain did not?" Angler's perfectly sculpted eyebrows rose.

Freddie bit her tongue. How did he know that? She'd just viewed the VDR footage the night before, alone with her staff. Did she have a leak? There was no time to delve into that now...nor did she have the patience to deal with Angler's political maneuvering. She would not let him use the deaths of good submariners to further his agenda.

"Unfortunately, Commander Raine performed below expectations." Freddie folded her hands and took a deep, calming breath. "We are six months into war. I will not deny that the demands of combat have revealed weaknesses in our pre-war training pipelines. My team is working to address those, but we cannot affect change overnight. Commander Raine had an adequate record on *North Dakota* prior to her sinking. He did well escorting convoys and in strike group operations. Unfortunately, he was not suited to independent command."

"So you admit that Admiral Trieu's methods of selecting commanding officers was flawed?" another senator asked.

"Senator, I cannot speak for Admiral Trieu. He is no longer here, and I did not work on his team," Freddie replied. "However, if you study history, you will find that this 'captain problem' is not unique. We experienced it in the previous world war, and I suspect our allies and our enemies are in similar situations. Peacetime performance is a poor predictor of wartime competence."

The senators murmured amongst themselves. It was clear they hadn't expected Freddie to *admit* to the problem. But she wasn't done. Freddie squared her shoulders and continued:

"Two-thirds of our sub losses can be traced back to their commanding officers. Commanders who looked like talented tacticians on paper or in exercises have proven otherwise during combat operations, and the excellent administrators that a peacetime navy promotes are frequently inflexible warfighters. And when those captains fail, they take an entire submarine *and* her highly trained crew with them. Of the sixteen boats lost, we have only recovered survivors from five."

More murmuring. Finally, Senator Angler—paler now, having done the math and thought about his son on a submarine—asked: "What are we *doing* to combat this, Admiral?"

"My first action upon assuming duties as SUBFOR was to empower submarine squadron commanders to relieve any commanding officer who they feel is unequal to the task. This is a no-fault relief; those officers can continue to serve in another capacity. Secondly, we have already enhanced training at the Submarine School for prospective commanding officers, executive officers, and department heads, adding more combat drills and stressful situations." Freddie smiled sadly. "But the reality is that we're only six months into the war. We haven't yet cracked the code on what *works*; we only know what doesn't. We're still operating on assumptions."

"Assumptions get people killed, Admiral."

"Yes, sir, they do. But finding good captains is not an exact science. There are too many intangibles. We never know if they'll handle the pressure until they're in the seat. We can provide them with excellent training, lessons learned, and the most skilled crews in the world, but in the end, it still comes down to the captain."

Angler's eyes narrowed. "That sounds like an excuse."

"No, sir, it is a fact. We are not the navy we thought we were pre-war." Freddie met Angler's angry eyes. "We will fix that. However, it will take time."

"Admirals don't always admit when the navy is failing." Angler sat back and crossed his arms. "I appreciate the honesty, but I would like to see your plans to fix the problems."

"You will have them as soon as they are drafted."

Angler exchanged glances with two other senators as Freddie fought back the urge to slump in exhaustion. She felt charbroiled, but this was part of her job.

The job she'd held for all of twenty-nine days.

Sometimes, she understood why Vice Admiral Trieu felt so defeated.

Twelve ships steamed quietly toward Australia at twenty-two knots. Wartime hadn't changed fuel consumption curves, and with much of the world's oil allied with the Freedom Union, *not* running engines at full speed was even more important than ever. Twenty-two knots was the most efficient speed for the majority of the convoy ships, so at twenty-two knots they stayed. For merchant ships, changing speed meant a watch change and major engine changes, not pushing a button like it did for a warship.

When the convoy commander, the captain of USS *Spruance*, expressed a desire to speed up, the senior merchant captain on board M/V *Tropical Express* told him to pound sand. And that was that. *Tropical Express* was owned by Hopkins-Llyod, a German shipping company—and thereby neutral; *Tropical Express* moved cargo for both sides—and her master was not going to waste gas because some brash young navy CO said so. Particularly without a threat out and about.

Burning extra fuel meant money, and even with a war on, shipping companies watched the bottom line. *Particularly* with submarines out to sink even neutral ships. Hopkins-Llyod had good insurance, but there was no reason to be stupid, *Tropical Express's* master said.

Spruance's captain grumbled and pretended it was his idea.

Midway between Hawaii and Australia, STS1 Wilson proved that he sure could *talk* like a real sonar tech. His voice echoed out of the speaker in control, crisp and confident:

"Conn, Sonar, got a group of high-speed surface contacts on the tail and the port side lateral array. Best guess on range is fifty-something thousand yards, inbound at...I think thirty-plus knots. Recommend coming left to resolve bearing ambiguity."

"What's the system answer?" the OOD asked.

That made Alex glance up, the navigation plan he and Maggie were reviewing forgotten. But he stayed silent, watching his team. Lieutenant (junior grade) Alvaro had the deck. She stood in the center of control, relaxed and confident, surrounded by a good team who knew their business. Elena Alvaro was the best of his division officers and never needed micromanaging—a point he was still trying to drive into George Kirkland's thick skull.

"Conn, Sonar, it's got no idea, ma'am." Wilson's drawl turned casual. "This new software's not so great at marrying up a strong signal with a faint one, and the lateral array is a hell of a lot older than the tail. But it sounds like several multi-screwed ships to me, and Doppler says they're inbound. I'm betting warships."

Alvaro glanced at Alex. "Are you good with the course change, Captain? We're still ahead of the convoy. It won't take us off station."

Alex's eyes flicked to the plot. "Do it."

Wilson could be wrong; a group of ships together weren't necessarily warships. Before the war, merchant ships didn't travel in company, but maybe commerce raiding was changing things. Sonar *could've* detected a group of oilers, but they didn't pay Alex to take chances. Besides, merchant ships were usually single screwed; it was cheaper. Warship designers liked multiple screws for maximum maneuverability.

Alex wasn't worried yet. They had time; the surface search radars of the surface escorts couldn't see the incoming contacts yet. Even in excellent weather, the average surface search radar didn't detect contacts at much past twenty-five miles, and *Jimmy Carter* was almost seven miles ahead of Convoy 3211. Wilson's targets were out of their range.

Jimmy Carter turned smartly, coming to the new course, and Alex finished his chart check as they waited for the towed sonar array, or tail, to settle out and regain contact.

"Conn, Sonar, it looks like we might have something here." Ensign Vincentelli, the sonar division officer, made the report this time.

"Looks, hell!" Wilson interjected before the OOD could reply. "It's two or three warships, with Prairie and Masker energized but going too fast for it to disguise their screw noise. Blade count is military, bearing is zero-seven-eight, range firming up around fifty-two thousand yards. We're getting some narrowband sound, too. I can't tell what it is, but the computer is chewing on it."

Wilson sure sounded like he knew what he was talking about, but could Alex trust him? He *talked* like a rock star, like the best of sonar techs whose ears and brain could beat the computer to the right answers. The other option was Vincentelli's caution, and Vincentelli was so new he squeaked. The kid graduated from Sub School less than a month before *Jimmy Carter* left Bangor.

But they were at war. The *cautious* option wasn't always safe. Besides, the hairs on the back of Alex's neck were standing up.

"Let's go to battle stations," he told Alvaro, pleased with how normal his voice sounded. Just giving the order was enough to make his heart race.

Alvaro's eyes went wide; she bounced on her toes. "Yes, sir! Chief of the Watch, battle stations!"

"Chief of the Watch, aye." *Jimmy Carter's* crew was full of junior sailors filling positions normally belonging to senior people. This "chief" of the watch was a fire control technician first class who qualified for the watch on the transit to Pearl. Still, FT1 Iceni didn't betray his inexperience until the last sentence:

"Man Battle Stations, Torpedo." The general alarm donged. "Man Battle Stations, Torpedo. And this is no drill!"

Alex cringed but said nothing. He had better things to do than chase Iceni's breach of procedure.

His heart pounded in his ears; Alex focused on controlling his breathing. Here they were, finally in combat, finally about to make a difference.

And it was all on him.

"Was that really necessary, Petty Officer Iceni?" George stalked toward the chief of the watch, who still had the 1MC microphone in his hand and froze like a deer caught in the headlights.

The young sailor flushed as red as his hair. "I just wanted everyone to know..."

"I'm certain that the crew is aware that we are both at war and escorting a convoy under combat conditions." George folded his hands behind his back, warming up for one of his favorite lectures. "Had we been in a training environment, there would have been a reason to clarify the situation, but since we clearly were *not*, there was no reason to pass extraneous words over the 1MC. Correct?"

"Yes, sir." Iceni swallowed.

The XO's frown deepened. "In fact, I think a thorough review of standard procedures for *all* chiefs of the watch is due. I've noticed several gaffs since we got underway."

Not this again. Alex cleared his throat, hoping to get George's attention without cutting his legs out from under him, but Kirkland continued:

"You'd be an excellent choice to hold that training, FT1. I want to see the outline of your presentation by—"

"Excuse me, XO, but I need to take the watch from FT1 Iceni."

Alex had been about to interrupt, but someone else beat him to it. Chief Pamela Hill, the chief of the watch assigned to the battle stations watchbill, moved to stand diffidently by the XO's side, her expression blasé.

"You—" George started, glancing around the space and finally realizing that every watch stander aside from Iceni had completed their turnover and manned their own battle stations. Iceni kept fidgeting and sending wide-eyed *help me* looks at Chief Hill. The chief, however, kept her eyes on the XO. George finally nodded. "Of course."

Well done, Chief. Alex watched for a moment to make sure that George headed toward his own station with the fire control party and then turned to Maggie, who was now the officer of the deck.

"You send off the initial contact report?" he asked, wishing his XO required as little supervision as the navigator.

"Yes, sir." She smiled. "The watch on *Spruance* seemed pretty excited."

Alex tried not to frown. The navy was still reeling from one hell of a bloody nose, or maybe a series of them. Everyone wanted to get some of their own back. Alex wasn't immune to the feeling—he'd lost numerous acquaintances and a few friends to the war already, and his *wife* was out here being shot at, too—but being *too* eager would get people killed.

Still, striking back at the enemy would be nice. The Freedom Union had free rein of the Pacific and Indian Oceans for too long already.

"Damn straight they are," someone muttered from the weapons corner.

George frowned, his brow creasing as he crossed his arms. Alex ignored the comment. Instead, he moved over to the speaker box that communicated with *Jimmy Carter's* other major watch stations, thumbing the key. "Sonar, Conn, what've you got?"

"Firming up now, Captain," Wilson replied. "Computer's ninety percent solution says we're looking at three French warships, one definite *Talisman*-class DDG from a narrowband match on tonals, a probable Fremm-type ASW frigate, and a possible *La Fayette*-class frigate." The sonar tech paused before adding, "I think the computer is right on the first two and dead wrong on the third. I've got a tick on the forty-five Hertz line and the *La Fayettes* don't have equipment operating on that freq."

Click. Abruptly, Wilson stopped speaking, but Alex could still hear voices murmuring from the sonar room. Cocking his head, he wandered aft to stick his head through the partially open door.

Ensign Vincentelli stood towering over where Wilson still hunched over a sonar console. "This isn't the time for one of your damn games, Wilson!" Vincentelli snarled. "I know you like to screw with the younger sonar techs, but dicking around with real world contact reports under combat conditions just so you can pretend you're smarter than the computer is—"

"Sir, I'm not stupid." Wilson leaned back and cut him off. "But this software upgrade ain't all that and a bag of chips, either. It's designed for the *Ceroes* and doesn't work so well with our hardware. I'm *not* wrong, sir. The *Talisman* destroyers have an air compressor that operates at forty-five Hertz—see that on the first contact?" His finger jammed into the top screen. "I think tracks 7034 and 7036 are both *Talismans*. Even if I'm wrong, it's better to overestimate them, anyway."

"But why would the computer be wrong?" Vincentelli's shoulders slumped, and Alex repressed a smile. Junior officers were taught to trust their systems. Eventually, they gained the experience to know when not to.

"Probably because the guys who wrote the software were in a hurry, and we're the only *Seawolf* left in service. It worked great on *Bluefish*, most of the time. It's better than what it replaced, sir, but it's still kind of a mess sometimes."

"You sound pretty confident, Wilson." Alex spoke up before anyone in sonar noticed him.

Every sailor in the space jumped, but none so high as Vincentelli and Wilson. The chronic drunk hit his knees on the bottom of the console and swore. "Yes, sir."

Alex considered the situation for about two seconds. Right or wrong, Wilson had a point. Erring on the side of caution was safer than the alternative. *Talisman*-class destroyers were more capable than the *La Fayettes*, and not only because the frigates were built in the early 2000s. The new destroyer class carried more missiles, more depth charges, and was a better sub hunter. Besides, sonar was still considered something of a black art, even in a navy that should know better.

"It sounds like a plan," he said. "Put the IDs in the system and punch the contacts out over Link to the escorts."

"You bet, Captain."

Alex headed back into control as Wilson went to work. A sub sharing real-time contacts with a surface ship was still kind of an alien concept, not to mention the number of tracks they received in return. Advances in undersea technology over the last decade allowed for increased communications to and from submarines, but Alex was one of the few COs who carefully monitored outward emissions.

Stealth was still the name of the game. Anything one warship put into the water, another warship could detect. But today, passing contact information to the escort ships was more important than escaping the slight chance of detection.

"Battle stations set, Captain," Chief Hill reported as he reentered the control room.

Alex blinked. "That took a while." *I can pull that string later.* He made himself shrug. "But I suppose we're in no hurry. Very well."

"What took so long?" George asked.

Jesus Christ, George, can you not take a hint?

Alex held up a hand. "Not now, XO."

He hated to contradict his second-in-command in front of the crew, but heading into combat wasn't the time to needle-dick things.

"Captain, I think—"

Alex shook his head. "We can deal with it later."

"Yes, sir." George frowned but shut up.

Man, having an XO who dealt with all problems right the hell away *should* be awesome, but George was on his last nerve. George's brain focused on events chronologically, instead of prioritizing by importance, and it made Alex want to bash his head into a wall. But now wasn't the time. He'd talk to George later, not in the middle of the first shooting incident of *Jimmy Carter's* long career.

"Why don't you head on over and see how the fire control party is doing?" he suggested.

"Right." Fists clenched, George stalked over to join Angler's team.

No one in the space met his eyes. *Jimmy Carter's* watch team did an admirable job of pretending they couldn't hear the tense exchange between their captain and XO, but control wasn't a big enough shoebox for anyone to miss it.

Moments ticked by, and then *Jimmy Carter* finally received orders to close with the enemy.

Electricity crackled in the air as soon as the radio watch passed the order along. Most of the crew, like Alex, had never seen combat. Wilson was probably the only person who'd ever been on a war patrol, and *Bluefish's* record wasn't exactly worth writing songs about. Even Wilson didn't wear the coveted submarine war patrol pin on the left side of his chest.

Alex's heart raced, but he shoved his excitement down. *Time to act like you're a real navy CO,* he told himself. Admiral Hamilton might've sent him here because he disobeyed orders and no amount of later good could erase that incident on *Kansas*, but he was all

Jimmy Carter had.

Squaring his shoulders, Alex reached for the 1MC. God, he hated public speaking. No matter how many times he rehearsed the words in his head, he felt stupid. But at least he didn't mumble. He conquered *that* problem back in college.

"Smiley, this is the captain." He paused, wondering if that was a foolish opening. *Of course it's the captain, you moron. They all know your voice.* But at least *Jimmy Carter* had a cool nickname? With an effort, Alex slapped the doubts aside. "We've detected three surface contacts on sonar that appear to be French warships heading toward the convoy. So we're closing to investigate."

Another deep breath. Should he try to say something motivational? He already forgot almost everything he rehearsed in his head.

"Anything can happen from here on out, so keep your eyes and ears open. We've trained for this, and I know you'll do fine."

Now hang up the mic before you sound like more of an assclown than you already have. Alex replaced the handset, almost missing its holder in his haste. A nervous laugh bubbled up, and he swallowed it with an effort. Combat didn't frighten him—not after being shot at on Armistice Station, which was one thousand percent worse than this—but talking to his own crew tied his stomach into knots. What kind of screwed-up idiot was he?

Maybe Admiral Hamilton was right. Maybe he didn't belong here.

Or maybe she wasn't.

Screw her.

"Okay, Maggie." Alex straightened, stuffing his hands into his pockets. "Let's catch these guys with a purpose. Give me an approach offset by thirty degrees and at…let's say twenty-eight knots."

The book mandated a slower and more cautious approach, and George frowned. "Captain, the probability of detection at twenty-eight knots is—"

"Negligible when they're moving at that speed," Alex cut him off, his nerves forgotten now that he had a problem to solve. "We'll slow before we turn toward the enemy."

The enemy. Just saying those words sent a chill racing down his spine. *And I thought convoy duty would be boring.*

"Yes, sir." George pursed his lips, then slinked off to stand by the sonar room door, looking no one in the eye.

Maggie ordered *Jimmy Carter* onto the new course, turning the sub's bow past the enemy's line of approach and bringing the starboard side sonar arrays into contact. Technically, approaching faster than his boat's rated silent speed was a risk, but Alex knew the

French warships' own speed would mask *Jimmy Carter's* noise. He'd slow before firing. The gamble was worth it.

The range spiraled downward quickly. Alex kept his eyes on the plot, waiting for the distance between his submarine and the French warships to drop to less than fifteen nautical miles. It didn't take long.

Time to dance.

"Firing point procedures: tubes one and two, track 7034." Alex forced himself to take a deep breath. *Get it right or don't do it at all.* "Tubes three and four, track 7035. Tubes five and six, track 7036."

He wished Benji didn't sound so surprised when he acknowledged the orders, but at least his voice was level. "Firing point procedures: tubes one and two, track 7034; tubes three and four, track 7035; tubes five and six, track 7036, Weps, aye."

In training, Alex always felt that the wait for the fire control team to work out a firing solution was interminable, but now his mind found a thousand and one other things to focus on. He was halfway through a mental progression of what-ifs, considering how *Jimmy Carter* should react to possible enemy actions, when Alex realized several minutes ticked by without the expected report from the fire control party.

Had he missed it? If so, George should've called him out. But, no—Angler and his team remained bent over their consoles, whispering furiously.

"What you got, Weps?" he asked.

It was George who answered. "We're refining the solutions, Captain."

Damn. That was slower than usual. *Much* slower than their drills. *Another thing to check on later.*

Alex chewed his lip. At least George wasn't admonishing Angler's team over something pointless, and they were still pretty far out from the enemy. Alex wasn't ready to shoot yet. He just had to be patient.

"Very well."

Another minute ticked by; they were in range. Alex glanced at Maggie. "Come left to your intercept course and slow to ten knots."

"Aye, sir." *Jimmy Carter* slowed noticeably, the slight tremor in her deck vanishing as she settled onto her new course and into textbook-perfect position to shoot. Again, Alex glanced toward the fire control party.

"Weps?"

A long moment of silence passed. "Solution ready."

Was he missing something? Alex turned in time to see Benji's shoot a mutinous glare at the XO.

"Ship ready." George's frown almost folded his face in half. Would he speak up if something was wrong? Undoubtedly. Alex burned to know what the hell drama was going on over there, but asking would only distract his team.

"Very well," Alex said. "Make tubes one through six ready in all respects, including opening the outer doors."

He didn't plan to fire all six torpedoes simultaneously, but the computer would continuously update the firing solutions once they were locked into the system. Angler acknowledged the order and a moment later reported:

"Tubes one through six ready in all respects. Outer doors are open. Firing key is red."

"Very well," Alex said.

Hot damn. It was time. Crossing the space, he reached for the firing key. It was a small plastic thing that looked like it was made by Fisher Price, but it was the most important thing on the boat. *And one of these puppies almost cost me my career back on* Kansas.

Firing keys were only placed in the firing system when you were ready to fire...or when the U.S. Navy was at war. The key was the final safety between the push of a button and armed torpedoes racing away from the submarine. Some COs kept the key in their possession and only inserted it when needed, but not Alex. Too much caution could get his sub killed as quickly as being too reckless. And he trusted his watchstanders.

A flick of his wrist turned the key, indicator lights shifting from red to green. "Key is green."

Jimmy Carter was ready to fire.

The speaker to his right crackled.

"Conn, Radio, we've got a no-fire order coming in from *Spruance*."

"Say again?" Alex gaped.

"Sir, we've verified it twice," the radio watch replied. "*Spruance* says that the surface ships are going to do a long-ranged Harpoon engagement. They want us to stay in stealth."

"Sonofabitch," he whispered.

Spruance was the senior ship, and her CO had every right to make that call. It wasn't even a *bad* order. But it should have been given long before *Jimmy Carter* worked her way in dangerously close to the enemy and was a hair's breadth away from opening fire.

Tightness gripped Alex's chest like a vise. If *Jimmy Carter* didn't get a chance, how was he supposed to prove to people like Commodore Banks that his boat could contribute to the war? Had *Spruance*'s captain decided to do a surface engagement because he thought *Jimmy Carter* was too old to do the job?

Alex shook himself and stepped on his disappointment. They'd barely entered the warzone. There would be other chances. He cleared his throat. "Conn, aye."

It was early in the war, Alex told himself. He said the same to his crew later. *Jimmy Carter* would have plenty of chances to prove herself, he promised as the sonar techs listened to French warships exploding. They had time.

Didn't they?

Chapter 20

Sprint and Drift

5 October 2038, Pacific Ocean, the approaches to Christmas Island (Australia)

The officer of the deck's voice crackled in Nancy's ear over the internal net: "All stop. Secure all main engines."

Nancy sat back in her command chair in CIC as the whine of *Fletcher's* four gas turbine engines spun down to silence. The stillness felt strange, even after sprinting and drifting their way through the Red Sea and halfway across the Indian Ocean. Speed and agility were life for a destroyer—particularly a lone destroyer without air cover or a submarine to protect her.

Nancy closed her eyes, wishing she could banish the burning fatigue. *Fletcher* had drifted for fifteen minutes every three hours, and she or Ying were stationed in the Combat Information Center every time. This was their best chance to hear an enemy submarine, not to mention their *only* chance to avoid getting their own asses shot off. But Nancy was so tired. She'd sprinted her ship all the way toward Diego Garcia, only to bypass the base—with barely a resupply via helicopter to say hello—to support a force gathering near Prince Edward Island.

Whatever brilliant planner assigned them that darling mission seemed to forget that Prince Edward Island was off the southwest tip of Africa. Like, *way* down there. Closer to Antarctica than anyone with a brain fought a battle. But they broke out the cold weather gear, inventoried to find the fifteen critical things *Fletcher* wasn't outfitted with when she was assigned a climate, *Mediterranean* deployment, and made the best of things.

Showing the flag would convince South Africa not to join the Freedom Union, the strategists said.

Sure.

A hundred miles out from Prince Edward Island—skipping distance for a destroyer traveling at thirty-seven knots—South Africa signed on with the enemy and Nancy's ship spun around for a new destination: Christmas Island.

But Christmas Island was thousands of miles north of Prince Edward Island, diagonally across the entire Indian Ocean. So off to the races *Fletcher* went, turning and burning through an ocean full of enemy submarines. Hopefully, they'd get to stay at their new destination for a few days. Nancy needed fuel, and her crew needed rest.

At least this island belonged to Australia. They could be reasonably sure *Australia* wouldn't change sides. Not after the blood America and Australia had already shed together.

The only good thing about the entire ridiculous transit was that her crew got to "cross the line" on the way down. Crossing the equator—not the norm for a ship based on the East Coast—was one of the navy's biggest rites of passage. *Fletcher* had been set to cross after transiting the Strait of Malacca the previous April. But that innocent passage turned into a shooting incident, and that turned into war...

Needless to say, Nancy's crew didn't get to become Shellbacks that day. Now, a year and a half later, when they finally crossed the line, Nancy's sailors went all out with the shenanigans and the ceremony.

Already a Trusty Shellback herself, Nancy was happy to sit back, laugh, and plot with the senior sailors on board to make the slimy wogs pay the price for crossing the line. It was a rare moment of levity in a war that left them all wondering when the next disaster would strike, and she could feel the pep in her crew's step afterward. It helped combat the fatigue a little, too, even if the adrenaline shot only lasted for a few days.

A week and a half after the fun ended, they finally entered the approaches to Christmas Island.

Nancy shivered and hunkered down in her chair, trying not to let her mind drift. Navy tradition said CIC had to be cold, dark, and quiet, but damn, she missed the warmer wind on the bridge. The weather was nice again now that they were back above the Tropic of Capricorn.

"TAO, Sonar, new contact bearing zero-one-five."

Nancy bolted upright in her seat, eyes flying open.

"TAO, aye," Lieutenant Viola Hawkins said from her right. "Submerged or surfaced?"

"Submerged, running quiet. Estimated range twenty-one thousand yards. Good bottom bounce contact," Chief Randstad replied from the sonar room further aft. "I've got 'em on the dome and the tail. Pushing to Aegis, now track 7098."

"Seven-zero-nine-eight, aye." Viola turned to her, speaking quietly. "You see this, Captain?"

"You bet I do." Tiredness forgotten, Nancy watched the track appear on the big screen Aegis display. It was the upside down "V" that represented a hostile submerged contact—a symbol she hadn't seen since those disastrous first moments in the Strait of Malacca.

The track blinked once and then turned red. "TAO, Sonar, tonals match an *Akula* III-class submarine, likely Indian."

Nancy stepped on her own microphone's foot pedal. "Sonar, Captain, what's his course and speed?"

"One-seven-five, speed fifteen. He's coming right for us, fat, dumb, and happy."

"Captain, aye." Nancy took a deep breath. She studied the contact again, thinking about what Alex told her. Conventional wisdom told her to close the range and prosecute, to launch her helicopter and hound this sub. What if she didn't need to?

"You want to start the engines and close the range, Captain?" Viola asked.

"Nope." Nancy shook her head. "I want to sit here and let this bastard come right into our laps."

"Winds are bad for launching a helo."

"But ASROC doesn't care about wind." Nancy grinned. "Let's firm up the contact and then drop a rocket-launched torpedo right on his head."

Viola laughed. "I am *so* here for that, ma'am."

"Yeah, it'd be nice to sink the right submarine for once." Nancy didn't like how quiet her voice got on that; she was glad *Fletcher* hadn't taken the shot that started the war, even if they'd been right behind *Belleau Wood* when the battle started. Captain Rosario rarely talked about how that made her feel, but Nancy could guess.

"Damn straight."

Nancy keyed her microphone again. "Officer of the Deck, Captain, sound general quarters."

"Officer of the Deck, aye!"

Nancy eyed the plot, wondering if that *Akula* had sunk any merchant ships today. Or yesterday. There were a few off to port, just out of *Fletcher's* visual range. Could the *Akula* think *Fletcher* was one of them?

"You think he's looking at AIS readouts?" Nancy asked as the general alarm donged through her destroyer's hull.

Viola blinked. "You think that's why he's headed for us? I mean, I know we're reporting a name that isn't ours and not much else, but that's what everyone around here is doing."

"We're the only one not traveling in company."

"Hm. I hadn't noticed that." Viola popped a piece of gum in her mouth; Nancy tried not to grimace. Alex loved the stuff, as well as candy and anything else that he could chew while he was thinking, and it drove her crazy. All that sugar was terrible for him, even if he had the metabolism of a dolphin.

"Makes us look like an easy target," Nancy said. "Except now he can't track us."

"He can probably dead reckon our course, though. Though he won't know where on it we are without going active."

"I'm not planning on giving him the time to make a bunch of guesses," Nancy replied. "Sonar, Captain, you have a solid track?"

"Yes, ma'am."

"TAO, Captain, kill track 7098 with ASROC." Nancy reached down with her left hand, turning the small plastic key in the console between herself and Viola. "FIS is green."

"TAO, aye, break, Subsurface, TAO, kill track 7098 with ASROC."

"Subsurface, aye. Killing track 7098 with ASROC."

Nancy's eyes flicked to the smaller screen above the large plot displays; it showed *Fletcher's* aft Vertical Launch System, or VLS, banks. All nine of the Anti-Submarine Surface Launched Rockets her destroyer carried were in the aft cells, awaiting commands from the Aegis weapons system to launch.

This command was accomplished in two key strikes from the subsurface warfare coordinator. Those transmitted the command to the aft VLS bank, where a hatch flipped open and the rocket boosters in the ASROC missile ignited. Moments later, the missile screamed into the sky, arcing brilliantly against the clouds.

The missile wouldn't kill a submerged submarine, of course. At its core, an ASROC was just a torpedo strapped onto a missile to give it longer range—and a much shorter flight time. The best torpedo in the American arsenal would take almost seven minutes to cross the twenty thousand yards between *Fletcher* and the *Akula*. An ASROC took fifty-three seconds...and the sub never heard it coming until it hit the water.

The torpedo dropped into the ocean less than a hundred yards in front of the Indian *Akula*, its screws already turning. With little time to react, the enemy captain did well, turning away from the threat and putting on speed—but all that did was let the torpedo hit her submarine broadside.

There were no survivors.

Razorback pulled into Perth, Australia, an hour before midnight, local time. John wasn't sure what they were trying to hide by having subs enter the harbor in the dark; the base was so well lit that it might as well have been daylight, with lights lining every pier and flooding them with florescent light. Further into the base, he spotted a few active missile defense batteries, and those were *also* well-lighted, almost as if the Alliance was asking someone to drop a bomb on them.

John shook his head. Any satellite worth the millions it cost to put in space had night vision, anyway. Maybe it wasn't worth trying to disguise anything. But then why bring submarines in at night? Thankfully, John was just a mere captain—and a submarine commander, *again!*—so it wasn't his problem.

Getting his boat tied up *was* his concern, but Patricia Abercrombie was so damned good at her job that John could just sit back and watch from the sail as she settled *Razorback* in. Why hadn't they just given her the boat when Commander Harney lost it? Sure, she was about as junior for the job as John was too senior, but she was clearly capable. It was another one of the navy's great mysteries, wrapped up in a war that was still so disorganized that John hadn't known what port he was returning to until halfway through the patrol.

He hadn't been to Perth, Australia, before. John was an East Coaster and spent his career in Groton, which usually meant he got deployed to the Persian Gulf. That didn't leave room for port visits in exciting places like Australia; instead, they got the Dubai-Bahrain-Rota route on most deployments, usually skipping Dubai because it was too much fun. John was excited to experience Perth, even with a war on.

John squinted. There was a thin figure waiting for them on

the pier, complete with nervous-looking aide. A surreptitious look through the binoculars pinpointed the stars on his visitor's shoulders, which could only mean one thing.

John Dalton and *Razorback* were important enough to make the commodore wait. Nice.

Razorback's third war patrol under John had the distinction of going better than her second, which had produced a big, fat goose egg in terms of results. But this time, intel proved good, sending John and his boat after a pair of Indian diesel subs busy hunting merchant ships in route to Australia. Sinking those was the easy part. The French frigate they caught between them was a little harder, but a patrol with three kills wasn't too bad.

John hurried down to meet his new boss as soon as the brow was across.

"Captain Dalton. I'm Commodore Banks." The man who greeted him with an outstretched hand was tall, with thinning brown hair and a rather pointed nose. He held himself ramrod straight, like he was terminally afraid of slouching, and his expression told John that he was a Very Important Person.

"It's a pleasure to meet you, sir." John saluted and put on his best kiss-ass smile. He'd learned to do that as a teenager. Any admiral's kid knew how to blow sunshine up someone's ass.

"I wanted to be the first to welcome you to Perth. *Razorback* will be a welcome addition to SUBRON Two Nine." Banks' smile seemed genuine enough, and his handshake was firm. Maybe John's snapshot assessment of him was wrong?

Probably not. John knew the type. This one had an ego that ballooned when all commodores—previously mere O-6 captains called "commodore" by courtesy because they commanded a submarine squadron—got an automatic promotion and swapped the eagles on their collars for stars.

Jaylen Banks was the sort to check for John's academy class ring, too. Not very subtle.

"Thank you, Commodore." John kept his smile in place and pretended he didn't want to crawl into bed. He was a creature of habit, and his sleep schedule would be sacred if he'd picked a more convenient line of work. *Stupid war getting in the way of my dream time.*

"I read your patrol report—thank you for sending it in on your way into port," Banks said. John made a mental note to thank Patricia for helping with the thing; patrol reports were old fashioned, but they beat answering forty-five emails about how things went. "Congratulations on your three kills. I'm impressed."

"I wish I was, sir. I'm not happy that we missed the two *Yasens*."

Banks cocked his head as a trio of *Razorback* sailors connected shore water to the submarine's topside hookup. "You don't think it was the same boat twice?"

"That'd be even worse. But their sonar signatures didn't line up, even if both outfoxed my torps in pretty much the same way." John scratched the back of his neck. "I would like to take a moment to highlight the point I made in my report: we need a change in tactics or weaponry if we're going to stand against enemy submarines that are faster than our torpedoes. Even with me sneaking in close, both *Yasens* were able to outrun my torps."

"Standard procedure says to fire from at least fifteen thousand yards." Banks pursed his lips. "I saw that you breached that and closed to ten."

"Sir, I didn't see another way to catch that second one, and it still didn't work." John wished he'd been ballsy enough to close to less than five nautical miles of the second Russian submarine, but he'd pulled the trigger too early.

For a submarine that couldn't see the enemy, five nautical miles *felt* close, but it really wasn't, was it? It was a hundred football fields. About seventy-six *Cero*-class boats stacked up end to end. Peacetime rules said getting too close to a potential enemy would be suicide, but getting his ass shot off by one would kill him just as quickly, wouldn't it? John grimaced.

"I'll pass your report along." Banks' eyes narrowed. "However, until procedures are changed, I would appreciate you following them."

"Sir, today the navy gave me a snowflake and ordered me to build a snowman. I can't kill enemy submarines if my torpedoes can't get there, and sooner or later, the Russians or French are going to figure that out and hammer us from outside our effective range."

"There's no evidence of that."

"Sir, I fear there won't *be* evidence because it's all on the ocean floor," John replied. He remembered the name of every lost submarine—eleven since last April, many of them commanded by friends.

Banks' frown was pointed enough to pop balloons. "That's quite enough, Captain. Your point is made."

"Any news on the rumors of those super-cavitating Russian torpedoes?" John asked instead of arguing. He knew having a silver star on his medal rack meant he had a lot more latitude than his fellows, but if he kept at this, he'd sink himself. Banks clearly didn't like his tactics, and calling him a conservative fool wouldn't help matters.

"Intel says they're still in prototype and failing." Banks' scowl now promised retribution.

Digging a hole would only lose him credibility, and Banks *had* promised to push his report upward. Annoying the man about the Russian's mythical three hundred–knot torpedo was probably not a good way to make friends.

John would just have to hope that someone with more stars on their collar would listen.

Preferably before America's slow torpedoes got more of his friends killed.

Chapter 21

Blood in the Water

13 October 2038, approaching Perth, Australia

Jimmy Carter was free of her first convoy escort and five miles out from the inbound lane to Perth when yet *another* argument started in the sonar room. Alex wasn't there to hear it, but he got filled in later by a shame-faced Benji Angler who couldn't figure out whose side to take.

On one hand, Wilson was involved. That generally meant trouble, because even when Wilson *wasn't* drinking, he was ragging on his shipmates or pulling practical jokes on the chiefs. On the other side was his division officer, Ensign Vincentelli, who generally *meant* well...but didn't know as much as he thought he knew. Fortunately, Maggie was on watch in control, and she was having none of Vincentelli's crap, particularly when everything sonar detected was recorded and could be replayed.

After listening to the replay, Maggie sent the boat to battle stations. Fortunately, Alex beat George to control—the XO was still on a rampage about completing every checklist in the exact proper order and would've had Maggie's head for not calling the captain first. But Alex didn't care. It was wartime, and he'd discovered that he was one hundred percent fantastic with having department heads who weren't afraid to make the right call.

Maggie was the best of them.

"What's up, Nav?" Alex asked, strolling into control with the last of his grilled cheese sandwich in his hand. He hadn't bothered to bring the plate, but if he left his sandwich, who knew when he'd next eat?

A quick glance around the space told Alex he wasn't the only one who'd brought lunch to go; hell, Master Chief Morton brought the whole damned tray out of the Chief's Mess and was still eating mashed potatoes with a spoon while he accepted turnover of his new duties.

Some captains would've reamed him out. They also would've yelled at Chief Stevens for the bunch of grapes lying on his console or wigged out over the industrial-size box of cheesy poofs in the electronic warfare corner. Alex just took another bite of his sandwich.

"Sonar detected an explosion and potential secondary explosions at medium range, sir. Bearing one-two-one at approximately thirty-seven nautical miles." Maggie stood in the center of control with a scowling Ensign Vincentelli at her side, and she smiled. "There was a little ambiguity about the existence of the explosion, but I had sonar play the tapes back, and we caught it on both the bow and port side arrays. It's faint, but it's there."

"Who's supposed to be in that area?"

"No patrol boxes assigned there, sir, but the explosion appears to be on a straight line with the northern lane into Perth."

Pinpoints of concern prickled up Alex's spine; he straightened. "Anyone reporting in Link out that way?"

Not every boat stayed in Link. Even Alex didn't like doing it all the time, but he thought it was smart to stay up in Link when coming into the inbound lanes to Perth. Those lanes changed every week and were specifically in place so that surface ships didn't sink friendly subs who they *thought* were enemies sneaking toward Perth. Coming up in Link was another layer of insurance.

"No subs up in Link 18 within fifty nautical miles, sir." Chief Stevens shook his head and popped another grape in his mouth.

Alex frowned. "Can you pull up a history?" He glanced at Maggie. "How long ago was the explosion?"

"About ten-and-a-half minutes, sir," Vincentelli replied before Maggie could open her mouth.

"There's your timeline, Chief."

"Looking back ten to twenty minutes, aye, sir." Stevens's fingers flew over the console.

"You're thinking someone got sunk," Maggie whispered.

"I'm not thinking anything yet." Alex chewed his lip. "Just...checking."

It could be an enemy boat, but if so, who sank them? Someone should be there—surface or subsurface—reporting the position of a sunken enemy. Alex frowned. The only for way a mystery explosion to exist was for someone *else* to sink a friendly sub or surface ship...and then for their victim not to get a message off.

None of the possible answers were good answers. In fact, Alex couldn't think of a single possibility that didn't represent a threat to Perth or ships inbound and outbound from the base.

"Sir, we'll get off schedule if we turn to investigate." George appeared to his right as the rest of the crew settled into their battle stations, his face marred by pillow creases.

Alex didn't comment; lunch was a great time to nap. "Slowing's a great idea, XO. We can always pick up speed in the lane. Maggie, let's slow to ten knots until Chief Stevens has an answer."

"No need to wait, Captain. System says *Georgia* was up in Link until ten minutes, forty-seven seconds ago," Stevens said. "System log says the Link hub is still pinging her, trying to reestablish contact."

Alex twisted to meet George's eyes as realization curdled in his gut. But his XO stood frozen, his mouth slightly agape.

"Radio, got any SUBMISS/SUBSUNK messages?" Alex asked when his tactical deputy couldn't get in gear.

"Nothing yet, sir," the radio watch said.

"They might be fine, and we're due in Perth in five hours..." George trailed off.

"And they might not be." Alex squared his shoulders. "There might be survivors...or we might find their killers. Maggie, lay in a course for *Georgia's* last reported location."

"Nav, aye."

Jimmy Carter swung away from the inbound lane and sprinted toward the enemy while Alex closed his eyes and prayed that his friend's command was all right.

He hadn't seen Tommy Sandifer since leaving Groton three months earlier, but a few classmates shared an email group where they exchanged news, gossip, and basically had a place to moan in ways captains couldn't in front of their crews. Tommy was sharp, one of the best, and if *his* boat was missing...

Alex swallowed his fear and got to work.

Christmas Island (Australia)

One look at the man told Nancy he was a firecracker.

She'd met her new boss in the helo hangar like a proper captain; only an idiot would embark an admiral and leave him to find his own way to the bridge. Nancy was there waiting when the helicopter touched down and wasn't surprised to see the admiral as the first person out.

Ding ding. Ding ding. Ding ding, came the sound over the loudspeakers. "Destroyer Squadron Two-Three, arriving!" *Ding!*

The man who led the new squadron *Fletcher* was assigned to was short, and his dark eyes were creased with laugh lines. He wore the uniform like a second skin, pulling off the flight helmet and handing it off without a second glance. His eyes scanned the hangar, alight with curiosity, and Nancy pushed down a sudden case of nerves. She knew her crew was good. Everything was where it should be.

Instead, she stole a second look at his staff as they filed in through the hangar door, gripping their bags tightly to stop the rotor wash from flinging them overboard. Where the hell was she going to put them all? The CH-53M Wild Stallion still spinning on *Fletcher's* flight deck held up to fifty-five; thankfully, the admiral didn't bring that many with him. But an additional fifteen officers and twenty enlisted would still strain *Fletcher's* berthing to the max. *O'Bannon*-class destroyers didn't exactly have a lot of space to spare.

But captains of United States warships did not grumble when accorded the honor of having their ship become the flagship of a brand-new task force. They made things happen, which was why she shot Ying Mai a look that told her XO to find holes for all these people to sleep in.

Ying nodded.

"Welcome aboard *Fletcher*, Admiral!" Nancy said. "I'm Nancy Coleman. This is my XO, Ying Mai. We're delighted to have you here."

"Spare me the ceremony, Captain!" Admiral Marco Rodriquez grinned as the sound of the CH-53's rotors faded. "We've got a shit-ton of work to do and not much time to do it in."

Nancy smiled. "We're two miles from the rest of the task group, sir, turning and burning to meet up with *John C. Stennis*."

"Fantastic." Rodriquez laughed. "Here's hoping things go better than the last time *Fletcher* rode herd on an aircraft carrier."

"Sir, I—" Nancy blanched.

"Oh, don't look like I fucking stole all your Christmas presents. I didn't mean that as an insult. Jeff McNally shat himself and screwed you in the process. Anyone with two goddamned brain cells to rub together knows that." Rodriquez's grin was infectious. "I'm just an ass with no sense of tact. You're going to have to get used to that. Tanya here"—he gestured at the slender captain by his side—"will tell you all about it. She'll probably even tell you my dick size, though lord fucking knows how she figured that out."

Captain Tanya Tenaglia chuckled. "A good chief of staff never tells her secrets, sir."

Nancy's eyes flicked between the pair, taking in the chief of staff's easy grin and the admiral's unabashed shrug. "I won't ask if you don't tell, COS," she said.

"With him, it's best that way," Tenaglia replied.

"I'm sure you'll find me a fucking handful, Captain," Rodriquez said. "But I work my ass off, too, so let's see if we can't make a happy marriage out of this, shall we?"

"Sorry, sir, but I'm taken." Nancy couldn't help but smile.

"Well, that's a good thing, because it'd be fucking complicated, and even in wartime, that'd be a hell of a thing to ignore, wouldn't it?" Rodriquez barked out another laugh. "I may be an uncontrollable urchin of an admiral, but even I'm not such a numb-nuts idiot as to commit frat with my flag captain. Sure, it'd be fun, and you look like you could keep the fuck up, but sooner or later, I'd do something stupid and you'd break my heart. *Then* we'd be a fucking mess, and who has time for that with a war on?"

Nancy didn't want to laugh. She didn't. But the once giggles burst out of her, they wouldn't stop.

"Don't worry," Tenaglia said. "He has that effect on people." She shot the admiral a glare. "But he'll behave when there's work to do, won't you, sir?"

Rodriquez snickered. "Lead me to the bridge, Captain, and I'll put my best big-boy face on."

"There's no one here, sir," George said after an hour of searching.

Did most captains regularly have to resist the urge to smack their XOs upside the head? No, Alex was pretty sure that was just him. "You're right," he said. "Whoever sank *Georgia*, they're long gone."

Jimmy Carter's control was unusually quiet. No one liked the thought of one of their own being sunk, and they liked the idea of letting the killer get away even less.

Even the snacks were gone now. Alex didn't have to say anything; he watched the food gradually be put away as watchstanders concentrated harder and harder, trying to find the mysterious ship or submarine that sank *Georgia*. After an hour of searching—and listening to the sonar recording himself—Alex grew increasingly convinced that *Georgia* was on the bottom...which meant that Tommy Sandifer, his friend from Sub School, went down with her.

And whoever had killed her was long gone. Alex's chest was so tight it felt like a giant was sitting on it, and he wanted to scream in frustration. Never mind the fact that *Jimmy Carter* was always too early or too late to make a difference. Now they had lost brothers and sisters to an unknown killer who they couldn't find.

"Assuming they sank *Georgia* at all." George's chin only jutted out like that when he was feeling peevish, and while Alex loved a good pedant himself, this was going a bit too far. There were *lives* on the line.

"I don't think we can afford to assume otherwise," he replied. "Officer of the Deck, let's take a look around topside. Make your depth sixty feet."

"Periscope depth, aye, sir." Maggie gave the rest of the orders while Alex watched the color drain out of George's face.

"Sir, you can't be serious. If there's a surface ship up there, statistics say *most* submarine sightings come when someone spots a scope!"

"And if anyone got off *Georgia*, they aren't hanging around down here," Alex replied. "I don't think we have a recent inventory of our rescue gear, do we?"

George blinked. "Uh, no, sir, I don't think we do. I can get on that if you want."

As always, bureaucracy and checklists calmed George right down. "Please do."

"On it, Captain."

Alex pretended not to notice the relief on his sailors' faces when George left control. He had a mission to focus on, and his XO's wonky eccentricities had to get better with time. This was their first real patrol. He'd get better, right?

Twenty minutes later, *Jimmy Carter* was at periscope depth, and Maggie slowed the submarine so that her periscope would create as small of a wake as possible.

That would decrease the possibility of eyes on the surface spotting them, because no matter what George thought, Alex *did* listen to him.

"Up scope," Alex ordered. He'd grown up in *Virginia*-class submarines with their "always up" periscopes, but something in him loved the old-school type 102 scope on his boat. Was it all the WWII movies he watched?

Jimmy Carter's periscope slid up with a soft hydraulic hiss, extending his submarine's eyes the old fashioned way, with mirrors and angles instead of cameras. Of course, the periscope *also* featured a camera—*Jimmy Carter* wasn't built in the Stone Age—but the bulk of the scope had the same design as those used in the previous world war, just updated a little.

Smiling, he grabbed the handles worn smooth by age. How many officers had touched these over the years? How many places had *Jimmy Carter* raised her scope to spy on and never been able to admit they were there? Smiling to himself, Alex leaned in close, doing the sideways duck walk to bring the periscope around in a circle. *Jimmy Carter* did have a monitor next to the scope where others could see what Alex saw—and enough technology to record video, too—but he liked looking through the scope, proper.

Yeah, Admiral Hamilton might've given him this old submarine as a punishment, but he'd grown to *like* his cranky old lady.

His slow walk through three hundred sixty degrees showed nothing but waves and sky, but Alex wasn't surprised. The scope's height of eye was only about twenty feet at this depth, but Alex didn't dare go shallower.

"No contacts." He leaned back from the scope. "Chief Stevens, what course was *Georgia* on when she dropped from Link?"

"Zero-five-one."

"Match it, Maggie. And calculate for set and drift so we know how a life raft would travel." Alex ordered just as a petty officer walked in from radio.

"Sir, we got a SUBMISS/SUBSUNK message."

A hand closed around his heart, and when Alex asked the question, he already knew the answer. "*Georgia?*"

"Yes, sir. Buoy launch was about two minutes after the explosion. Wilson gave me the data."

"Well, at least we know what we're doing out here." This shouldn't be another fruitless effort, not like setting up on those French destroyers. If anyone had gotten off *Georgia*, they'd be around here.

Alex settled in to wait as *Jimmy Carter* crept along *Georgia's* last course. He could see the grim certainty in his peoples' expressions; no one joked, and no one smiled. They all knew.

Twenty minutes later, George returned to control. "Search and rescue gear inventory complete, sir. But Petty Officer Ness has a sprained wrist."

"Say again?" Alex's stomach dropped. Ness was one of *Jimmy Carter's* two divers, one of the few people qualified to save anyone who went over the side. Surface operations required two swimmers—one ready to go in the water, and the other ready to go after them if something went wrong. "How bad?"

"Bad enough that he went to see Doc about it this morning. Apparently, he tried doing a handstand on a table on the mess decks and it didn't go well." George scowled. "Some stupid dare."

"Shit." Alex shook himself. "Well, that's only a problem if we find survivors, so let's classify that under 'problems I want to have,' shall we?"

"Sir, it's not safe to—"

"Contact off the bow! Bearing zero-three-two!" Maggie had taken over the scope while Alex talked to George, and she zoomed in on the black specks on the horizon. "Looks like it could be a raft, sir. Range is...about six thousand yards."

"Kick it up to ten knots and let's find out."

It took an agonizing ten minutes to get close enough to see details of the shredded life raft on the surface—and the people bobbing in the water around it.

"Surface the ship!" Alex said. "Emergency surface, Nav—we already know who is and isn't around here. Get us up there now."

"Nav, aye!" Maggie spun to relay orders as George grabbed Alex's arm.

"Sir, we can't put a swimmer in the water without a backup!" George flung a hand at the periscope display monitor, which showed dozens of people clutching whatever they could to stay afloat. "And we can't rescue them without putting *someone* in the water! We need to call this in and—"

"And what?" Benji Angler approached from the weapons corner. "Pardon me for interrupting, Captain, but I've looked at the Link picture. There's no one within a hundred nautical miles, and I don't know about you, but I sure couldn't swim long enough for another ship to get here."

"We need *two rescue swimmers*," George hissed.

"We have two," Alex said grimly.

"Ness can't go in the water with a sprained wrist," George said just as Benji asked, frowning:

"You want Ness to be backup for MM1 Ruse and assume nothing goes wrong?"

Alex's eyes flicked back to the screen of his own accord. He couldn't see faces from here, thank God, but he could only imagine how horrible *Georgia's* sailors felt right now. How many were on the surface? A dozen? Two? Had others drowned while *Jimmy Carter* searched for their killer and the wheels of bureaucracy delayed the naval message announcing their sinking?

No way was he wasting any more time.

"I'm a qualified diver and rescue swimmer. I re-upped my cert before I left the sub school." He held up a hand to stop both Benji and George from speaking. "And I have my gear on board. Ruse is primary, and I'll be secondary. And if *I* have to go in, Doc splints the shit out of Ness' wrist for him to be another backup. Got it?"

"Sir, you're the *captain*!" George yelped.

"I'm glad you noticed. XO, you'll be in charge of the rescue operation topside. Nav," he raised his voice to make sure Maggie heard him, "will keep the deck and drive us as close to the survivors as she can, because I *hate* long swims in the ocean like I hate asparagus. Weps, you're Nav's backup down here in control. Keep an eye on the tactical picture and call a fucking audible if anything at all happens. Got it?"

Three sets of wide eyes stared at him. This wasn't the kind of careful planning the sub force was known for, but they were out of time.

"I can't talk you out of this, can I?" George asked.

"No. All you can do is waste time our friends in the water don't have." Alex looked at his team. "Anyone have any questions, or can I go throw my swim gear on?"

Maggie and Benji exchanged a glance. "We've got it, Captain," Maggie said.

He considered sending a tweet about his latest target's sinking, but there was a small rub—*Barracuda's* sonar computer wasn't sure if it was USS *Georgia* or USS *Alabama*. The two sister ships were both so new that France didn't have a lot of sonar data on either, and Jules Rochambeau was not about to suffer the embarrassment of announcing he'd sunk the wrong submarine.

This time the Americans could wonder, he decided. How was it his duty to tell them when their submarines sank? Really, they should keep better track.

But that last sinking had been so *easy*, and there were no other targets in the vicinity. So Jules left the area and contacted his fleet headquarters, looking for an idea. It took mere hours for it to bear fruit. By then, he was lounging in his stateroom, watching a popular French drama series.

It was a good show. He was four episodes in, already wondering if the mistress would murder her benefactor, when the knock came twice, sharp and quick.

Camille opened the door without waiting for permission. "Satellite update received, *mon capitaine.*"

"And?" Jules paused the show.

"And their course remains as predicted by the naval group. The new American task force is on course toward Perth, just as our last target. They appear to be running EMCON."

Transiting under EMCON, or Emissions Control, meant radiating no radars or radio signals. It protected warships from detection by most conventional means...except the old-fashioned eyeball. Or the newfangled one attached to satellites, which could see you as well as a lookout, but at much further range.

Further out than sonar, too. Jules' new idea had promise.

His sculpted eyebrows rose. "Our range?"

"Eighty miles from the task force."

"Closest point of approach?"

"Two miles in four hours on current course and speed." Camille grinned. "This new way to stalk is very peaceful."

Jules laughed. "Indeed. We must sent our compliments to *l'Armée de l'air et de l'espace* satellite group for watching our foes," he replied. "Maintain course and speed and set battle stations in three-and-a-half hours. Let the crew relax until then."

"Gladly." Her eyes gleamed. "And then our enemy will sail right into our trap—for the second time in one day."

"*Précisément*. Right into a watery grave."

Chapter 22

So Others May Live

The sky was blue turning to gray as *Jimmy Carter* surfaced as close to the swimmers as her crew dared. The sub's giant black form rose from beneath the waves about two miles out from the swimmers and began creeping forward as her rescue-and-assistance detail hurried topside to tie themselves off to the submarine.

Everyone wore safety harnesses and lifejackets; submarines were not safe surfaces to stand on while underway, and the faster *Jimmy Carter* went, the more waves washed over the deck. Unlike a surface ship, the sub didn't have sides or railings to protect the crew. No, she had a round hull that was only slightly flattened on top...and was at the mercy of wind and waves. No sub handled surface weather well, which was why sub COs preferred to stay submerged as long as possible. Weather meant sailors getting tossed around in a metal can. Inevitably, that led to seasickness.

Today, however, *Jimmy Carter* had little choice. So her handpicked rescue detail inflated their small boat, readying it to pick up survivors who couldn't swim to the boat as it slowly approached. The boat slowed to a crawl to put the inflatable in the water; once its coxswain started the engine, *Jimmy Carter* eased her way back up to five knots. Only then did the rescue detail start tying nets off for the survivors who could get to them.

But the former spy submarine wasn't only limited to her boat and nets. *Jimmy Carter* was commissioned with four small airborne search and rescue drones. One of them still worked, and its feed was visible from both the sail and the rigid-hulled inflatable boat, or RHIB. For an emergency man overboard, the rescue swimmers would've got out of the port-side diver lockout, but putting the inflatable boat was a better choice for rescue operations.

"XO, Captain, how're the rescue nets going?" Alex used a handheld radio to ask as he scampered down the hull to jump into the boat, fins clutched in one hand.

Machinist's Mate First Class Ruse caught him before he could bounce right out of the small boat, and Alex shot him a smile.

"Two mikes and we'll be ready to deploy," George replied.

Alex glanced over his shoulder. *Jimmy Carter* was equipped with three search and rescue nets—two more than his last boat. They were basically big, vaguely triangular-shaped nets with inflated sides, designed to curve over the sides of a submarine and help people climb up. There were also pockets at the bottom where survivors could rest, which meant they shouldn't be dropped into the water until the sub was as close to the survivors as possible.

His eyes flicked to the drone monitor while the boat bounced alongside his submarine. Hovering above the water, its camera picked up survivors perched in the floating end of a half-sunken life raft, while others swam around the edges or clung to that same life raft. Two even held onto an empty life-raft canister, while another person bobbed on top of a life-raft canister that looked like it never deployed. Counting quickly, he picked out thirty-six bobbing heads—or thirty-seven? His stomach clenched. Barely a third out of a crew of over one hundred twenty.

Poor bastards.

Yet there would be none of them if *Georgia* had been deep, a traitorous voice inside him told Alex. Tommy must've shot for the surface when the torpedoes were after him. They'd spent a few hours speculating back then about how that was the only way to survive...but Alex didn't want to be proven right like this.

"Let's do this thing," he said to the coxswain. Much to his surprise, it was *Wilson*, of all people, who turned out to be the most experienced small boat coxswain on board. It turned out Wilson was the only one on the sub qualified as coxswain aside from two junior officers, neither of which Alex wanted on the job for something like this.

He just hoped to Christ that Wilson wouldn't screw this up.

"Killer Rabbit, this is Paws," Wilson said. "Requesting permission to shove off."

"Paws, Killer Rabbit, shove off," Maggie's voice replied immediately.

Alex smiled grimly. Like *Jimmy Carter's* callsign of "Killer Rabbit," the boat's callsign was a callback to the incident where a swamp rabbit went after then-president Jimmy Carter while he was fishing. "Paws" referenced a comic released in newspapers at the time, and while Alex wasn't old enough to remember it, there was a signed and framed copy on the mess decks.

Wilson eased the boat way from the submarine and then gunned the engine, heading straight for the closest survivors who weren't clinging to the semi-working life raft.

"Here's the plan!" Alex shouted over the roar of the waterjet engine. "MM1 Ruse is first up as rescue swimmer, and I'm his backup. CS3 Orama and I will be primary for pulling the survivors out of the water. *We have to prioritize those in extremis.* This is a twelve pax RHIB and there are four of us. That means we can only ferry eight at a time to the boat."

Thirty-seven survivors meant five trips, four long waits for people who'd been in the water for over an hour. Some of them were scattered to hell and gone. Alex squinted. Were those specks on the horizon people? Could there be more?

"But the boat's right behind us, right, sir?" CS3 Orama, a mess attendant who served as the bow hook, turned to look at him with huge eyes.

"As quick as a giant lumbering beast can be." Alex flashed her a smile. "Worst case, we let the survivors cling to us until *Jimmy Carter* arrives."

His sailors chorused understanding as the boat slowed near the first cluster of swimming survivors. These six clung to what looked like a piece of a life raft—on second glance, Alex realized it *was* a life raft, just partially submerged and hanging vertically in the water with the one inflated side up.

"Shit," Alex whispered.

"Sea state's picking up like bitch, sir," Wilson said in an undertone. "Got to make this fast or we'll roll like a drunk whale. This tiny-ass rubber boat don't have a keel worth shit."

"You're metaphors are whackadoodle, but you're not wrong. When the hell did you qualify coxswain, Wilson?"

"Got bored on *Bluefish* and it got me off the boat. I made a bet with Weps. She thought I couldn't do it, and she bought me McDonald's when I did." Wilson shrugged. "Besides, I was on restriction at the time."

"For drunken antics?"

Wilson grinned. "You know me so well, sir."

Alex ignored Ruse and Orama snickering; *everyone* knew Wilson. Craning his neck, Alex saw the shadow of *Jimmy Carter* approaching, but the sub was still a good fifteen hundred yards out. At five knots, she'd still need almost ten minutes to reach them.

"Killer Rabbit, Actual, pop the drone over to three-five-two relative," he said into the radio. "I think I see something over there."

"Three-five-two, aye," Benji's voice replied just as Wilson steered the boat into the first group of survivors. Alex didn't watch as one of them waved an exhausted arm; he watched the drone monitor.

"Sonofabitch."

A mattress floated, half-submerged, far away from the rest of the survivors, with one lone figure clinging to it as the waves washed over both man and mattress. Not far away, two others held onto what looked like a piece of shredded life raft.

That's forty.

"Pan right," Alex ordered as something caught his eye.

Shit, there was another survivor, not far behind the two at the shredded life raft, draped exhaustedly over what looked like another piece of it. He was barely above the water, but face up—was he alive?

Forty-one.

He didn't dare hope Tommy might be one of them.

"Let's grab these guys fast." Alex stowed the radio and matched action to words as a survivor came in reach, grabbing the woman's hands and pulling her aboard. Ruse and Orama followed suit, and they repeated the actions until they'd pulled the first group of six into the boat.

"You're American, right?" the waterlogged petty officer at Alex's feet whispered. She was young, maybe early twenties, with freckles and curly red hair plastered tightly to her skull. "Please be American."

"*Jimmy Carter*," he replied, watching her slump in relief. Alex tapped Wilson on the shoulder. "Head for those three."

The next closest sailors were a group of three clinging to a pair of mattresses.

"They might overload the boat, sir," Wilson replied. "Then again, some of 'em are pretty skinny."

"We'll have to take that risk."

"Kickin' it up." Wilson jammed the throttles forward before Alex could yelp at him to take it slow, but he reversed thrust on the waterjet just in time to coast to a stop next to the mattresses. The boat's wake hit the mattresses-made-float, and they rocked precariously, but all three *Georgia* survivors—two chiefs and a junior officer—hung on doggedly.

Ruse gestured their current passengers to port while they pulled up the newcomers. Wilson grabbed the radio as he wheeled the small boat around left-handed. "Killer Rabbit, Paws, inbound with nine pax, over."

"Paws, Killer Rabbit, you are clear to approach starboard side to the nets. We will slow for a lee, over," Maggie replied.

"Paws, roger."

The boat skipped across the waves as Alex glanced back at the big knot of survivors. Could *Jimmy Carter* reach them while the boat picked up the smaller groups?

"How'd you guys find us?" one of the chiefs asked, wiping saltwater out of his eyes. "None of us have a radio."

"We saw your Link track vanish, and Wilson here caught bottom bounce on the implosion," Alex replied.

"Fuck me." The chief slumped against the boat's center console, his eyes sliding out of focus. "Thanks. Wasn't sure those mattresses would hold much longer."

"Wasn't sure *I* could hold much longer," the other chief said, looking at her companion. "Did you see Sally?"

"She climbed out before me. Hopefully she's in a raft."

"You've got a bit of a climb left yourselves," Alex said as Wilson cut the engine and coasted up to the nets draped down *Jimmy Carter's* side. "We've got to kick you all out so we can pick up the others."

"Right. Only one boat." The junior officer from the mattress stood, panting. "Let's go."

"Stay on deck, Petty Officer!" George's screech carried down to Alex as Petty Officer Tillman—the boat's "first lieutenant," or senior petty officer in the deck work center—scampered down the net to help pull *Georgia* sailors over. Three more of Alex's crew followed him to do the same.

The boat was empty within minutes.

"Which group next, Captain?" Wilson asked.

Alex's eyes swept over the remaining clusters of survivors. The largest group was straight ahead, but they were the ones in or around the half-inflated life raft. They'd last the longest. A hundred yards or so to their left was the pair on the open life-raft canister and the singleton clinging to the non-deployed canister. *Further* away, several hundred yards at least, was the other mattress rider, plus the three beyond him.

Heaven help him, there were no right answers here.

"Head for the furthest group." Alex pointed to the four to the right. He'd have to gamble that the three on the canisters could hold on.

Shit, they talked about command being full of hard choices, but did his gut have to roll like this?

Alex snatched the radio off the console. "Killer Rabbit, Actual, make a slow approach on the raft, over."

"Killer Rabbit, roger, out," Maggie replied.

It would be a hard maneuver and was a big ask for an officer of the deck that Alex hadn't served with for long. Maggie was the best shipdriver out of the department heads, but was she good enough? *Jimmy Carter* was an ungainly beast, and the winds were all wrong to get that raft on her starboard side where the nets were rigged.

He'd expected better of George.

Wilson shoved the throttles down, and Alex held on tight as the boat turned its bow into the waves. The sea state *was* getting worse. Alex grimaced. They weren't near the limits for rescue operations yet, and the water temperature was still in the low eighties. That was good for survivability, but the wave height was a worry.

The boat jumped a bit in the chop, and Alex could barely see the pair of survivors behind the man on the mattress as they approached. There was no way to calculate a formal closest point of approach, but instinct screamed at Alex.

"You need to slow—" he started to say, just as Wilson miscalculated.

It was understandable. Urgency ran through *Jimmy Carter's* sailors like a current, and Wilson was trying for the fastest approach possible. So he bled his speed off in a last-minute turn, twisting the boat to a stop and using the waterjet like a brake. But he underestimated the wake that would cause, which swept the sailor clinging to the mattress right into the water.

He went down with a gasp, flailing, and didn't come back up for several agonizing seconds.

"Fuck!" Wilson struggled to hold the boat straight and then gave up, letting it spin three hundred sixty degrees until the bow pointed back at the now-sinking mattress.

"Swimmer one deploying!" Ruse slammed his mask on and kicked over the side before the boat stopped moving, swimming with strong strokes.

His eyes never leaving Ruse, Alex reached down and pulled his own fins on. He hadn't been needed as a rescue swimmer since his division officer days—excepting that insane incident rescuing a marine while on a secret mission last year, which was best left unmentioned. Saying he maintained all his qualifications wasn't a lie; Alex was a recreational scuba diver and loved the water. Captains just didn't *do* this.

Alex could do nothing other than watch as the *Georgia* petty officer flailed in the water. Ruse needed long seconds to reach him and then longer still to calm him and drag him back to the boat. Orama and Alex pulled the petty officer in while Ruse rolled over the side on his own.

"Swimmer recovered!"

"Moving to next pair." Wilson matched actions to words, bringing the boat around quickly—but not as fast as last time. Clearly, he'd learned his lesson and didn't want to swamp the shredded pieces of life raft holding this pair up.

It was a good thing, too; these sailors were young, panicking, and almost drowning each other in desperation to stay above water. They didn't notice the boat's approach.

"Hey," Alex said, trying for gentle until one shoved the other under. "*Hey!*"

Startled, one shied away from the boat, splashing water in Alex's eyes. The other lunged forward, allowing Ruse and Orama to grab her under the arms and pull her aboard. She landed like a sack of wet potatoes, gasping.

"Puller's trying to drown me!" She coughed up seawater right in Orama's face. "Bastard!"

Meanwhile, Puller continued thrashing in the water, his arms windmilling around him as he screeched and babbled.

"Got 'em," Ruse said and was over the side again before Alex could blink.

When the rescue swimmer approached Puller, he tried to calm him down to put him in a normal tow, but Puller just started screaming. Alex couldn't pick up everything Ruse said, but he caught pieces of Puller shouting that he was trying to drown him. Alex's eyes narrowed. How long had the tug-of-war for survival gone on between these two sailors? Something told him both ingested enough saltwater to make them crazy.

"Leave him," the young sailor panted. "He's nuts. Always has been. Fucker."

"Oh, shut and let us do the rescuing," Wilson replied before Alex could say anything.

"Who the fuck are you to tell me what to do?" She glared up at Wilson from the deck, and Alex finally glimpsed the name patch on her soaked uniform. It read *Singh*.

"I'm the fucking coxswain, and Orama here will throw you back overboard if I ask." Wilson winked. "Won't you?"

Orama cringed. "Leave me out of this, will you?"

A yelp carried across the water before Singh could reply, followed by the wet squish of flesh hitting flesh. Alex caught sight of Ruse just in time to see his head snap back, nose bleeding, from Puller's wild blow.

"Oh, fuck," Wilson said and started to turn the boat toward the pair.

Alex grabbed his arm. "Relax. Ruse is trained for this."

Puller might've hit first, but Ruse hit harder, rising out of the water to tackle Puller and then clobber him into insensitivity. Two quick blows and the *Georgia* sailor was out of commission; Ruse towed him back to the boat without trouble.

Still, Ruse was bleeding impressively when he got back, the blood thick and shiny against his dark skin. He'd split a lip and broken his nose, and his mask was cracked, too.

Damn, he needed to give that kid a medal, Alex thought as he and Orama dumped Puller's semi-conscious form into the boat. Ruse pulled himself in again, yanking his mask off to glare at it. "Mask's no good." He spat blood. "And my spare's on the boat."

"That's my cue, then. Tip your head back and try not to bleed all over yourself."

Ruse laughed out a wheeze. "Thanks, sir."

"Heading for the next one." Wilson pointed the boat to the furthest survivor. Picking him up was almost anti-climactic compared to the last pair, though he eyed Ruse's bleeding face and Puller's semi-conscious form with unease.

"What the hell kind of rescue is this?" he slurred.

"Welcome to *Jimmy Carter*," Wilson said before Alex could answer. "We're messy bitches."

"Jesus Christ, Wilson," Alex muttered.

Wilson grinned. "Last three singletons, sir?"

"Do it."

Gunning the engine again, Wilson cut around behind *Jimmy Carter* as the sub maneuvered toward the life raft. Alex could see Maggie leaning over the side of the sail, crabbing the giant submarine sideways using nothing but her thrusters. Damn, she was good. Alex grinned.

Messy his people might be, but they got the damned job done.

With the boat aiming for the largest group, that left the three hanging onto life canisters. Unfortunately, Maggie's maneuver *had* left a wake behind, and slight though it was, the wash from *Jimmy Carter's* propulsor still swept over the single survivor hanging onto the closed life-raft canister, pushing him further away from the boat.

It also rocked the open canister two women clung to, knocking one free.

Then a wave rolled over her as she struggled toward the surface, sending her right back down. The other survivor clung doggedly to the life-raft cannister, her fingers bleeding as she gripped its safety line.

"Gentle with the approach," Alex said.

"Looks like you're got a customer, sir." Wilson's eyes never left the two closest survivors. "I'll try to get close enough that we can pull this one aboard if you want to deploy to port."

"Good call."

Alex shifted to sitting on the boat's inflated port sponson, checking his mask one last time as Wilson eased up on the throttles. Wilson had done a pretty good job of splitting the difference between the survivors, but the one in the water had no support, and her struggles only combined with the current to push her further away.

"Help Orama pull her in, will you, Singh?" Alex said to the first survivor they'd picked up. Puller was still sprawled in the middle of the boat, lying dazed on the deck, while Ruse was still leaning back, holding his nose to stop the bleeding.

Singh scowled at him. "Aren't you a little old for a rescue swimmer?"

"Isn't it a bit of an asshole maneuver not to help your *drowning* shipmate?" Alex retorted.

Beet red, she turned away and reached down to help as the boat coasted to a stop. Alex, meanwhile, pulled his mask down.

"Swimmer two deploying." He slipped over the side, feet first, into the water.

Alex always noticed the temperature first, even when the water was warm. Luckily, these were good conditions for a rescue; the water was warm in the Indian Ocean this time of year, almost eighty degrees. That made survival twelve hours or greater, which at least meant *Georgia's* people were safe from hypothermia, which could happen, eventually, even in the warmest seas. He also wouldn't have to watch his own time in the water.

Orienting himself as his body adjusted to the change in environment, Alex spotted the struggling swimmer and zeroed in on her. He swam to her side with quick and powerful strokes, letting his fins do most of the work. Open-ocean swimming was hard, particularly with a growing sea state.

Thankfully, Alex was *with* the current right now. The swim back would be another matter.

She was still above water when he reached her...barely. His field of view was narrowed with his mask on, but she looked about his own age, with dark hair escaping what used to be a bun. "Relax. I've got you."

"I—" She caught a gulp of water and gagged.

"This is where you stop doing the work and I start," he said, swimming close so he could wrap an arm around her diagonally. "Just stop swimming."

She might've nodded or choked on more water; Alex couldn't tell the difference. He just started towing her back to the boat, keeping his strokes steady and even. There was no use wasting energy, not other potential rescues to make.

They still reached the boat in good time. By then, Orama and Singh had the other survivor from this pair on board, and they helped pull Alex's rescuee on board.

"Last one's bobbing in and out of sight, Captain," Wilson said as Alex draped himself over the rubber sponson.

"Get me close and I'll grab 'em."

Wilson nodded and steered the boat that way. Alex risked pulling his mask off long enough to look around and then grimaced. The sea state wasn't worsening fast, but waves were up to four or five feet. That was nothing for the sub, but bad for the small boat he was in—and even worse for the partially inflated life raft the other survivors were clinging to.

He couldn't deal with that problem right now. First, the other man in the water.

"I can't get close to that busted canister, sir. It'll rip the rubber sponsons right open," Wilson said as the boat approached.

Shit, he was right. That last canister never deployed because it was broken on one end, the same end that had the automatic depth sensor. Its jagged edges would rip the hull of their boat right open, spilling everyone in the drink, and with the waves higher than the boat was tall, controlling its position relative to a non-hydrodynamic, half-sunken life-raft canister would be well-nigh impossible.

"No need. Swimmer two deploying."

Alex reentered the water by rolling off the side of the boat feet first. By then, he had a line on the survivor's back, and Wilson had stopped the boat less than twenty feet away. It was an easy swim.

Only once he reached the survivor did he recognize Tommy Sandifer's waterlogged face. His friend from the Sub School clung to the canister with white-knuckled and shaking hands; he wasn't quite able to get his body over it and balance, which meant he had to hold onto the canister or have no buoyancy. It wasn't like submariners wore life jackets, after all, and there wasn't time to grab one when a sub sunk.

"Hey, Tommy," Alex said. "How's it going?"

Tommy blinked sunken eyes several times before he recognized him. "Alex? What the hell are you doing out here?"

"Rescuing your ass, it seems. Let go of the canister and I'll haul your ass in."

"My crew—"

"Mine are all over it, and you're the last one out here not on or around a raft," Alex said. "Let the fuck go, Tommy."

Tommy's nod looked numb. Would Alex feel like that if he'd lost his boat? Probably. Best not to think of that now; he had a friend to buddy swim back to the boat. So Alex did, helping Tommy into *Jimmy Carter's* small, rubber rescue boat before hoisting himself back aboard.

"Hey, Captain," the last survivor Alex picked up said. Her smile looked relieved. "I wasn't sure you got out."

"I was right behind you, Master Chief. For all the good it did." Tommy slumped against Alex as he pulled his fins off.

"Let's get them back to the boat, Wilson."

"On it, sir."

Now Alex could look up and see how the recovery operation between his sub and the raft was going. Maggie had aced the difficult maneuver; *Jimmy Carter* was nestled up right against the life raft, and about half the sailors from it seemed to have been transferred already.

"How many?" Tommy croaked, following Alex's gaze.

Alex swallowed. "I counted forty-one."

"God." Tommy dropped his head in his hands. "Torpedoes just came out of nowhere. It was just like *Moray*, but I went for the roof instead of the deck." He coughed up water. "Their warheads must be smaller than ours, because we didn't explode to hell and gone right away. Just took the aft end out and killed all of engineering, but the emergency blow took us topside long enough for people to get out the forward hatches. Then I…"

"Captain was the last one out," the master chief—likely *Georgia's* chief of the boat—next to Tommy said. She snorted. "Practically had to drag his ass. Told him going down with the ship was old fashioned as fuck."

"She's right, Tommy," Alex said quietly. "You did the right thing."

"More than half my crew is dead," Tommy whispered.

"And the others aren't because of you."

"And you guys." Tommy looked around. "Why'd they send a sub after us? No offense, but attack subs are terrible rescue platforms."

"We saw your Link track vanish when we were inbound Perth. Thought I'd check it out." Alex pursed his lips. "The SUBMISS/SUB-SUNK message came out when we were already on our way."

"Thank you, Alex." Tommy swallowed. "For my crew."

Alex reached down and squeezed his friend's shoulder. "You'd do the same for me."

An hour later, *Barracuda* set up silently on the USS *Pearl Harbor* (CG 80) Surface Action Group, newly in route from Pearl Harbor to reinforce the fast-growing American fleet presence in Perth, Australia. Consisting of the cruiser, two destroyers, a frigate, and a littoral combat ship, the first four ships were all stuffed with brand new SM-6 anti-air and LSRAM anti-ship missiles, all ready to take the fight to the enemy.

What they lacked in air cover they made up for with their own embarked helicopter squadron, with two helicopters buzzing around the SAG at all times. The cruiser CO thought that kept them safe from approaching submarines, but he never imagined one might sit like a mine in his path, waiting.

One by one, *Barracuda* slammed torpedoes into each ship. Their anti-torpedo maneuvers failed, and despite enthusiastic—and increasingly desperate—prosecution by both helicopters, Rochambeau gave them the slip before either could launch a torpedo.

One made it to Perth before running out of fuel. The other ditched twenty miles offshore. Two of its three-person crew were never recovered.

Meanwhile, Rochambeau waited until the next day to send his tweets. Stealth was still paramount, and Jules would not endanger *Barracuda*, not even to brag. Besides, after sinking a Canadian frigate—also in the approaches to Perth—he was critically short of torpedoes. It was time to head toward Saint Denis.

Part of Jules regretted how easy this was…but had he wanted to spend a career dodging satellites, he, too, would have chosen to command a surface ship. Why pity the fools who chose their fates foolishly in a modern world?

Once inbound in friendly waters, he tweeted off news of all three victories.

14 October 2038, Perth, Australia

"Welcome aboard," John said as Alex plopped into the couch in the captain's cabin on *Razorback* the day after rescuing *Georgia's* crew. "I just got told to shut up and color for the second time in two weeks."

"Sounds like kindergarten. Where do I sign up?"

Alex resisted the urge to mention how much *nicer* John's cabin was than his. For one, the carpet was intact. Hell, it was even plush! Alex would've loved to sink his toes into this carpet, unlike the worn-smooth or worn-off carpet back on *Jimmy Carter*. The furniture all looked like it belonged, too. John had a table with three chairs, all decorated with *Razorback's* crest. And the fold-down couch that turned into a bed wasn't broken; the one back on Alex's boat was stuck in the bed position, which limited seating options if he wanted to hold a meeting in his stateroom.

Even the computer monitors on John's desk were nicer, with bigger screens and brighter resolution. He had a TV, too, instead of an empty set of brackets that Alex hadn't tried to fill.

Yeah, the *Ceroes* were the place to be, weren't they? Alex pushed back a surge of envy. John had earned this boat, and then some. Besides, being mad at his friend for success—and survival—was a dick move.

"Very funny." John kicked his feet up and scowled. "I told you about the torpedo problems?"

"Yeah. It doesn't take much imagination to figure out that we can't shoot subs faster than our torps," Alex replied. "You getting flack for pushing it up?"

"More than I expected, especially with 'Commodore' Banks being about two-point-five seconds senior to me. How the hell am I supposed to make a difference out here when they send me out with weights tied to my ankles?"

"Hey, at least someone's given you a chance," Alex said before he could stop himself. "I've got an oversize weapons room full of fifty Mark 48s, and I haven't even managed to shoot *one* of them."

John grimaced. "God, we're a peacetime navy. Some admiral gets a hate-on for you, and someone else somewhere—higher than Banks, I'm sure—loves whatever Congressional district the Mark 48 is manufactured in, so we're both screwed."

"It can't last, right?"

John shrugged. "Shit, I'm still getting requests for paperwork my predecessor forgot before his meltdown."

Alex groaned. "At least my XO takes care of that stuff for me. He's an admin monster."

"According to my XO, he's not great for much else," John replied. "Pat says he's twitchy as a nun in a brothel and twice as lost."

"No comment."

It was as good a way as any to describe George Kirkland, who half the crew hated and the other half despised, but Alex wasn't going to badmouth his own XO. Not even to his best friend. George was *trying*, even if his best efforts usually ended up as useful as a tutu on an elephant.

And it wasn't like Alex was going to have to take the guy into combat and watch him freeze up. Not on *Jimmy Carter*.

Chapter 23

Bull in the China Shop

Months passed; senior officers dithered, ships were lost, and subs sank. Some tried to fight against the rising tide, but it seemed to matter little. John Dalton pointed out torpedo problems in four consecutive patrol reports before Commodore Banks finally kicked it upstairs. Meanwhile, other sub captains encountered the same problems. Some tried to follow standard procedures and shoot from a distance, which did little good. Others closed with the enemy and died.

A few died in less glorious ways, like the entire convoy Annette Garnier and the French attack sub *Amazone* took out in November. *New York*, a relatively new Block V *Virginia*, got assigned to escort that convoy of military supply ships when the convoy's senior officer objected to *Jimmy Carter's* age. That freed Alex's boat from the duty, but Commander Towers' newer and theoretically shiny *New York* never even got a shot off. Garnier sank his submarine, a frigate, and three precious supply ships in less than an hour.

Alex wasn't sure if he should be relieved or infuriated; he *thought* he knew how to take the fight to the enemy but would anyone give him a chance? Not in *Jimmy Carter*.

Mark Easley from the *Post* wrote another two scathing articles about submarine losses, going head to head with Admiral Hamilton every chance he got. She did an interview with him and almost came out even; the *Post* reporter was sharp and fair, but he could smell blood in the water better than anyone. Easley was out to prove that the U.S. Navy had never been ready for this war and their leadership *still* wasn't... and the damnable thing was that no one knew if he was wrong.

Jimmy Carter spent October escorting convoys. Then they were sent to check on out-of-the-way Alliance underwater stations in November when no convoy wanted them, picking up a pair of downed aviators out of the water on the way back from Wharton Basin High, a natural gas mining station full of jaded Australian miners and not much else. The pilots were fascinated, but Alex's crew was bored within two hours.

Once they were back in Perth, they were treated to a no-notice visit from the SUBRON 29 maintenance officer, who announced she was there to inventory spare parts and survey *Jimmy Carter's* general condition. She brought along two obnoxious petty officers who tried to steal anything not nailed down, and the visit was a roaring success until Wilson got in a fistfight with the nastier of the pair. That landed Wilson in medical and the petty officer at Commodore's Mast—all accounts said she started it, no matter how annoyed the maintenance officer was to admit that. Alex went easy on him, though it was hard not to throw the book at the kid when he smirked like that.

It would be great if he could just concentrate on his job, Alex wrote in an email to his wife. *But he seems to have enough bandwidth to run sonar and get in trouble.*

Sounds like he's not busy enough, Nancy replied. *Got any time-consuming collateral duties to hand the kid? Morale, Welfare, and Recreation are always a blast. And he might do some good there...assuming your crew ever gets a break. I miss running into you.*

Running gun battles with the Indians and French are great, but I'd rather be in port with you if we can't have missiles to finish them off. It's like a game of hide and seek out here. Everyone's using satellites to find each other, so unless we want a battle...no one's chasing one.

Alex, sitting in one of the few warships that *could* avoid a satellite, grimaced and went back to work.

Jimmy Carter rounded out the season with a little spying over Thanksgiving. It was a mission that *should* have been challenging, but no one thought for a moment that North Korea was going to shoot at anyone. Not with China still engaged in their four-way civil war and Russia gobbling up territory left and right. Even despots weren't that dumb.

Sure, sneaking into the East China Sea was a tad exciting, but they got there right as ships clashed in the La Perouse Strait. That meant there was jack for enemies in the vicinity. After a touch-and-go contact with a Russian *Yasen* that disappeared into the shallows before they could firm up a firing solution, the rest of their contacts were merchants and Chinese warships of questionable allegiance.

And on the way back...well, there just wasn't a lot of fighting up there now that the Japanese Navy was toast, not with the British making faces at the Russians in hopes it kept them bottled up in the north. It was a more interesting mission than convoy escorts...but it still left Alex on the bench, waiting to make a difference.

To add insult to injury, intelligence eventually got around to telling them that the two destroyers they weren't allowed to sink way back when escorting Convoy 3211 hadn't even been after the merchants. They'd been legitimate military targets in wartime, so there was no reason *not* to sink them, but their presence didn't indicate a shift in enemy posture. Escorted convoys were still safe.

Three months into their time in the war zone, *Jimmy Carter* hadn't fired a single shot. If not for message traffic and chats with his fellow COs over drinks in the Officers' Club, Alex might've forgotten that they were at war.

Unfortunately, he knew of what was happening to the rest of his navy to worry.

I spend most of my time chasing ammo, Nancy said in her email dated December 6th. *There aren't enough missiles to go around, or even surface-launched torpedoes. Your crystal ball was right, though; they installed old-style depth charge launchers on* Fletcher *last week. Not that it's done me a bunch of good. I think I got a piece of one Indian diesel sub before it snuck off and we lost it.*

We haven't had one significant surface ship battle in the last two months, and don't get me started on La Perouse Strait. Everyone has ships, but no one's got missiles. I guess it's nice to know that <u>all</u> the bean counters messed that one up, not just ours. I hear that the manufacturer stood up another three production lines to try to get more SM-6s out, but right now, I'd settle for SM-2s. Even expired ones usually explode when they hit.

On the bright—if you can call it bright—side, our task group has a new name. Fletcher *is the official flagship of Task Group 23, the Little Beavers. It's nice to know someone's read their history, but we've got a real admiral in charge, so we must be more than a plus'd-up destroyer squadron. Makes me willing to forgive the new boss for being a submariner, particularly since he seems sharp as a box of knives.*

He joined us right before La Perouse Strait, and he's the only reason why we were in range to help when the Japanese Navy needed it. He was the reason we had weapons, too, though I shot pretty much all of them off. I suppose that makes me ungrateful, but alive. Still, the admiral kept his head on worlds better than the last submariner I served with. I guess not all your flag officers have bird shit for brains. Do you know Rear Admiral Marco Rodriquez?

I think you'd like him if you don't. He's determined to kick the shit out of someone, so hopefully that'll get me more than the handful of missiles they handed me here on Christmas Island. I feel like my VLS cells are whistling.

Either way, we'll be in Perth soon. I hope to see you there, assuming you're not out escorting another convoy. Give the girls a call when you get the chance. Bobbie's fretting college choices, and Emily's grades dropped a little. They could use a little dad-brand love and encouragement.

Reading Nancy's words left Alex feeling a strange mixture of affection, envy, and gut-wrenching worry. His wife remained one of the top surface commanders in the war—Nancy served with distinction everywhere she went, including the recent Battle of La Perouse Strait, where half of Japan's surface navy went down in flames.

The grapevine said it would've been a lot worse if one Rear Admiral Marco Rodriquez hadn't had the weird urge to do exercises in the Sea of Japan with his shiny new Task Group, which put him in range to help when the Russians came south in force and everything went straight to hell.

Fletcher escaped with empty magazines and minor damage, mostly from fragments of Russian long-range missiles that were hellishly hard to stop. Nancy won a second silver star for sinking two Russian frigates and a destroyer, but the actual hero was the British submariner, Ursula North.

Captain North and HMS *Gallant* somehow slipped through every Russian submarine screen, sprinting through Russian-held waters to defend the combined Japanese-American fleet against a veritable fleet of Russian submarines. She sank all four submarines with the Russian strike group, as well as two of their "super" frigates that the rest of the world considered destroyers.

She also sank two surface ships as the Russians withdrew, turning the battle into a bloody draw. Her eight kills in one day were by far the best of the war on the Alliance's side, and North turned into an international sensation overnight. While the Alliance's losses continued mounting faster than the Freedom Union's, North's actions proved one thing: stealth was the most important game in town.

And it was a game only submarines could play, with satellites and aircraft everywhere.

So *Virginias* and the *Ceroes* struggled to take the fight to the enemy while *Jimmy Carter* did the boring jobs.

Like his current glorious task of escorting battle-damaged warships back to Perth from all the way the hell across the Indian Ocean after the Battle of the Agalega Islands.

The Agalega Islands had been the last of Mauritius' possessions to resist the Freedom Union, but located as they were north of Tromelin Island and Saint Denis, both firm French possessions, it was only a matter of time before the French closed in on them. Particularly after Madagascar joined the enemy. For a while, however, people clung to hope that the Agalega Islands might maintain their independence, if not outright ties to the Alliance. After all, the Seychelles, north of the Agalega Islands, were neutral. And Diego Garcia was not far to the west.

But the war came to the Agalega Islands around Thanksgiving, and local forces were hammered. Alliance reinforcements arrived too late, only to find the islands already in the hands of the enemy. The ensuring battle went poorly…and left *Jimmy Carter* four damaged warships to escort back to Perth.

On the surface, it seemed like a more honorable job than a convoy escort and way more likely to give *Jimmy Carter* a chance to see action. Yet all it had done so far was give Alex the glowing opportunity to deal with cranky surface officers whose ships had been shot halfway to shit and who hated admitting that.

Dealing with *them* was almost as entertaining as juggling his crews' increasing hostility toward the XO, whose inability to take a joke had grown to epic proportions.

"I got to give the junior officers credit, Captain. That stunt with the medical dummy at lunch was *funny*, and it ain't hurt no one. Wasn't even a bit humiliating to the XO, or shouldn't have been, anyway," Master Chief Morton said.

The pair sat in Alex's threadbare cabin, which he *still* hadn't bothered to get re-carpeted. The idea seemed pretentious with a war on. Alex sighed. "It probably would've helped if the XO hadn't screamed like a little girl."

"Or if the entire boat hadn't heard him." Morton snickered. "Begging your pardon, sir, but it was pretty fucking legendary."

"You know that. *I* know that. But—" A knock on the door cut Alex off, and he straightened out of his slump in his desk chair. "It's open!"

STS1 Wilson stuck his head in. "Do you have a moment, Captain?"

"Sure, Wilson. What's up?" Alex leaned back in his chair, exchanging a curious look with Morton.

"Sorry to bother you, sir, but I wanted to let you know the results of the test we were working on the port-side lateral array." Wilson shifted from one foot to another, studying the holes in the carpet.

"How'd that work out?" Alex asked.

The sonar techs had been trying to repair the port-side sonar array for three days, trying to fix the hydrophones' disturbing tendency to blank out medium-strength signals. Ensign Vincentelli told him that there was nothing in any technical manual to explain the problem, and the slow process of emailing back and forth with the repair shop in Pearl Harbor hadn't helped so far.

"I think we got it fixed, Captain." Wilson grinned. "We're clearing tags now, and we're ready to optest the system with your permission."

Alex smiled. "Permission granted. Let the EOOW and the OOD know."

"Yes, sir." Wilson turned to go, until Alex asked:

"One last question, STS1. Why are you briefing me instead of Mister Vincentelli?"

The young petty officer twisted back to face him, shrugging. "He's got his pre-board for his dolphins with the department heads in the morning, sir, and he's been up for a day and a half. I told him to get some sleep and that I'd handle things."

"Be careful, STS1. You're starting to sound responsible."

"Ain't it crazy, Captain? I'll have to work on misbehaving more."

"Oh, get out of here!" Alex laughed.

Together, the captain and the master chief watched their delinquent sailor duck out of the stateroom. Finally, Morton shook his head and chuckled.

"Well, shit, Captain. It looks like he's turning out better than I hoped. Certainly better than I expected."

"I imagine that last bit isn't hard to accomplish."

"Nope." Morton leaned back in his chair. "But hell, sir, I didn't expect more than a warm body and an okay watchstander out of the deal. Master Chief Baker didn't exactly speak highly of him, and *Bluefish* was so glad to see the back of him I thought they might pay me."

"Well, as surprises go, I suppose I'll take the good ones. God knows there've been enough bad ones."

"You mean like winding up on this old boat, Captain?" Morton asked.

Alex grimaced. "Was I that obvious?"

"Nah, you hid it pretty well. But I've been around the block a couple of times, and no CO like you wants to wind up on a boat like this, doin' jobs like these. You're a lot better than the sort they *should've* sent here, no disrespect intended."

"None taken." Alex gulped.

"Hell, I could see the writing on the wall when I was dumb enough to volunteer for another COB tour and *Jimmy Carter*. I came here because otherwise they'd have sent some numbskull who'd have been too inexperienced to figure out what to do with this old boat and the funky crew the Bureau decided to saddle us with. But there ain't no way they sent us a captain like you on purpose, sir. You're too good for the shit jobs they want *Smiley* to do."

"Thanks. I think."

Knowing his crew thought highly of him was flattering, but hearing the sentiment spoken aloud made him want to hide in a corner. What was he supposed to say in response?

"D'you mind me asking who the hell you pissed off to wind up here, Captain?"

Alex surprised himself by laughing. "The list is long, Master Chief, but at least it's distinguished."

"Sounds like one hell of a story."

"Well, it's something." For the first time, Alex smiled at the memory. "You ever been to Armistice Station? The first time I was near the place—"

The speaker next to his desk crackled.

"Captain, Officer of the Deck, you might want to come up to control."

Marty's drawl was higher pitched than usual, and the whispers in the background were urgent. That got Alex's attention. The engineer had the deck right now, and he wasn't exactly prone to overreacting. An engineering casualty wouldn't phase him, and pending combat would send them to battle stations, so what was going on?

"I'm on my way," Alex said.

Out the door and a few steps forward, and then Alex was in the Attack Center, Master Chief Morton on his heels. Watch section two was on right now, full of familiar faces in familiar positions, but there was a certain tension that Alex did *not* recognize.

"What's up, Marty?"

Marty Sterling was, in spite of—perhaps because of—his portly build, a perfect fit to the stereotype of the navy engineer. His coveralls were baggy, a rag peeked out of one pocket, and at least two flashlights always hung from his belt. He was the oldest of *Jimmy Carter's* department heads, the most experienced, and the least bothered by minor setbacks. Marty often joked that he'd lost most of his hair battling with his ex-wife, so there was no use letting *Smiley* steal the rest of it.

Now, however, that dry sense of humor seemed to have been replaced by sheer disbelief. Marty looked as stunned as if someone had smacked him between the eyes with a baseball bat.

"You're not going to believe this, Captain," he said.

"Hit me with it."

Marty sighed. "*Safeguard* had a complete reefer plant meltdown. They lost almost *all* their frozen and chilled foods."

"Okay...?" Alex glanced around the space, noting the other pale faces and wide eyes. A casualty on the rescue-and-salvage ship they were escorting shouldn't create this level of tension.

Obviously, the situation sucked for those on board *Safeguard*, particularly since the salvage ship was carrying about half of *Chesapeake Bay's* crew, too. Parts of the damaged cruiser were uninhabitable from battle damage, and *Salvage* had taken her under tow two days earlier. Still, it was hardly a tragedy to make his people look so shell-shocked.

"The captain of *Chesapeake Bay* has ordered us to pull alongside and replenish *Safeguard's* stores with some of ours."

"*What?*"

Alex's jaw dropped. He'd never worked under a cruiser's CO before, but he'd assumed that a full bird captain on their second command would be smart enough not to come up with an idea so flamingly moronic that it was likely to spontaneously combust.

Submarines didn't simply rig fenders and pull alongside surface ships while underway. The only ships they ever moored alongside at sea were sub tenders, and only then when the tender was making no way through the water! And there was a *reason* for that. Driving a submarine in close vicinity of other ships was dangerous. Doubly so in the open ocean.

It was an article of submariner faith that subs handled like drunk elephants on the surface, prone to wallowing in the waves and ignoring rudder commands. A modern submarine was a steel tube with a propulsor—which was a fancy propellor—and a rudder stuck on its ass. They weren't designed to drive above water and generally didn't, except when pulling into and out of port.

"Why the hell can't one of the destroyers do that?" Alex stumbled back a step, shaking his head.

Marty threw up his hands.

Alex resisted the urge to groan. Most surface warfare officers were smart enough, and even brilliant in their own fields, but they didn't know jack about submarines. Even Nancy was weak on the topic, and she had his brain to pick. Of course, he didn't know much about surface operations, either, but it was a pain in the ass that just kept revisiting *Jimmy Carter*.

"I'll take care of this," he said instead of swearing up the storm he wanted to. Steeling himself, Alex lifted the handset for the convoy command comms channel.

Don't babble, he told himself. *And don't be an ass. Just stick to the facts.* God, he still hated public speaking. The fact that the people on the other end couldn't see him barely helped at all.

"*Chesapeake Bay*, this is *Jimmy Carter* Actual for *Ches Bay* Actual, over." Some convoy commanders liked to use call signs, whereas others trusted their communications' encryption enough to speak in plain voice. This guy was one of the later.

"*Jimmy Carter*, this is *Ches Bay*. Standby."

A minute of nothing ticked by, and then finally a new voice came over, sounding way too jolly.

"*Jimmy Carter*, this is *Ches Bay* Actual. I don't see you on the surface yet, over."

Alex gritted his teeth. *God, these idiots really do think you can surface a submarine in two minutes flat, don't they?* Surfacing was a complicated procedure, even using the shortcuts approved for wartime. While moving between deep water and the surface, a sub's sensors were almost blind to what they might find topside. Although a good link picture passed from the surface ships alleviated the danger some, every sub CO worried about surfacing beneath something he couldn't see.

That was a kiss goodbye for a career in peacetime. Even in wartime, it was a great way to disable your submarine…or sink it, if you were really unlucky.

Not that *Chesapeake Bay's* captain considered such mundane concerns. Alex waited a heartbeat before responding, fighting back the urge to offer to surface right under *Chesapeake Bay* and ruin the cruiser's day, too.

"Ah, *Ches Bay*, this is *Jimmy Carter*. We've got a, um, couple of lengthy procedures to get through down here before we can come up and join you," he said. "It'll take us fifteen or twenty minutes to surface, even following wartime procedures. Over."

A long silence echoed on the other end. Should Alex tell Captain Hickman that a *peacetime* no-notice surface took around an hour? Technically, without an emergency declared or the convoy in danger, the longer procedures were the proper ones to follow, but so long as the surface ships stayed clear of his submarine and kept transmitting their positions, coming up the fast way should be safe. Should.

"I find that...inconvenient, *Jimmy Carter*," Hickman said.

That was probably the closest the senior officer would get to calling Alex a liar on a circuit every other ship was listening to. For a moment, Alex almost hoped that *Chesapeake Bay's* captain would *order* him to breach procedure—but no, pulling the safety card and refusing to follow a foolish order would only start a fight he didn't need.

And he'd already disobeyed orders once in his career. No, he'd have to pray logic worked.

"May I suggest you call one of the destroyers alongside *Salvage* to provide assistance?" Alex said. "That'll get them help a lot faster."

And then he wouldn't have to try to explain how dangerous it would be to bring a four-hundred-fifty-foot-long submarine alongside a rescue-and-salvage ship that couldn't stop without endangering the cruiser she was towing.

Never mind what my propulsor could do to that tow line if it gets sucked in! Smiley *is heavier and longer than that piddling little salvage ship and a whole lot less maneuverable.*

"Negative, *Jimmy Carter*. You've got the most frozen food left on board, and *Salvage* is also providing food to half my crew. You're best suited for the job."

Yeah, *Jimmy Carter* had more food because a submarine couldn't exactly have stores delivered via helicopter. Alex snarled a curse under his breath. The convoy wasn't due in port for another two weeks, and although *Jimmy Carter's* freezers carried enough food to provide a comfortable safety margin, that wouldn't last if she was expected to provide for the rescue ship and the cruiser. Together, those ships carried over three times as many personnel as Alex's submarine.

This was a disaster just waiting to happen.

5 December 2038, Washington, D.C.

It took far too long for the torpedo issue to land on Freddie Hamilton's desk. But it only took her five minutes to decide what to do with it.

Getting an appointment with the CNO took longer, but having three stars and most of the war on her shoulders meant Freddie was on the short list of people who could walk in on Admiral David "Scrap" Chan unannounced. She wasn't that impolite—not yet—but his aide snuck her on a Sunday. They were all working weekends.

"Seven months of war and sixteen boats sunk, sir. It's a terrible record," Freddie said in lieu of saying hello.

Scrap squinted at his coffee behind his long and shiny desk. "Isn't it your job to fix that?"

"That's why I'm here." Freddie sat down and crossed her legs, not bothering to turn her tablet on. She knew the facts. "We have two problems: one, more admirals than submarines. I trust you'll fix that one. Two: our torpedoes are too slow, and the enemy's boats are too fast. I can't touch the latter, but there's a faster torpedo out there, and we can have it now."

"Say what? How?"

"Lazark and AIB got together and married the British Spearfish to our Mark 48. Then they gave it a sexier battery and screw. The result is the Mark 84 Advanced Spearfish Variant. It's compatible with British *and* American firing systems, 32 knots faster than the Mark 48 and for the same range. Even better, Lazark says they can start manufacturing it next week."

Scrap blinked. "How much will that cost us?"

"A lot less than another sixteen new *Ceroes*, sir," Freddie replied.

"But will it *work*? I can read World War II history as well as anyone else. We fired a ton of duds in that war." Scrap rubbed his chin. "We can't afford to do that, Freddie. Even if they're fast duds."

Fast duds might give our boats a chance to get away, she didn't say. Telling Scrap that current submarine tactics didn't work would be like lecturing her cat about depth contours.

"The test results are convincing." She took a deep breath. "And we have to do something, sir. Our boats can't get in close enough to get kills with the Mark 48s. They're too slow. That's one of the main things getting our people killed."

Scrap sighed. "Why didn't we see this coming? Surely we knew how fast enemy torpedoes were before the war. We have intel."

"Honestly? We've been the best so long that it never occurred to us that we might not be anymore."

Christmas Island (Australia), East Indian Ocean

USS *Fletcher* swung gently at anchor, a warm night breeze carrying the smell of baking bread across her decks. It was wartime, so some watches were manned in her engineering spaces and CIC, but her main engines were on standby, and there was only an officer and two enlisted sailors on the bridge. Protected by two ready-duty ships—tonight, a cruiser and a destroyer—most of *Fletcher's* crew could sleep.

That included her captain...until the general alarm started blaring.

Commander Nancy Coleman jerked awake just in time for her cabin phone to ring. She snatched it out of the plastic cradle so fast she almost broke the cord.

"Talk to me!"

"Captain, it's the CIC Watch Officer. *Cold Harbor* reports multiple missiles inbound bearing two-seven-seven. Profiles match BrahMos NG. Range one four zero nautical miles, speed Mach 7. Time to impact one minute, thirty seconds."

"*Shit!*" Nancy threw herself out of bed, grabbed her boots in one hand and coveralls in the other, and sprinted for CIC.

Fletcher's Combat Information Center—the beating heart of her warfighting capability—was one deck down and forty feet forward of the CO's cabin. Nancy needed twenty-five seconds to get there, never noticing how the metal ladder rungs stung her bare feet. She flung herself into the captain's chair, dumping her coveralls on the deck to her left.

Fletcher shuddered.

"Birds away, targeting hostile tracks in sector." Chief Warrant Officer Anna Nagel was *Fletcher's* Systems Test Officer, a gray-haired and steel-willed prior enlisted sailor who knew the Aegis Weapons System like the back of her hand. Her eyes never left the screen, not even to glance at the captain who now sat by her side. "Doctrine launching ESSM."

"Captain, aye."

Nancy's eyes swept over the three tactical screens at the front of *Fletcher's* CIC. The missile storm aimed at the twelve ships anchored in Christmas Island's harbor was too dense to count individual tracks; fortunately, Aegis could do that for the mere humans operating it. *Fletcher's* watchstanders were mere passengers now that Nagel had engaged doctrine. It was the right call—there was no way the reduced watch in CIC could keep up.

Now that the battle stations watchstanders were streaming in, that would change. But *Fletcher* had to survive the first minutes of the battle before that mattered.

She wished that the other ships around them would activate Link Doctrine, but the blinking light on Nancy's console told her that no one had. Months of war taught them that the major weakness of Link Doctrine was that it needed a cruiser's Aegis brain to be effective—or at least three destroyers working in tandem. One destroyer's Aegis weapons system couldn't shoulder the processing load alone.

Pushing the thought out of her mind, Nancy pulled a headset on and keyed into the internal communications net. "Central, Captain, come to full power."

"Cheng, aye! Full power in one mike," her chief engineer replied. "GTM one-alpha and two-bravo started, split plant, max speed available two-six knots. Ready to answer all bells."

"Captain, aye, break, bridge."

"Bridge, aye," Commander Ying Mai, *Fletcher's* XO, said. "Weighing anchor now."

"Captain, aye."

Nancy glanced at the clock. She'd entered the CIC less than a minute ago. Maybe they still had a chance.

The ships around *Fletcher*—five destroyers, one frigate, and a cruiser—still weren't moving. Safe at anchorage, with two shooters to guard them, some crews stood down more than others. Would it kill them?

Fletcher shuddered.

Evolved Sea Sparrow missiles burst out of vertical launch tubes forward and aft, joining the SM-6 standard missiles in the air. Nancy *could* count the white icons representing friendly missiles, and they appeared in three groups, all dwarfed by the tidal wave of destruction inbound.

The first and smallest launch was from the guard ships, steaming three miles from the anchorage. The next was standard missiles from *Fletcher* and her fellows, with *Fletcher's* missiles in the lead, despite her position toward the rear of the anchorage. The last was the short-ranged ESSMs.

They weren't enough.

Nancy gripped the arms of her chair, white-knuckled, as *Fletcher's* Close In Weapons System opened up in full auto. Firing 4,500 rounds per minute, the destroyer's two phalanx guns, one forward and one aft, were her last line of defense. Every destroyer and cruiser had two CIWS mounts, with a maximum range of about two thousand yards.

Tracer rounds glowed against the night sky, spitting defiance against the incoming missiles as they dropped low to the deck to avoid the standard missiles and sea sparrows launched to stop them.

The Brahmos NG was the fastest ship-killing missile in the world. Almost four hundred of them roared in on the nine ships at Christmas Island, countered by just 144 standard missiles and 72 ESSMs.

Nancy gritted her teeth and got to work.

Chapter 24

Laying Traps

Western Indian Ocean, 100 nautical miles from Madagascar

Okay. This cruiser CO was clearly an idiot. So, if subtle wasn't working, Alex would go with blunt. It was only a few hours before sunset, and he was driving a goddamned *submarine*. Who in their right mind thought a submarine could resupply *anything?*

He cleared his throat and spoke into the radio to the cruiser captain who had rice for brains. "You do know that a submarine isn't designed to—"

"I expect you to make it happen, Captain."

Alex blinked.

He opened his mouth to argue and then snapped it shut. Judging from the tone of Captain Hickman's voice, *Chesapeake Bay's* commanding officer didn't care how logical an argument Alex could muster; he wasn't going to listen. And in wartime, odds were that even the most reasonable admiral would take a full captain's side over the screwup who got *Jimmy Carter* seven days a week and twice on Sundays.

It wasn't like he had a habit of finding reasonable flag officers, was it? From Admiral Hamilton to Commodore Banks—who he'd never even met—Alex was super popular with submariners with stars. Double bonus points went to Banks, who just wanted *any* excuse to decommission his boat. Alex couldn't afford to put a foot wrong.

Not again.

"*Jimmy Carter* copies," Alex snapped. "But it *will* take time. There is *no* safe way to do this, but if I have to execute this goat rope, I'm going to do it with as little danger as possible. Out."

Ending the transmission like that was the equivalent of hanging up on Hickman, but Alex was beyond being worried about that. He *hoped* the jackass felt insulted.

"Easy there, Captain," Morton muttered from his side. "No need to make enemies."

"Eh, my enemies outrank him." Alex shrugged.

"You really owe me that story now, sir."

Alex shook himself. "Later." He turned to Marty, forcing his voice to be level. "All right, Cheng. Let's bring her up about five hundred yards off of *Safeguard's* beam, slightly astern of her." He forced a smile. "But do try to avoid the cruiser. Wouldn't do to surface under her and tear a hole in her ass."

"Aye, sir." Was that a smile on Marty's face? It was hard to tell with Marty so pale.

Everyone knew how dangerous and stupid this was. Everyone wearing a submariner's dolphins, anyway.

Slowly, *Jimmy Carter* worked her way toward the surface, clearing her baffles on the way up to make sure no underwater contacts could creep up on them. The process took the entire twenty minutes Alex promised it would. Under other circumstances, he might've cut some corners, but the fool in command had drawn the formation in tight. And of course, he wanted Alex's boat right in the middle of all those pesky surface ships.

Surfacing under these conditions was like climbing a set of stairs while blindfolded, without knowing if there were people on the steps or just near them, and with no way to prevent a collision except a quick glance through the bottom of a glass cup before the blindfold went on.

The radio was crackling again by the time *Jimmy Carter* broke the surface, but Alex ignored it. Instead, he headed up to the bridge on Marty's heels, trying to ignore the way his heart jumped into a knot in his throat.

Getting up into the sail didn't help; heavy and warm salt air smacked him in the face as soon as Alex climbed the ladder and his head popped into the light. Then *Jimmy Carter* rocked port, and Marty stumbled right into Alex, knocking him into the side of the sail. Gripping the handrail, Alex studied the seas, watching his boat roll. This was worse than usual, but the waves hadn't looked this bad through the periscope. Seas were worsening rapidly.

Oh, this was going to be a fantastic fucking day, wasn't it?

Alex looked up from the water and gulped. "Shit, Marty, that driving was a bit on the nose."

Marty grimaced. "Sorry, Captain. I guess I misjudged that one a little bit."

Marty was an excellent engineer and a dependable officer, but he wasn't the best ship handler on Alex's crew. He had a habit of winding up just a bit *off* from where he aimed the submarine...and today was one of those days.

Instead of five hundred yards away, *Jimmy Carter* was barely a hundred yards off *Safeguard's* starboard side. Nancy would've called this precision ship handling and been impressed.

In a submarine, it was dangerous.

But Marty was miserable enough already, so Alex didn't mention it. Did he get seasick in rough weather? Alex supposed he'd find out if his engineer puked on him.

"Four hundred yards is more than just a *little* bit, Lieutenant Sterling," a new voice said.

Joy. Just what he needed. George had scurried up the ladder, joining Alex, Marty, and the lookouts in the cramped bridge area. The XO was already all but wringing his hands.

Marty twisted to glare at George. There was no love lost between these two; Marty resented the XO's micromanaging, and George claimed Marty wasn't a team player when he tried to run his own department without interference.

"Afternoon, XO," Alex said cheerfully. The best way to cut the tension was to make everyone go along with the captain's good mood. Sometimes, it was good to be king.

Or it would be if his XO played along.

"Captain, this is dangerous." George really wasn't wasting time today. "This is *insane*. No one in their right mind would actually want to—"

"They call them orders for a reason, George," Alex said. "Pulling alongside *Safeguard* really isn't how I planned to spend my afternoon, either, but let's just try to get this over with as quickly as possible."

"I'm very uncomfortable with this, sir."

"You think I'm not?" Alex grimaced. "But we've got a job to do, so let's complain less and do more. Understood?"

George heaved a sigh, staring pointedly at *Safeguard*. But at least he nodded and shut up.

Marty brought *Jimmy Carter* around as George headed below to coordinate a working party to hump the frozen food and stores over to the rescue ship once the sub got alongside. Keeping George busy was the only way to manage his nerves. Alex was becoming a pro at finding non-demeaning tasks for his ever-twitchy XO.

Marty, however, seemed to have his own case of the shakes and looked at Alex with owl-like eyes.

"Captain, I'm not sure how you want me to approach this one."

Alex smiled. "You want me to take her in?"

"Well, if one of us has to smash her up, I'd rather it be you." Marty fidgeted. "The XO's right. This is...crazy. Even for wartime."

"Crazy's not quite a strong enough word," Alex said, taking the sound-powered handset from Marty, anyway. No department head enjoyed admitting that they couldn't do something, especially to their CO. He patted Marty on the shoulder. "I got it." Alex spoke into the microphone. "This is the captain. I have the conn."

The reply came back from control on the speaker to his right, muffled a little by the rising wind. "Diving Officer, aye. My rudder is left fifteen degrees, coming to course three-one-seven. Planes are at zero. All engines are ahead one third for three knots."

"Very well."

Alex's eyes sought out the rescue ship, barely one hundred yards to port and pulling ahead of the submarine. Still calculating angles, he glanced over his left shoulder to study the cruiser wallowing in the waves about a mile astern of *Safeguard*. The tow line between the two appeared to be riding correctly, which at least meant he could avoid it by staying clear of *Safeguard's* stern.

The speaker crackled. "Steady on course three-one-seven."

"Very well. All engines ahead two-thirds for eight knots."

He tuned out the repeat back. The rescue ship was making five knots, which meant that three knots of overtaking speed would allow *Jimmy Carter* to close the range within three minutes or so. Meanwhile, he grabbed the handheld bridge-to-bridge radio with his other hand.

"Rescue Ship Five-Seven, this is Warship Two-Three," he called up *Safeguard*, using both vessel's hull numbers on the unencrypted radio circuit.

"This is Five-Seven, go."

"Five-Seven, Two-Three, my intention is to approach from astern and come along your starboard side, over."

"We're standing by for you, Two-Three, and we're grateful for the help."

Alex could already see sailors moving to *Safeguard's* starboard side to receive the submarine. And yet—something was missing. *Shit.* "Uh, Five-Seven...do you have lines for us?"

"Say again?"

"Five-Seven, this is Two-Three. Subs receive lines, we don't send them over. There's no space on deck to store them," Alex said, his heart pounding.

There was a long pause on the other end while Alex fought down the urge to break something in frustration. The disaster just kept growing.

"Standby Two-Three," *Safeguard* said after too long.

"Two-Three standing by." Alex pulled his finger off the transmit key. "Fuck." He gritted his teeth against the urge to swear more. It wouldn't do to let his crew know their CO was done with this pointless game.

"All ahead one-third for four knots," he said when he trusted his voice again.

Halving their speed made *Jimmy Carter* start dropping back. They were still dangerously close to the rescue ship, with the sub's bow already in the edges of *Safeguard's* wake. If Alex wasn't careful, the forces generated by the rescue ship's screws churning through the water would suck the submarine in, causing a collision neither vessel could afford.

Yeah, that'd make this sparkling day even better.

Two long minutes passed before the salvage ship's CO's voice came over the radio. "Two-Three, this is Five-Seven Actual. We've been ordered to bring you alongside immediately, so go ahead and commence your approach. We'll have lines ready as soon as possible."

Bile churned in Alex's throat, and visions of his submarine kissing *Safeguard* danced through his mind. Damn Hickman to every hell there was.

"Two-three copies," he said, his voice hoarse.

"That cruiser CO is a flaming moron, Captain," Marty whispered.

Alex snorted. "Ours is not to reason why." He licked his lips. "Let's just do this thing so we can go back down where it's safe again."

"Roger that, sir. I'll call the line handlers topside."

"Make sure they double check their safety tie-offs," Alex said. "These seas are only getting worse, and I don't want anyone going overboard."

Taking another deep breath, Alex returned his attention to the approach and ordered *Jimmy Carter* back up to match *Safeguard's* speed. Hickman could be as impatient as he wanted; Alex wasn't going alongside until his line handlers were all secured. *Jimmy Carter* had been on the surface for just ten minutes, and the waves had already grown by a foot.

The rescue ship's deeper draft meant she wasn't rolling too badly, but the round hull of the submarine was really taking a beating. A few waves splashed high enough to spray Alex right in the face, and by the time the line handlers were assembled on the sub's deck, all of them were soaking wet.

"You think we should get some safety harnesses up here, Captain?" Marty asked.

SOP said yes. Alex made a face. "I think we're using them all on deck."

Over the whistling wind, Alex could hear Master Chief Morton yelling: "And if any one of you unlucky sunzabitches goes overboard, you can bet I ain't comin' after you, so secure those damn lanyards!"

"Aye, aye, Master Chief!" the crew on deck echoed.

Morton turned to check his own lanyard before giving Alex a thumbs-up; Alex nodded and swallowed back his nerves.

Enough delays. It was time to get going with this goat rope before the weather got even worse.

Waltham, Massachusetts, USA

An early morning flight delivered Freddie to Massachusetts around noon, and Lazark had a car waiting at the airport. Freddie didn't believe in bringing a large staff along, but she did drag along her brand-new operations officer, Captain Conrad Croft, and Commander Maria Vasquez, still her aide.

The drive to the factory was blessedly short. Lazark had facilities all over the eastern seaboard, but this one was in a suburb of Boston, which meant they only had twenty minutes. That was barely enough time for Freddie to get bored. After they arrived, a veritable who's-who of Lazark managers fell all over themselves to show Freddie this magical new torpedo.

The factory smelled like plastic and welding. The latter smell was one Freddie liked; it said they were busy. She pushed hope down ruthlessly; so much could go wrong. She could not depend upon Lazark to do the right thing.

Companies looked out for their own bottom line. There was no room for patriotism in that. Freddie *knew* how the world worked, and no three-star admiral was going to change that. She just had to figure out how to work within its confines.

"We tried inviting Admiral Trieu out here," Lily Garcia, the site manager, said as they walked out onto the production floor. She was a tall woman, taller than Freddie, with graying red hair and thick glasses. "But he never found time in his schedule."

"I see." Freddie pursed her lips, exchanging a glance with Maria. That was a nice way of saying that Trieu was too overwhelmed to get off his behind and look at the solution right in front of his face.

They walked down one production line while an engineer rattled off the new Mark 84's specs. Freddie, who'd already recited them for the CNO, only listened with half an ear. Manufacturers always said good things about their weapons, and these were the same guys who'd been building one variant or another of the Mark 48 for *fifty* years.

But the thing was shiny. She had to admit that once face-to-torpedo with the great big fish. Most civilians thought torpedoes were *small* because they only saw them on television screens, but this sucker looked the same length as its predecessor, about nineteen feet. It probably weighed the same three thousand pounds, too.

The torpedo was painted gray, though, not the green she was familiar with. That was a nice touch.

"Is it as fast as you say?" Freddie ran a hand down the smooth body of the torp.

"Tests say a fifty-five knot minimum, Admiral," Garcia replied. "Some have reached as high as sixty in their terminal run."

"It looks like the same basic torpedo body as the Mark 48," Captain Croft said. He was a tiny man, thin, with steel gray hair and horn-rimmed glasses. He was quiet and meticulous, too, just like the boomer captain he'd been on his last tour. Freddie liked him. "Are all the connections compatible?"

Garcia smiled. "Plug and play, sir. All you need is a software upgrade."

"Hm." Croft frowned.

"How fast can you roll it into production?" Freddie hated asking that question. Proper procedure was for live fire testing by the navy, validations, and then more testing. But...they didn't have time.

November saw three boats sunk. Six days into December and

they'd already lost one. Captain Dalton's scathing but politely written reports were very clear: her submariners needed better tools than they'd been given.

"We started the line up already and have fifty in stock," Garcia replied, her face a little pale. "Once the contract is signed, we will start another three lines up here in Waltham and another two in Rhode Island. Working three shifts, that will give us the ability to produce six torpedoes a day."

Maria whistled. "That's one hell of an increase."

"And a hell of a lot of money," Croft said.

"Submarines cost more," Freddie said. "Let me see this contract."

It went without saying that Lazark—and their partners, AIB, who would build the same torpedo for the Brits and the Aussies—would make bank off this. But Freddie was fine with that. Lazark was confident enough in the Mark 84 to put their own money on the line by making fifty of the things without a contract, which meant fifty torpedoes that could go to the fleet *now*. They were entitled to a little profit.

Freddie just wanted the goddamned torpedoes.

The Western Indian Ocean

The hunt was always the best part. After a mouth's leave in Toulon, during which his beautiful submarine received upgrades to her fire control system and sonar processors, Captain Jules Rochambeau was back in the thick of things. He made four warship kills in November, an excellent performance by anyone's standards—except for one thing.

Ursula North had sunk *ten*.

Six of them in one infernal afternoon.

She'd beaten his record. Jules knew he'd set the record for most warships and submarines sank in one afternoon at the Battle of Cocos Islands back in late July. He'd been certain no one would top *five*, and then Ursula—his old friend and competitor from across the Channel—sank six Russians in that bloody stalemate over a worthless atoll.

Short of another major surface battle—those were the best shooting galleries—or perhaps another task force he could track by satellite—Jules was not likely to find another day so profitable. So he needed a month to top Ursula's October. And he needed to unnerve his old exercise opponent.

Tweeting her was out of the question. Ursula wouldn't dirty her aristocratic fingers on Twitter if it was the last social media platform on Earth. That left email. On the bright side, he doubted the Brits changed their email addresses upon the arrival of war any more than his navy had. Reconfiguring servers was just too much work when the tech geniuses had so many better things to do with their time.

So Jules waited until the dead of night—always the quietest time on his submarine, particularly when not on the hunt—to sit down and type an email to his old friend.

Dearest Ursula,

I would congratulate you on your spectacular month in October had you not decided to send some of my compatriots to the bottom with your torpedoes. Did you think of them when you gave the command to fire? Commander Fortin shared that memorable dinner with us in Marseilles—she was the one your tall PWO flirted with so shamelessly.

It is strange standing against old allies, is it not? I still remember all the exercises we engaged in, each striving to "kill" one another with our practice torpedoes. I always enjoyed the stories and drinks afterward, but I imagine there will be no meeting after if we clash now.

Rumor says you remain in northern waters. Perhaps you should come south, and we will renew our friendly rivalry.

Your old friend,

Jules Rochambeau

Smiling, he clicked send.

She would not take the bait this time. No, not Ursula. She would rant and rave and then return to her duty. She would probably not even answer, at least not the first email. Jules estimated it would take another three or four emails before Ursula sent him a string of creative swear words and a demand that he leave her alone.

She'd be too proud to block him, of course. And Jules would not abuse that. Not often.

He'd work on her slowly, little by little, until she came out to meet him.

And then they'd find out who was better.

For good.

Christmas Island (Australia)

Missile met missile in the darkness, painting the sky red, orange, and yellow with fire. Voices filled the command circuit, reporting as some ships ran out of missiles and others struggled to get underway.

"Forward CIWS empty," Lieutenant Commander Davud Attar, the general quarters tactical action officer, reported as Chief Warrant Officer Nagel sprinted back to her station as air warfare coordinator. "Reloading now."

Nancy didn't even have time to swallow. "Anyone in Linked Doctrine?"

"Negative."

"Aye."

"Own ship doctrine launching forward ESSMs," Attar said.

Nancy punched a button and brought the forward camera view

up, just in time to watch the missiles race into the night. Then her eyes flicked back down to the V-shaped missiles inbound toward her destroyer. *Fletcher* was toward the back of the formation, which meant any missile aimed at her had to get through all the other ships' point defense along the way...but it also meant *Fletcher* had a duty to help defend them.

Her standard missiles took out two Brahmos, missed three more, and then the forward ESSMs destroyed those in an eye-bleeding flash of fiery missile-on-missile fury. Another Brahmos jinxed past *Jason Dunham* and dove for *Fletcher*, only to be caught by a single round from the aft CIWS mount and tumble end over end into the water.

"All stations, *Cold Harbor*, I am Winchester, I say again *Cold Harbor* is Winchest—" There was a yelp, then static, and the previously calm voice turned high-pitched. "*Cold Harbor* is hit. Two hits forward. On fire and taking on water. Unable to maintain tactical command."

"Shit, she was one of the ready-duty ships," Attar said.

"Here's hoping they can keep her afloat." Nancy didn't have time to worry about how someone else's cruiser did damage control. She stomped on her voice pedal. "Bridge, Captain, get me some maneuvering room to the west. We've got more missiles than almost everyone else, and we need a clear shot at the next wave."

"Bridge, aye," Ying Mai replied. "Coming left to one-two-zero."

"Captain, aye."

Nancy's eyes flicked to the Link 18 ammunition readout, and she grimaced. Yeah, *Fletcher's* twelve remaining SM-6 missiles were more than anyone except *Okinawa* had left, and she was a cruiser. The *Bull Runs* had a lot of magazine space, but *Okie* had still used up almost all of her ESSMs. She only had one quad-pack left; *Fletcher* had seven quad packs for a total of twenty-eight.

"All stations, *William Charette*, one hit midships, fire under control. Lost power aft," another voice reported on the net.

Nancy's heart clenched. That was Commander Mina Markusson. They'd gone to the Prospective Commanding Officer's Course together. Mina made great martinis and had twin sons in middle school. Her wife was in the Air Force, and—

"All stations, *Jason Dunham*, took one missile through the helo hanger with casualties. Fully mission capable." Was that Todd Kellner's voice? She hadn't known he'd taken command of *Dunham*.

"All Stations, *Middendorf*, *Farley* is going down."

Nancy closed her eyes. That was expected; *Farley* was still under repair from the Battle of La Perouse Strait. A ship with little luck, she'd been hammered in the Sunda Strait, only to be repaired and sent back into the meat grinder again.

Grieve later. Focus now. Nancy's destroyer picked up speed, sprinting around her maimed fellows as they finally weighed anchor. They knew the threat bearing, and while Nancy didn't yet have a track on the enemy, she was sure as hell going to find a way to hit them back.

"Well, this is no goddamned fun," a voice said from her left. "Give me a headset and let's see if I can't straighten out this clusterfuck."

Nancy twisted to see Rear Admiral Marco Rodriquez looming over her—though not by much, given how short he was. She extended a headset plugged into the external net and—

"Vampire, vampire, vampire, missiles inbound bearing two-seven-one, range one four zero nautical miles, speed Mach 7. Time to impact one minute, thirty seconds."

"All stations, *Fletcher,* activate Linked Doctrine," Nancy said over the net.

Immediately, the voice of the other cruiser in their group replied: "*Fletcher*, this is *Okinawa,* your recommendation is noted—"

"*Okinawa*, this is Task Group Two-Three Actual," Marco Rodriquez cut in. "Do as the lady says, and we might live another day."

"*Okinawa,* roger, activating Linked Doctrine, out."

Nancy didn't bother to thank her admiral. She didn't bother to think about how she'd overstepped her authority, either. She just watched the icons of enemy missiles blossom on the plot and added up the missiles the Americans had to counter them.

Even with Linked Doctrine, it wouldn't be enough.

Chapter 25

Someone Else's Mess

Christmas Island (Contested)

Admiral Marco Rodriquez watched with growing horror as American ships were blown apart.

This wasn't his kind of warfare, but he'd sure seen a lot of it over the last nine months. A submariner by training, Marco commanded a fast-attack boat and a submarine squadron before earning his first star and getting an Amphibious Strike Group. Granted, that command got all twisted out of shape when the war started and he wound up taking over for a shell-shocked Jeff McNally after the Battle of the SOM, but he'd bounced from one surface command to another ever since.

Somehow, he always ended up cleaning up someone else's mess.

Today, it was for Rear Admiral Chucklefuck Ingram, who was dead, dying, or somehow incapacitated over on *Cold Harbor*. Or maybe he was in the water. The cruiser was busy sinking, and Marco'd inherited the disaster.

Only two of the destroyers involved in the raging Battle of Christmas Island were his: *Jason Dunham* and *Fletcher*. He'd spent the last month trying to assemble the rest of Task Force 23, only to find that his Little Beavers were little indeed; every ship he was supposed to be assigned seemed to be needed somewhere else.

Until this fucking battle, where the entire mess was now his.

"Task Force Two-Three, this *J William Middendorf, Middendorf* is Winchester, over."

"Task Force Two-Three, roger, out." Marco tried not to grit his teeth at the news that *Middendorf* was out of missiles. "Fuck, that's another one."

Nancy Coleman, still clad in nothing but a smiley face shirt and Norwich University sweatpants, snarled under her breath. "The only ships with missiles left are us, *Dunham*, *Truxton*, and *Okinawa*, sir. And we don't have much."

"No shit. It's time to blow this popsicle stand and go home." Marco scowled. "Tanya, did we ever get that air cover?"

"Optic Six says eyes in the sky in fifteen minutes," his chief of staff replied. "We won't have fighters overhead for four hours, not until they can get a carrier in place. *Abe Lincoln* is too far south."

"In hours, we'll be fucking dead, and information in fifteen minutes won't buy us much. These shit waffles can see us, but we can't see them. Either they've got a stealthy friend in the sky or a friendly satellite—and don't fucking tell me *again* about how there are no satellites available." He wanted to break something, but he'd barely been on *Fletcher* for two months. Disassembling things in CIC was rude. "Time to retreat and let them have the islands. Comm the base and tell Commodore Woodward to evacuate. If these ass nuggets are a hundred miles away, she's got time to get her people out if she's smart about it."

Marco *hated* the idea of retreating, but he hated the idea of dying for nothing even more.

And he sure as hell wasn't going to drag anyone else down with him.

Not with missiles still flying and his four remaining ships trying to beat them off with a shoestring, shielding their damaged and empty-magazined counterparts as best they could. Marco watched in helpless fury as *Nicholas* took two hits amidships; they tore the lightweight frigate apart like paper, spewing fire, bodies, and metal everywhere.

Truxton, tucked in close to try to defend *Nicholas*, took a flaming piece of superstructure to her bow, and it ate through her decking like a giant hell creature. That forced her to deluge some of her forward vertical launch system cells, cutting the old *Arleigh Burke*-class destroyer off from the rest of her ordnance. She made the Winchester call a few seconds later.

Okinawa surged into the gap, launching her last missiles to defend her comrades. The cruiser took a glancing blow to the stern that destroyed her empty Harpoon brackets—none of the ships had Harpoons; the supply shortages were too severe—but left her largely intact. Then it was *Fletcher's* turn, and Marco braced himself for death and pain when a missile snaked past the best her CIWS mounts had and took the forward gun mount straight off.

Nancy swore and fires raged, but *Dunham's* last missiles took out the rest of the third wave, buying time for the four remaining warships to retreat.

There was no saving *Nicholas* and *Middendorf;* both burned brightly against the steadily lightening sky. *Farley* was already gone, and *Cold Harbor* was sinking bow down, with her screws sticking out of the water. Marco slowed to pull as many survivors on board as possible, but he only dared linger for two hours. By then, two helicopters from *Okinawa* got eyes on the enemy fleet and confirmed they had fucking *tenders* alongside.

The assholes were reloading missiles at sea. Who did that?

Apparently, no one told the Indians that was a bad fucking idea, even in good weather and in near-dawn darkness. At least it slowed them down long enough for Marco's four ships to pull hundreds of survivors out of the water and sink *Nicholas* when the frigate stubbornly refused to go beneath the waves on her own. Sending her to the bottom took more five-inch rounds than he wanted to waste, but that was better than leaving her secrets for the Indians to find.

What a time not to have submarine along. Marco would've given his right arm for a Mark 48 right now, but surface ship–launched torpedoes were in short supply *and* needed to ward off any future attacks by submarines. Guns were a better option, even if they took longer and made him feel like this hellscape was some weird, alternate World War II they were losing.

Meanwhile, the base on Christmas Island loaded everything they could carry on the one unlucky supply ship moored at pier two and shredded everything they couldn't.

Then Marco and his five ships ran, metaphorical tails between their fucking legs, while ten Indian destroyers and sixteen corvettes took sovereign Australian territory.

"Watch out!"

Master Chief Morton's shout made Alex's head snap around; he'd been focused on maintaining a slight distance between *Jimmy Carter* and *Safeguard*, but he turned in time to see a petty officer third class slip on the submarine's slick deck and almost fall, only to be caught by a shipmate just in time to keep her from cracking her head open on the hull.

"This is getting damn ugly," he muttered to George, who'd rejoined him on the bridge when Marty headed down to engineering.

"Getting?" George's laugh was nervous, but at least he wasn't trying to put his fingers into everyone else's pot today. Perhaps he really was getting better.

I hope to God he is, because the weather certainly isn't!

The skies hadn't quite opened up yet, but it smelled like rain. This wasn't a part of the world Alex had deployed to before, but it didn't take a genius weather-guesser to search the internet and know they were about to get a late-season typhoon.

Jimmy Carter had been alongside the rescue ship for almost ten minutes, and *Safeguard* still hadn't managed to get lines across to the submarine. The salvage ship's crew had rigged fenders between their ship and the black behemoth that was Alex's command, but the rubber bumpers were riding badly in the heavy seas, smacking between the vessels with a wet *squish* sound that got louder with each hit.

Worse yet, *Safeguard's* deck wasn't much higher than *Jimmy Carter's*, which meant the sub couldn't use the lee of the larger vessel to hide from the weather. Instead, she bounced and twisted like a cork bobbing amongst the waves, at the mercy of the seas.

Safeguard wasn't much better off. Cringing, Alex watched the surface sailors slipping and sliding as they struggled to hand the first line over to the submarine. Four efforts later—and a soaking wet line—the thick wire rope finally made it across. Alex's sailors caught it deftly and immediately started making the line up under the COB's supervision.

"That's one." Alex let out a breath he hadn't known he was holding.

"I don't like that they started back aft, Captain," George fretted.

"Me neither, but I'll take what we can—*Jesus.*"

One of *Safeguard's* sailors overbalanced, clearly trying to keep the forward line from dropping into the drink like the last one. As Alex watched in horror, the sailor toppled headfirst over the side of *Safeguard* and into the narrow gap between the two vessels.

Were he a little luckier, it might've ended there. But a sub was considerably wider below the waterline than above it. And with the line back aft attached, *Jimmy Carter* was closer to the rescue ship than she'd been moments before.

Thonk.

The wet sound of flesh hitting metal was audible even though the impact happened a few feet underwater.

"Hard right rudder!" The order was automatic.

"Captain, the stern!"

But Alex's eyes were already riveted on it, watching the stern grow ever closer to the other ship. He'd had to throw the rudder over to keep the overboard sailor from being crushed between the two vessel's bows, but when the bow came out, the stern went in—

Shouting came from forward, and suddenly Master Chief Morton was flat on his stomach on the deck, dangling over the side to reach for *Safeguard's* semi-conscious sailor. A second later, Ruse, *Jimmy Carter's* rescue diver, was next to him, and together they hauled the other man out of the water while Alex's other sailors pulled the two of them back up.

"Shift your rudder!" Alex said, just in time. Ponderously, *Jimmy Carter's* bow swung left, and the stern stopped inches away from hitting the rescue ship.

Someday his heart would stop trying to hammer its way out of his chest. Really, it would.

"Doc, XO, we've got a personnel casualty on the forward deck," George said into his radio.

"On my way."

Alex tuned the exchange out. "Get that goddamned line across!" he shouted down to Morton.

Captain Hickman's ego had already injured one sailor, and Alex would be damned if he let it hurt another.

Another giant wave swept over *Jimmy Carter's* deck before the forward line could be passed from *Safeguard*, but the sailors finally got it secured as Alex straightened the boat out. After the first two lines were across, getting the next two tied off was much easier.

Rigging a makeshift brow between the two vessels was more complicated than getting the lines across, however, because subs and surface ships didn't roll the same way, even when they were attached to one another. *Jimmy Carter* out-massing *Safeguard* by a factor of two didn't help, either. By the time the brow was secure enough to use, forty-five-knot winds were whipping across both vessel's bows.

"Looks like we've got a monsoon brewing, Captain," George said. He looked distinctly green.

"Tell me something I don't know." Alex twisted to glance at the pair of lookouts. "If either of you to are going to puke, try not to do it on anything critical, okay?"

"You got it, sir," the senior one said with a wan smile.

The rocking and rolling was worst on the sail, but sailors on deck were already sick. Unlike their surface counterparts, submariners weren't used to *weather*. Normally, subs dove deep to avoid this crap. *Jimmy Carter's* sailors swayed drunkenly, staggering back and forth as they struggled to lug boxes up from below.

The only good thing about the bucking seas was that they washed the vomit off the deck almost as soon as it hit.

Midway through the transfer, Maggie's head popped up through the hatch, and she scrambled up next to Alex.

"Captain, the barometer's dropped again, and winds are almost up to fifty-five knots," she said. "Fleet weather is predicting a typhoon with winds up to ninety knots."

"This day's just getting better and better, isn't it?" Alex said. "All right. Patch me through to Convoy Command on the phone up here, will you?"

"Yes, sir." Maggie passed the orders and handed him the red-colored phone. "You're up."

"Thanks, Maggie." Alex sucked in a deep breath; this wasn't going to be pleasant, but that was why the navy paid COs the big bucks. "*Chesapeake Bay*, this is *Jimmy Carter* Actual for *Ches Bay* Actual, over."

"Standby."

Alex glanced back at the cruiser following in the dual wakes of his sub and the rescue ship. Despite not maneuvering under her own power, the big warship rode better in the rough seas than either of them, probably because of her deeper draft. Could Hickman even see how badly the transfer was going from back there? He didn't strike Alex as the type to pick up a pair of binoculars and watch.

Six minutes ticked by—Alex timed it, growing increasingly annoyed. During that time, two other sailors lost their footing. A third slipped but caught herself, tearing her forearm open on the edge of the brow and splattering blood all over the box of frozen vegetables she'd been trying to pass off. The next sailor in the daisy chain decided not to catch the vegetables and opted to steady his shipmate instead, and the box tumbled overboard, bouncing off of *Jimmy Carter's* cylindrical hull before vanishing into the churning water between the two vessels.

Thunk. Alex heard the muffled sound of wood hitting metal, and then the box was gone.

Enough was enough. Every instinct Alex had was screaming at him to stop this madness before someone else got hurt.

"Secure the transfer!" he shouted down to Morton.

Morton twisted to look at him, gesturing blankly. It took Alex a moment to realize the winds were too high for the Master Chief to hear.

"Kill the transfer!" He punctuated the words by slashing his free hand across his throat and almost lost his balance when a wave hit *Jimmy Carter* and he wasn't holding on.

Morton waved an acknowledgment, but it took Alex's soaking wet COB three tries to get the message across to *Safeguard*. Meanwhile, sailors hurried to pass the last few boxes over. Last of all, the injured *Safeguard* sailor limped across the brow, supported by shipmates on both sides of the divide.

"*Jimmy Carter* Actual, this is *Ches Bay* Actual, send your traffic, over."

Alex bit back the urge to snap at Hickman. Eight minutes. Where had the cruiser captain been, asleep? Nice to know he cared about the ships executing dangerous orders under his command. Yeah, it wasn't combat, but weather could kill as easily as a torpedo.

"*Ches Bay*, this is *Jimmy Carter*. The weather's gotten worse out here, and we're seeing personnel injuries. I've secured transferring supplies to *Safeguard*." Suddenly, the sub took a wild roll, and Alex couldn't catch himself before his left shoulder slammed into the edge of the sail. Pain shot through his arm, and he bit back a curse. "They've got about sixty-five percent of what we intended to send them, but it's dangerous out here. I'm going to break away."

An almighty *crack* punctuated his last sentence, and one of the lines holding the brow in place snapped. It whipped backward toward the sailors on *Jimmy Carter's* deck, who dove out of the way. Thankfully, the lines used to tie the brow down weren't long, because snapping back lines could cut sailors in half. This one ripped across the deck like a rapid snake but finally landed on *Safeguard's* quarterdeck without hitting anyone.

"Jesus," Alex whispered.

"Stand by on that, *Jimmy Carter*." Despite the buzz of the radio, Hickman's voice sounded damnably normal. "I'd like to get a higher percentage of stores across before securing."

Wide eyed, Alex watched the bow go under as a wave rolled over the submarine. That made the brow between the ships rock precariously with only three lines holding it in place. Unfortunately, *Safeguard* was handling the seas better than *Jimmy Carter*, which turned the brow into a seesaw.

Another wave hit *Jimmy Carter*, and the brow bucked wildly, almost dropping a *Safeguard* chief petty officer right into the drink.

Then, just to make things better, it started to rain. Not to sprinkle, but real rain, with fat, warm raindrops that made the watchstanders below close the hatch to control in a hurry.

"Get them off that brow!" Alex shouted down to Morton. "Get everyone clear, and cut that damn thing loose!" He mimed cutting lines with an axe in case the COB couldn't hear him, which seemed to work. Morton's orders were lost in the wind, but sailors moved away from the sub's port side.

"*Jimmy Carter*, this is *Ches Bay*. Did you copy my last?" Hickman sounded like he was ready to lecture Alex on something utterly unimportant.

Wartime necessitated taking certain risks, but this was *stupid*. Alex mashed the talk button on the phone almost hard enough to break it.

"I copy, *Ches Bay*. However, I've got lines snapping and my deck is awash. We're way outside the envelope for submarine surface ops. I'm breaking away as soon as *Safeguard* pulls the brow back. Over."

Wham. The brow jumped up again and came down hard on both decks.

"My people on *Safeguard* need those supplies, *Jimmy Carter*. Under the circumstances, I think..."

Alex tuned the rest out. A violent roll jerked *Jimmy Carter* to starboard, tossing him into the opposite side of the bridge and straight into George. He'd forgotten his XO was still there until they both yelped. Something cracked distantly, and someone down on deck shouted.

Staggering, Alex tried to catch his balance, only to be thrown back to where he'd started when the submarine rolled back the way she'd come from. Alex had lost the handset and didn't look to see where it fell.

Crack.

Alex's head snapped up. Another line tying the brow down had snapped, but now the metal of the brow itself bent, sheared, and *broke.*

Crack!

There was no time to say anything. As *Jimmy Carter* rolled back toward the rescue ship, the last line on *Safeguard's* side of the brow snapped, leaving only one line attaching the brow to the submarine and nothing to the surface ship. The heavy metal walkway reared up and swung over *Jimmy Carter's* deck, sweeping sailors aside like a giant scythe. It hit three of Alex's people full-on, snapping the lanyards holding them to the boat and throwing them overboard like rag dolls.

"Man overboard, port side!" Alex bellowed down the hatch, distantly hearing the word passed over the 1MC.

But the boat couldn't maneuver while alongside *Safeguard*, and both rescue divers were already topside. If they could find the three sailors that went over, they had a chance—but Alex was a trained rescue swimmer and knew how slim that chance was in weather like this. And he wasn't sure he'd ask anyone to go in the water, even after a shipmate. Odds were he'd lose them both.

He held his breath.

One of the sailors who went overboard came up immediately, and those still on deck scrambled to throw him a line. But after several agonizing seconds passed, the other two did not reappear.

Vomit rose; Alex barely managed to force it back. His gaze flicked to *Jimmy Carter's* wake, searching desperately for his other two sailors, but no sign of them appeared amidst the waves.

On deck, it took two tries for the others to haul the one survivor out of the water; he'd almost been washed right by the submarine by the time Master Chief Morton managed to get a line on him. His struggle up the sloping side of the submarine was a long one, and just watching him clutch his ribcage painfully made the bottom drop out of Alex's stomach. Only then did he recognize the waterlogged sailor as his miscreant sonarman, STS1 Wilson.

Belatedly, he realized that Hickman was calling him. Again.

"*Jimmy Carter*, this is *Chesapeake Bay* Actual. What the hell is going on up there? Are you disobeying my direct orders?"

"What the hell is his—?" Alex chopped the words off, groping for the red phone. "I apologize for the delay, *Ches Bay*. I just lost three sailors overboard and recovered one. I am breaking away now. *Out.*"

He slammed the phone down without waiting for a response.

"Master Chief, cut those lines right now!" he shouted down to Morton, who was standing mercifully close to the sail.

"Cut the lines, aye!" Morton turned to the linehandlers. "Get moving!"

Four sailors surged forward with axes, chopping through the lines *Safeguard* had passed over less than an hour before. Had it only been that long? God, it felt like a lifetime. Back aft, two corpsmen helped Wilson through the hatch.

Lines cut, *Jimmy Carter* rolled free of the rescue ship with a giant lurch to starboard, her bow digging into the trough and sending spray all the way up to the sail. Saltwater stung his eyes, but Alex ignored it. Morton was ushering the other sailors below decks without waiting to be told to do so, and within seconds, only Morton and one other chief were left on deck.

This was the moment of danger. Without anything holding her in sync with *Safeguard*, *Jimmy Carter* could very well roll into the surface ship, causing irreparable damage to both. Alex couldn't just stop his boat, either; the tow line between the tug and the cruiser had vanished into the waves, and wrapping it around his screw would doom his submarine.

"All ahead two-thirds for eight knots!" he said into the sound-powered phone connecting him to control. "Right five degrees rudder!"

"Captain—" George was greener than ever.

"Not now!"

He had to do this as gradually as he dared, yet instinct told Alex that there wasn't much time to spare. Another wave hit the watchstanders in the sail head-on, making George sputter. The decks were clear. His bow was edging away from the salvage ship, and *Jimmy Carter* was slowly pulling ahead. *Too slowly.* Alex had underestimated the seas and how hard it would be for the sub to gain speed with the waves beating on her like this.

"All ahead standard!"

There just wasn't time to dick around with this. "Rudder amidships!" He had to keep the stern from kissing *Safeguard*, but at least the increased speed let him get past quicker. The moment the stern was clear, Alex ordered: "Hard right rudder!"

The turn plowed his submarine into the waves almost immediately, re-soaking everyone. George and the lookouts sputtered as Alex ordered another increase in speed. All too soon, the silhouette of a destroyer loomed up out of the growing gloom, less than a mile away and directly ahead.

"Damn this close formation," he whispered.

"Sir, the destroyer..." George's swallow was audible over the wind.

"I see it."

Of course, Alex couldn't just race for open water. The other ships in were arrayed close in to protect the rescue ship and the disabled cruiser. Continuing on this course guaranteed a collision with the destroyer.

"Clear the bridge!"

Both lookouts shot through the hatch. George shot him a

wide-eyed look before following, but if there was one thing Alex really didn't have time for, it was soothing his XO.

"Officer of the Deck, Captain, take her down fast," he ordered, waiting for acknowledgment before dropping through the hatch himself. A petty officer secured it for him, and Alex continued down into control.

Only after he was standing there, dripping and with the deck sloping under his feet did it sink in that *Jimmy Carter* was submerging with two fewer sailors than she'd surfaced with. His chest felt tight. He'd been in command of *Jimmy Carter* for four months of war, and he'd yet to lose a sailor...until now.

God, what a failure he was. He couldn't make a goddamned difference in the war, and now he couldn't even keep his own sailors alive.

Jimmy Carter dropped beneath the waves as Alex thought about the letters he needed to write to their families. He spent the next forty-eight hours alternating between replaying that disastrous evolution in his head and trying to make sure they were just right.

Finally, Master Chief Morton marched in, read the letters, and declared they were fine. He clicked *send* on the emails before Alex could stop him and ordered his captain to get some sleep.

Alex dreamed of storms and sailors going overboard.

Chapter 26

Eternal Patrol

7 December 2038, Commander Submarine Forces Atlantic HQ, Norfolk, Virginia

Freddie Hamilton was *not* in the mood for an interview, but they came with the job. And she didn't mind keeping the public informed; there was a war on, and if *she* hadn't been getting Top Secret briefings every day, Freddie would've wanted the news to tell her what was what. It was a just pity that she had to sit down with this shark.

Why was the *Washington Post* still relevant, again? Freddie couldn't ask.

"I'm generally a human-interest reporter, Admiral," Mark Easley said with a smile they both knew was fake. "I'm not really someone who's into military facts and figures. So that's the angle I'm going to take here, if you don't mind."

"Of course not." Freddie tried to look relaxed. They were in *her* office, after all. She should be comfortable here. Having made Easley drive to Norfolk from D.C. was a small and petty victory, but one she enjoyed, too.

"It's becoming apparent that this war will be focused on submarines," Easley said. "There are a thousand and one articles on why—from stealth, to missile shortages, to underwater habitats being half of what we're fighting over—so I won't belabor the point. What I'm interested in is the *people* on those submarines."

"The U.S. Navy has a proud tradition of having the best trained submariners in the world. Speaking as one myself." Freddie smiled.

"Trained, yes. But ready?" Easley asked. "Could anyone have been ready for this war?"

Freddie opened her mouth to say *yes*, but her heart skipped, and she closed it. She took a deep breath. "Our record is public. You've reported on it many times. Unfortunately, our training—technically complete though it is—did not prepare us adequately for the war."

"Why not, Admiral?"

Because pushing paper doesn't mean you can fire torpedoes, Freddie couldn't say. She'd spoken about the captain problem six *months* ago at the Sub School, and she was only halfway closer to solving it.

"Submarine command is a beast like no other. You must be highly trained, a technical expert on every aspect of your boat, and yet independent-minded enough to come up with creative solutions to unexpected problems without support. There's no help to be had on a submarine. The captain is on their own."

"And you're saying that some of them don't live up to that?"

"I'm saying that prewar training did a poor job of determining who could function under an unprecedented level of *wartime* leadership stress," Freddie replied. "As you said, this war is likely to move underwater...which puts even more pressure on each individual submarine captain. Some of them break. Some don't."

Easley's eyes narrowed. "And we can't tell which ahead of time."

"We've adjusted our training methods. There's more time spent in the simulator under higher-stress scenarios. We're digging into officers' careers to look at how they've handled themselves in hard situations instead of just looking at their official records." She sighed. "But yes, it's hard to tell. Everyone's human."

He perked up, and Freddie realized that Easley could be an ally if she played this right. She'd been trained not to trust the media, but the CNO insisted on this interview, so she might as well use it.

"We don't want robots commanding our submarines. Robots aren't flexible, and a certain degree of flexibility is required to get the job done. That's at odds with our nuclear training, of course, which requires one hundred percent procedural compliance...so it's a hard balance to strike. They had the same problem in World War II, you know. Minus the nuclear reactors, of course."

"How did they solve it then?"

"They didn't." Freddie grimaced.

Easley frowned. "We won that war, and submarines made a huge impact in the early days in the Pacific theater."

"Take a look at how many didn't come home, Mister Easley," she said quietly. "They solved the captain problem in the same grisly way we're solving it now...by culling out those who couldn't do the job."

Easley blanched. "That's a lot of dead crews."

"That's what I'm trying to prevent."

Jason Dunham steamed parallel to *Fletcher*, the two destroyers at the center of the formation. *William Charette* and *Truxton* were on point, which paired their second-newest destroyer with the oldest. Both were *Arleigh Burkes*, but *Truxton* was a Flight IIA with an AN/SPY-1D radar, whereas *Charette* carried the newer and much more powerful AN/SPY-6(V)4.

They looked similar from the outside—rather like Steph Gomez's own *Dunham*, also a Flight IIA and just a year younger than *Truxton*—but the innards counted most. *Charette's* Aegis Baseline 14.2.1 brain was faster and could see further. However, *Charette* took one hit amidships during the battle, knocking an electrical generator clean off its housing, which meant her electrical plant was a bit dodgy. So she couldn't be trusted on the front end by herself. Not when she tended to drop out of Link with no warning and leave everyone with a big honking blind spot up front.

Fletcher, to *Dunham's* starboard side, had a hole where her five-inch gun had been, and the secondary explosions from that hit mangled her forward CIWS mount, too. That meant someone—namely *Dunham*, whose hole in her helicopter hanger miraculously only destroyed one of her helicopters since the other had been sitting on deck—had to cover the gap in the flagship's defenses.

Okinawa, their lone cruiser, lagged behind the destroyers. Only *Okie* had a second set of SPY deckhouses back aft, so she was ideal to bring up the rear. She was slower than the others, though. Even *Dunham* and *Truxton*, both almost thirty years old, could hit thirty-three knots in good weather. *Okie* struggled to make it past twenty-nine on a good day.

Today wasn't a good day. Due to flooding on *Charette* and damage to *Okie*, they were limping along at twenty-two knots, which was hardly fast enough to outrun a teenager on a bicycle. They were a ragged little fleet, beat seven ways past Sunday and with the scars to prove it.

Not that any of it was Lieutenant Commander Steph Gomez's problem to solve. She was just the lowly executive officer of the third most senior destroyer in their group, keeping an eye on things so her captain could sleep. Commander Todd Kellner was a good sort, or seemed to be so far, quiet and thoughtful. He pretty much let her have her way, which Steph liked, and he kept his head on in the battle, which kept them alive.

Two afternoons after the Battle of Christmas Island, Steph sat curled up in the XO's chair on *Jason Dunham's* bridge. The windows were broken again, this time because of the concussion from a missile strike on the now-sunken *Middendorf*, so a slight breeze wafted in. Normally, she liked the smell of sea air, but today it carried too much burned metal.

"Longbow nine-four-one is on approach and requests green deck, ma'am," the officer of the deck said, startling Steph out of her reverie.

"Winds in the envelope?" She hadn't been paying attention while the officer of the deck ran the flight operations checklist, and Steph wanted to kick herself. Not that she didn't trust the OOD; Lieutenant (junior grade) Barry was a solid watchstander.

"Yes, ma'am. Relative wind is zero-zero-seven at five knots."

"Very well. Green deck."

Steph was glad that the captain trusted her enough to make this call without waking him up. They were both fried after the battle, but she'd gotten a nap in after settling the survivors they picked up. It was his turn.

She flicked the talk button on the "bitch box" used for internal communications with CIC. "TAO, XO, did Longbow see anything new?"

"Negative. Looks like the Indians are moving into Christmas Island lock, stock, and barrel. They're anchoring, not coming after us."

"XO, aye."

Steph grimaced. It wasn't that she wanted another fight—at least not before they could get more missiles, since *Dunham* had exactly three ESSM left. She had a full magazine of five-inch rounds for her gun, but no way were the Indians getting in close enough for a slugging match. They weren't that dumb.

Shifting her gaze to the aft camera, Steph watched Longbow line up for their approach. The MH-60 helicopter was a mainstay of the surface Navy. One variant or another of it had been in service since the 1970s, although thankfully the aviators were pretty good about upgrading. Most destroyers carried two, but *Dunham* would be down to one until the aviation gods shipped out a new one.

Now on final approach, everything looked normal for Longbow 941. Yawning, Steph watched the helo creep in diagonally over the deck, approaching from *Dunham's* starboard quarter. Everything was in accordance with SOP.

Then the helicopter did a little wiggle.

"TAO, ASTAC, Longbow reports a chip light on engine number two. Lining up for emergency landing," the air controller in CIC said, her voice clipped and tight.

"TAO, aye."

"Oh, shit." Steph bolted upright in her chair, suddenly awake. "OOD, pass the word for the crash-and-smash party to stand by."

"Officer of the Deck, aye!"

A chip light was aviator speak for *something is wrong with my engine and I don't have time to care what*. Steph might've been a surface warfare officer, but she'd supervised enough helicopter landings to understand the danger.

"Don't drop out of the sky," she whispered. "Please don't drop out of the sky."

Every eye on the bridge was riveted on the camera as Longbow 941 made a mad dash for the destroyer's small helo pad. Steph burned to do something, to give some order to help, but she knew the best thing *Dunham* could do was maintain course and speed. A change now could kill everyone on that helicopter.

The right side of the helo bobbed down; the pilot compensated with power, and it jumped too high, making the helicopter jiggle in midair. Then there was a sudden *poof* of black smoke, and Steph's heart jumped into her throat so quickly she thought she might vomit as Longbow 941's second engine died completely.

The pilot did the only thing he could, firewalling his throttles, aiming to get the helo over the deck before it dropped like a rock. And his aim was almost perfect: two of the MH-60's three wheels landed on *Dunham's* flight deck.

The third did not.

"I'm sick of *running*, Admiral." Nancy spoke the words as softly as she could, safely in the privacy of her at-sea cabin.

It was just her, Admiral Rodriquez, and Captain Tanya Tenaglia. While Nancy wanted to pace, even the captain of task group flagships didn't get that privilege. Not when admirals were around.

Instead, she sat on one couch with Tanya while their admiral slumped on the other. Even his aide—a poor, traumatized lieutenant who didn't know how to cope with the hard-charging, colorful admiral—wasn't present for this skull session. Not that they had any great ideas so far.

"Me, too." Rodriquez scraped hands over his face, looking like he hadn't slept the thirty-six hours since the Battle of Christmas Island. For the first time since she'd met him, he seemed too tired to swear.

"But we're not fit to do much right now, not when we're stuffed to the gills with survivors and down to a handful of missiles," Tanya said. "We need to offload them before we can do anything."

"There's nowhere closer than Perth." Nancy sighed. "At least nowhere friendly that can take on twenty-five hundred waterlogged sailors."

"And we're lucky we saved that many." Tanya looked down at her tablet. "Last count is twenty-five thirty-five. That's almost seventy-five percent of the crews from—"

The screeching *whoop* of the flight crash alarm cut her off, and Nancy snatched the phone off her desk before it even finished the first ring. "Captain!"

"Ma'am, Longbow Nine-Four-One just crashed on *Jason Dunham*," the junior officer of the deck said. "Oh holy Jesus—the helo's half over the side, caught in the flight deck nets!"

"I'm on my way."

"Did I sleep through you putting a helo up, Captain?" Rodriquez asked as Nancy hung up the phone.

"*Jason Dunham's* just crashed."

"Well, fuck me with a frozen turkey. Let's go."

The trio sprinted up to the bridge. They reached *Fletcher's* port bridge wing just in time for Longbow 941's port fuel tank to explode; the shock wave rocketed across the five hundred yards between the two destroyers, rattling *Fletcher's* windows.

Marco swore. Tanya gasped.

The helo on *Jason Dunham's* deck burned, swaying precariously as fire teams raced forward. Two specially outfitted rescue crew, distinctive in their shiny silver fireproof suits, rushed into the flaming wreckage to free the helicopter's crew of three. But the helo was at a terrible angle; hitting the deck on only two wheels left it listing left, leaning on a broken wheel and part of a cockpit door.

It lay diagonally across the flight deck, too, with its tail sticking off the edge. The rotors weren't turning, but the aircraft was still unbalanced, leaning against the metal nets—several of which were already bent.

The pilot in the right-hand seat managed to free herself, kicking the door open and climbing up and out. Her sudden motion made the helo rock just as the rescue crews reached the other side, and someone on the fire party chose that moment to spray aqueous firefighting foam at the helo's underside.

Unbalanced, the pilot toppled out the open door. The flight deck nets might've caught her, but they were already overstressed, and the wrong one gave—dumping the pilot right into the water.

"Man overboard, port side!" Nancy shouted into the bridge, grabbing a bridge-to-bridge radio. "Warship Eight-Five this is Warship One-Five-Five Actual. One-Zero-Niner has a man overboard, their starboard side, just lost an aviator in the drink, over."

"One-Five-Five Actual, this is Eight-Five. I have visual and will recover, over."

"One-Five-Five, roger, out."

Nancy let out a breath, and it rattled acidly in her chest. God, could anything *else* go wrong today?

Glancing back at *Dunham* and the burning helicopter, she realized what a foolish question that was to ask, even silently. She watched helplessly as the rescue team pulled the other pilot out of Longbow 941, but when they went back for the final crewmember, a second explosion blew them right off their feet. Only luck and good flight deck nets on *Dunham's* port side kept them from going overboard.

Eventually, there was nothing for *Dunham* to do other than put the fire out, retrieve what was left of the body, and then dump the wrecked helo over the side.

Meanwhile, their battered task group headed for Perth, Australia, full of survivors and not much else.

The typhoon lasted three days, after which Alex surfaced the boat to hold a memorial service.

He passed word to Captain Hickman that *Jimmy Carter* had to conduct a bow to stern inspection for topside damage after the disastrous supply transfer and offered no further information. It wasn't a lie, and he *was* worried about damage, but Alex was still too pissed off at the convoy commander to say more. Hell, he had George send the message because he *still* didn't trust himself not to tell Hickman what he thought of the damn fool stunt he ordered Alex's submarine to carry out. Seventy-two hours later, Alex still wanted to say things that might ruin his career.

Under other circumstances, Alex imagined none of his sailors would be happy dusting off their service dress blues and assembling on *Jimmy Carter's* deck just aft of the sail, but he didn't hear a single complaint as he climbed the ladder to join them.

"Attention on deck!" Morton ordered, his voice subdued.

"Floor's yours, XO," Alex said as he took his own place.

George had organized the ceremony with his usual efficiency. For once, Alex found his obsessive attention to detail comforting. He listened with half an ear as George and a few other sailors spoke, his eyes sweeping over the rest of his crew.

The mood on board was both sad and angry, with a strong sense of disbelief thrown in for good measure. Subs rarely lost crew members outside of freak accidents—combat under the surface was an all-or-nothing proposition. No one was used to losing friends or shipmates.

Alex hadn't made attendance at the ceremony mandatory, and but looking around, it seemed like everyone not on watch was there. Alex was so proud of them and so gutted that he let them down. How could they not hate him?

It was his turn. Stepping forward, Alex cleared his throat, shoving his nerves aside and focusing on his grief. It wanted to drown him, to drag him under like a riptide.

How had he failed his sailors so badly that he lost two overboard during an evolution he *knew* he shouldn't commit his sub to? Not screaming obscenities was hard; it was either that or break down weeping, and a captain could do neither. Alex knew that his job wasn't to keep his crew safe, but he was equally expected *not* to waste their lives needlessly.

And that stupid supply exchange had been a waste.

What a *fucking* waste.

Now two sailors, two damned good sailors who tried their best, wouldn't be going home. And not because the enemy killed them in combat. No, because Alex Coleman was too much of a coward to say no to someone just because they were senior to him.

Never again, he promised himself.

"Eric Jennings and Felicia Zarowa were more than just shipmates—they were our family. Both had been with us since before we left Bangor and shared memories and hardships with every one of us. The gaps they've left will not be easily filled.

"Though they were not killed by enemy action, we trust that they will join our brother and sister submariners lost to the deep. Today they accompany the likes of Mush Morton, Howie Gilmore, and

Samuel Dealey, forever on eternal patrol."
   Alex would not forget their loss.
   He would not repeat it.
   Never again.

Chapter 27

Changing Tides

15 December 2038, Perth, Australia

"You are not serious."

"Yes, sir, I am." Commander Fletch Goddard wished he'd gotten a haircut. Or worn a nicer uniform. His coveralls were rumpled and his hair was askew, and he probably needed a new pair of glasses if he was going to look presentable, too. But he hadn't exactly expected to wind up in front of the head of the entire Royal Australian Navy today.

But backing down wasn't in Fletch's nature, even when his boss kicked his idea upstairs like a lava-flavored potato.

Vice Admiral Gray glared over his horn-rimmed glasses like Fletch had grown a second head. *Out of my posterior, maybe. He thinks I'm mad.* Fletch wasn't sure he blamed him. How many officers tried to give away the brand-new destroyer they'd been handpicked to command?

Maybe I am mad.

"Let me get this straight, Commander." The admiral crossed his arms. "You are *volunteering* to leave *Warrego* and take command of *Parramatta* when she leaves the shipyard—*and* you've convinced most of your wardroom to go with you?"

Fletch swallowed. "Yes, sir."

It sounded barking insane when phrased that way.

"You want to trade a top-of-the-line guided missile destroyer for a thirty-five-year-old *frigate*?"

"A recently upgraded frigate, sir," he said. "Aside from the hull, she might as well be brand new."

It would be impolite to mention how many hull sections were also new. Gray's beady eyes grew comically large, but Fletch wasn't wrong. God knew *Parramatta* had been gutted at the Battle of Cocos Islands, and the shipyard had thrown in a thousand upgrades while they repaired her. Calling her *young* was a tad optimistic, but *Parramatta* had most of the same bells and whistles a modern frigate did.

"You've lost your ever-loving mind!"

Fletch fought the urge to shrug. "Possibly, Admiral. But *Warrego* hit another production delay, and our navy needs our officers *fighting*, not waiting. I'm ready to fight, sir, and so are my people."

Gray gaped. Then he tried to talk Fletch out of it. By the end, however, there might've been a certain amount of satisfaction in the admiral's expression. After all, Fletcher Goddard wouldn't have been given *Warrego* if he wasn't already one of the RAN's rising stars. He was right in saying that their navy needed people to fight and to lead...and *Parramatta* was almost ready to leave the shipyard.

Eventually, Gray agreed. The navy might have wanted Fletch in command of a brand-new destroyer, but they *needed* him on the frontlines now. *Parramatta* might not have been the ship Fletch dreamed of commanding, but she'd get him into the fight.

That was particularly important with Christmas Island lost. First Cocos Island back in August, and now Christmas Island—Australia was rapidly losing all her forward bases, and with it much of her fleet. A buildup unheard of since World War II wouldn't be enough to save her if they couldn't start winning battles...and Fletch couldn't help win battles if he was stuck on the damned beach.

Parramatta was almost as old as he was, but she'd do the job.

AUSTRALIA ON THE ROPES

Vaska Woodrow, Washington Post

THE WAR NO ONE WANTED

December 23, 2038—These days, everyone knows that the "Grand Alliance" of the United States, Great Britain, Canada, and Australia isn't exactly the powerhouse we expected. Repeated loses throughout the first nine months of the war—with far fewer victories than anticipated—have proven that.

Multiple smaller nations that signed on with the Alliance in the early days, including Indonesia, the Philippines, Singapore, and Papua New Guinea, have been re-evaluating their relationships with the "big four" considering the recent loss of Christmas Island. This follows the bloody Battle of the Cocos (Keeling) Islands in early July, in which the Alliance's hard-won victory saw the deaths of over four *thousand* Allied sailors and marines. And that's just in the Australian sphere of influence.

The undersea war goes just as badly, with both First Station and Cartier Combine—Australian-owned and operated—falling to the Freedom Union in the last few weeks. With these two critical stations lost, what's next?

Australia's GDP growth in the years before the war, in large part because of undersea resources and Australian-owned stations, supported a significant naval buildup. Without these resources, will Australia soldier on?

Without Australia, could the Alliance continue at all?

Should it?

Christmas came and went; most of December after the Battle of Christmas Island passed in an eerie quiet caused by mutual exhaustion. Even the Christmas Eve sinking of USS *Gato* by *Barracuda* didn't rouse the Alliance out of their bone-weary slumber, perhaps because Jules Rochambeau's victorious tweet was unusually subdued.

USS *Fletcher* and her battered compatriots from the Battle of Christmas Island went into shipyards around Australia; sending them home to the U.S., even to Pearl Harbor, just took too long. The navy didn't own enough floating dry docks, so civilian-owned companies in Australia picked up the slack, doing a good job despite politicians back home screaming about security concerns.

Freddie Hamilton ignored the politicians where she could—surface ships weren't her problem—and quietly bought every Mark 84 ASV torpedo she could get her hands on, loading them on a C-130 heading to Pearl Harbor, Hawaii. By New Year's Eve, there were two hundred torpedoes on the way—enough to fill seven boats' torpedo rooms with some left over. That wasn't nearly enough...but it was something.

Pick your boats carefully, she said in an email to Vice Admiral Doug Brown, her Pacific Ocean counterpart. Brown was senior to her in rank but inferior to her in position; as Commander, Submarine Forces Atlantic, Freddie was dual hatted as Commander, Submarine Naval Submarine Forces. That meant COMSUB*PAC* worked for her, a fact she knew Brown hated.

Freddie didn't care. She was too worried he'd send a handful of torps to every sub he had and none of them would do any good—or that he'd fully load some idiot who'd get sunk in three days flat. *We can't afford to have anyone take a full weapons room of Mark 84s to the bottom*, she added to the email as an afterthought.

It was a sentence she would later regret.

8 January 2039, Perth, Australia

Ding, ding. Ding, ding. The ringing of bells echoed over the 1MC, followed by:

"*Fletcher*, arriving."

Alex's head snapped up as soon as he heard the announcement. Before he could even reach for his radio, George's voice crackled over *Jimmy Carter's* main "net."

"Officer of the Deck, XO, is there something I should know about?"

Hearing the XO's panic made Alex cringe. George hated schedule changes. He hated creativity and chaos. Sure, he was a hell of a planner, and no commanding officer could ever complain that Lieutenant Commander Kirkland wasn't on top of things, but man, his jitters were exhausting.

Jimmy Carter had only been in port for three days since dropping Convoy 6548 off—a task they acquired five seconds after they were free of that idiot on *Chesapeake Bay*. The unexpectedly long underway left Alex glad he hadn't given an iota more canned food to *Safeguard*, because the cupboards and freezers were damned bare by the time his boat crawled into Perth. It took almost two *days* to fill them up again.

George, still jittery from that chaotic at-sea stores transfer, complained that the job would've been done faster if they secured liberty, but Alex's crew had been through enough. He put down liberty call as soon as the brow was across and stuck around to help the duty section hump the stores on board. To George's credit, he stayed, too.

Alex hoped a little rest might bring his XO back to an even keel, but now this unexpected visit threw him into a tailspin. George didn't even give the OOD a chance to respond.

"You know all visits need to be cleared through me. Why wasn't I notified? What's going on?"

"Sir, we just had a Commander Coleman show up on the quarterdeck and—"

George cut the OOD off: "Ask the commander what he wants, and I'll be right up."

"XO, Captain, there's no need for that." Alex tried not to let his smile carry through his voice and failed. "Officer of the Deck, Captain, if you'd have the messenger escort my wife to my cabin, I'd appreciate it."

"OOD, aye," the quarterdeck replied.

Snickering, Alex put his radio down. It was very like Nancy to show up with no warning and torment—err, *challenge*—his watchstanders a little. She'd been doing that sort of thing since college, and even if it wasn't his favorite aspect of her personality, Alex could live with her quirks.

Besides, he hadn't seen Nancy face to face since she'd deployed. Emails and phone calls weren't the same, and their in-port periods never seemed to line up. Now that they did, *Fletcher* was almost seventeen hundred miles away at Osborne Naval Shipyards, which might as well have been another planet when they were both in command.

Warship captains couldn't go gallivanting off during wartime. Leave was something you gave your subordinates, not yourself.

A sharp rap on his door interrupted his thoughts, and Alex pushed back from his computer. "It's open!"

Nancy walked in, wearing service khakis that contrasted sharply with Alex's working uniform. He would've been wearing coveralls if he hadn't had to go over to the SUBRON earlier that morning, but even during wartime, leaving the boat in coveralls was prohibited. The brass probably didn't like the fact that the uniform felt too much like comfortable pajamas.

"Thank you, ET3." Nancy smiled at the messenger and slipped inside.

The door clicked shut, and Alex didn't recall standing up before she was in his arms. Breathing in the faint smell of her made Alex smile; it was the same lotion she always used, and it felt like home.

"Hey, babe."

"Hey yourself."

They stood in silence for a long moment. They'd married their senior year in college, nearly eighteen years ago. Separations were old hat by now, but with a war on, neither could forget that each moment could be their last. One out of every three American submariners still weren't coming home...and the odds for destroyers weren't much better.

At least there's more of a chance of getting off a destroyer before it sinks, Alex told himself for the thousandth time. He couldn't disparage Nancy's choices—he'd love her a lot less if she was anyone other than the independent and bull-headed woman she was—but he still worried.

Finally, Alex pulled back and grinned. "I'm so glad you called ahead and let me know you were coming out to Perth."

Nancy laughed. "You know I like to keep you on your toes."

God, he'd missed her.

"How long can you stay?" he asked after they separated and sat down in two ugly green chairs that added to *Jimmy Carter's* charm.

"Three days," Nancy replied. "I made a deal with Admiral Rodriquez that Ying could mind the store while *Fletcher* is up on the blocks getting her rudders replaced."

"Both rudders? That sounds ominous."

Nancy shook her head. "It's not as bad as it sounds. It's a class issue—the rudder pins on the *O'Bannons* shear off if they encounter a combination of high-speed turns and underwater concussions. They're trying to replace everyone's."

"Must be nice to have a ship that isn't in a class by herself." Alex shook his head. "All my problems are so unique that no one knows what to do with them."

"Comes with the territory when your boat is old enough to drink."

"So does doing jack shit and nothing." Alex tried to sound casual, but he knew the effort had failed when Nancy punched him lightly in the arm.

"Don't be a dumbass. I'm perfectly content with you staying safe and bored. Bad enough that I'm dancing where the fire is hottest."

"At least you get to make a difference." Alex scowled.

"Difference? Ha!" Nancy snorted. "So far, I've mostly managed to survive long enough to run away and get medals for it. Sometimes I sink someone else before I do that, but we haven't exactly done great things out there."

"Story of the war so far, babe." Alex wasn't sure which was worse: fighting and losing, or not getting to fight at all. Both he and Nancy were frustrated, worn out, and trying to do their duty in a war where that was incredibly hard.

"Things back home are a mess, too. Mom tells me that no one's talking about rationing or anything crazy, but the War Powers Act has been invoked to focus the economy on the war."

"Really? I hadn't heard about that."

"Just happened this morning, our time. So last night back home," Nancy said. "This twelve-hour time difference is murder."

"This everything is murder." Alex rubbed his eyes. "We've been at war since April, but it feels like all we've done is retreat, fight losing battles, and watch friends die. Or just pick up survivors, in my case."

"Will it help you forget for a bit if I told you I got us a room at the Pan Pacific Hotel?" she asked.

Alex grinned. "Damn straight it will."

"Good." Her smile turned wicked. "Because once we get there, *you're* the one who gets to call *your* daughter."

"What'd Bobbie do this time?" Because it had to be Bobbie. Roberta Coleman was the troublemaker. Emily was much better behaved.

Nancy sighed. "She's decided that she wants to go to the Academy, according to Mom."

"Ah." Alex *was* proud that his eldest daughter had received an appointment to the Naval Academy. Competition was fiercer than ever with the war on, but Bobbie had never really shown any inclination to go anywhere other than her parents' alma mater. Alex frowned. "What brought this on?"

"You did."

"Huh?"

"She's pissed at you," Nancy said. "When I talked to Mom, she pointed out that *someone* hasn't called the girls as often as he should and that *someone* didn't congratulate Bobbie when her team won the soccer championships."

Alex groaned. "I've been underway on a submarine! My internet connectivity is spotty, and phone connectivity is even worse. *Smiley* is an old boat. We don't have the latest tech."

"She's used to what you had on *Kansas*. It's hard on the girls, Alex. I know you call when you can, but Bobbie's stressing about college. She's not going to be rational about this."

"She must get that from you," he grumbled, earning himself another playful whack.

"Alex."

He sighed. Bobbie had inherited his impulsive nature. Worse yet, his tendency to go off at right angles was more pronounced in his elder daughter than it was in Alex, because Bobbie combined her mother's outgoing nature with his insolent streak. Still, at least they weren't fielding regular calls from the high school about Bobbie acting out. All in all, both of their daughters were remarkably well adjusted...but both parents at war was hitting them hard.

Knowing she'd been conceived at Norwich University didn't help Bobbie, either. Her parents married before she was born, and Bobbie was the best mistake Alex had ever made, but there was no way to pretend they'd *meant* for Nancy to get pregnant their senior year.

Emily had followed a more regular fashion two years later, but the first few years of parenting, marriage, and juggling two brand new naval careers had been messy.

And now things are messy again, Alex thought with a sigh. *Damn war.*

"I'll talk to her and make sure it's what she really wants," he said. Neither wanted to force Bobbie to go to Norwich, but Alex also didn't want Bobbie to back herself into a corner because she was pissed at him. He snorted. "But I'll never hear the end of it from John if she goes."

"Janet will keep him in line." Nancy laughed.

John Dalton was an Academy graduate, but Janet Dalton, nee Yu, was a Norwich girl. She and Nancy had been in the same company at "the Wick," as the cadets called the nation's oldest private military college. Alex had introduced his then-shipmate to Nancy's best friend on a whim, and the rest was history. The pair had been an unofficial aunt and uncle to the Coleman girls ever since.

"She'd better."

Alex hated admitting he was envious of his best friend. John had raced right to the number one spot on the list of American sub COs by enemy tonnage sunk shortly after taking command of *Razorback*, despite rightly complaining about the inadequacies of their torpedoes. John was the best they had…and Alex just wanted a chance.

Just one.

8 January 2038, the mid-Indian Ocean

Razorback broke away from the convoy they were escorting and hovered near the surface long enough for John to answer the phone call. Instinct told him to transfer it to his cabin; any time COMSUBPAC's office called a captain personally was irregular enough to make the hairs on the back of his neck stand up.

He picked up the phone. "Captain Dalton speaking."

"Captain, this is Commander Angel Rivera, aide to Vice Admiral Brown, SUBPAC. We have new orders for you."

"New orders?" John perked up. Anything beat convoy duty, which was what *Razorback* got underway for two days earlier. He didn't often get stuck with the boring jobs, for which he was grateful, but pickings had been slim since *Razorback* sank an Indian supply convoy on Thanksgiving.

"We have intel that indicates Annette Garnier and *Amazone* will be sent after Convoy 45979, which is why we pulled you off the escort," Rivera replied.

"What? That makes no sense. You'd want us there to stop her, unless—this is a ploy, isn't it?" John asked, his mind working furiously.

"Yes, Captain, it is. Your reassignment was slipped to a known enemy intelligence asset. Garnier will expect the convoy to be undefended by undersea assets. Feel free to maneuver independently but keep the convoy in range. Your orders are to sink Garnier and protect the convoy."

John swallowed. Doing both would be hard, particularly given that Garnier's torpedoes were both faster than his *and* longer ranged. "Which mission takes priority?"

"Both are equally important."

"I understand." John was glad the man on the other end of the line couldn't see his scowl. *I understand you've never tried to fight an enemy who can outrun your torpedoes, anyway.* Was Rivera even a submariner? Asking wouldn't help.

Hell, Jeff McNally had been a submariner, and he'd still proven incapable in combat. Understanding how subs worked didn't grant anyone grace in wartime. John's predecessor on *Razorback* proved that when he froze up and let enemy aircraft carriers sail on by without shooting. Rank didn't guarantee competence.

"Good luck and good hunting, Captain."

"Thank you," John said.

He hung up the phone and sat for a long moment, contemplating the impossibility of these orders. He could have pushed back, but that wasn't John Dalton's style. Not if he wanted to make his way to the top.

Besides, he had faith in his people. They were damned good, and if anyone could pull off protecting a convoy *and* hunting France's second best submariner, it was his crew. So perhaps his orders were not impossible. Just...difficult.

He would have to be smart. Smarter than his adversary. That would necessitate a good plan and the flexibility to put it down as needed. John closed his eyes, wishing he could talk to his wife. Janet would probably have some crazy idea for him, one he'd translate out of ex-air force and into submarine tactics. But calling his wife while underway was selfish. Personal calls were prohibited, even if he knew some sub captains who got away with it.

Much to his shame, John contemplated it for a long moment. Commodore Banks probably wouldn't say anything. Not to his top captain. Banks knew he needed good COs to rise to the top, which meant he needed John a lot more than John needed him.

Man, the urge was strong. But John pushed it aside. He needed to concentrate on the mission, not spill classified information to his wife. *That* was against the law, and for good reason. Shaking his head, he called his XO's stateroom.

"Patricia, you better grab Nav and get in here. We've got some fiendishly clever planning to do."

Pat's cheerful competence was always reassuring: "On my way," she said.

Maybe they could pull this off.

Chapter 28

Old School

10 January 2039, the mid-Indian Ocean

There was no way to know when Annette Garnier and *Amazone* would intercept Convoy 45979. Their route from Perth to Diego Garcia was almost three *thousand* nautical miles long, and it wasn't like John could just set up an ambush in a canyon or something. Navigating underwater didn't work like that.

"You think intel might've been a bit more specific about where *Amazone* is?" Lieutenant Commander Patricia Abercrombie glared at the plot in *Razorback's* attack center. "Telling us she's coming down from the northeast leaves a metric shit ton of water to search."

"Tell me about it." Captain John Dalton rubbed his eyes, wishing the display would change. It didn't, and he sighed. "We're in the best possible position here. No reason to change yet."

"What if she sneaks around behind us? Pardon me for saying so, Captain, but that hairbrained order from SUBPAC about protecting the convoy *and* using it as bait sounds like it sprung from the brow of a half-witted two-year-old."

"I've known smarter toddlers, that's for sure." John smiled wryly. "But ours is not to reason why, right?"

Patricia snorted. "That's what they say."

Razorback was parked three miles out from the convoy off its starboard bow, angled to meet the most likely approach *Amazone* would make. John didn't have a lot of confidence that the wily French submariner would come in fast enough for him to hear her if he raced around out here, though, so he chose not to use the classic submariner tactic of sprinting and drifting.

Instead, he trusted the designers at Electric Boat when they claimed the Improved-*Ceroes* had a top silent speed of twenty-nine knots. No one'd really tried to test that outside of exercises—war turned sub captains into conservatives mighty fast—or if they had, they hadn't lived to talk about it.

John shook his head to chase those optimistic thoughts away. "At twenty knots, she should lose our sonar signature against the convoy behind us, and at least this range gives us room to maneuver. It's the best I've got, Pat."

"You want to pull the tail in to a short stay?" Patricia fidgeted. "I worry about it getting tangled up in combat."

"I think this is going to be a short fight, one way or another. We need the extra detection capability."

Razorback's "tail," or Tactical Towed Sonar Array (TACTAS), was a long string of hydrophones deployed behind her to extend her passive sonar range. Leaving it out in combat was a risk that most COs wouldn't take, but John needed to detect *Amazone* as early as possible. Sure, he could snap the array, but the odds of that were low. The worst-case scenario was getting it wrapped around one of the convoy ships' screws, and if he stayed deep enough, that wouldn't happen.

He just needed to remember that he was dragging a mile of hydrophones behind him when he started maneuvering.

He caught Patricia's frown and added: "But feel free to reel it in to a short stay once we fire. Then she'll know where we are, and she'll probably be going too fast to lose her on the lateral arrays, anyway."

"You got it." Her smile was wan and did little to hide the butterflies marching around in her stomach.

John knew they were there because he had them, too.

Hours passed, and John wished he dared nap. It was the middle of the night by *Razorback's* clocks—they were still on *Perth* time, since they didn't plan on pulling into any ports and swapping time zones every few days was a pain—and interruptions to his sleep schedule always put John Dalton in the worst mood.

One of the best things about being a captain, even in wartime, was that he could generally sleep when he needed it. Yeah, people woke him up at odd hours with tactical updates, but that was the job. So were moments like this, when he was needed in control, despite the sleep weighing his eyes down like sandy lead.

Thank goodness there was a fold-down seat next to the chart table. Only the Improved-*Ceroes* had it; the original ones, like *Cero*, which John commanded in his first command tour, didn't. But *Razorback* had a sweet little chair, complete with smelly blue padding. It allowed John to squeeze himself in between the chart table and the diving officer, leaning on the former to stay out of the latter's way.

He wasn't stupid enough to keep his boat at battle stations for days on end. That was a good way to wear the crew down, and going into combat with a worn-down crew was a good way to die. However, sonar got their first long-range sniff of *something* four hours earlier, which meant *Razorback* was primed and ready to fight. They just had to wait for the mystery contact to firm up, and then...

"You're looking peaked, boss," Patricia said, handing him a cup of coffee.

"Thanks." John smiled, inhaling the too-strong scent of chocolate and feeling the caffeine go straight to his brain. "I suck at this all-nighter crap."

She laughed. "You'll wake up just fine when the shooting starts."

John sipped the coffee instead of answering, trying not to think about the Battle of the SOM. He'd been exhausted before that battle, too—but hopefully the similarities ended there. For one, *he* was in command today, instead of working for an admiral who sank the wrong submarine before freezing up and starting World War III.

John didn't want to think about the friends he lost that day. He still dreamed of them, sometimes, even when he knew he—

"Conn, Sonar, aspect change on track 7589. She's coming in, sir. Speed now three-zero knots, closest point of approach with the convoy will be two thousand yards in thirty minutes."

John's head snapped up. "I think we've got her! Range?"

"Approximately forty-three thousand yards. Rate of closure is forty-five knots on present course and speed."

A chill ran down John's spine. He had to be patient, but his enemy was in his sights—and he'd *trained* for this. There was no evidence *Amazone* knew his submarine was here, so John had to resist the urge to adjust course or speed and give the game away.

His eyes traced over the plot. *Razorback* and *Amazone*'s combined speeds and courses meant they were closing with one another at fifteen hundred yards a minute. If John meant to shoot inside ten thousand yards—to hell with what Commodore Banks said—that meant he had to wait another twenty-two minutes before he could shoot.

Talk about a lifetime.

"Sonar, Conn, any indication she's spotted us?" John asked.

"Negative, sir. Computer has a tentative ID now, *Requin*-class fast attack, probable hull number S671."

"Conn, aye." John exchanged a grin with his XO. "That's her."

"Do you want to come right and speed up a little, sir? We can close the range," Patricia said.

John shook his head. "Rushing into this seems like a good way to get heard and then a faster way to get killed. If she hasn't heard us yet, we'll stay right here and let her keep closing the convoy." He grabbed the tablet that held *Razorback's* copy of the *Classified Jane's Addendum*, an unofficial document that the sub force held near and dear to its heart. John thumbed through it until he found the page for French *Requin*-class subs. "If this is right, thirty knots is her best silent speed. That means we only got a whiff of her because we have the tail out. The surface ships don't have a chance of detecting her, and she knows it."

"So, while she doesn't know we're here, she has no reason to change course." Patricia chewed her lip. "Might work."

"It requires an old school stalk and wait, but we're the best at that," John replied. "I think it's time we started playing to our strengths instead of letting the other side play to theirs, don't you?"

Patricia wiped a tired hand over her face. "Will it get me a nap, sir?"

"I wish."

It wasn't time to sleep yet. Not for anyone on *Razorback*, though John did tell Patricia to rotate people through meals and bathroom breaks. He couldn't give them much, not with battle so close—and against such a skilled foe—but at least they could go in with full bellies and empty bladders.

Finally, after those twenty-two minutes ticked by, the speaker box next to him crackled.

"Conn, Sonar, range is ten thousand yards. Contact bears zero-two-niner. Speed steady at thirty knots."

"Conn, aye." John straightened and kept the smile off his face. He'd done this before, but he'd never let an enemy get so close. Particularly not with such a high closure rate—every minute he waited, *Amazone* got 1,500 yards closer to the helpless convoy John had to protect.

And yet his torpedoes, the slow as molasses Mark 48s, were only five knots faster than the *Requin*-class submarine he hunted. John knew he was lucky on that front, too. If *Amazone* were one of the Advanced *Requins*, that speed advantage would be narrowed to a mere three knots.

THE WAR NO ONE WANTED

Death by a thousand cuts would be faster than letting a Mark 48 get in a stern chase with *Amazone*. If Garnier played it smart, she could run them out of gas, and then all of John's careful planning would be for nothing.

Now was not the time to think about the hundreds of civilian mariners topside. The ships themselves were full of precious metals and, most importantly, unrefined oil. Both were desperately needed back home; the American war machine was a hungry beast, and American industry could out-build any country in the world. But to do that, they needed resources, which Australia had to spare.

The gross value of the fourteen ships' cargo was somewhere north of astronomical. John wasn't a math lover and didn't want to add the numbers up, but he knew it was in the billions. That was probably why SUBPAC gave him the idiotic order that included two number one priorities: protect the convoy and hunt *Amazone*.

Minutes ticked by. Every instinct John had, every bit of training he'd ever been given, told him to fire. But wartime experience told him to wait.

"Range now six thousand yards."

"Captain, it's starting to get cozy out here," Patricia whispered from his side.

John smiled. "Don't worry. I won't let her shoot at the convoy."

"Never thought for a moment that you would."

"I just don't want to get our slow torps in a damned stern chase, either," John said. Then he squared his shoulders. "Firing point procedures, tubes one and three, track 7589."

Razorback had been constantly updating a firing solution on *Amazone* ever since gaining contact, but the formalities needed to be observed.

"Solution ready," his weapons officer reported.

Patricia's response was immediate: "Ship ready."

"Very well. Match bearings and shoot, tubes one and three."

Razorback shuddered ever so slightly; a long heartbeat passed.

"Conn, sonar, two fish running hot, straight, and normal."

"Very well," John said. "Cut the wires, close the outer doors. Right full rudder, steady course zero-two-nine."

"Right full rudder, steady course zero-two-niner, aye," the diving officer replied. "My rudder is right thirty degrees, coming to course zero-two-niner."

"Very well." John took a deep breath and contemplated coming up in speed; *Amazone* would shoot back, but how quick off the trigger would Garnier be?

John's tactic of coming right and closing with *Amazone* was what submariners called shooting her stern; by pointing at where *Amazone* had been, John could both open the distance with her and draw the French sub away from the convoy. It was a risk, of course—Garnier could choose to turn toward the convoy and shoot—but who would aim for the defenseless surface ships when there was an enemy right here torpedoing them?

"Contact is maneuvering, breaking right and dropping noise maker—torpedo in the water! *Two* torpedoes in the water bearing zero-two-zero!" Sonar reported.

"All ahead flank!" His heart thundering his chest, John twisted to look at the plot. "Weps, are our torpedoes in acquisition?"

"Both have *Amazone* cold, Captain. Range now five thousand yards and closing fast."

"That won't last. Once she gets up to speed, this is going to take a while." John tore his eyes away from the torpedoes he'd fired; he had to trust them to do their job, because *Amazone's* torpedoes could kill him if he wasn't careful. It would be a crying shame to die in a mutual kill. "COB, stand by your countermeasures."

"Standing by," the chief of the boat replied.

Another glance at the plot confirmed John's suspicions; *Amazone*, as one of France's older *Requins*, was armed with older torpedoes, too. The ones chasing John's submarine had stopped accelerating at fifty knots.

"Sonar, Conn, confirm torpedo signatures?" Patricia asked, her mind clearly on the same track as his.

"Conn, Sonar, enemy torps match F21 Artemis torps. Max speed five-zero knots, max rage thirty-one nautical miles."

"Conn, aye," Patricia replied.

"Rudder amidships." John watched the speed gauge as his submarine leveled out, her speed roaring up to sixty-three knots. Damn, his baby was fast. "Sonar, Conn, range to enemy torpedoes?"

"Sixty-five hundred yards and opening!"

John glanced around control, taking in his team's wide eyes and white knuckles. "Breathe, people. We've got a thirteen-knot speed advantage over those torps. They can only hit us if I do something *really* dumb."

"Saints preserve us from that, Captain." Patricia's smile was wan.

"Hey, it's nice to know that the other side has slow torpedoes, too." John grinned. "I could get used to this."

"You just want to run them out of gas, sir?" COB asked.

"Probably safer. We could try some fancy driving and use the noisemakers to try to blow them up, but I'm not sure I want to take the chance of spoofing them off and having the torps go after the convoy." John glanced at the clock on the bulkhead. "I'm okay with this taking a while. We still have another twelve minutes before our fish can catch *Amazone*."

Running torpedoes out of gas wasn't a glamourous way to end a battle, but it worked. John slowly brought his sub around to the left, heading parallel to *Amazone* in case he needed to shoot at the *Requin* again. That also kept *Razorback* roughly in step with the convoy, though nowhere near close enough for the torpedoes on her heels to decide a fat, lazy merchant ship was a more tempting target than the swift submarine.

After ten minutes, *Razorback's* lead on the French torpedoes widened to almost eleven thousand yards. John turned his attention to *Amazone*.

"Here she goes," someone muttered.

The French sub jinxed left and right, trying desperately to avoid the two Mark 48s slowly gaining on her. They didn't have much of a speed advantage—only five knots—but it was enough. And the Mark 48 might not have been a terribly fast torpedo, but it was *smart*. Both torpedoes ignored multiple noisemakers and course changes, boring in on *Amazone* tenaciously.

Nineteen minutes after *Razorback* fired, both slammed into *Amazone's* aft end. The first explosions tore her screw right off and opened her engineering spaces to the seas; the secondary explosions burst through her watertight bulkheads and sent the sub diving toward the bottom like a rocket.

There were no survivors.

Eighteen minutes after that, *Amazone's* last two torpedoes ran out of gas and dropped to the ocean floor, allowing *Razorback* to lope back to join Convoy 45979.

Chapter 29

Old Friends

25 January 2039, Perth, Australia

The Mediterranean was one of the "best" restaurants in Perth, or so said the list the Officers Club kept. Sick of drinking the same beer and eating the same fries, Alex and John decided to be daring and try somewhere further away two weeks after John sank *Amazone*. Since Alex had just bought a used Jeep—it was a good deal, he loved Jeeps, and he had to spend some of that hazard pay on *something* fun—they decided to make the half-hour drive across the city and try a new place.

At first glance, the restaurant was fancy. The décor was tasteful, the staff dressed to the nines, and the wait was long. But once they were seated, the glittery veneer started peeling back.

Alex's chair was missing a rubber foot, making it creak while it rocked back and forth. The menus were leatherbound and embossed, but the entrees listed inside were from here, there, and everywhere. It was more like an American joint pretending to be fancy than what Alex expected. Somehow, he thought Australia would be...better.

"This place really is a dump, isn't it?" John glanced up from his menu. "Talk about pretensions of grandeur. I think that's *supposed* to look like expensive artwork on the wall, but I'm not impressed."

Alex snorted. "You wouldn't be. I don't know the difference between finger painting and fine art."

"Trust me. *That*"—John gestured with his wineglass—"isn't fine art. I'm not even sure it's art. And this isn't fine wine, either. I can't believe this damn glass cost me twenty-nine bucks."

"That's why some of us drink beer." He grinned. "The Aussies make a good brew. If you weren't a pseudo-aristocratic ninny, you'd know that."

"If I wasn't a *what?*"

"You heard me." Alex laughed. While he wasn't sure he'd call The Mediterranean a dump, the restaurant *was* a dive, despite its claims to the contrary.

The food was ridiculously overpriced, too. Alex wasn't hurting for money, and there was nowhere to spend it on a sub, particularly one underway as often as *Jimmy Carter*. The Coleman family wasn't exactly rich, but they were doing pretty well these days, even with daughters looking at colleges.

He and Nancy both pulled down commander's pay and combat pay, not to mention command bonuses and Alex's sub pay. He'd never dreamed of being in this position; Alex hadn't grown up *really* poor, but his parents' deaths in a car accident when he was in high school meant he and his older brother went from mostly comfortable to scraping by. He made it through college on a scholarship; his brother never even tried.

"You're just pissed off because Bobbie got accepted to the Academy instead of going to your bat-shit insane army-flavored alma mater."

Alex scowled. Damn it all if his elder daughter wasn't set on attending the Naval Academy. Not long ago, she'd sworn up, down, and sideways that she'd follow in her parents' footsteps at Norwich University. But Bobbie was a rebel. And Alex was proud of her, particularly since *his* grades had never been high enough for the Academy.

He just wished he could be there to see her off for plebe summer, but there was no way he'd get back Stateside short of the war ending or *Jimmy Carter sinking*. Right now, the latter seemed more likely, given how little combat he'd seen.

"You *do* remember that your wife attended that 'batshit insane army-flavored' school, don't you?" He arched an eyebrow.

"Where do you think I learned to call it that from? All you Norwich people are nuts."

Alex grinned. "No argument."

The snazzily dressed waiter returned, and Alex broke down and ordered a steak, hoping that the place couldn't screw that up too badly. It was the simplest thing on the menu. John called him a chicken and ordered something fancier.

"You've got no sense of adventure."

Alex shrugged. "Escorting convoys sucks it all out of me."

"Yeah, it's not my favorite gig, either." John looked away.

A cynical part of Alex wanted to bitch and moan. John was one of the Alliance's golden boys; even when he was assigned to a convoy, he got to do important things like hunting down *Amazone*. But it wasn't John's fault that Alex had enemies in high places, so he sighed.

Besides, the chances of John not coming home one of these days got a hell of a lot higher the longer he danced on the razor's edge. The recent example of Kurt Kins hung silently in the air between them. Kins had been one of the best—ahead of John for enemy ships and subs killed—and where had that gotten him? Adventure equaled danger in wartime.

"So, uh, in other news, you wouldn't believe the phone call I got right before I stepped off the boat," Alex said, mostly to end the silence.

"Oh?"

"Commodore Banks' chief of staff called me to poach an HMC off *Jimmy Carter*," Alex said. "I kind of ruined her plans when I pointed out that I don't *have* a chief corpsman."

"Someone's an idiot if they didn't check that ahead of time." John frowned.

Alex shrugged, trying not to think about the undertone in that call: *Jimmy Carter* didn't do enough to matter, so why did they need a chief corpsman? He shook himself. "If I interpreted the ranting and raving coming from the other side of the pier correctly, they wound up stealing one from *Bluefish*."

"Where'd they send him?"

"*Kansas.*"

"Ah. Your favorite boat." John's smile was sad.

"I've got nothing against *Kansas*." Alex kept his voice as level as he could.

"Not the boat, sure," John replied. "You could do more than they're letting you. Don't argue with that. If Kennedy hadn't screwed up so spectacularly, *you'd* be pulling the missions I am—in a hell of a different boat than you have now."

That made Alex roll his eyes. "Keep flying so high and I'll wonder if you pre-gamed."

John laughed. "You know, I've got a spare HMC, if you need one. My HM1 recently put on Chief, and she's high speed. As soon as Big Navy catches on to the fact that I have two HMCs, I'll lose him, anyway. So if you want him...?"

"You don't have to twist my arm, John. I'll gladly take him." Then he couldn't resist adding: "You need a sonar tech first class?"

"Not if it's that Wilson you keep emailing me about!"

Alex laughed and then sobered. "Speaking of sonar and things that go boom, any news on the new torpedoes in the pipeline?"

"No." John's brow furrowed. "But you know where Janet works. I know the damned things are out here somewhere, but they're sure as hell not in *my* weapons room."

"You're afraid they're sitting in a warehouse gathering dust."

"Or in a supply ship on the bottom of the Indian Ocean." John downed his wine and grimaced. "I'm not sure which would be worse, frankly."

Alex felt a crooked smile twist his lips. "If that's where they are, navy'll never tell us."

"Not officially, but the rumor mill probably would've by now. Which is why I'm thinking warehouse," John replied. "And isn't that a kick to the gut? You know how close I had to get to Garnier to sink *Amazone* with a Mark 48? I let her get to six thousand yards, and she still almost outran the damned things. That's spitting distance."

"Is that why your hair is going gray?"

"Oh, shut up." John laughed. "I should've known you wouldn't commiserate with me properly."

"I hear they're going to pin the Navy Cross on you for that. It's hard to feel sorry for you." Alex grinned. "But I'll try to cry some crocodile tears if you want. Great big ones."

"I think Commodore Banks might have an aneurysm. He told me to stay outside fifteen thousand yards."

"Disobeying orders?" Alex arched an eyebrow. "Am I wearing off on you?"

John shrugged. "It was the only way to get the job done."

Playing political games was a waste of goddamn time, but here Marco was, waiting in the foyer of the brand new—or not so new, but they pretended pretty well—headquarters building for Seventh Fleet. He'd even had to dust off a *nice* uniform for this rigmarole, as had Tanya. Though he hadn't put his damned whites on. Khakis should be good enough when there was a war on.

A couple of the SUBRONS turned what should've been a small

welcome into a real dog-and-pony show, with decorations, side boys, and all that jazz. Marco wasn't sure which commodore was trying to show off more, but Jaylen Banks had the shiniest shoes of the bunch, and damn that was hard when you were wearing whites. He'd tried sucking up to Marco, too, until Marco brushed him off with a profanity-laden excuse about needing to call his flag captain.

Unfortunately, Nancy Coleman was the efficient sort, so that call lasted two minutes flat.

So here he stood, with his entire mother-loving staff, waiting for an admiral who was late. Marco would love to blame a superior for this one, but he figured he should be fair; any plane flight from point A to point B was likely to be delayed by tactical considerations. Flying from Japan to Australia wasn't a quick hop; even in military aircraft, it took twelve hours if you did it in a straight shot. And no one wanted to fly a valuable officer over all that disputed—and sometimes outright hostile—territory, so it was likely that it took even longer.

Marco was lucky that he'd done most of his traveling via ship these days, even if it was something of a step sideways from his submariner roots.

God damn, he missed the boats. Sure, being an admiral and commanding task forces—he couldn't quite call his units a fleet—of ships was pretty fucking cool. Sometimes, he felt kind of like Nimitz, just with more swearing and fewer stars. It wasn't a bad life, and it was a damned good way to take the fight to the enemy...while the missiles lasted.

"Any news on missile reloads?" he asked Tanya in an undertone, scraping a hand over his face.

"Not a peep, sir. Everyone's still crying that there aren't enough missiles to go around," she replied.

"Fucking A."

"Pretty much." Tanya grimaced. "I'm more disturbed by the news of the French using satellites to track our forces. It's not great for real-time attacks, but if it gives them a general location..."

"Then they fucking localize and go to town." Marco sighed. "We're stuck in a weird-ass pattern, and I don't like it. Whoever shoots first has the advantage, and that's usually the other guy, since we're not in the conquest business. They pick up this atoll, that island, or cousin Franco's underwater station, and then we either have to live with it or fight to get it back. Insert a double complication if the station was independent to begin with, because then we have to wait for them to ask for our help. We've been on the back foot for *months*, and no one's done a good goddamn to change that."

"Maybe this change will help us better focus our efforts?"

Marco twisted to look at his chief of staff. "Since when has the navy implemented a change that *helped* instead of making work harder?"

She held her hands up in surrender.

"Seventh Fleet, arriving!" the petty officer near the door announced.

Vice Admiral Kristensen was wearing his whites, of course. As was his entire staff. Oops.

Taking a deep breath, Marco stepped forward and held out his hand. At least he was a two-star admiral. He didn't have to be intimidated by Kristensen the way mere humans did, and he could get in before the show-off commodores.

"Admiral, I'd say it's a pleasure, but anything that brings you out to Australia is bad fucking news for me and mine." Marco didn't bother with a fake smile. By now, no one in the navy thought he was someone's yes-man. They did, however, know he got the job done, and that counted during war time.

Vice Admiral Kristensen, Commander, Seventh Fleet, frowned. "I'm here to transfer Seventh Fleet to Perth."

"Well, that's a raw-ass admission of defeat that I didn't want to be party to."

"Thank you for the colorful summary." Kristensen grimaced. "Be it as it may, for now, Task Force Two-Three is under my command"—the way he spoke, it sounded like he hoped he wouldn't have to put up with one Marco Rodriquez for long—"including the effort to re-take Christmas Island. Which will be your primary mission."

"Great." He'd expected that ever since they lost the goddamned place. Not that the island had been Marco's to hold, but he'd been the senior guy left holding the bag when Admiral Ingram had the bad grace to die during the attack. "How many units am I getting?"

"I'm afraid I can't give you much more than you've already got. We're scraping the bottom of the barrel as it is, and new ships won't be here for at least two months. But we need a victory now," Kristensen said. "You have a reputation for pulling off difficult tasks. Can you do it again?"

"You're asking me to make a pie without filling, sir." Marco crossed his arms. "Even if I manage, it's going to be ugly. And taste like dog shit."

"We need a win, Marco."

"Don't I fucking know it." Marco sighed and looked around the still-empty building. "I'll get to work."

Regan's Rooster was cheerful and bright, just the kind of bar STS1 Bud Wilson picked back in his worst drinking days. He liked places that made him smile, but even more so, he liked a drinking establishment that was well-off enough to endure the hurricane of his drunkenness.

Not everyone thought that sober Wilson made decent decisions, but he generally tried not to screw over *everyone* in drunk Wilson's vicinity. He'd learned that young and early, when his first chief took him on a ripper around New York City during Fleet Week. Now he avoided places with swim-up bars, dancers, and karaoke. The Rooster had none of those, but it did have two bars, lots of tables full of happy and semi-drunk patrons, and a bartender who generally didn't cut people off.

It was a legend in the naval service after just a couple months of war, and Shore Patrol had picked Bud up here twice.

"Weps is going to kill you dead if you keep drinkin', Bud," his companion said as he picked up his beer.

They sat at a corner table, enjoying the music and the general vibe. The food was good, too; Bud never had eaten much here before, or at least not that he remembered, but the homemade chips were fantastic, and he couldn't get enough.

"What?" He tried looking innocent but knew that wouldn't help much. Bud Wilson looked more like the hockey player he'd been during his two years of aborted college than some sweet little cherub, and he had no problems playing rough. Pretending to have virtue fit him about as good as a tutu. "This is only my second drink!"

ET2 Maria Velasquez scowled. She was a tiny Puerto Rican firecracker who had somehow become his best friend and liberty buddy, probably because she could keep up and gave Bud as much crap as he did her.

"*I'm* not dragging your sorry ass back to the boat if you get drunk," she said. "*Or* bailing you out of the brig. You know what'll happen if the captain has to bust your ass out again. He ain't laid back all the time, and you'll get kicked off the boat quicker than you can shit if you try your stupid finger-painting thing again."

"Give me a little credit. I never do the same dumb drunk antics twice."

She rolled her eyes. "Cause that makes everything so much better."

"C'mon, Maria. I'll be good. I promise." Bud had no desire to sample the mattresses in Perth's brig again. They had lumps, and he wasn't sure there weren't bedbugs.

Ooh, maybe he left bedbugs on *Bluefish*. That was a happy thought.

He'd spent five months on his best behavior, and *Jimmy Carter's* officers were starting to trust his judgment as a sonar tech. Ensign Vincentelli had finally warmed up to him...and that trust meant more to Wilson than he enjoyed admitting.

And yeah, he'd gotten drunk a few times on liberty since his trip to the brig in Pearl, but never drunk enough to be extra stupid. He hadn't forgotten the captain's warning, and for once in his life, he didn't think an officer was bluffing when they threatened to hand him his head on a platter.

"I'll believe that when I see it," Velasquez said.

"Cross my heart and hope to— Ah, for fuck's sake."

"What?" She twisted in her chair to follow his gaze, but Bud just slumped and groaned. Sadly, he wasn't drunk enough to hallucinate. He'd done that, and it was kind of fun, as long as you stayed drunk. The aftermath sucked, though, and Bud had tried to drink his way through *that* once with no success. But today was not that day, and the trio of newcomers marching into the bar was from *Bluefish*. Even better, they were old drinking buddies of his...until Bud's antics got them tossed in the brig for building a fort out of barstools, among other silly crimes.

Yeah. Add that to the list of reasons Bud was delighted to leave *Bluefish*.

Bluefish might've been a hell of a lot newer than *Jimmy Carter*, but Bud would bet his mama's restaurant that crew was just as miserable as they were when he left. He didn't know what idiot went and gave Commander Peterson a state-of-the-art boat when they handed Commander Coleman the dinosaur...but he'd stick to the dinosaur every time. At least *Jimmy Carter's* crew felt like a team, and their captain didn't treat them like children.

Or criminals.

"Nothing." Maybe he could hide. "Just some old shipmates I don't want to hang out with."

"Then don't deprive me of your entertaining company, darlin'." Maria smirked.

Bud laughed. "I know it'll break your heart if I leave."

It almost worked. They spent the next hour ignoring glares from the three *Bluefish* sailors; pretending he didn't notice them was even kind of fun. Nursing beers slowly was less enjoyable, but Bud kept his promises, so he'd just started his third drink when the first of the trio swaggered up.

"Hey, Gary, Borreson, look who's here!" Machinist's Mate Second Class Steve Krennick swayed a bit, waving his shipmates over. "STS two—or is it STS *three*, now?—Wilson. Our old friend."

Bud shrugged as innocently as he could manage. "Still STS1, actually. Miracles do happen."

"No shit."

"Yes, shit. Sorry to disappoint."

The foursome got busted together two years back, and while Wilson and Borreson both managed to make first class petty officer again, the other two were both still second classes. There was nothing worse than watching your friends advance while you were stuck in place. That was something Bud knew from experience.

"How the hell did you avoid being busted after that last bout of stupidity?" Ramona Borreson demanded, her voice growing shriller, just like it always did when she was drunk.

Am I this annoying? God, I see why sober people drink. Then the drunks are less painful to be around.

"Guess I was lucky. Just like I was damn lucky to get off *Bluefish*." Bud regretted those words immediately. Sailors might complain amongst themselves, but if an outsider insulted a submariner's boat, there was hell to pay.

Even if the sailor in question used to be on the same miserable boat as those who were currently offended.

Surprisingly, it was Corpsman Second Class Ryan Gary who spoke up. He usually was the sensible one. "Bring my old shipmate a drink! *Two* drinks!" he yelled to the bartender. "We'll drink to *Bluefish*!"

If there was one situation where drinking might've been the smart idea, this was it, but Bud Wilson never claimed to make smart decisions. He'd spent most of his career being damned for making the stupider choice whenever two were available.

The bartender delivered a pair of tequila shots; Velasquez eyed them like they were poisonous.

"Don't you dare."

Bud licked his lips. Maybe they were poisonous. Maybe he should be good. Sure, he'd drunk a hell of a lot more than three beers and two shots before—and made a royal-ass mess out of things—but he'd promised to be better, hadn't he? And he didn't want to let *Jimmy Carter* down. Not this time.

"Actually, uh...I've reached my limit for the night, Ryan. But thanks."

"You've what?"

Bud took a deep breath. "I was about to head back to the boat." He'd planned on having another drink before these morons ruined that, but not anymore.

"You're gonna insult your old shipmates and your old boat by not drinking with us?" Ramona demanded.

"Well, it's not exactly an insult, but I'm—"

The first punch came out of nowhere.

Lieutenant Bobby O'Kane was in the middle of an email to one of his brothers when the call came, sitting at the small foldout desk in his cramped stateroom and minding his own business. It was a bit early in the evening for any of *Bluefish's* sailors to have gotten in trouble now that Wilson was gone, so he answered the phone with his usual aplomb.

His good mood evaporated when a chief from Shore Patrol was on the other end of the line, but Bobby agreed to take custody of three miscreant sailors so that they weren't sent to the brig. He scrawled their names and their misdeeds on the back of an old nav plan, and then he called Harriet Ainsworth on the quarterdeck to let her know what to expect. After that, Bobby had to stop putting off the inevitable.

The one good thing about the captain deciding that he didn't want to talk to anyone lower than the XO was that Bobby got to call Vanderbilt instead of Peterson. Still, he knew he'd face Peterson's wrath the next day. No amount of fancy dinners with his wife were going to make the captain forget this one.

Vanderbilt wasn't on the boat, but he answered on the first ring. "XO."

"Sir, it's the navigator. I've got the duty tonight, and I just got a call from Shore Patrol that we have three sailors inbound for a courtesy turnover."

"What'd they do this time?" Even Vanderbilt couldn't hide his sigh. Then again, if being the hapless navigator on board the good ship *Bluefish* was miserable, Bobby could only guess how the XO felt most days.

"Drunk and disorderly at Regan's Rooster. Something about a fight."

"Anyone hurt?"

"Not that Shore Patrol mentioned," Bobby replied. "They're still on their way back."

"Very well." Vanderbilt sounded like he was sucking lemons. "I'll call the captain."

"Aye, sir," Bobby said and hung up.

He knew where this would go. The entire crew would probably be on restricted liberty.

Again.

Now, all Bobby had to do was wait for Gary, Borreson, and Krennick to show up. He might as well finish his email while he still had time. And while his head was still on his shoulders. Forcing himself to stop fretting, he read what he'd written to Derek.

I really hope that the aviator life on that carrier is treating you better than sub life is going for me. Not gonna lie, I'm starting to consider begging Peter for a job. Working for Dad and Peter at the car dealership can't be worse than crap on BLF right now. We're still stuck to the pier, and of course it's all my fault. Yeah, the outboard breaks, but the thing was a piece of junk before I arrived! I don't get it. I don't get Peter blaming me for Carter deciding he wants to be a fireman, either. How's it <u>my</u> fault that he's setting fires all over the house just so he can put them out? I told him about how subs fight fires last year, and he's not my kid. So not my fault. Anyway, got any ideas on what to get Cole for his birthday? I've searched the internet up and down and can't find anything. You're the oldest uncle, so it's your job to figure out gifts.

His radio crackled. "CDO, Officer of the Deck. Shore Patrol is here, sir."

Harri always had such great timing.

"I'm on my way."

Bobby popped up out of his chair and headed topside. Did he slam his stateroom door shut on the way out? Maybe. This wasn't a good day, and no amount of pretending would stop that. Even the sailors he saw on his walk forward looked glum, but that was life on *Bluefish*, wasn't it? He started whistling a happy tune in self-defense, which made two sailors laugh and one roll their eyes.

Better.

Bobby was only halfway up the ladder when an angry voice floated up to him.

"I'd like to speak to your CDO. Immediately."

"He's on his way, ma'am." Harri sounded unhappy, but Bobby frowned.

Ma'am? Since when did the base send officers out on Shore Patrol? Harri had just been promoted to lieutenant (junior grade), so the visitor had to be at least a lieutenant.

"And here I am!" Bobby hated the way he resorted to manic cheerfulness under pressure, but he couldn't help it. He scrambled up the ladder onto *Bluefish's* quarterdeck, determined to save Harri from whatever angry fate was after her. *Someone* should protect the younglings, after all.

Bobby spotted the interloper immediately, just from her scowl. She was indeed a lieutenant, slender and trim like a gymnast and with curly black hair vying mightily to work its way free of her bun. She wore a *Jimmy Carter* ball cap over that hair and a narrow-eyed glare that transferred straight to Bobby.

"You're the CDO." Her flat voice made it sound unbelievable.

"Bobby O'Kane." He held out a hand. "Nav. And CDO, obviously."

"Obviously," she said. "Maggie Bennett. I'm the nav and CDO from *Jimmy Carter.*"

There'd been no way to miss the behemoth pulling into the pier behind from *Bluefish* that afternoon. Rose and Bobby had gaped as the big boat came alongside without using a single tug, sure it would hit *Bluefish* and then Peterson would have another tantrum. But it hadn't, so why would their command duty officer would pay him such an angry visit?

"So, uh, what can I do for you this fine evening?" he asked. The weather was nice, too. Real nice, if you forgot about the war. Too nice to be dealing with liberty incidents.

"Three of your sailors beat the holy hell out of one of mine, and now *my* sailor is in the brig because of it." Bennett crossed her arms.

"Can't you give them a verbal release and have Shore Patrol bring your sailor back?" Bobbie frowned. Perth was one of the easier bases to deal with, and hadn't he done just that?

"*I* can't. He's a repeat offender."

Subtlety really wasn't Bobby's strong suit. "So how do you know it was my sailors that started it?"

"Because another one of my sailors was right there, and *she* wasn't drunk!" It was too bad Bennett was so angry; if she hadn't been furious, she would've been cute. "And neither was Wilson, for that matter."

"I'm not sure what I can— Wait a minute. Did you say 'Wilson'? As in, the sonar tech that we traded to you, *Wilson?*"

She heaved a sigh. "Yes, that one. But look, all I need is for you to call the brig and say he wasn't at fault, and then they'll release him. Probably."

"Give me a sec, okay?"

Knowing Wilson's reputation—and that his three miscreants were his former drinking buddies—Bobby wasn't sure that it *wasn't* Wilson's fault, but he was willing to ask what had happened. Stepping away from Bennett, he walked over to where Shore Patrol held his three drunk and bruised sailors. At least Harri had already taken care of the paperwork.

"Okay, Borreson, what's the story?" he asked. She was the senior one of the bunch and *usually* the reasonable one. Bobby figured he had the best chance of getting an answer out of her.

"Well, sir, it's like this." She hiccuped, leaning on the brow for support. "We ran into Wilson, and he was getting all bell...bellig...uh, angry and insultin' *Bluefish*. An' we couldn't let him do that."

Bobby fought back a groan. "Who started it, MM1?"

"I don't really...recall, sir."

"Great." It was Bennett again. She'd stalked over to listen and looked ready to do murder. "Look, O'Kane, those three have had enough that I could get drunk just breathing around them. You really think you're going to get sense out of them?"

"Look, no offense, but I can't slam my sailors for something your sailor says they did. Particularly since I have experience with Wilson."

"You want to ask my ET2, then? Compared to these three, she's a rock of sobriety."

"Talking to her isn't going to help. I'm sorry, but I'm not just going to throw these three under the bus. They're only trouble when Wilson's around, so it kind of figures that the same thing as always happened." He was babbling, but even if these three *were* guilty, it was his job to protect them as best he could. There was no way Peterson wasn't going to bust them down a rank, but if the captain thought they were at fault, it would only make things worse.

"Shore Patrol had to haul your sailors *off* Wilson, and suddenly it's his fault?" she asked.

"Look, I'm not saying you're wrong. Just that I want them to sober up before I start assigning blame, okay?" Bobby only earned himself another glare of death. Feeling helpless, he turned to Harri. "Get those three below."

"Yes, sir."

"And send...ah, crap. HMC already left, didn't he?"

"Two hours ago," Harri said.

"Then find what's-his-name, the new guy who's an EMT. Send him down to look at them." Because of course, HM2 Gary was now *Bluefish's* only corpsman, with their chief corpsman stolen by *Kansas*. Fortunately, one of the fire control technicians was a qualified EMT.

"I'll send Cesari down."

"Thanks, Harri."

Taking a deep breath, Bobby turned back to Bennett, only to discover she was on her phone.

"Yes, sir...I'm over on *Bluefish*, now talking to their CDO. He won't call the brig." She scowled at Bobby again, then gave him a half-apologetic shrug. "Honestly, I'm not sure if it'd do any good. The sailors from *Bluefish* are pretty trashed, and I don't think they even remember who started the fight."

The other sub's CDO paused, and then a look of alarm crossed her face. "Sir, I'm sure we can do—" Bennett bit her lip, listening. "Well, no, but...Benji's probably going to die of embarrassment if you bail Wilson out again."

Bobby could hear the laughter from the other end. Bennett's tense expression eased, and she *was* cute.

Maybe Bobby should try making her acquaintance when she wasn't mad at him.

"Yeah, I do." Another pause. "Then I'll fish Baby Doc out of his rack and have him standing by for when you get here. Thanks, Captain."

She hung up; Bobby got in before she could speak, trying to keep his jaw from dropping. "Is your captain really going to bail *Wilson* out of the brig?"

"I *tried* to get you to call." Bennett's glare was back. "And yes, he is. It's not the first time, either."

She stalked off *Bluefish* before Bobby could find a response.

Chapter 30

Sacrificial Lambs

16 February 2039, Perth, Australia

They crammed into the small planning room like teenagers at a concert with the body odor to match. Unfortunately, the room wasn't nearly as well decorated as the raves Nancy Coleman's elder daughter wanted to attend; it held two computers, an electronic charting system, one wall-size big screen monitor, and a conference table barely big enough to hold half of Rear Admiral Rodriquez's staff. There wasn't even a coffee maker, an unforgivable sin in the navy, so Tanya Tenaglia brought in a portable one that now sat next to the door on a folding tray table.

Nancy scowled as the coffee maker beeped after filling her cup. House rules said that the last person to use it had to refill it, so she set to work refilling the water reservoir while her compatriots filed in. Their little hidey hole was attached to an out-of-the-way maintenance building out by a disused helicopter pad, near nothing except a parking lot. No one came out here, which made it doubly secure...and the technology was one generation short of state of the art.

Nancy didn't want to know a classified planning room existed way out here or why it was so small. The planning room was a great metaphor for this entire operation. Done on a shoestring and hidden away where most decision makers couldn't see them. This was their second week of planning, and so far, they'd come up with exactly zero brilliant ideas to win back Christmas Island. But they did have a hundred innovative ways to get their entire task force killed.

Marco Rodriquez turned to her, his brow furrowed. "Can you target Tomahawk missiles off of GPS data from another unit instead of a satellite? Like, passed in real time?"

"I can't see why not." Nancy sipped her coffee. It was lukewarm, as usual. That coffee maker was on its last legs. "The system isn't exactly designed to shoot quickly, but we can make it work. What are you thinking?"

"I'm thinking that we have a metric shit-ton of Tomahawks left, and their warheads are big enough to rip ships apart."

"Yeah, but satellite pictures are time late, and ships *move*, Admiral," Captain Tanya Tenaglia, Rodriquez's chief of staff, replied.

"That's why I asked if you could use GPS coordinates from another unit." Rodriquez smirked.

Tenaglia shook her head. "No way can anyone get in that close."

"You're thinking about a sub." Nancy shivered. "Someone to sneak in at periscope depth and send us targeting data."

"Right the fuck from the middle of their formation." Rodriquez nodded grimly. His brown eyes met hers unflinchingly.

"They'll get hammered the moment they start transmitting."

"Likely." A shrug. "You got any better ideas?"

The LED lights made his eyes burn, and the speeches went on forever, but John cut his teeth on events like this when he was a kid. With two parents wearing stars—one a navy admiral, and the other an air force general, a challenging marriage if there ever was one—John Dalton was no stranger to ceremonies. He just wasn't used to being the star.

The crowd was pretty impressive for it being wartime, though half of it was his crew of a hundred thirty. The rest was a mix of submariners from other boats, friends—including a few from the ill-fated staff on *Enterprise* he'd served on—and some reporters. They all stood behind a hastily erected and not-so-attractive line of bunting a dozen feet from the temporary stage. There wasn't a seating area because no one wanted to haul chairs out by the sub piers, but there were flowers and flags, so it looked nice enough.

John wished to hell his wife could've made it out for this, but Janet was knee deep in torpedo design out at Lazark, and he'd found out about the ceremony yesterday. That wasn't enough time for her to make the cross-continental flight, even if she'd been able to leave.

Janet, a senior engineering manager, had just moved off missiles and onto the *next* generation of torpedoes—the one John wasn't supposed to know about, beyond even the Mark 84s coming out to the fleet—and they agreed that Massachusetts was the best place for her right now.

No matter how much he missed her.

At least Nancy Coleman was here, hiding in the back and winking at him. Alex was underway, but it was good to see *one* of his best friends in the crowd. And Jeff McNally, still running for the Senate, *wasn't* here. He'd called with congratulations that morning, but if John never had to see his old boss again, it would be too soon. He was done kissing that particular ass.

Unfortunately, there were still admirals who required a certain degree of...handling. Five minutes of listening to him speak was enough to tell John that Vice Admiral Doug Brown, Commander, Submarine Forces Pacific, was the type to leave exactly one cookie in the jar when you told him not to eat them all. He was twenty years John's senior, white-haired, eagle-eyed, and a politician to his core.

John exchanged a glance with Patricia. He and his XO didn't need words to understand each other: those almost-impossible-to-execute orders to protect the convoy *and* take out *Amazone* had come straight from Brown. No way they didn't. This man hadn't seen a minute of combat and didn't have the imagination to figure out what it was like.

"...Captain Dalton's inspiring leadership and devotion to the fulfillment of his hazardous mission reflect great credit upon himself and the United States Naval Service," Brown said, finally pinning the blue-and-white ribbon Navy Cross on John's dress blue uniform.

John accepted the offered hand and shook it firmly. "Thank you, sir."

"Thank you, son. You've done your country proud."

"I am honored to have had the opportunity to do so." John knew the right words to say, and besides, he was damned proud of himself—and especially his crew, who'd been awarded the Navy Unit Commendation for the same mission.

"Keep up the good work." Turning, Brown smiled for the cameras, and the two struck a pose while reporters snapped pictures.

John smiled, nodded, and did his job. That included a short interview with two officious-looking reporters, one from the *Navy Times* and one from the *Washington Post*, and then posed for another dozen pictures with his crew. Vice Admiral Brown butted into all of them. *Razorback* gleamed on the pier behind them, recipient of a fresh coat of paint just for this occasion.

All the camera operators worked for the navy, however, so at least John didn't have to worry about them snapping pictures or video they weren't allowed to take. Even with the reporters around. Finally, he and Patricia put down liberty call, and the crew disappeared in a flash, leaving the captain and the XO alone on the pier.

"That was fun." John looked down at the medal on his chest, hardly able to believe it was there.

Patricia shook her head. "I can never tell if you're being sarcastic or not."

"Neither can I." John smiled.

"Congratulations on the Navy Cross. It's nice to know you survived getting it," she replied, reaching out to finger the medal.

John laughed. "You say that because you like not feeding the fishes."

"Since we'd be feeding them side by side if it was a posthumous medal, you can count on that."

They both had too many friends on the bottom of the ocean, too many boats lost and too many posthumous medals. Sinking one French submarine, no matter how successful, shouldn't be worthy of a Navy Cross—a *Navy Cross!*—but John knew the navy needed every victory it could get. Particularly ones from boats that came home.

Humping stores was no one's idea of fun, but Bud Wilson found himself supervising a lot of it on *Jimmy Carter*. Supervising. Him.

Today, it was a long line of food that needed to get on the boat. Nothing new. They were *always* humping stores on board and finding places to hide it. Torpedo tubes seven and eight were the crew's favorites for egg and milk overflow; the tubes were nice and cold, great for storing things that shouldn't get warm. Besides, the weapons guys said those tubes were a bitch to load, anyway, so might as well stick boxes of milk, eggs, and taters in them.

As usual, *Jimmy Carter's* sailors formed a sailor-powered conveyer belt to schlep the food onto the boat, handing off box after box until it went down the aft hatch and to wherever the supply officer decided it should hide today. On long underways, the floors of passageways and berthings were lined with boxes that the crew just walked on, which sucked if you were tall. That was after they filled up every little fan room with food, of course. There was never enough storage space on a fast-attack submarine, something Bud was coming to appreciate more and more as he gained responsibility.

Now that he was a couple months into his time on Smiley, he was smart enough to have spare parts for the ancient sonar computer hidden in his *rack*. They weren't in the stock system. Those were ones he bought off eBay or scrounged off another ship, trading this and that, including an old *Jimmy Carter* plaque that he hoped no one would miss off the mess decks.

The boat was still chronically short of chief petty officers, though, which meant he stood in for one on a lot of occasions. It was a weird-ass feeling, being respected. People even listened to his opinion and *trusted* him not to get drunk and stupid. Like when he got bailed out of the brig a second time around, only this time for a fight he really hadn't started.

"Why the scowl, Bud?" Maria Velasquez asked.

"Thinking about *Bluefish*," he replied as he tore into the pallet of sodas their supply officer indicated was ready to go aboard.

"Best you don't do that. Always puts you in a black mood, and I like you better when you aren't a fucking asshole," she replied.

"Yeah, me, too." He sighed. "It's embarrassing to get bailed out of the brig for something I didn't do, okay?"

"More embarrassing than all the times you got thrown in there for things you did?" She tossed a flat of sodas to the next sailor in the chain.

"Way more. Then I could take perverse pride in whatever artistic disaster I created."

Maria laughed. "You're fucked up, you know that?"

"I was a destructive child. The doctors always said it was because I was bored, and it cleared right up once I started playing hockey." Bud grinned.

"Pity you can't do that on the boat," she muttered just as a newcomer approaching the boat caught Bud's eye.

The fact that the chief petty officer was in nicely pressed khakis was the first giveaway that he didn't belong. Nobody on the boats had time for that bullshit during war; they wore their coveralls every chance they got and changed into a semi-rumpled working uniform if they had to leave the pier. This guy, however, had creases in his fucking pants and was wearing *all* his ribbons. Those were all sure-fire signs of a shore weanie.

He had silver dolphins on, though, which meant he'd qualified in submarines at *some* point. Probably years ago, Bud decided, stepping forward.

"Can I help you, Chief?"

"I'm looking for your combat systems duty chief. I'm here from SUBRON Two-Nine to evaluate your spare parts inventory and see what systems you have on board."

"No chief today, just me." Bud offered his hand; the handshake he got in return was unsurprisingly limp. "STS1 Wilson, Sonar Sup. We just got the latest upgrade to the integrated combat systems suite. Sonar software's a bit dodgy because it was written for *Virginia* hardware, but we threw some extra memory in the system, and it's running okay now."

The strange chief pursed his lips. "I'd like to go aboard and see your spare parts inventory."

"Sure. You here to see if we need anything?" Bud gestured for him to follow up the brow as sailors humping stores shifted to make room for them.

"More like seeing what you've got on board in case this old boat is decomm'd and we need to parcel it out to newer boats." The chief looked across *Jimmy Carter's* deck with a critical eye, frowning. "Looks like your topside preservation could use some work."

Bud felt his eyes narrow. "She's forty-one, Chief. Be nice to the lady."

"That's exactly why she shouldn't be at war." The chief wrinkled his nose. "You're lucky she's still seaworthy."

"Hey, now. We do pretty good."

"Doing what, exactly?"

"More than some boats," Bud snapped. Like *Bluefish*, he didn't add. "We rescued *Georgia's* crew back in October and those two pilots in November. And none of the convoys we've escorted have got sunk, either."

"Escorted convoys are rarely attacked."

"Tell that to *Amazone*." Bud snorted.

"STS1, I'm just here for facts. If you'll take me to your storeroom, I'll be about my business," the chief replied, gesturing at the down ladder by the quarterdeck.

"And what business is that?"

Bud whirled, surprised to see Commander Coleman topside. "Captain!"

Salutes were exchanged, though Bud noticed the chief's was stiff. "I'm here to do a fore-to-aft survey of your combat systems spares," he replied.

"Like the one my Weps already submitted to the squadron, as per request?" Coleman cocked his head.

"A physical inventory is always preferred to—"

"So you don't trust my crew to do our own inventory. Is that what you're saying?" Oh, Bud knew that tone. That was the deceptively calm tone that came right before the captain *fucked you right up*.

He decided to help. "I didn't realize you wanted to do a keel-to-keel inventory, Chief. I'd need Weps' permission for that, and he's off the boat today. You just said you wanted to *see* our spare parts inventory. I was going to pull that up on a computer."

Best not to mention that Weps was visiting with his senator dad, who'd apparently come out to Australia under the radar to see his one and only kid. They could leave that one in their back pockets. Besides, would Bigwig Senator Angler help out the oldest boat in the fleet, or would he sink them? Weps was pretty decent, but maybe he got that from his mom.

"Is there another request for parts in the works?" Coleman asked before the chief could respond. "We already sent over the two VMS cards requested by *Florida*."

"As you know, Captain, the squadron is doing a potential decommissioning survey of your boat. Just to be prepared," the chief said after a long silence.

"Well, if you don't mind, I'll continue being prepared for war right now." Coleman's smile was sharp enough to cut glass. "Do you have an official request for anything other than the inventory you were already sent?"

"No, sir, I do not."

"Then perhaps it's best if you trust the sailors and officers assigned to ships in the squadron," Coleman replied. "Sowing seeds of distrust between the squadron and *Jimmy Carter* is in no one's best interest."

"That was not my intention, sir. However, given the quality of the crew assigned to—"

"It's best that you don't finish that sentence, Chief." Coleman's voice went cold.

"I'm here to help the squadron prepare for the future, sir." The chief crossed his arms. "This is my job."

"Then you can kindly get the fuck off my boat and do your job elsewhere."

Time to add this to the list of reasons why Bud Wilson would follow Alex Coleman off a cliff. Bud had a hard time not smiling as he watched the chief trundle back down the brow and away from *Jimmy Carter*.

Did assholes like that really make chief? How dumb did you have to be to insult a crew in front of their captain—and the twenty-something sailors humping stores onto the ship. The handful who could hear would tell everyone else, and now everyone knew that the squadron had it out for *Jimmy Carter*.

Not that the captain was surprised. Bud guessed that from the look on his face. How long had he carried that weight around by himself? Shit, Bud was glad he'd never gotten a degree and decided to be an officer. Command had to be lonely as shit. Of course, *good* chiefs were supposed to help take some of that burden, but that no-load chief back there seemed like a pro at making things worse.

Shit, if that dude could make chief...maybe there was hope for Bud yet.

26 February 2039, Main Harbor, Christmas Island (India)

Luck was with Marco Rodriquez, or for some definition of luck. There were two attack submarines within range of Christmas Island, both finishing up their current missions. SUBPAC hesitated to hand both over, but in the end, Marco's arguments won, and USS *Pacu* and USS *Florida* CHOPPED, or changed operational command, to Task Group 23.

Florida was closer and thus drew the short straw. Fortunately, or unfortunately, her CO was also a former protégée of Admiral Rodriquez's, having served as one of his department heads back when he commanded an attack submarine. Guilt churned in Marco's gut when he passed the order along, but he still sent *Florida* into the belly of the beast.

Like the bulk of America's inventory, *Florida* was a *Virginia*-class submarine. She was newer, one of the modified Block VI boats that traded organic special operations capability for twenty-eight additional vertical launch missile tubes. Those tubes could either carry ship-killer missiles or ship-to-shore missiles and gave her an offensive punch equal to most destroyers. But where she beat destroyers was stealth.

"Damn shame we're loaded with Tomahawks," Lieutenant Commander Alicia Abbott, *Florida's* XO, said, watching the sleepy ships swinging at anchor from the combat systems display in control. "It's a beautiful shooting gallery up there."

"Great way to get dead fast, you mean," Commander Nuru Okafor replied. "We start shooting up there, and they'll find us right quick."

Florida's control room was eerily quiet; everyone who was briefed in on this new mission knew how hard it was going to be, and there were no secrets on a submarine. Alicia guessed the truth needed twenty minutes to get around the boat once the mission was briefed.

It would've been half that if they hadn't just downloaded the Super Bowl. After being submerged for over a month without good connectivity, the crew was eager to see who won—not to mention watch all the commercials.

Now, four days later, they'd snuck underneath the enemy fleet in the harbor at Christmas Island, creeping along so the boat didn't broach in the shallow waters. Anywhere shallow enough to anchor was shallow enough to run aground…or run afoul of a ship's anchor chain. Plotting the course in had been hair-raising. Alicia just wished she thought they'd use the course she and the navigator had plotted out.

"Going to be bad enough the moment we start rotating and radiating, boss." Alicia grimaced. She wasn't looking forward to this mission, not one bit. But it was the job, and she was the XO. Her task was to make it happen—she just wished she could accept it as calmly as the captain.

"I know." Okafor's dark features were serene. "But we have a job to do. Periscope depth."

"Periscope depth, aye," the officer of the deck replied.

Florida rose silently from the depths, moving through three hundred feet, two hundred, and then leveling out just above one hundred. There she hovered while Abbott directed the scope in a circle, counting enemy ships on the horizon. They stood out as steadily lightening silhouettes against the fading orange-and-pink lights of the dawn. This was an ideal time of day to take periscope bearings. Submariners trained endlessly with warship silhouettes, even in these modern times.

The Indian fleet that swung gently at anchor was far bigger than the American one it had displaced. Seven destroyers, four frigates, two cruisers, two amphibious warships, and…were those submarines on the surface? She squinted at the periscope display screen.

"I think they got two French destroyers here, Captain," she said. "And it looks like one of those submarines might be a *Requin*, too. Look at the sail."

"I believe you might be right." Okafor chewed a nail. "I believe those cargo ships have missile pods on deck, too."

"Damn." Alicia whistled. "We going to paint them as targets?"

"You bet we are," Okafor replied. "Five minutes to go time."

"General quarters set, Captain," Lieutenant Commander Davud Attar, *Fletcher's* tactical action officer, reported. "Condition II-Strike set."

"Very well." Nancy took a deep breath and turned to Rodriguez, sitting to her left in *Fletcher's* darkened CIC. With only blue lights and computer screens providing illumination, her crew in combat was almost unaware of the time topside, but they'd been on station for the last two hours. Just sitting on go. "We're ready when the call comes, Admiral."

Nancy's breathing was steady, though. She sat back in her chair, watching the plot with a practiced eye, radiating competence. This was not her normal battle, but what was *normal* in this war?

"*Florida* will come through." Rodriquez's hands were busy dismantling a calculator.

"It's a suicide mission," Nancy whispered. A strange feeling stole up her spine.

"I know." Rodriquez closed his eyes briefly. "Would you do it, if ordered?"

She bit her lip, eyes staring blankly at the large-screen displays. "Of course I would."

"So would I." He grimaced. "We all fucking would. It's the goddamned job, because there's a mother-loving navy war on. And we're losing. We've got to change the rules, Nancy. And we don't have enough ship-killing missiles to turn this into a slugging match."

"I know, sir." Nancy still felt guilty, and she could tell Rodriquez did, too. But Rodriquez wasn't wrong. They didn't have another way to take Christmas Island back, at least not quickly.

And the Alliance needed a quick victory. Really, they needed any victory that *lasted*. Nancy had retreated one too many times, had picked up the pieces of dead or drowning friends. Enough was enough. They had to do something different.

That was how this crazy, straight-out-of-left-field plan had developed. Not out of good tactics, but out of desperation. And more than a few ounces of creativity.

Nancy let her eyes drift over the icons representing the other ships in their task group. *Jason Dunham* stuck close to *Fletcher's* side, with *Nitze* to port. *Truxton*, *Farley*, and *Caron* were aft of the trio, with two Australian frigates, the brand-new *Bogan* and ancient *Parramatta* out on either flank, already searching for submarines.

Seeing a surface ship even older than her husband's submarine was flat-out weird. *Parramatta* had looked like she was in decent shape lying against the pier back in Perth—she wore a fresh coat of paint and every line was faked out with precision—but she was still an *Anzac*-class frigate, commissioned in 2003.

Nancy had been *three* in 2003. Ships almost as old as those commanding them were not supposed to go to war...but then again, no one really planned for this war, did they? If they had, no one in their right mind would've come up with the current battle plan.

Sitting a mere thirty miles away from her target, steaming in radio silence, just waiting for a submarine to tell her where to shoot, was barely short of insanity. *Fletcher's* surface search radars were almost this long ranged, but Tomahawk missiles weren't built to take radar input. Once, a lifetime ago, there had been a ship-killing variant of the TLAM, but budget cuts killed it, and those missiles were converted to the Block IV TLAMs now in *Fletcher's* launch cells.

Tomahawks were designed to go after land-based targets, targets that didn't *move*. Once fired, they could be updated for a new, GPS-specific target, but Tomahawks didn't do terminal maneuvers like ship-killing missiles. They just bored in on their targets with the inevitability of rocks falling from the sky.

Rocks with really, *really* big warheads.

Jimmy Carter, newly underway, was actually the third-closest submarine when Marco Rodriquez put out the call, but they dodged the bullet that ended up landing squarely on USS *Pacu*.

Much like *Florida*, *Pacu* spent several days creeping in close to Christmas Island, though in her case, she didn't enter the harbor. Instead, she lurked right outside, inside torpedo range of the ships guarding the entranceway. The irony wasn't lost on her crew; not long ago, the Indians started a battle by taking out the Alliance ships

in this same position.
Now maybe they could return the favor.

"*Florida's* going in close, boys and girls. It's our job to draw fire away from her for as long as possible," Commander Steve Munson told his crew on the 1MC. "And we're going to do that by sinking as many of the enemy as possible. As fast as we can load torpedoes."

Unlike *Florida*, *Pacu* was a *Cero*-class boat, the fourth one off the line. She wasn't as advanced as later boats like *Razorback*, but she was quick, quiet, and well-led. Munson had also read John Dalton's patrol reports and had a healthy respect for the tortoise-like nature of his Mark 48 CBASS torpedoes.

He hung up the microphone to the 1MC and returned to studying the plot, standing in the center of a soft buzz of activity in *Pacu's* control room. This was what the instructors at the Sub School called a *target-rich environment*, but unease bubbled in Munson's gut. He had a full weapons room. Twenty-eight torpedoes were enough to sink fourteen of the seventeen enemy ships on the surface if he shot two at each target, but Munson doubted he'd get the chance.

If all went right, Admiral Rodriquez's plan would work, and missiles from the surface ships would sink anything *Pacu* couldn't. If things went wrong...well, *Pacu* wasn't likely to get the chance to reload seven times.

Munson licked his lips and tried not to think about that. At least they didn't have *Florida's* mission.

"How do you want to play this, sir?" Lieutenant Commander Courtney Hatcher slid up next to him, elbowing Munson lightly in the side.

Hatcher could've been Munson's twin, born a handful of years too late; both were tall, dark haired, and green eyed. Random luck and the Bureau of Personnel brought both native Alaskans to *Pacu*, even though they hadn't seen one another since their Academy days.

"Right around the edges. We're the distraction, so it needs to be explosive." Munson gestured at the plot, consciously controlling his breathing. "We take the two guard ships out first with two torpedoes each. Fortunately, a destroyer and a frigate aren't going to outrun our torpedoes."

"That's not what worries me," Hatcher replied. He leaned into the speaker to his right. "Sonar, Conn, any sign of a sub out there?"

"Conn, Sonar, just the two on the surface. Both have reactors hot and main circ pumps going."

"Conn, aye." Hatcher frowned.

"We'll need to watch them. Particularly that *Requin*." Munson grimaced. "I'm not as worried about the *Akula*. They're slower."

"And louder."

"That too." Munson glanced at the clock; three minutes to go time. His heartbeat quickened, but he raised his chin and tried to sound commanding. "Firing point procedures, tubes one and three, track 7088. Target the first destroyer, Weps."

"Weps, aye. Tubes one and three ready in all respects. Solution ready. Weapons ready."

"Shoot!"

Weps' hand slapped down on both buttons. "Tubes one and three fired electrically."

A moment later, sonar reported: "Two fish running hot, straight, and normal."

"Very well." Munson shivered. This was *Pacu's* first shot with him in command; he'd spent two months escorting convoys, waiting for a chance. Here it was. "Line tubes two and four up on track 7089. We need to take the other guard ship out next."

"Tubes two and four ready in all respects. Solution ready. Weapons ready."

"Shoot!"

"Tubes two and four fired electrically," Weps reported.

"Very well." Munson took a deep breath, debating his choices. His eyes drifted to the clock.

2:35

2:34

2:33

A quick look at the plot told him that his torpedoes would need less than a minute and a half to reach their targets, which meant they'd hit one minute before go time. Right on schedule.

"You want to cut the wires and reload, Captain?" Hatcher asked the same question he'd been wrestling with.

Cutting the control wires decreased accuracy. It meant that the torpedoes would be on their own, using only their onboard sensors to track and kill the destroyer and the frigate on guard duty at the mouth of the harbor. As long as the wires were still connected to *Pacu*, the submarine's fire control team could give real-time updates to the torpedoes using the submarine's better sensors.

But Munson couldn't reload his torpedo tubes until he cut the wires and closed the outer doors, either. And every moment he waited carried a chance that the surface ships topside might find him.

And every one of those ships carried at least a pair of rocket-propelled depth charge launchers, which could *really* ruin a submarine's day.

"Yeah." He shook himself, wasting precious seconds. "Cut the wires, close the outer doors. Reload all tubes."

1:51.

"Officer of the Deck, bring us right and come up to twenty knots. Follow in the torpedoes' wake so we can get a better shot at the next targets," Hatcher ordered.

Munson nodded. "Good idea, XO. Let's find our next two."

"Stand by to crash dive on my command," Okafor ordered as the timer hit one minute. How could she stand there so relaxed when everyone in *Florida's* control room was staring at her? "Fire control, stand by to radiate."

"Officer of the Deck, aye."

"Fire control, aye."

A chill ran down Alicia Abbott's spine. She'd done some downright stupid things in her time, going all the way back to college at Texas A&M, where pranks were the name of the game and Alicia was a frequent player. But this took the cake. Coming to periscope depth in the middle of an anchored enemy fleet and then intentionally giving away their position by turning on their radars? The plan was so insane it might just work.

"Conn, Sonar, explosions to port! Multiple explosions on the bearing of the guard ships!" Chief Kavka's voice was almost loud enough to hear in control proper.

Okafor's smile remained serene. "That would be *Pacu*."

"Glad we've got friends on our side, ma'am," Alicia whispered.

"As am I."

Alicia would've given her eye teeth to have *Pacu's* mission instead of *Florida's*, but they called them orders for a reason. It wasn't like they got to pick and choose, and there *was* something thrilling to being in the middle of an enemy fleet, lurking right beneath the surface. No one knew they were here.

Yet.

She stood by Okafor's side at the navigation table, watching the plot. None of the Indian ships were moving, at least not as far as sonar could detect, but Alicia could imagine the chaos on board those formerly sleeping ships. *Serves you bastards right*, she thought.

How long would it take sleeping crews to raise anchor and go sub hunting? Their focus would be in the wrong direction, with every sensor pointed out to sea, hunting *Pacu*. That would give *Florida* a small window of opportunity. Would it be long enough?

Her heart pounded in her ears like bongo drums.

"Fifteen seconds to go time," the navigator announced.

"Stand by, fire control," Okafor ordered. "Radiate surface search radars at go time and start transmitting in Link 18 immediately. Do not wait for my order."

"Radiate surface radars and go active in Link immediately, fire control, aye," Weps replied.

Okafor turned to meet Alicia's eyes. "I want to shoot anything that localizes us, XO, but *not* unless we have a reasonable belief that they know where we are. We have to play this smart."

"Yes, ma'am." Alicia *wanted* to start shooting anything that moved, like *Pacu*, but that would give away their position. It wasn't like they could run and hide; they needed to stay near the surface so they could keep their radar antenna up.

That same antenna restricted how fast *Florida* could move, lest she risk ripping it straight off. This mission signed them up for a whole parcel of bad options. Bad and worse.

God, how long did *Pacu* need to reload?

"Time!" Nav's voice broke the stillness, high-pitched with nerves. A glance that way told Alicia that Nav was white-faced but steady; lord, they all knew what they were about, didn't they?

"BPS-17 radiating! Tracks coming in!" Weps said. "Link 18 handshake in process with *Fletcher*."

"Very well." Okafor was still dead calm.

Alicia felt her heart skip a beat as she looked at the plot. The AN/BPS-17(v)2 radar was a strange hybrid for the later *Virginia*-class boats. It was a surface search radar with fire control capabilities that could merge tracks with sonar signatures to determine precise, GPS-accurate locations for enemy contacts. Combining sonar and radar data meant *Florida* knew the Indian ships' locations down to a few feet—the accuracy needed for Tomahawk missile launches.

"Link established! Transmitting contact data!"

"Conn, Sonar, another explosion to port bearing two-nine-one. Looks like *Pacu* nailed a cruiser."

"Conn, aye." Alicia took this one, smiling. "Sounds like Munson doesn't want the skimmers to take all the glory, Captain."

"There'll be glory enough to go around, XO."

"TAO, IDC, Link tracks from *Florida!*"

"TAO, aye, break, Captain." Attar's voice was level, but he turned to look at Nancy with a gleam in his eye.

She didn't even have to pass the word to Admiral Rodriquez, still seated at her left shoulder; he was on the task force command circuit in a flash. "Little Beavers, this is Task Force Two-Three Actual. Commence firing plan on all tracks passed from *Florida*. Out."

"TAO, Captain, you have batteries release for Tomahawk engagement," Nancy said.

"TAO, aye, break Strike. Batteries release per Tomahawk firing plan," Attar replied.

"Strike, aye."

Fletcher's strike warfare officer was just an ensign. Although she was highly trained, no one really expected land-attack missiles to be a large part of this war. Civilians just wouldn't put up with missiles landing on highly populated areas—a fact proven in multiple small conflicts throughout the 2020s. Governments of major nations couldn't afford to drop a thousand-pound warhead on Grandma and Grandpa. Not if they didn't want riots in the streets.

Because of that, Ensign Marcy Wilner clearly never expected to hold the fate of a task force in her hands. Tomahawk planning was not meant to be done on the fly. Targets were pre-selected by military planners, not a mere ensign on a destroyer. Coordinates were checked, rechecked, and then verified by an independent third party before a ship even *saw* them.

Not today.

Today, Ensign Wilner's flying fingers designated targets not just for *Fletcher's* forty Tomahawks, but also for thirty from each of the other five destroyers. The two frigates didn't carry land-attack missiles, but they were there for ASW defense. That still left 240 Tomahawks for fourteen ships.

Was it overkill? Maybe. But Tomahawks weren't designed for this, and no one wanted to risk too many being shot down by point defense. Nancy watched out from the corner of her eye as Wilner, chewing her red hair, designated seventeen missiles per ship—and twenty for the remaining cruiser.

"Looks like *Pacu* got three already," Admiral Rodriquez said.

"Yes, sir." Nancy grinned. "I'll even forgive them if they make us drop good missiles in the drink by killing a few more."

"From your mouth to God's fucking ears, Captain."

"TAO, Strike, missile launch in five...four...three...two...launching now!"

Missile hatches on six destroyers snapped open and boosters ignited. No destroyer could launch forty missiles at once; they launched in stages out of each eight pack of missile cells. But Tomahawks were smart missiles, and they could be programmed to linger and wait for their compatriots, which these did.

Within a minute, all 240 missiles were in the air, and they turned to roar toward the Indian task force at almost 500 knots.

But a lot could happen in their three minutes and thirty-one seconds of flight time.

Chapter 31

Suicide Mission

"Tubes two and four reloaded, Captain," *Pacu's* Weps finally reported.

Commander Steve Munson wiped sweaty hands on the legs of his coveralls and tried to hide the way his breathing wanted to become short little gasps. They were out here, naked as the day they were born, but *damn it.* The reloading drills his crew practiced all the way out to Christmas Island weren't paying off. That reload took thirty seconds longer than their average time before the drills. It was nerves, he supposed.

He couldn't blame them.

"That's three down, Captain," Lieutenant Commander Courtney Hatcher said. The XO was calmer than Munson. Hell, he looked calmer than anyone in *Pacu's* control room, like a rock everyone could lean on. "Let's get another one while the torpedo room reloads the starboard tubes."

"Good idea." Munson swallowed. But it took him a moment to focus when he looked down at the combination navigation and tactical plot.

For a moment, he wished he was on an older sub, like the ones he'd grown up on back in the day. Back then, all contacts had been labeled Sierra or Master with a number, and there'd been none of this combined warfare nonsense. No flatscreen displays that *synergized* all sensor information into one place. Sure, it was nice to have, but it wasn't the way he'd been trained.

"Captain?" Hatcher whispered.

"Right." He shook himself. "Let's line up on track 7056, Weps."

"Firing point procedures, track 7056, Weps, aye," the weapons officer replied. His face was stark white, too, but he started calculating the fire control solution right away.

Thank God they still did *that* the old-fashioned way and didn't let this crazy new combat systems suite do everything for them. There had to be flaws in all this networking. He didn't trust it worth a damn.

"Solutions ready," Weps said.

"Ship ready." Hatcher's response was crisp and confident; Munson wished he felt that way.

He squinted at the display. Track 7056 was only a frigate, closer than the second cruiser. The cruiser was a higher value target, but it was harder to hit with a frigate and a destroyer in the way. Should he maneuver to go for the cruiser? Or would the Indians be underway by then?

What if there was no time?

"Captain?" Hatcher was at his side again, nudging him.

"Right. We should—"

"Conn, sonar, high-speed screws! Torpedoes in the water bearing one-two-four! Range unknown, speed approximately...*one hundred thirty-nine* knots!"

"What?" Munson spun, heart in his throat.

"Impact in twenty seconds!"

Barracuda was almost close enough to kiss the enemy submarine at just three quarters of a mile away. Jules considered wandering closer for a moment, doing something reckless like launching one of his drones and taking pictures of the American submarine's hull. That would be fun, but alas, business called.

"The F27 Rafales are impressive, *mon capitaine*." Commander Camille Dubois turned to him with a smile as the new torpedoes roared out of *Barracuda's* tubes with amazing speed. "Every bit as fast as the naval group promised."

"*Oui*." Jules Rochambeau nodded, his eyes already searching for his next target. His silly imagination could wait. He leaned over the plot and studied the traces of enemy contacts. This was a time for business.

Barracuda was not officially part of the task group at Christmas Island; Jules was too talented and his crew too proficient to waste by chaining them to some unimportant little island. But he was also no fool. Jules knew the Alliance would try to take the island back. It was a point of pride for Australia, if nothing else.

So, lurking *under* the sleepy, anchored formation—anchored! How foolish could you be?—*Barracuda* waited for the enemy to arrive.

He did not expect the enemy to be two submarines, one of which snuck right past him. Smarting, Jules maneuvered his submarine between the pair as quickly as he could, firing two of his brand-new F27 Rafale torpedoes at the first *Cero*-class. After all, it was the one attacking his allies.

The other was simply at periscope depth. Were they a scout? Jules did not know or care. The *Cero*—his computers could not identify which one it was before he killed it—had taken out three ships already; Jules was not a compassionate man, but letting it sink more of his country's allies reflected badly upon him.

"Impact, *mon capitaine*," his sonar supervisor reported. "Two excellent hits."

"Well done." Jules smiled. "Come left to zero-nine-zero. Prepare to fire upon the *Virginia*."

"*Oui, mon capitaine!*"

Camille led the firing party while Jules mused over what he would tweet later. It was bad luck that the *Cero* was close enough to attack the fleet before Jules could stop him; he'd need to spin this into a victory.

Minutes ticked by as they closed *Florida*. Jules watched on the plot as the unsuspecting American submarine slowly descended from periscope depth, creeping back toward the safety of the deep. Did they think their mission was complete and they were safe? Fools.

"Firing solution ready," his weapons officer reported.

Jules did not look up; his team knew their business. He merely checked the range, watching it spiral downward as *Barracuda* glided toward the American. Yes, he would fire this torpedo from even closer range. This enemy had no idea he was here.

Another minute. Two.

"Fire."

"Remaining flight time two minutes, thirty seconds, Captain," Ensign Wilner reported.

"Thank you, Strike." Nancy sat back and tried to look calm, but *damn* if Tomahawks weren't slow. They only traveled at about Mach

.74, a little under five hundred knots. Standard missiles were almost five times that fast. Seven if you counted the next generation SM-6 Block 1B that had barely made it out to the fleet when the shooting started.

"This takes goddamned forever," Admiral Rodriquez growled. "It's as bad as Dalton says our fucking torpedoes are."

"What's that?" Nancy turned in her chair to look at her admiral.

"The Mark 48 is as old as my dead grandmother. Older, probably. The latest version—the CBASS—is only about thirty, but the original torp entered service in nineteen-fucking-eighty-two. It was state of the art when it came out. Now it's slow as an elephant dick and a monument to government asshattery."

Nancy blinked. "How bad is it? I hadn't heard anything."

Marco snorted. "How many submariners do you talk to?"

"My husband, for one."

"Ah. That's right the fuck out of what I expected. He in command?"

"*Jimmy Carter.*"

"Interesting." Marco pursed his lips but said nothing for a long moment. Then he shrugged. "Anyway, the goddamned things are slower than shit stuck to a frozen telephone pole. Fifty years ago, fifty-five knots sounded spritely. Nowadays, half our enemy's boats are faster."

"That's a problem." Nancy didn't have to drive subs for a living to do that math or to figure out how it could get people killed. Including Alex.

"A *big* fucking one, yep. We've got to get newer torps. I just hope it's fucking fast enough. Just like these goddamned missiles. The Indians have to have seen them coming by now."

"Probably." Nancy realized she was gripping the armrests of her chair and forced herself to stop. "We did program them for a sea-skimming approach, so their radars should have a hard time tracking them. And with two subs in the middle of their formation..."

"Yeah, their eyes might be elsewhere. You really think we're going to get that fucking lucky?" Rodriquez laughed. "It's my plan. I sold it to SUBPAC. But even I'm not such a fucktard as to think it'll come off all roses and glitter."

Despite the seriousness of the situation, Nancy smiled. "We can always go in with guns if it doesn't, sir."

"Might have to." His eyes drifted downward, and he started disassembling yet another grease pencil. Nancy made a mental note to have her crew order the things in bulk if the admiral was going to keep breaking them. "How many standard missiles do we have?"

"Task group wide? Forty-seven. Nothing near enough to saturate their defenses."

"Could be enough if the TLAMs tear them up, though." Rodriquez frowned. "Strike, how long we got?"

"Two minutes, three seconds, sir."

"All right, let's stop sitting around like cancerous lumps." Rodriquez stomped his foot pedal. "Little Beavers, this is Little Beaver Actual. Immediate execute, course three-zero-zero, speed two-five knots, over."

Fletcher and her consorts turned left, increasing speed and dashing away from their previous position. This kept the Indians from determining their firing position and sending missiles back down that bearing.

Not that Nancy thought the Indians had enough spare missiles to fling them around indiscriminately. No one did.

She was more worried about submarines.

"Scope's awash," Commander Nuru Okafor said on board *Florida*. "Down scope. Make your depth two hundred feet. All ahead full for fifteen knots."

"Make my depth two hundred feet, aye," the chief of the boat—acting as diving officer at battle stations—replied. "All ahead full for fifteen knots, aye."

Fifteen knots was as fast as they dared go in the harbor. In fact, it was a faster submerged speed than anyone would've chosen under other circumstances; the chances of broaching—accidentally surfacing—or running into the bottom were pretty high. Particularly when turning. But *Florida* didn't have a lot of choices.

Not if she wanted to live.

"Conn, Sonar, new explosion bearing three-three-zero! Multiple *underwater* explosions!"

Lieutenant Commander Alicia Abbot's head snapped up. "Christ, that's *Pacu's* bearing."

"All ahead flank!" Okafor ordered.

Someone had killed their fellow submarine, but who? There were no surface ships on that bearing, and they would have heard splashes if one of them dropped a torpedo or depth charges in the water—

"Conn, Sonar, torpedo in the water! Torpedoes in the water bearing three-zero-zero! Range twenty-three hundred yards, impact in thirty seconds!"

"Snapshot tube one, bearing three-zero-zero! Hard left rudder!"

Alicia knew it was the right command to give, but she also knew it was too late. One wide-eyed look at the tactical plot told her that the torpedoes were incoming at over 130 knots—more than *ninety* knots faster than a *Virginia* like *Florida* could manage. No submarine was that fast.

Torpedoes weren't supposed to be, either.

Florida shivered as she picked up speed, her propulsor cutting through the water as she raced toward the nearest Indian destroyer. Alicia immediately spotted what her captain was trying to do; if they could cut under that destroyer, there was a slim chance that the torpedoes might target the Indian instead of them.

"You thinking torpedoes this fast have to be dumb?" she asked.

"Hoping, more like." Okafor's expression was still calm, though a bead of sweat finally appeared on her forehead. "Steady as she goes."

"Steady as she goes, aye. Steady course two-five-two," the chief of the boat replied.

"Very well."

Alicia glanced at the speed indicator. *Florida* was up to her top speed of fifty-five knots. That bought them time, but only a little.

"Sonar, Conn, time to impact?" she said into the speaker.

"Forty-two seconds!"

Her heart clenched so hard that speaking was difficult. "Range to nearest destroyer?"

"Conn, Sonar...about eight hundred yards."

"Conn, aye." Alicia did quick math in her head. They could do it. She looked at her captain. "That's less than twenty seconds to spare."

"Any more and this can't possibly work," Okafor replied. "Stand by the countermeasures."

"Countermeasures, aye." Hands clammy, Alicia rushed over to the countermeasure control panel. *Fifteen seconds.*

Submarine-launched countermeasures were just noisemakers. Designed to create underwater noise and bubbles, their entire purpose was to distract torpedoes for a few critical seconds, allowing a submarine to make a course change and get out of the torpedo sonar's range. Onboard sonar on a torpedo was limited by the space it lived in—the head of the torpedo.

Alicia swallowed. "Countermeasures ready."

"Very well. Countermeasures on my mark." Okafor turned. "Chief of the Watch, pass the word to brace for impact."

Her eyes found the clock. *Ten seconds.*
"Conn, Sonar, range to destroyer three hundred yards!"
"Conn, aye; water depth?" Okafor asked.
"Four hundred feet!"
Okafor did not respond to that. Alicia could barely breathe. *Five seconds.*

She couldn't see the moment when *Florida* passed underneath the Indian destroyer; neither could the Indian destroyer. It was too busy with the cascade of Tomahawk missiles raining from the sky—an attack Alicia completely forgot about. But the tactical plot showed when they crossed under the destroyer's keel, and Okafor's razor-sharp eyes noted the exact second they were clear.

"Hard right rudder, emergency blow! Launch a full spread of countermeasures!"

Alicia tuned out the other watchstanders' replies, slamming the levers on the countermeasure control panel up to eject four noise-makers out of their tubes. Two popped out of *Florida's* port and starboard sides, spiraling in the water, hoping to distract the torpedoes.

"Countermeasures away!"

Florida cut under and up around the Indian destroyer, heading for the surface at breakneck speed. It was a reckless, desperate move, one bound to break both equipment and bodies in the American submarine. But it should have worked. Torpedo sonar just wasn't that smart.

Except *Barracuda* never cut the control wires to the torpedoes.

"Breaching the surface in three, two, one—" The chief of the boat cut off as *Florida* slammed into the surface in the middle of the Indian formation. Her low black form went unnoticed during the light show topside, even with a white wave of foam contrasting against her round bow. *Florida's* Indian enemies were too busy fighting off Tomahawk missiles with their own counter missiles and point defense weapons; by now, they'd forgotten all about the submarines in the middle of their formation. The glow of tracer rounds split the sky between missile explosions and launches, leaving *Florida* a dark shadow cresting out of the waves.

Florida's bow reared up, thrusting out of the water at almost a forty-five-degree angle before slamming back down. Her propulsor kept churning, pushing her forward on the surface, cutting holes in the water as sailors, equipment, and over-stressed metal groaned in pain.

Alicia lost her balance, slamming into the countermeasure controls. Sharp needles of agony flared in her shoulder, but she barely noticed, hissing and catching herself. People cried out as the sudden impact with the surface threw crew members forward; Okafor clung to the navigation table, but Weps crashed into the COB, and the chief of the watch hit the periscope display screen headfirst, falling in a heap of blood and sparks and water leaking from the overhead.

"Conn, Sonar, torpedoes are still incoming!"

The last thing Alicia Abbot felt was a second almighty *jerk*, and then white light flared as two F27 Rafale torpedoes slammed into USS *Florida*.

Watching a surface battle without taking a hit in exchange was surreal.

Nancy wasn't sure she liked it.

"Damn," Rodriquez said. "Those Tomahawks might be slow, but their synchronized time on top is a thing of fucking beauty."

Nancy smiled thinly. "We knew their speed wouldn't get them through, so it had to be saturation. Even if the Indians had full magazines—which we were pretty sure they didn't—they're like us. They can only fire so many missiles at once. If we hit them with enough simultaneously...well, you can see how that's working out."

Farley's drone footage was up on the big screens, and it showed missile after missile hammering down on the Indian fleet. All the Tomahawks were programmed to hit within a one-minute window, and while the Indian ships fought back valiantly, with seventeen synchronized missiles coming at each ship, they could only launch their Barak 9 air defense missiles so fast.

Nancy's eyes narrowed as she watched hit after hit strike. "One out of three getting through. Maybe one out of four. Not bad."

"Is that enough?" Rodriquez asked. "I'm used to one torpedo and done."

"A TLAM has a big warhead, about seven times the size of a standard missile's. You probably only need one or two to ruin even a cruiser's day in a big way." Nancy shrugged. "We have to use a *lot* of them to get through, but it's working."

She'd expected the Indians to shoot down most of the Tomahawks. They'd even planned for that. But Nancy had hoped for a lot better than a twenty-five percent hit ratio. She grimaced. Once the computers tallied up the final score, it looked like the TLAMs might be hitting at a rate of one out of every five.

But they shot an average of seventeen missiles at every ship for a reason, coming from every angle imaginable so last-minute point defense couldn't possibly target them all. It paid off, too. Every Indian ship was burning.

All fourteen of them.

"Damn good planning, ladies," Rodriquez said to her and Captain Tenaglia, seated on his other side. "This might've been my ass-backward hairbrained scheme, but you made it work. *I'll* make sure my bosses know that."

"Thank you, sir." Nancy glanced at the screen one last time, fighting back a smile.

Not taking a shot in exchange felt like cheating, but damn, it was nice to see Indian ships sinking for a change.

Tanya grinned. "You want to head toward Christmas Island and start collecting survivors, Admiral?"

"Bet your ass I do, Captain. Let's pick the poor bastards out of the water and show them some good, old fashioned American hospitality." Rodriquez laughed. "And someone find my wayward submarines so we can start planning what medals to pin on the assholes."

There was one factor Marco Rodriquez had not counted on.

To be fair to the admiral, no one had reported *Barracuda's* presence to him. In fact, he still thought *Florida* and *Pacu* were in the game. So perhaps he was to be pardoned for not realizing the wolf that hid among the sheep.

"Shall we set up on the American surface group, *Capitaine*?" Camille's question was almost a purr.

Jules steepled his fingers, watching the ships sweep into Christmas Island's harbor. It would be so simple to target them. They clearly had no idea he was here, almost dead center, lurking amid the carnage they'd caused.

"Five destroyers and two frigates. Hm."

Math was not with him. Jules had seven torpedoes left, and while it only took one torpedo to sink a ship...hit probabilities were not that good.

"It is almost a pity we sank those supply ships last week," he murmured.

"We could skirt their formation and sink one or two," Camille said.

"They would not catch us."

"No. Surface ships are too easy to sink." Straightening, Jules waved a hand. "This little island means nothing to France. We have not the torpedoes to take it back singlehandedly, so we will not make a feeble attempt. We will find another enemy submarine." He smiled. "Or two. Someone worthy of our new torpedoes."

Camille's teeth flashed in a bloodthirsty smile. "I look forward to it."

"As do I."

HMAS *Parramatta* steamed on the task force's flank, a quiet blue-gray shadow against the lightening sky. Aging frigates had little place in a missile battle; unable to carry Tomahawks, *Parramatta* was relegated to defending the group from submarines. It was something she was good at, so her commanding officer didn't mind. He wasn't out here for glory. He wanted to make a difference.

"That was about as anti-climactic as battles get," Charlie Markey said, leaning on the bridge wing railing.

Commander Fletch Goddard grinned. He was back on *Parramatta's* bridge now that his frigate had secured from action stations. There were no Indian ships to threaten them, just survivors to rescue and one burning destroyer that stubbornly refused to sink. He'd had his doubts about Admiral Rodriquez's plan to shoot land attack missiles at an anchored Indian fleet, but it wasn't proper to voice them when his aged frigate was merely along to be an ASW screen. Now he was glad he hadn't.

"Particularly since they were so discourteous as to send the anchored submarines to the bottom, too?" he asked.

Charlie, his first officer, laughed. "That was mighty rude of them. Might put us out of work."

"There's always more subs to sink." Fletch shrugged, staring at the burning Indian ships on the horizon. "Let's keep the array out, just in case."

"Of course, sir."

Fletch popped his feet up while Charlie headed down to the operations room, watching the destroyers head in to rescue survivors. His orders were to remain on the task group's right flank, keeping an eye out for anything that might make Admiral Rodriquez "twitchy."

Despite himself, he liked the colorful American admiral. Or

maybe Fletch just enjoyed getting out of the damned shipyard. He spent far too long there waiting for *Warrego* to be finished, and while a part of him still missed the sleek and beautiful destroyer—his no longer—*Warrego* wouldn't join the fight for another year. *Parramatta*, old or not, was here now.

Thinking of older ships made instinct prickle. Fletch leaned forward and keyed his internal communications console. "Ops, Captain, have we heard anything from the two American submarines?"

One of them was an older *Virginia*, he remembered. Not nearly as old as *Parramatta*, who was just a mite younger than her captain, but older than most every other ship out here.

"No, sir. The flag's been trying to raise them on Gertrude with no effect."

"Very good." Fletch sat back in his chair, scanning the horizon as a chill raced down his spine. "Neither of them?"

"Neither, sir."

"Officer of the Watch! Come right to zero-zero-zero. Ops, go active on sonar."

"Sir, under the Geneva Conventions, I am obligated to treat all surrendered and rescued personnel with dignity and respect," Marco said for the third time, gripping the radio like he wanted to strangle it. "I assure you that my country has no interest in committing war crimes, over."

Not swearing at the captain of INS *Chennai* was difficult. Marco had no doubt that the poor bastard was in a bad place; his ship was on fire, a good portion of his crew had to be dead, and every other Indian ship nearby was on the bottom. But did he have to keep asking the same damned questions?

When there was no answer, Marco continued: "*Chennai* Actual, this is Task Force Two-Three Actual. I personally guarantee the safety of your personnel if you surrender. USS *Farley* is closing to provide firefighting and rescue assistance. Do you accept, over?"

He could see *Farley* from where he stood on *Fletcher's* port bridge wing. The other American destroyer approached the maimed Indian destroyer cautiously, with fire hoses faked out on deck and ready to help with the fires still raging on *Chennai's* aft end.

Their purpose was half humanitarian, half tactical. Capturing an Indian destroyer—even a half-burned one—would be the intelligence coup of the century. Even though *Chennai* was an older *Kolkata*-class ship, that didn't mean she wasn't full of modernized technology. The Race to the Ocean Floor increased India's already significant GDP by a factor of almost four, enabling them to more than double their navy's size and strength in the 2020s and early 2030s.

They started freezing America out at the same time. *Chennai* would have hundreds of stories to tell if Marco could grab her, but he had to convince her terrified captain first.

Thank fucking God the man was more worried about his crew's safety than guarding national secrets. Marco was okay with this war thing, but he didn't like the idea of butchering people who couldn't fight back.

"Two-Three, this is *Chennai*, I accept." The voice on the other end was thick with grief. "Please have medical personnel standing by. My casualties have been heavy."

"We will take care of your people, Captain. You have my word," Marco replied. "My chief of staff, Captain Tenaglia, is on board *Farley* to coordinate with you. She will make sure you have everything you need."

"*Chennai*, roger, out."

Letting out a huge breath was not as satisfying as swearing, but Marco didn't have time. "Captain Coleman! Pass the word to *Farley* to commence firefighting efforts and send their rescue and assistance teams over. And send *Jason Dunham* in to take *Chennai* under tow."

"Aye, sir." Nancy turned to with her normal competence, but she didn't take two steps before word blared out of the speaker between them.

"Bridge, TAO, *Parramatta* has gone active on sonar and is prosecuting a submerged contact bearing zero-one-six, range ten thousand yards!"

"Where the fuck did they come from?" Marco twisted around. "Get me secure comms to *Parramatta!*"

Chapter 32

Old but Golden

26 February 2039, Christmas Island (Australia)

On second thought, the formation was a tempting target, despite his lack of torpedoes. Jules *could* make the Americans bleed for Christmas Island. It would be nice revenge, he supposed. Should they let the Americans take back territory without repercussions? Of course not. Yet Jules had to be smart about this; he was not in the best position to exact revenge, given his dwindling supply of torpedoes.

Also...would doing this gain him any notoriety at all?

"Capitaine, we have a contact to port," *Barracuda's* sonar officer reported. "It is a *Scorpene*, Indian-built. Early model. *Karanji*, I think."

"Is that so?" Jules cocked his head, sitting back in his seat and crossing his legs. This changed the equation, didn't it? "Were they here the entire time?"

"*Non*. They are approaching recklessly. Speed is twenty-plus knots."

Jules laughed aloud. "Our friends on *Karanji* want revenge."

"Should we help them?" Camille's beautiful eyes gleamed, and her face twisted in a mocking smile. "Like the good friends we are?"

"With the careless way they're racing about?" Jules shook his head. "No, they might mistake us for a target, and I would *hate* to sink an ally. Or to be sunk by one. What an inglorious way to go."

Rushing into combat like the Indian sub was doing was foolish.

Worse than foolish. They would be heard before they did much damage, and for what? Revenge? Jules tapped a finger against his lips. Revenge only tasted sweet when you lived to savor it. Otherwise, you were just dead.

He glanced at his sailors, poised and ready to jump from stealth and attack the enemy. *Barracuda* was not manned by such fools as their Indian friend, *Karanji*, but like him, his people wanted a piece of the action.

"Shall we continue outbound?" Camille's lip curled.

"Oui. But since things are growing so confusing topside, let us find a ship to target with a passing torpedo. No need to let our Indian friend get all the glory in a French-designed submarine. But please do make it something worthwhile—not this old frigate closing in on *Karanji*." Jules gestured at the plot. "Find me something newer. Something that will hurt the Alliance much more."

Camille's face twisted into a glowing grin. "It will be my pleasure."

"Launch a full spread!" Fletch leaned over the starboard bridge wing of his frigate as *Parramatta* swept into a crash turn. His stomach dropped down to his ankles, but he ignored it.

Charging into the teeth of a submarine attack was against conventional wisdom, but Fletch was driving the oldest frigate in the task force, he didn't have any rocket-launched torpedoes, and his helicopter wouldn't be ready to launch for another ten minutes.

In ten minutes, torpedoes could make a mess of every ship at Christmas Island.

A salvo of four rocket-propelled depth charges burst out of the launchers on the frigate's stern, crashing into the water less than a mile away from Fletch's command.

BOOM!

The charges detonated at their programmed depth of four hundred feet, making his ship shudder. Fletch hardly noticed, instead glancing over at the tactical display relayed up from his ops center. Many COs hunted submarines from in front of a console down in Ops, but Fletch believed in driving the problem and pushing the opposition. That was why *Parramatta* was close to the enemy submarine and Fletch was on the bridge.

"Shift your rudder!" *Parramatta* swung back the other way.

"Captain, the admiral is on task force command for you!" The junior officer of the watch stuck her head out onto the bridge wing, pointing at the secure phone.

Fletch swore under his breath and yanked the handset out of the cradle. "Task Force Two-Three, this is *Parramatta* Actual, over."

The musical crackle of crypto syncing up filled his ears before the voice on the other end said: "Actual, this is Rodriquez. What the hell are you doing over there?"

"Sir, we have a track on presumed Indian diesel, likely *Scorpene III*-class. Range is ten thousand yards from *Fletcher*."

"And right under your goddamned ass," the American admiral snarled. "What the hell are you doing up so close?"

"My helo isn't ready, and I don't have rocket-launched torpedoes." Fletch paused to watch his plot.

The track they had on the Indian diesel sub was iffy, but Fletch knew the enemy was close. By maneuvering quickly and forcing the sub to do the same, Fletch could keep the bad guy from developing a firing solution—but the same rules applied to his ship. He had to get a good fix on the sub to kill it. Right now, they were just dancing.

"Steady as she goes!"

"Steady as she goes, aye! Steady course zero-nine-four!"

"Very good." Fletch returned his attention to the phone in his hand. "My apologies, Admiral. We're a bit busy here."

"Well, don't let me waste your fucking time. I'll have helos up to support you in five. Rodriquez, out."

Charlie Markey moved to stand by his right shoulder. "This guy's pretty good."

"Quiet as a bleedin' mouse, too." Fletch grimaced, dropping the phone and letting it dangle as all thoughts of irate American admirals left his mind. The icon representing their track on the sub started to blink. "What are you doing up here, anyway? I thought you were down in Ops."

"It's more interesting outside." Charlie shrugged as the officer of the watch ordered another course change, standing on the step of Fletch's empty chair to look over the edge of the bridge wing. "Besides, I think I was driving the PWO crazy. Can't do much good babysitting Red. He doesn't need it."

"Ah. The truth comes out."

Fletch glanced at the display again. The track was still flickering. *Damn it.* They'd lost contact. Without a sonar contact to tell them which way the sub was moving, the error in the estimated position grew by the second.

"Damn." What were the odds they'd sunk the Indian? *Not high.* He leaned over to speak into a communications box. "Sonar, Bridge, any breakup noises?"

"No, sir."

"Hoping to get lucky, Captain?" Charlie grinned as Fletch swept his eyes across the deceptively calm blue sea.

The rest of the task group was less than five miles away. He couldn't let this sub get past *Parramatta*. Keeping its attention kept the rest of the ships safe.

"One time or another, something will go our way." Fletch rapped his knuckles on the wooden bridge wing railing. Turn right or left? Continue to hunt the sub within its own torpedo firing range, or back off and hope he could bag the *Scorpene* when it sped up? Fletch knew which the safe option was, but if he waited too long, the Indian would pickle off torpedoes at the other ships.

His eyes shifted back toward the display. "If I was a canny diesel boat skipper, I'd try creeping along aft of us..."

"Because you blasted the towed array to pieces by launching depth charges back aft?" The XO grinned.

"A sonar array's cheaper than a bloody frigate, even an old one." Fletch frowned at their wake. "If I were him, I'd be hoping I could open the range enough to shoot when the damn frigate stopped dancing about—because every surface officer eventually gets impatient and figures the sub has left."

There'd be hell to pay if he really had blasted his own "tail" of hydrophones off with depth charges. Fletch had ordered it pulled in, but he hadn't had time to check if his crew managed before he started sending rocket-propelled depth charges off the stern.

But even the ever-cranky Admiral Gray would probably understand if he nailed this submarine.

Markey grimaced. "Meanwhile, he can hide in the sonic layer and keep us from getting active contact. We know where he *might* be, but... Hell. If one of those bleeding helicopters ever launches, we'll have him cold."

Fletch shook his head. "Five minutes is an eternity if we can't find this guy." Then the thought hit him like a bolt of lightning. "To hell with that. We don't *need* an exact position, Charlie. We don't even need a good estimate—we just can't afford to let it get any *worse*."

Markey blinked. "I'm not following where you're going, Captain."

"Can't make the goal if you don't kick the ball." Fletch turned back to the communications panel. "Ops, Captain. Standby to fire four—correction, five—full spreads of depth charges, bearing one-zero-zero to two-six-zero relative. Make the range for the odd numbered salvos four hundred meters from own ship, two hundred meters for the even numbered. Standard depth dispersion."

That would give him thirty-five depth charges to blanket the area astern of the ship, covering a huge amount of water. He was betting the sub was close in to *Parramatta* now. That was the best way to hide from all the *other* ships out here, after all. If he was wrong, Fletch would waste an awful lot of ammunition...

"Chancy." Charlie frowned. "But why not? Worst case, we only kill some fish, and I doubt the government will shoot you at dawn for wasting depth charges. They certainly cost less than frigates."

Fletch grinned. "Damn straight."

"Ready to launch," his principle warfare officer reported a few moments later.

"Very well." There was little time to spare. "You may launch when ready."

Lieutenant Red Weston's finger must have been on the button, because the launchers started moving before Fletch could even glance aft.

Whoosh!

Seven depth charges rocketed in the first salvo, heading off *Parramatta*'s starboard side.

Splash. They hit the water, sinking to the pre-programmed depths.

Boom. Parramatta trembled and the surrounding water churned and bubbled. The second salvo left the launchers even as the first one detonated.

Whoosh. Splash. Boom.

These charges exploded even closer, and *Parramatta* jumped in the water, almost like driving over a bump in the road.

Whoosh. Splash. Boom.

Nothing. Three shots, three misses. Perhaps this wasn't the best—

Whoosh. Splash. BOOM.

Parramatta jumped violently this time. Water boiled furiously off of *Parramatta*'s port quarter, and the deck trembled under his feet.

"Bridge, Sonar. Hull breakup noises bearing two-four-zero! Secondary explosions, same bearing—whoa! *Big* secondary explosions!"

The fifth salvo left the launcher superfluously, but the spreads were programmed too closely together to be stopped. No matter.

BOOM! The last explosion was in no way related to the salvo of depth charges and made *Parramatta* buck even harder. Catching himself on the bridge wing railing, Fletch didn't need the sonar watch to confirm the kill on the submarine. He could see the water churning almost directly aft of the frigate, where the Indian attack sub had set up for a perfect shot at his ship.

Another few minutes, and I'd have been a goner. Damn.

"I think we just got luckier than we had any right to be, Captain," Charlie whispered, reading his mind like a good XO always did.

Fletch let out the breath he hadn't known he was holding. "Indeed."

The Mid-Indian Ocean

"Another day, another convoy." Alex knew his smile was crooked when he walked into *Jimmy Carter's* attack center, but it was the best he had.

It was morning on *Jimmy Carter's* clocks, so Maggie had the watch as officer of the deck. Her team was a sharp one—and was expected to be, since the navigator should be *the* pro at navigation and driving the boat. Fortunately for Alex, Maggie was. She ran a tight watch but wasn't against her team having a bit of fun, whether it was through trivia games to stay awake or sharing snacks around the control room when things were quiet.

Unfortunately, life was quiet every day on *Jimmy Carter*.

"I think this one is Convoy 1402, sir, but they're getting so hard to tell apart." Maggie's laugh sounded more natural than Alex felt as she leaned against the periscope stand. "What is it, our seventeenth?"

"Twenty-first. Our convoy escort cred is now old enough to vote."

Maggie laughed. "I'm sure we'll get a medal for that when the war's over."

Alex managed not to scowl, but it took all the self-control he had. What a fool he'd been to accept Admiral Hamilton's offer of command instead of a medal. He'd thought he could make a goddamned difference, yet here he was, escorting convoys from point A to point B, doing jack shit and nothing, with the ever-present worry that he'd *lose* his boat to the breakers in the back of his mind.

Accepting a medal would've been worse, he supposed. Then he'd be stuck in an office somewhere, unable to even pretend there might be an opportunity to—

"Excuse me, Captain, we just received a SUBMISS/SUBSUNK message," the radio watchstander said.

Alex froze. "Another one? For who?"

"*Skate*."

"Shit." A proper captain probably wouldn't swear aloud, but Alex wouldn't be on *Jimmy Carter* if he was some proper captain, would he?

He met Maggie's eyes and read the horror on her pale face.

Maggie swallowed. "*Skate's* one of our best."

"In the top three, yeah." Alex didn't need to rattle off the stats; Maggie knew them as well as he did. Commander Annabella Santiago was quiet but efficient. She didn't grab the limelight like John Dalton or Rico Sivers, but she'd still been responsible for sinking fourteen enemy combatants in the last ten months.

Only Kenji Walker on *Idaho* and Rico Sivers on *Guam* were better. Maybe John, too, but he was still behind in the totals.

"Just when we thought things were looking up," Maggie whispered.

Alex accepted the message tablet, his eyes skipping around control to look at his watchstanders' expressions. Yeah, this was hitting them hard. And why wouldn't it? Another hundred-plus brothers and sisters on eternal patrol, lost while they escorted convoys.

Sure, keeping convoys alive was important. Convoys carried the materials that allowed them to continue fighting the war. And yet it still felt like taking the safe option. Like they were...not cheating, but doing less than they could.

His eyes flicked down to read the message.

SUBJ: SUBMISS/SUBSUNK UPDATE ICO USS SKATE SSN 854

RMKS: 1. INITIAL SUBMISS/SUBSUNK BUOY SURFACED 260714Z FEB 39 AT POSIT 13°30'35.6"S 79°18'13.2"E.

2. COMSUBPAC RECEIVED DATA/LOG UPLOAD VIA SATELLITE AT 260714Z FEB 39. LAST LOG

UPDATE AT 240714Z FEB 39, FORTY-EIGHT (48) HOURS BEFORE SUBMISS/SUBSUNK BUOY RELEASE.

3. TWENTY-FIVE (25) EMERGENY ATTEMPTS TO CONTACT SKATE FAILED. ALL SCHEDULED COMMUNICATION TIMES MISSED SINCE BUOY LAUNCH TEN (10) HOURS AGO.

4. USS SKATE SSN 854 OUT OF CONTACT THREE (3) DAYS.

5. STATUS: MISSING, PRESUMED LOST.

Alex had read too many SUBMISS/SUBSUNK messages during this damned war. Too many of them were boats commanded by people he knew, and every time he opened one, he lived in fear it would be a close friend like John Dalton or Teresa O'Canas. He'd been damned lucky when he fished Tommy Sandifer out of the drink. No way would he get lucky like that again.

Feeling relieved this wasn't John or Teresa made guilt bubble up like acid in his gut. He'd gone to SOAC with Anabella Santiago on their way to be department heads. She loved practical jokes, hated getting up early, and cooked a mean steak.

Or had.

His gaze drifted over the position listed in the message again, and realization hit Alex like a lightning bolt. He lunged for *Jimmy Carter's* navigation plot—one of the few brand-new pieces of equipment on the boat—and punched in *Skate's* last known latitude and longitude.

"We're practically right there."

"Captain?" Maggie peered over his shoulder, her eyes going wide as he twisted to look at her. "We're less than thirty nautical miles away. That's...call it fifty minutes at flank speed."

"Their buoy just launched ten hours ago." Hope warred with grief to tighten Alex's throat tight. "And if there are survivors..."

Maggie whistled. "I'll punch in a nav plan."

"And I'll call the boss." Alex grimaced. He hated talking on any radio circuits, though he'd gotten a *bit* better at it since his days on *Kansas*, when Chris Kennedy liked to make him do it for his own twisted amusement. But there was no way around this little bout of public speaking; *Jimmy Carter* couldn't go haring off station without permission.

Alex walked over to the communications console and punched in the network for the convoy command circuit. He licked his lips. "Sheriff, this is Killer Rabbit, over."

USS *Truxtun*, a destroyer, had the senior captain and was in command of the convoy. Their callsign, "Sheriff," was a reference to Commodore Thomas Truxtun's later civilian career—a bit of trivia Alex only knew because a classmate of his from Norwich had chosen *Truxtun* as their first ship and had been obsessed with weird facts.

Alex wasn't sure he understood the surface ship obsession with callsigns, particularly on a secure channel like convoy command. The net was encrypted, which meant any sane ship driver would've just used their ship names. But half the surface officers Alex worked with insisted on using callsigns instead.

As usual, *Jimmy Carter* was the only submarine in the convoy escort. There just weren't enough attack subs to go around, not with half of them off on independent operations trying to hunt enemy subs. There was another destroyer and two frigates along to protect the sixteen merchant ships, but all of them answered to *Truxton*.

Alex tapped his foot, waiting for a response and watching the icons of sixteen merchant ships sail along their programmed track, fat, dumb, and happy. All were en route from Australia to the Suez Canal. Unlike the destroyers, Alex didn't have to stick around through the canal transit—always a security risk for a submarine. Then the ships would sail east through the Mediterranean Sea, through the Straits of Gibraltar, and across the Atlantic to hit the East Coast of the United States.

Most of those ships carried various ores or other raw materials, all of which fed the American war machine. Now that the industrial base back home was up and roaring, ships, spare parts, and weapons were being built faster, which would eventually give them an edge in—

"Killer Rabbit, this is Sheriff, roger, over."

"Sheriff, this is Killer Rabbit Actual. I have received a message indicating an American submarine has sunk two-nine nautical miles from my present position." Alex knew most surface ships didn't pay attention to SUBMISS/SUBSUNK messages—the fools thought they had little reason to. "Request permission to break off from the convoy and search for survivors, over."

"Standby, over."

An ominous silence followed; Alex tried not to fidget. Instead, he turned to Maggie. "Nav, give Suppo a call and determine how many extra racks we have. Probably good to look at food, too—we might be bringing on a whole lot of friends. And tell the XO to break out the rescue plan again."

"You got it, Captain." Maggie grinned. "If there's one thing we have here on *Smiley*, it's space."

"It helps that we were designed to lug a bunch of SpecOps people and their crap around, yeah."

Jimmy Carter's giant midsection, known as the Multi-Mission Platform, was useless. After the special operations gear was removed—along with all the cool toys Alex didn't have the clearance to play with—the "garage" and SEAL lockout areas were sealed off. Alex wasn't *too* eager to play with those areas; anything meant to be flooded on a submarine was asking for trouble. But his boat still had more racks and more internal cubage than any other attack sub afloat.

They made good use of them after rescuing *Georgia's* sailors. Now it looked like they'd have a second chance. Stomach rolling, Alex glanced back at the convoy's icons on the plot and listened to the silence.

Damn it all, *Truxtun's* captain was going to be a conservative fool and chain *Jimmy Carter* to the convoy, wasn't she? Alex started marshaling his mental arguments, thinking of *Skate's* crew.

Ten hours had passed since the SUBMISS/SUBSUNK buoy activated. The buoys were programmed to go off if a submarine reached a certain depth—always beneath their class's crush depth—and war had proven they were almost never launched by mistake. Some subs sank without the buoy launching...but if the buoy hit the surface, it was damn near a sure thing that the boat hadn't.

Ten hours was a shit amount of time to wait in the water for rescue. Alex loved the water and looked for any excuse to dive...which meant he appreciated what ten hours in the water could do to people.

"What's the water temperature?" Alex snapped.

"Seventy-five Fahrenheit, sir."

"Shit." Seventy-five degrees *sounded* warm. But as a diver, Alex knew it wasn't. He memorized standard hypothermia tables years ago. Swimmers in water that was in the high seventies could expect exhaustion or unconsciousness in anything from three to twelve hours. *Skate's* crew could survive far longer than the ten hours they'd been in the water, but if they weren't all in rafts, like *Georgia's* sailors hadn't been...

People didn't usually think about what the difference between the body's temperature of 98.6° and the water temperature did to the human body. Disorientation always came first. Shivering started just two degrees below the normal body temperature. Amnesia could set in around temps as high as 94°F if someone was left there for too long.

They'd been lucky to pick up *Georgia's* sailors so fast, but even if they left now, *Skate's* sailors were facing a minimum of eleven hours in the water.

Alex swallowed.

The command circuit chirped, making him jump.

"*Killer Rabbit Actual,* this is *Sheriff.* Permission granted to search for survivors. Remain in contact with convoy command, over."

Alex let out a breath he hadn't known he was holding. "Hot damn, I was starting to think they'd say no," he said to himself. Then he lifted the handset before *Truxtun* could change their mind. "This is *Killer Rabbit,* roger, thank you, out."

"Right standard rudder, steady course zero-zero-five," Maggie ordered without waiting for Alex to tell her what to do.

Why the hell couldn't George be so efficient under pressure?

No, Alex would not ruin his good mood by thinking about his XO's shortcomings. George was an organizational monster, and rescue operations were something he was *good* at. He'd done well with *Georgia's* crew and even better when they'd fished two downed pilots out of the drink in November.

Yeah. George would be fine. Just like he was useful during that disastrous replenishment operation with *Safeguard.*

"Maggie, pass the word for all department heads to assemble in the wardroom and find yourself a relief," Alex said, shaking those thoughts away. "We've got a rescue operation to plan and not much time to do it in."

Her smile was infectious. "You got it, Captain."

Not too far away, another ship turned to close with the survivors of USS *Skate*. Intelligence having relayed the message a mere ten hours after the submarine's sinking, it was passed to *Yantar*, one of Russia's many intelligence trawlers—or, in the common vernacular, spy ships.

Yantar was the first of her class, now a relatively old lady, having commissioned in 2015. But intelligence-gathering ships did not need to be new hulls to cram advanced technology, listening devices, and other cryptological toys on board. In fact, her aged appearance was often her greatest asset. From a distance, she looked like a worn-down research or survey vessel, which was exactly what she pretended to be.

Today, her automated identification system labeled her as *Knorr*, a cable layer out of the Seychelles. Stringently neutral, the Seychelles remained a popular vacation destination and tried to stay out of the fight—but didn't have the strength to protest when Russian ships "borrowed" their flag for a few days or weeks.

Now *Yantar* turned west, heading for *Skate's* last known position.

"What shall be our excuse if someone else approaches, Colonel?" her captain asked the man to his right.

"There was a report of survivors in the water on the bridge-to-bridge radio, of course," was the serene response.

The speaker was a tall man, pale in that Russian way, with dark eyes made darker by his light blond hair. He wore the uniform of a colonel in intelligence and was clearly in command, despite the presence of a captain second rank on the bridge.

"The usual, then," the captain said.

"Of course. No one has caught us yet." The colonel smiled. "No one will."

The captain twitched, trying not to think about the holding cells belowdecks and the prisoners inside them. "As you wish."

"Make best speed, Captain." A thin smile. "There is no knowing when American rescue forces will arrive, and I wish them to find no evidence of survivors."

"None at all."

Chapter 33

Bad Luck and Worse

26 February 2039, Christmas Island, Main Harbor (Australia)

Steph Gomez wasn't sure how *Jason Dunham* drew the short straw. Sure, *Arleigh Burkes* had more raw shaft horsepower than the newer *O'Bannons*—and a hell of a lot more of it than either of the frigates—but towing ships was no officer's idea of fun.

Particularly when that officer was the XO and had to supervise this goat rope.

"All set, First?" she asked the first lieutenant.

They stood on the ship's fantail together, watching the boatswains mates at work. Technically, the "fantail" was also the flight deck, but it was the furthest aft part of the ship and where both the towing padeye and capstan were located. Later-model *Arleigh Burkes*—really, anything still in commission, in Steph's mind—weren't really built for towing. Their towing padeye was off center to port, and that sometimes shoved the *tow* itself off center...which was not what an experienced officer wanted.

But an *O'Bannon* would've made a worse mess out of it, so Steph supposed she just had to live with her fate. Besides, the captain agreed to this, trusting her to get the job done.

Lieutenant (junior grade) Ben "Bear" Kibbe nodded. "Yes, ma'am.

Towing hawser is over and tested. We're ready to take strain on the line and get *Chennai* underway."

"Finally!" Steph grinned. "No offense, First. Or to you, Boats," she added to the watching chief boatswain's mate. "You've done a bang-up job here. I just hate towing with a passion I usually reserve for coffee creamer."

"That sounds like a story."

"You'd better believe it, but it's one I'm in no way telling." Steph grinned. "Now get your butts to work and let's haul this Indian destroyer to Perth like the prize she is."

"Has anyone captured an enemy warship yet, XO?" Kibbe asked.

"Not that I know of. It's nice to be first on something good, isn't it?" *Jason Dunham* was a good ship, with a great crew, but after losing their captain to a missile strike when he was walking down a passageway and then dropping a helicopter in the drink, the reputation for bad luck stuck to them like skunk stink.

Maybe that was why Admiral Rodriquez gave them the job of towing *Chennai* in. The admiral was a strange one, full of profanity, off-the-wall ideas, and irreverent attitude, but he was a fair son of a bitch.

Steph could live with the tow job if that was the reason. Even if it meant a long, *slow* slog back to Perth.

Meanwhile, *Barracuda* crept around the edges of the Alliance formation, unnoticed and deadly. Keeping on the edges of the harbor accomplished two things. One, it opened the distance between *Barracuda* and that idiot commanding *Karanji*. Whoever he or she was, they were currently engaged in a duel with a frigate near Jules' age. Not a good look.

Two, it let Jules maneuver in deeper water. This was better for avoiding detection and also gave his three hundred-plus-foot-long submarine adequate depth to avoid broaching, even if Jules made a mistake. Which he would not. But he was not the best in the world because he was stupid or reckless. Every choice he made was well-measured.

"We have a frigate in our sights, *mon capitaine*," his watch officer reported. "Or there is a destroyer further away, but that shot is harder. The frigate might hear us if we try."

Jules tapped his fingers against the tactical plot, thinking. Usually, he embraced calculated risk. The appearance of daring and dashing escapades captured the public's imagination, and he enjoyed having the people's acclaim. Success in war was not enough. History proved that military glory was fleeting. Who remembered the great submariners of the last war except the naval officers who followed in their footsteps?

Jules Rochambeau wanted to be more.

Yet he also needed to *think*.

That ancient Australian frigate on the far side of the formation was far too good at flinging depth charges. And his original problem remained: he only had seven torpedoes. Hit probabilities were not in his favor, even with the new torpedoes. He could not sink all of his enemies.

That meant a passing blow at the formation while he retreated to get more weapons. Jules sighed. As nice as it would be to singlehandedly sink a task force, today was not that day.

"Is it the new Australian frigate?" he asked. His estimation of the older one increased when its captain nailed that *Scorpene* so neatly with depth charges, but an old *Anzac* was still worth only the cost of the metal sold at scrap. Any government would prefer to lose that to a newer Type 26 *Hunter*-class.

"*Oui*," Camille replied.

"Very well. Match bearings and shoot. Two tubes, *s'il vous plaît*."

"Range is ten nautical miles. Torpedo run time, four minutes, fifteen seconds," his weapons officer reported. "Firing."

Jules smirked.

The shooting was done, so Marco headed for the bridge. Being able to handle a lot of operations in the light of day still struck him as weird. He was used to operating in a world where only subs wanting to die came to the surface. Not that he'd ever faced submarine combat, but Marco'd snuck into a tricky place or two in his time.

Fortunately, the complicated stuff was done for today. So he headed out onto *Fletcher's* port bridge wing, relishing the taste of the sea air on his tongue.

"Looks like *Dunham's* finally got that Indian under tow," he said to Nancy. "Does it make me a bad person to wish we'd fucking sank the thing? I didn't need the crown of being the first admiral to take an Indian destroyer intact." Marco eyed *Chennai*, his lip curling.

She laughed. "And here I thought admirals were in it for the glory, sir."

"Glory's for goddamned politicians and ass lickers. I'm just trying to keep you people breathing." He shrugged, eyes still on the torched-up Indian destroyer. "Besides, she's a *Kolkata*-class. Those little shit cans have been around since 2014. We probably stole most of their secrets already."

"Do you ever stop complaining?" Nancy cocked her head. "I think my teenagers are happier with their lot in life."

Marco laughed. "A bitching sailor is a happy sailor, Captain."

"If this is you happy, I hate to think—"

Light flashed to the left; Marco's head whipped around just before a *boom* shook the air and the shockwave hit him.

Marco staggered as it hit, but he almost didn't feel it. Four miles away, out on their flank, the remnants of a ship—with her keel now broken and fuel, sailors, and God knew what spilling out of the breach amidships—burned brightly against the horizon.

"Was that *Bogan*?" he asked like an idiot.

"Oh, no," Nancy whispered.

They stood in shocked silence for five heavy seconds. Numbers whirled through Marco's mind. *Bogan* had a crew of almost one hundred fifty, and torpedo hits caused fires, flooding, and conflagrations that turned men and women to ash. Even worse, the Aussies had just lost another frigate on top of the territory, people, and ships they'd already lost. How much more could Australia—

"That was another sub!" The words burned off his tongue like acid. Marco whirled to face Nancy. "That was a fucking torpedo! We've got an enemy left out here—launch the ready helo and all ships commence search!"

Nancy darted into the bridge. Marco stole one last look at *Bogan's* burning grave, just in time for the crashing and splintering of more metal to split the air with a metallic scream.

His stomach dropped, vomit rising, as he thought about another one of his ships being torpedoed. But then Marco turned to see *Chennai's* bow stuck in *Jason Dunham's* stern, and he almost laughed out loud.

"Could today get any fucking stranger?" he asked the air. "What the hell are those ass clowns up to over there?"

Fletcher's port lookout, a young boatswain's mate with freckles, red hair, and horn-rimmed glasses, stared at him with wide eyes. "Wish I knew, Admiral."

"You and me both, kid." Marco shook his head. "Time I headed down to CIC and sorted out this mess. You hold down the fort here, okay?"

"I, uh, think that's the OOD's job, sir."

"Good kid." Marco grinned, slapped the girl on the shoulder, and darted through the door before sprinting down the ladder to *Fletcher's* CIC.

The hunt for *Bogan's* killer was fruitless, despite four hours of searching. But it didn't shoot another one of his ships, so Marco chalked that up to a dubious win. Recovering *Bogan's* fifty-two survivors fell to the surviving destroyers, however, and Marco forced himself to look them in the face and apologize for missing another enemy submarine just minutes after *Parramatta* sank the other.

At least no one died when *Jason Dunham* and *Chennai* kissed. The hole from *Chennai's* bow was even above the waterline and easily patched, so Marco didn't even bother to write home about that mini disaster.

How could winning a battle end with such a bad feeling? Shaking himself out of the funk was hard while the rest of the task force celebrated. Marco could only think of the dead sailors on *Bogan* and wonder where that mystery sub had gone. Still, reporting a victory was nicer than calling the boss to report a defeat.

These days, his standards for a good day were so low that the bar was looking for the fucking Mariana Trench.

The slight vibration under the soles of his sneakers was a nice feeling.

Submariners always wore sneakers. While the "skimmers," or sailors on surface ships, might wear steel-toed boots to protect them from bumping their precious toes on metal bulkheads or equipment, silence was of the essence on a boat. Steel toes meeting metal meant metallic-sounding *clomps* that an enemy could hear, which was why sneakers were the name of the game underway.

Alex loved going to work in coveralls that felt like well-worn pajamas and sneakers...even when work was war.

Thirty-five knots was the fastest Alex ever dared push his aging submarine. With her keel laid in 1998, *Jimmy Carter* had hit a few bumps—and redesigns—on the road on the way to her commissioning in 2005. Conventional wisdom said not to keep a nuclear submarine in service more than thirty years, but here she was, rolling through the water thirty-four years past her commissioning—and *forty*-one years after her keel was laid.

"Captain, I'm nervous about sustaining this speed for so long," George said for the fifth time since *Jimmy Carter* started her sprint.

"Do you have a faster way to get to *Skate's* survivors?" Alex asked, popping a hard candy into his mouth. Chewing things always helped him think and, in this case, stopped him from saying things to his XO that a captain shouldn't.

George wrung his hands. "Sir, we can't help them at all if we go to pieces on the way."

"I think that's being a bit dramatic." Alex smiled. "We'd pop a few leaks first for sure."

"*Captain*." The word was a whine fit for the puppy Alex had never bought his daughters.

He sighed. "We're three minutes out. It's a little late to slow down now, and Smiley's taken the load like a champ. She's done so well that I almost wish I'd pushed her all the way to full power."

George shuddered. "I'm glad common sense prevailed."

Alex chose not to reply, thinking about *Skate's* crew. This wasn't the previous war; they wouldn't be bobbing in the water without survival gear. Or at least they *shouldn't* be, not if the lifeboats stored in watertight compartments along the topline of *Skate's* hull automatically deployed. But they hadn't on *Georgia*, had they?

Some captains feared the explosive bolts in those compartments would activate if they dove anywhere near test depth—thereby giving the boat's position away—and welded them shut. It was a dumb choice, in Alex's opinion. Sure, getting off a sinking submarine was unlikely. But if anyone *did*, they needed those life rafts to survive. Tommy Sandifer had been one of those captains who welded one of the compartments shut because it rattled when deeper than eight hundred feet, and it hadn't done *Georgia* any favors. The damage was only compounded when the compartments he left alone failed to open properly. The life rafts that made to the surface had been damaged, barely enough to keep Tommy's crew alive.

But they *had* survived the sinking, mostly because Tommy was wise enough to hit the roof with his boat when the torpedoes were incoming and because *Jimmy Carter* got there fast.

As nations developed faster submarines, they needed faster torpedoes. Those torpedoes had to fit in the same tubes the old ones did, which meant *something* had to give in terms of space. Miniaturization was great, but they could only downsize engines so much and fuel still required the same amount of space.

That meant smaller warheads and increased survival rates.

"All ahead one-third," Maggie ordered.

"All ahead one-third, aye," Master Chief Morton replied. "Engines ahead one-third for five knots."

George's sigh of relief was audible as he sagged against the bulkhead.

"Very well." Maggie turned to Alex as *Jimmy Carter* coasted down in speed. "We're approaching *Skate's* position, Captain."

"Very well. Make your depth two hundred feet and stream the comms wire. Scan bridge-to-bridge radio on all frequencies." He turned to George. "Stand by for the rescue-and-assistance detail."

"Aye, sir." At least George didn't argue with that, heading aft to get the team together at the hatch aft of the sail.

Maggie conned *Jimmy Carter* upward, the gigantic submarine easing her way into shallow water. Once there, they streamed their four-hundred-foot "wire," which was really a long, waterproof antenna designed to drag behind the submarine and allow her to communicate with the surface.

"Nothing on bridge-to-bridge, Captain," comms reported.

Alex nodded, meeting Maggie's eyes. "That was always a Hail Mary. Let's come to periscope depth."

"Periscope depth, aye, sir." Maggie did her usual bang-up job of bringing the submarine the last few feet to the surface, at which point Alex raised *Jimmy Carter's* old-fashioned Type 2 periscope himself.

Somehow, over the months he'd been in command of his ancient beast, he'd come to find that hydraulic hiss comforting. The *Virginias* Alex grew up on had always-up periscopes. You didn't have to look through the traditional eyepiece for those; instead, you got a high-tech, high-definition monitor. The periscope stand didn't even take up an ungodly amount of real estate in control because the scope didn't have to go back down. It just stayed up.

Compared to a *Virginia*, *Jimmy Carter's* attack center was cramped full of old equipment and the aforementioned periscope stand, which was huge and always in the way. But Alex didn't mind. Looking through that eyepiece felt *real* as he pulled the handles down and started the sidestepping walk that brought the scope through a 360-degree look at their surroundings.

"It's getting dark," he said without pulling his eye away. "What time is sunset?"

He heard Maggie pulling up information on the computer. "Not for another two hours. But last METOC report says we might get storms."

"Good thing we're here to find these poor bastards, then." Alex shuddered, trying not to think of the last storm he'd faced topside on *Jimmy Carter* and the sailors they'd lost in that horrible evolution with *Safeguard*. "Sitting on the surface through a storm is a special kind of hell."

"Isn't your wife a destroyer driver?" Maggie asked.

"Yeah, she's got some weird kinks."

Maggie giggled. "I so didn't need to know that, Captain."

Alex grinned. "Ask bold questions, get unexpected answers, Lieutenant. You don't want to know what they say about Norwich— Got 'em! Bearing two-four-four!" His fingers danced over the controls for the laser rangefinder. "Range thirty-three hundred yards and change. Come left and calculate intercept."

"Left standard rudder, steady course two-three-zero," Maggie ordered.

It seemed to take forever for *Jimmy Carter* to settle onto the new course. Alex spent that time studying the survivors on the periscope. His heart sank.

"There's only one raft," he whispered.

"Captain?" Master Chief Morton turned away from watching the helm, his brow wrinkled in concern.

"She should have three rafts, each able to carry about sixty. There's only one on the surface...and it doesn't look full." Alex swallowed.

Were there swimmers in the water? He couldn't see them. Hopefully the people in the raft were relatively dry.

"Shit," Morton said. "Well, we all know that it's hard to get off one of these puppies when they go under, no matter what they say at the Sub School. Those Steinke Hoods make for nice stories home to Ma and Pop, but you got to get close to the surface to use 'em—and have enough time."

"Not to mention the poor bastards who probably ate it when the torpedo hit," Chief Pamela Hill, the battle stations chief of the watch, said with a grimace.

"Yeah, let's not talk about them." Maggie looked a little green, much to Alex's surprise, but she shook it off.

They'd all talked to the *Georgia* sailors about the chaotic hell of getting off their boat while it sank...and no one wanted to think much about that experience.

"COB, will you head back aft and join the R&A detail? We may have some wounded up there, and I'm sure the XO won't mind an experienced hand," Alex said.

"You got it, Captain," Morton replied, handing his watch over to Chief Hill.

No one commented on Alex's sudden desire to give George some forceful backup; no one needed to. Control was largely silent until *Jimmy Carter* settled on her new course, creeping toward the survivors.

Alex leaned into the bitch box and said: "Conn, Sonar, anyone around us?"

"Conn, Sonar, conditions are going down the shitter," Wilson replied. "Is there a storm brewing topside?"

"The weather weanies seem to think so, yeah. Give a shout if anyone approaches."

"Sonar, aye— Wait, I've got a distant contact, barely making any way. Surface ship, but tonals match a Russian *Yantar*. Range over thirty thousand yards, probably outside visual range."

"A spy ship?" Maggie's head jerked up from looking at the chart.

"Affirmative. They've got a tick on the sixty hertz line due to a wonky generator design. Hard to disguise. TACMEMOs say they like to pretend to be fishing vessels, assuming you can see one up there."

"Fuck." Alex's eyes flicked to the plot, where a diamond-shaped icon blinked to life fifteen miles off *Jimmy Carter's* port bow. Here it was. An enemy ship he could shoot. "What's the max speed on a *Yantar*?"

"Twenty-five knots, give or take a few," Maggie replied without looking it up.

Alex chewed his lip. He didn't need to do math. Fifteen nautical miles was the Mark 48 CBASS torpedo's maximum range. Even if he stepped a torp's speed down to conserve fuel, it wouldn't have terminal speed to *catch* the *Yantar* after reaching it. Of course, if the *Yantar* didn't see it coming and didn't move and a fucking miracle happened, he might just get *Jimmy Carter's* first kill.

Mights and maybes did not equate to good tactics. If he missed, the *Yantar* could call for help...which might arrive right when his boat was on the surface and at her most vulnerable.

Alex's stomach twisted and gurgled, tying itself into a knot of anxiety. He'd have to close the range to prosecute...and that meant leaving the survivors in the water with bad weather coming in. That could kill them, and what would he gain? A little notoriety for sinking a spy ship that couldn't fight back? The odds of that *Yantar* changing the course of the war were infinitesimal.

There was only one raft. How much had *Skate's* sailors suffered already?

Alex straightened. "Officer of the Deck, surface the ship."

"Surface the ship, aye!"

Jimmy Carter's matte-black form broke the surface just minutes later. Wartime procedures were much faster than the peacetime ones they'd replaced. Back then, it took an hour to get to the surface. Now, you could do it in less than fifteen minutes if you were in a hurry—and Alex was.

"It's not worth the risk of creeping in to shoot that *Yantar* first, is it, Captain?" Maggie leaned in close to ask.

His smile was thin. "You read my mind, Nav."

"Someone's got to." She shrugged and didn't insult the XO, which he was grateful for.

In a just world, Maggie would be his second-in-command. She had the guts and the brains, not to mention the tactical acumen, but she was worlds too junior. And no one would listen to Alex if he complained about George, anyway.

George had been sent to *Jimmy Carter* because he was on the bottom of the barrel. It wasn't like the bureau of personnel would be *surprised*.

Alex put his eye back to the periscope to hide his scowl. "Deck's awash! Down scope."

The periscope slid away without complaint, which was more than Alex could say for himself. But he had a job to do.

Yantar had crept in to ten miles away by the time the American submarine breached the surface. Her captain swore.

"Colonel, we do not have any weapons to overcome a submarine." He wiped sweaty hands on his trousers, not liking the narrow-eyed glare his superior directed his way.

"Not even a surfaced one?"

"No." He shook his head a little too convulsively and had to force himself to stop. Colonel Nikolin was unnerving, even when one was his countryman—and his all-too-constant companion. But the captain knew that Nikolin viewed *Yantar* as a transport vessel, nothing more. He was polite to the crew, but a statue would have been warmer.

Not to mention far less terrifying.

The captain did not want to know what happened in the holding cells belowdecks. He had long since ordered his crew to stay away from them, instead letting Nikolin's intelligence personnel take care of things. It was better that way.

Russia had a history of dealing harshly with her enemies. The captain could understand that without wanting to *watch* it.

When those cold eyes did not leave him, the captain shook his head again. "A surfaced submarine can still shoot us, Colonel. We have a few depth charges, but no rockets to fire them with." *They're expensive*, he didn't say. Nikolin had almost endless funds, but no one was putting visible weapons on intelligence trawlers that frequently disguised themselves as fishing trawlers or private yachts. "We would have to be directly above the submarine to drop them."

The colonel pursed his lips. "That seems unwise."

"*Very*. They can shoot at us there." The captain was a surface officer at heart. If he commanded *Yantar* well—and avoided pissing off Nikolin and his powerful patrons—his next command would be a destroyer.

"Very good. We will watch from here."

The captain did not have the courage to mention the submarine might see them. Instead, he stopped his engines and counted on drifting silently and the submarine's low height of eye to save his life.

Meanwhile, Nikolin watched the enemy submarine with rapt fascination.

"All stop. Initiate station keeping," Alex ordered.

The wind was picking up. It was easy to feel from where he stood in the sail, crammed up there with Maggie and two lookouts. But the weather wasn't bad yet, and *Jimmy Carter* was close enough to *Skate's* lone raft that Morton got lines to the survivors on the second try.

His eyes searched the horizon, but *Jimmy Carter's* height of eye was too low. There was no way to see the *Yantar* from here, which was a pity. If he could see it, he could shoot it. That would've been a nice two-for-one special...but Alex put it out of his mind. He had fellow submariners to rescue.

Today, both of *Jimmy Carter's* assigned rescue swimmers were hale and healthy, so Alex was in a captain's traditional place on the bridge. With only one raft to recover from, there was no need to launch their small boat, either. It stood ready on deck, in case anyone went over, but the rescue ladders faked out on *Jimmy Carter's* port side could reach the raft, so why bother with the boat?

"Wow, they look like they've been out here a lot more than eleven hours," Maggie said.

Alex followed her gaze. The sailors—he counted forty-one—in the raft were huddled together, some wearing exposure suits, but most in coveralls. Most were wet, pale, and several cradled limbs that seemed to be broken.

"Shit, I think you might be right," he whispered, suddenly feeling better about ignoring the spy ship. "What if the buoy went off late?"

Maggie swallowed. "They're not supposed to do that."

"Lot of things aren't supposed to happen." Alex couldn't help looking aft to where *Jimmy Carter's* SUBMISS/SUBSUNK buoy was barely visible just forward of her rudder. It was a little black thing, round and innocent looking. But that buoy was the only thing that would tell the world that they *might* be alive if Alex went and got Smiley sunk.

"I don't like thinking about that." Maggie shivered. "You know, I wanted to lateral transfer into intelligence, right?"

"You did?" Alex twisted to look at her, his eyebrows rising. "Why?"

"You're asking me that when we're looking at those poor guys?"

"Since I haven't seen a request from you, I assume you meant before the war."

"Yeah." She grimaced. "I was on *Parche*, and I like the intel business. I think I'm pretty good at it, too. But the war started and needs must." Maggie shrugged. "My detailer told me I was a great candidate for a lat transfer, but it wasn't going to happen until the shooting stopped."

Alex felt his smile go crooked. "Well, you're a damned good submariner, too. I'm lucky to have you."

"Thanks, Captain." Maggie sighed. "I don't hate being a submariner. And I'm not afraid to do my duty, even when I see things like this"—she gestured at *Skate's* bedraggled crew struggling out of the raft—"or when friends die. It just wasn't the way I wanted to serve my country, that's all. I think I'd be better at other things."

"I can understand that."

Alex swallowed, also watching the survivors. Here they were again, doing what no other sub had done: rescuing what remained of their brothers and sisters from another boat. Saving forty lives *mattered*, even if it wasn't taking the fight to the enemy and helping end the war faster. There was no way of knowing what would've happened to *Skate's* people if *Jimmy Carter* hadn't come for them.

Maybe a surface ship would've found them. Eventually, Big Navy would've assigned someone to go looking, but assets were hard to come by, and subs didn't always leave survivors.

But he still wanted to do more. This wasn't the way he'd envisioned serving his country…and could even repeated rescue missions prove *Jimmy Carter's* worth?

His radio crackled. "Captain, XO, last survivor on board."

"Captain, aye. We're getting good at this." Alex shook off the morose thoughts. "Let's submerge the ship and get back to the convoy, Maggie. Then we can both get back to doing the things we didn't think we would."

She snorted. "I can't imagine how you haven't gone crazy with all this, Captain."

"I have no idea what you're talking about."

Yantar swung quietly in the wind as it picked up, her engines providing enough power to her screws so that she was barely making way. That held her mostly stationary, so that her captain and her…visitor could watch. Not that the colonel appreciated the sight.

"They are picking up the survivors, Colonel."

Yantar's captain had waited long moments before speaking, hoping irrationally that something might change. Alas, the American submarine had not made some stupid mistake.

"I can see that, Captain." Another man might have stressed the word *see* peevishly. Not Nikolin. His tone was even.

Deadly.

The captain swallowed. "What are your orders?"

"We will gain nothing by remaining here, so we will move south. Closer to where enemy submarines will sink so that we may reach their survivors faster." Nikolin walked over to the chart and studied it through narrowed eyes. "If the Americans are now sending submarines—which are quicker than we are, are they not?—to rescue their people, we must be less distant from the action."

"That does increase the danger." The captain licked his lips. He was not afraid of battle, but courting discovery in an almost-unarmed intelligence trawler was…foolish.

"We will pull into one of our friendly French ports to further disguise the ship as an innocent civilian vessel. Perhaps a new paint job." Nikolin's smile made him shiver. "I need more prisoners."

"May I ask why?"
"You may ask. But I will not answer."

Chapter 34

Declaring Victory Too Soon

Later, with *Jimmy Carter* back on course and heading for the convoy at a speed that made George twitchy, Alex headed aft to the mess decks. It was the one space large enough to hold all the survivors at once, and even then, it was tight. However, it was a lot bigger than the closet HMC "Doc" Chester and his junior corpsman called medical. Peeking in revealed *Skate's* waterlogged crew wrapped in blankets and wearing borrowed coveralls. Most clutched hot drinks, speaking quietly among themselves as *Jimmy Carter* sailors handed out food.

"Hey, Captain." Master Chief Morton stood outside the open doorway, his eyes missing nothing. "We've got some real worn-out friends here."

"They looked like it from the sail."

"Doc's worried about a couple of them." Morton grimaced. "XO is fretting like a mother hen. Want I should find something useful for him to do? I could grab him for a spot check of the midships port sonar array. Wilson says it's been twitchy."

Alex grimaced. "Does it have to be near Wilson? He and the XO are like gasoline and a match."

"Good point." Morton laughed. "I'm sure the engineer has something that needs clucking over if I ask him."

"Please do."

Was this routine for a captain? Conspiring to keep his XO busy so the man didn't drive him insane? Alex had no idea what normal looked like.

Shaking his head, he stepped into the wardroom while Morton made a beeline for the nearest phone to drag Marty into the conspiracy. Chief Chester stood off to the right, splinting a young man's arm as its owner gritted his teeth.

"How's it going, Doc?" Alex asked. Tradition demanded that the chief medical type on any seagoing vessel went by "Doc," even if they didn't have a medical degree. In Chester's case, he was a chief corpsman, which meant he was a cross between a nurse practitioner and a trauma expert. Chester spent most of his time doling out Motrin for random aches and pains, but sometimes, he really earned his keep.

"Could be worse, sir." Chester always wore an easy smile; he had the best bedside manner of any corpsman Alex had ever met. "Nothing life-threatening, though I'll be monitoring all our new passengers for heat stroke, dehydration, and the other fun things that come from escaping a sinking submarine."

"There's no need to be so casual about it, Chief." Chester's patient turned a dark glare on him and then flushed when he glanced at Alex. "Sorry, sir. I'm Lieutenant Steffano Seymour, Assistant Weapons Officer from *Skate*. Or I was." He grimaced. "I'm the senior survivor."

"No need to apologize, Lieutenant. I'm Alex Coleman. I can't imagine any of you have had a fun time these last couple days," Alex said. "I'm going to guess that you were in that raft for almost sixty hours?"

He'd checked the SUBMISS/SUBSUNK message before coming to visit, cursing himself for not noticing the key piece of information. The message indicated a *buoy launch* barely eleven hours before *Jimmy Carter* reached *Skate's* survivors, but the last video data recorder entry from *Skate* had been forty-eight hours before that.

Seymour swallowed. "I'm not sure why that's much of a guess, sir."

"I think your buoy stuck when you sank," Alex said as gently as he could. "It only launched eleven hours ago. We got the message about an hour ago after multiple attempts to reach you."

"Eleven *hours*?" All color drained out of Seymour's face. "We...yeah. We didn't..." He shook his head.

"I thought as much." Alex swallowed. "Can you tell me what happened?"

"Not too much to say, sir. We were hunting a pair of *Scorpenes* that were going after merchies traveling between Australia and the Red Sea. We got them cold, sank both, and then boom, out of nowhere, torpedoes bracketed us. The captain outfoxed the first pair, but the next ones got us." He shuddered. "She did an emergency blow right beforehand, and I think that's what let some of us get out. I don't remember much. Master Chief Waskiewicz dragged me out after I hit my head."

"And your arm," Chester put in. "It's broken in at least three places, Lieutenant. We'll need to x-ray it to make sure, but I don't have one on board."

"I'm sure we'll be able to transfer the survivors to one of the destroyers after we rejoin the convoy." Suddenly, George was by Alex's shoulder. "That would be proper, and they have better medical facilities."

"Not by much." Alex shoved down the need to glare at his XO. "I'm not sure if they've got x-ray machines or not, but destroyers don't have doctors, either."

George started. "They don't? Are you sure?"

"My wife commands one, remember?" Lord, for a man good with minutiae, George really only remembered trivia he *liked*.

"Right. Of course. But we'll still have to offload them." George shrugged. "No offense, Lieutenant."

Seymour cringed at George's dismissive tone, but he was young, wounded, and a little lost.

"We'll discuss that later." Now Alex did spear George with a *shut the hell up* glare before turning back to Seymour. "For now, if there's one thing *Jimmy Carter* has, it's plenty of space. We were designed to lug around a bunch of extra people, so we've got racks to spare for all of you. A few of you may have to put up in the torpedo room, but here on Smiley, the weapons room is rather palatial, so even then, you'll be in comfort. We'll take good care of you. No matter what happened, you're our brothers and sisters. Consider yourselves at home here."

"Thank you, sir," Seymour whispered.

"You concentrate on feeling better, Lieutenant." Alex smiled as reassuringly as he could. "We'll take care of your people. Doc Chester here may smile a lot, but he's good at what he does, and if you let him, he'll fix you right up."

"I will, sir."

"Excellent."

Nancy wasn't sure how she felt about mooring *at* Christmas Island.

The tiny harbor had two working piers, only one of which was big enough—and deep enough—for *Fletcher*. Admiral Rodriquez would've sent *Jason Dunham* in after that stupid little collision, but *Dunham* had a deeper draft, and she wasn't likely to leave again if low tide visited while she was moored.

Besides, the admiral really needed to talk to the people ashore. Ospreys from distant amphibious warships threw enough marines at the island to convince the Indians to surrender, which meant Admiral Rodriquez now had a lot of *other* Indians to haul around.

"You keep collecting prisoners, sir," she said as they walked down *Fletcher's* accommodations ladder two hours after sunset. "I'm starting to think you like it."

Rodriquez rolled his eyes. "Oh, go piss up a rope."

Nancy laughed. "Hard for a chick to do, Admiral."

"You're creative. You'll find a way."

"Looks like our marine friends are punctual." She pointed at the group walking toward the pier. "That's a new skill for them. Must be on the syllabus after shooting and coloring between the lines."

"Ha! Behave yourself, Captain. They've got guns, and I don't fucking fancy scraping you off the ground when that giant flattens you."

A grin split Nancy's face as she spotted the so-called giant leading the group of marine officers. "Oh, I think I'll mock that one extra hard."

"You got a death wish, girl, or is there something you're not telling me?" Rodriquez eyed her.

"Maybe both?" She put on her best innocent expression.

"Damn, you've gone salty. I'm going to guess you know that lurking tower of humanity, unless you're out to play David and Goliath or some other biblical nonsense," he said. "Give you a couple of victories, and then you get all uppity. Careful, or they'll go and make you an admiral."

Nancy shuddered dramatically. "I'll behave myself, sir. I promise."

"Ah ha! I found the threat that works!" Rodriquez returned the marines' salutes. "Gentlemen, I'm Admiral Rodriquez, commanding Task Force Twenty-Three. This here salty lady is Commander Nancy Coleman, captain of USS *Fletcher*, that lovely destroyer you see behind us. We've both had an extremely long day, so let's cut to the chase. Is the island secure?"

"Yes, sir, it is," the senior marine replied. "Lieutenant Colonel Paul Swanson, Commanding Officer, Second Reconnaissance Battalion."

Nancy tried not to snicker when Rodriquez grimaced over the strength in Paul Swanson's handshake. The hulking marine did it on purpose in first meetings, she knew. Even with flag officers.

"Paul." She grinned and offered her own hand, only to be swept up in a bear hug.

"Nancy! It's great to see you!"

"Put me down before I kick you in places unmentionable!" But the threat was ruined by a very un-captain-like giggle.

Paul obeyed. "I'll have you know that I *mightily* resisted the urge to swing you around."

"Good idea." Her glare was wasted on him.

Rodriquez cleared his throat. "I take it you two know each other."

"We're old classmates from the Wick, sir," Nancy said.

"Norwich University, class of 2022." Paul beamed. "We get around."

1 March 2039, off the coast of Christmas Island (Australia)

"You know, Freddie, there's such a thing as declaring victory too soon," Marco said. He was up in a rare video call with his old friend; Marco generally hated the things, preferring old-fashioned phone calls, but *Freddie* liked them, so he humored her.

Anything to get what he wanted.

She outranked him, too, which meant a "please" from Freddie was a polite kind of order, and while Marco thought she respected him enough—and there wasn't that much of a difference between two stars and three when you were one of the few admirals in the navy with a decent combat record and a head outside your own ass—he wasn't stupid.

Just ill-tempered and sometimes rude.

Freddie heaved a sigh that was obvious even over the bad connection bred by a destroyer's sliver of satellite bandwidth. It was amazing what they couldn't get right in the twenty-first fucking century.

"Last I checked, no one's saying we won anything," she said, trying to spear him with a glare. "Particularly the media."

Marco shrugged, unrepentant. "I saw that speech from the secretary of state about how we've won Australian territory back. Christmas Island has changed hands three times already. No promises it won't happen again."

"You going to run away that easily?"

"If they outnumber and gun me, bet your skinny ass I will. I don't have a fucking death wish. You've got to live so you can hand the piss-nuggets their head *next* time."

"Please God tell me you aren't calling the enemy that in public."

"No one's dumb enough to let me talk to the media, Freddie. I'm on a destroyer floating around in the middle of nowhere. The best part about Christmas Island is the lack of reporters."

Freddie laughed. "Definitely better for the navy." Then she sobered. "Why are you angry about the speech?"

"Because two good subs died to get us that shiny-assed victory, and I just watched their VDRs." Marco swallowed down bile. He hadn't enjoyed watching the video from either *Pacu* or *Florida*, though he'd forced himself to sit through both twice.

Nuru Okafor's loss burned; she'd been his protégé for years, and now a brilliant naval officer was fish food in the same harbor *Fletcher* occupied. Nuru's stoicism under pressure led directly to his success in destroying the Indian battle group that held Christmas Island just three days earlier...and as far as he could tell, none of her crew survived.

"Damn," Freddie whispered.

"You have no idea." The whisper sounded harsh even in his own ears; Marco blinked back the urge to weep. "They both never even got a chance to shoot at their killers, Freddie. Whoever shot them—probably the same cat, judging from the bearings—had super-fast torpedoes. Not as quick as the ones we still can't prove for sure the Russians have made work, but ones that go almost a hundred forty fucking knots." He forced a smile. "One-thirty-nine, to be exact."

"*What?*"

"Proof's in the pudding. Or in the video data recorders, if you want something less goddamned clichéd." Marco shook his head. "Our piddling old CBASSes go fifty-five knots, Freddie. For the love of fucking everything—God, Satan, the ancient Greeks if you want—please tell me there's something else coming. Otherwise our younger brothers and sisters are going out there with nothing but their dicks in their hands."

That earned him a narrow look. "Some of them don't even have that."

"Metaphorical dicks, then. Thanks for reminding me I'm a sexist prig."

"Don't change the subject," she said and then slumped in her chair in faraway Norfolk. "There are new torps on the way. In fact, they should be in theater now. The new Mark 84 Advanced Spearfish Variant, built by Lazark and AIB. Lazark has been manufacturing them since December."

Marco started, unable to believe his ears. "Then where the fuck are they?"

"I—I'm not sure." Freddie blinked.

He couldn't remember ever having seen Freddie Hamilton so uncertain, not even as a brand-new division officer with sexism stacked so high around her she couldn't see over it. Marco remembered those bad old days and didn't miss them.

"They better than what we currently got?" he asked, mostly to give her a chance to think. Marco Rodriquez would be the first to admit that he was an all-around asshole, but Freddie was his friend.

Maybe his best friend. She certainly put up with his crap better than most.

"They're not exactly a super-cavitating torpedo, but they top out at eighty-seven knots and have the same range as the Mark 48. They're already working on the next generation torp, but the 84 can fill the gap," Freddie replied. "At least it's faster than the subs it's chasing."

Marco snorted. "That's something."

Freddie looked down, checking something on her tablet. "There are hundreds in theater, some in Pearl but mostly in Perth. Let me get back to you on this."

"I'd appreciate that. I'm assuming I didn't get briefed in on these things earlier because I'm riding around on surface ships these days?"

"Need to know, Marco. You didn't."

"Let me sing you the song of how much I fucking love bureaucracy."

22 March 2039, Perth, Australia

They didn't manage to offload *Skate's* survivors, despite George's best efforts. Alex put them to work—gently, at first, and then had them join the watch rotation to keep their training current and their minds busy. Submarines didn't really have room for "shipriders," and it wasn't like there was a lot of entertainment—by the time he got them on the watchbill, *Skate's* sailors were ready to rip the bulkheads down in frustration.

Still, he hadn't expected it to take almost a month for *Jimmy Carter* to reach port again. If he had, he might've tried much harder to hand the survivors off to another ship—preferably one going back to Perth—much, *much* sooner. Making *Skate's* people ride around in *Jimmy Carter* was yet another way that Commodore Banks said he didn't care.

Would this be enough? A cold chill raced down Alex's spine. Three rescues, multiple downed aviators...

"Moored. Shift colors." The words echoed over *Jimmy Carter's* 1MC, drifting forward to where Alex and Maggie still stood in the sail of the giant submarine, which was now nestled against the least desirable pier in the Perth basin.

"One more in the bag." For once, Alex felt like he could smile after a convoy escort. They were finally back in Perth—after escorting *another* convoy all the way back—and the sun felt brighter than usual.

"Better than the last couple, sir," Maggie said. "I don't even feel like drinking myself into an early grave tonight."

He chuckled. "You read my mind."

Rescuing *Skate's* survivors put a pep in his crew's step, and Alex felt rejuvenated by it, too. He was sad that they couldn't rescue more of their fellows, but only pulling forty-one sailors out of the water wasn't anyone on *Jimmy Carter's* fault. Those who went down with *Skate* went down fast, and he couldn't do anything about that.

At least he'd saved those who made it out.

"Captain? New change of operational command message for us," the radio watchstander said, holding out a tablet.

"Thanks," Alex said absentmindedly and then almost keeled over.

"You hear the good news? We're CHOPping to SUBRON three-one. No more random visits from the squadron talking about decommissioning us," Alex said. The farewell message from SUB-

RON 29 had arrived that morning, and Commodore Banks hadn't even bothered to tell them *job well done* for rescuing *Skate's* crew. He just sent along reassignment information for them.

Good riddance to Jaylen Banks. Alex had never even met the man face-to-face, and he hated him.

But the threat to *Jimmy Carter* was gone. Sure, they'd probably continue to get the short end of the stick when it came to missions...but at least his boat would survive. That was something.

Hell, with a war on, that was *everything*.

"I did, sir. But then, I do own radio." Maggie flashed him a smile. "I also read the Convoy 687 formation message, unfortunately."

"Yeah, I couldn't hide from that one, either." He grimaced. "A two-day turnaround—just enough time to load up supplies and get the *Skate* crew safely to the hospital."

"Pity we're not one of those 'fleet boats' they send out on war patrols. Rumor says COMSUBPAC is talking about mandated rest periods between patrols now," Maggie said.

"You hear all the best rumors."

Alex didn't doubt it was true, though. He'd read enough patrol reports—and seen enough VDR dumps from dead subs—to know that fatigue was a killer. John sure talked about it often enough, and *his* boat got genuine breaks between the action.

Not that *Jimmy Carter* got to see action. Their two rescues, *Georgia* and *Skate*, were probably going to be the highlights of their war. Not breaking things in frustration was hard, but he was sure as hell not going to be Chris Kennedy.

Particularly not with *Kansas* sitting across the pier. Idly, Alex wondered who Kennedy pissed off to get stuck out here on the ass end of nowhere, but the list was probably long.

"Well, I've got a good one for you now. That's a sea lion sitting on *Bluefish's* ass."

"What?" Alex twisted around to look at the sub aft of *Jimmy Carter*, and sure enough, a giant brown sea lion with a golden mane lay sunning itself on the back end of the other boat.

He blinked. And then he blinked again, but the image didn't disappear.

"Is that an Australian sea lion?" Alex asked when Maggie only giggled.

"Is there a difference?" she asked.

"Yeah, these puppies are endangered." He shrugged. "My younger daughter's big on saving endangered species. Used to get all kinds of junk mail about it."

"Junk mail." Maggie sighed. "One of the few constants of the universe. I had a weird mortgage refinancing thing find me *here* for a house I sold two years ago."

Alex chuckled, leaning against the edge of the sail to watch the sea lion. It seemed to be asleep—not that he was an expert—basking in the afternoon sun on *Bluefish's* flat aft deck.

"You still thinking about lat transferring to intel?" he asked.

Maggie made a face. "I'd love to, but I don't think they'd let me."

"I'd offer to put in a good word for you, but my opinion doesn't hold much weight these days." Alex's eyes drifted right, landing on *Kansas*, before he could stop them.

"I thought you had a good tour on *Kansas*, sir."

Alex rubbed the back of his neck. "Most of it. But let's just say that Commander Kennedy and I aren't exactly exchanging Christmas cards."

"Oh."

Lord only knew what bullshit Kennedy was up to these days. His hotheadedness hadn't yet led him to killing the wrong people…at least as far as Alex knew. But he wasn't exactly what Alex would call *strategic*, either.

I wonder if Admiral Hamilton is still his fairy godmother? The thought stuck in his mind even when Alex tried to shake it away. Hamilton sure had been quick to take Kennedy's side in the first fiasco at Armistice Station, and the second one sure hadn't done anything to change her mind about Alex.

At least he had command. And he hadn't gone crazy, either, which had to be worth something. Alex forced a smile. "I think I'm going to sneak off the boat for a little bit—I've got a good friend who's in port, and we're meeting at the O-Club. Got any plans?"

Maggie's eyes crinkled. "You've gone and forgotten that I've got the duty tonight, haven't you?"

Alex chuckled. "I had. But it's good to be king."

"Gee, thanks, Captain."

"Not a problem."

Captains didn't stand duty, but it went without saying that Alex was always on call. Today, however, he planned on getting away from *Jimmy Carter* for a bit. *Fletcher* was underway, so he couldn't hang out with Nancy, but Teresa O'Canas was a good second choice.

"Anything I need to know before you head out, sir?"

"Nah, let everyone bounce for the night. Tomorrow will be the stores on load to end all stores on loads." Alex sighed. "A two-day bender and they couldn't even have food lined up for today and weapons tomorrow. Everything's coming at once."

"You didn't hear, sir? No extra torpedoes coming our way. We'll still sail with the twenty-eight we have. Benji just got a message."

"And the good news keeps on coming." Alex glanced up at the sky and made himself smile. "Forget I'm whining, Nav. It's un-captain-y of me."

She snickered. "Your secret's safe with me."

"Call me if you need anything. I'm heading down."

"Yes, sir. Hopefully, it'll be a quiet night. I could use some sleep."

Maggie did look tired; there were dark circles under her eyes, and her hair was even more unruly than usual. She didn't look bad enough to worry about—part of their job included functioning on too much coffee and too little sleep—but her fatigue only underscored how important it was to give his people some time off.

If only Alex could find some.

"I think we all could."

Patting her on the shoulder, Alex headed down the ladder and for his stateroom. He had a few emails to check before he could bounce.

Norfolk, Virginia

Admiral Winifred Hamilton spent entirely too long staring at the paneled wall in her office before she cleared her throat.

"You got any friends in the fleet, Maria?" Freddie asked.

It was an act of desperation, and she knew it. Admirals weren't supposed to lean on their aides for information like this—particularly not when said aid was due to depart in less than a week. But Maria smiled.

"I've got a couple, ma'am. Where are you looking for them to be?"

"Preferably on COMSUBPAC's staff." She scowled. Spying on one's fellow admiral and subordinate was *not* the right thing to do.

But it was necessary.

"Sure. I know his ops officer. Karla McCoy was my CO on *Oklahoma*. We stay in touch."

Freddie pinched the bridge of her nose. Captain McCoy had a reputation as a straight shooter. That was why she was the N-3, or Operations Officer, for Commander, Submarine Forces Pacific.

Asking a good officer to betray her superior was a risk, because good officers were generally *loyal* officers—at least when their bosses were worthy of loyalty.

But *was* Vice Admiral Brown worthy of that loyalty?

Freddie worried her lower lip between her teeth. Not if he was doing what she thought he was.

She wanted him to be worthy. She *hated* the idea of incompetent admirals making a hard war even harder. But she didn't always get what she wanted, did she?

"Ask Captain McCoy if Admiral Brown is sitting on a cornucopia of Mark 84 torpedoes," she said. "And ask her to keep the fact that we're asking to ourselves, if you would."

"I'd be glad to, ma'am. They're six hours behind us in Pearl, so I'll call before I leave today."

"Thank you."

Freddie turned back to the thorny problem of America's submarine war and felt no regrets.

Finally, Alex had time to settle in and catch up on some email not associated with work. Sitting down sideways in his stateroom chair, he pulled up his wife's latest and started reading.

Nancy's battle had gone well, and she even got to hang out with Paul Swanson in the aftermath. Alex pushed down a surge of jealousy as he read her latest email, grimacing. Damn, he was proud of her, but when was his chance going to come?

Rescuing *Skate's* survivors felt nice, but Alex burned to—

His radio crackled. "Captain, Officer of the Deck, uh, you might want to come up here, sir."

"On my way." Staring at Nancy's email wasn't going to improve his mood, anyway, so Alex headed topside to the quarterdeck.

Jimmy Carter had been in port for two hours, and Alex was almost done digging his way out of the email hole. That meant the in-port watch was set, and Lieutenant (junior grade) Elena Alvaro was the officer of the deck. Elena was Alex's damage control officer and easily the top division officer on board. She was usually solid as a rock, too, which meant the urgency in her request set Alex's teeth on edge.

Warm Perth air hit him in the face when he arrived on the quarterdeck, carrying the ever-present smell of the salt, sea life, and diesel fuel. But Alex paid it no mind, instead focusing on the knot of sailors gathered on *Jimmy Carter's* outboard side, staring at *Bluefish*.

A shout carried over from the other boat as a chief petty officer raced aft toward the open engine room hatch. "Is anything broken?"

"How the fuck should I know, chief?" a young officer, probably their officer of the deck, replied.

"Is anyone down there?"

A cry echoed up from the engine room, only to be drowned out by a roar.

"What the hell is going on, DCA?" Alex asked. "Anyone care to tell me why we haven't called away security alert yet?"

Elena Alvaro turned to face him, her dark face red with the effort of holding back giggles. "The sea lion fell down the engine room hatch, sir."

"The what?"

"The one that was sunning itself on *Bluefish*." A snicker exploded before she smothered it. "It rolled over in its sleep and fell down."

Alex's jaw dropped. "Oh, shit."

"You want me to call away security alert for this, Captain?" Elena gestured vaguely at the sailors running back and forth on *Bluefish*'s deck.

"No." Alex shook his head. "No, we might as well watch the show."

No one bothered to tell Lieutenant Bobby O'Kane that every other sub on the pier was watching the Best Entertainment Since *Down Periscope 2*. They didn't need to. He could feel their beady little eyes watching as he stood helplessly on *Bluefish's* aft deck along with half of the boat's duty section.

Everyone stationed forward in the boat thought it was hilarious. The engineers were busy experiencing their worst nightmare. Bobby, however, was having the worst day by far.

"What a day to be the command duty officer." His shoulders slumped.

"Hey, at least it's not your engine room, man." Lieutenant Lou Cooper heaved a sigh. "That beast's going to make a royal mess down there."

"I'm still the unlucky guy who gets to tell the captain. He's going to be doing cartwheels."

"Has he picked up yet?"

"Nah. He's out with his wife. Probably turned his phone off." Bobby didn't mention that Commander Peterson would probably blame them for that once he *did* realize there was a thousand-pound sea lion hammering at precious equipment in his submarine's engine room. He didn't need to. *Everyone* knew.

Flesh hit metal; more thrashing came from below, and Bobby inched forward, peering down two levels into *Bluefish's* engine room. He glimpsed the sea lion's tail as it whipped into something, and then the creature grunted in pain before howling in fury.

"Poor guy. He must feel like a ship in a bottle."

"Sucks more for our ship to be the bottle," Lou said. "I hate to think about what he's breaking down there."

"At least the reactor's cold?"

"You do know that nuclear reactors are hard to break, right?" Lou eyed Bobby like he was an excitable child. "You graduated from power school."

"Yeah, but it was a while ago. I'm a navigator these days. I dumped that knowledge like the One Ring going into Mount Doom." Bobby shrugged as innocently as he could. He loved getting a rise out of his roommate; unlike his predecessor, Lou was a good friend and a brilliant officer.

Lou rolled his eyes. "You really are—"

The *Star Wars* theme belting out of Bobby's phone cut him off, and he almost ignored it until he saw Commander Peterson's name on the display. "Hey, look, it's my funeral theme." He grinned before sobering and answering the phone. "Lieutenant O'Kane, sir."

"What's this I hear about a *sea lion* in the engine room?" Peterson's voice couldn't have been more nasally if he held his nose. "I do hope the shutdown reactor operator is still on station."

Bobby gulped. "Sir, there's a thousand-pound enraged marine animal in there." He hit the mute button and looked at Lou. "You got the SRO out, right?"

"Of course I did."

"And that's a multi-*million* dollar nuclear reactor, Mister O'Kane." Peterson said Bobby's name like it was a curse. "Put the engineer on."

"Yes, sir." Bobby licked his lips and handed the phone to Lou. "He wants to talk to you."

Lou took the phone with a resigned expression. "Engineer here, sir." He paused to listen, grimacing. "Sir, the SRO evacuated the space—no, sir. Captain, I believe it is unsafe—"

Bobby could hear Peterson's biting tone without being able to understand the words, but he could imagine the insults to Lou's professionalism rolling off the captain's tongue. And yeah, the crowd staring from the pier made everything *so much* better. What a great time to feel small.

Finally, Lou said: "Respectfully, Captain, I believe it is unsafe to send any of my sailors into the space with a sea lion present. We are monitoring the reactor remotely from control for now."

"I gave you an order!" Now Bobby could hear Peterson's snarl. "If you won't send someone, *you* go take the watch!"

Lou's face twitched so hard Bobby thought he might spit. "Aye, sir. I will take the watch."

"Good!"

There was nothing left to say, because Peterson hung up and Lou handed the phone back to Bobby.

Bobby stared. "No way are you going down there."

"I said I'd take the watch. I didn't say when."

"I, uh...wow. Yeah. Here's to another day, saving *Bluefish* from *Bluefish* Actual." Bobby forced a smile and then checked his texts. "Good news is that the guys from the aquarium should be here in ten. Might've told the captain that if he'd given me the chance."

Lou snorted. "I'll take the watch after they tranq yonder angry beastie. Someone should be down there to make sure the crane operators don't swing it into anything vital, anyway."

"Yeah, that reminds me to call port ops and schedule that crane." Bobby glanced at the crowd. "At least then we'll have safety reasons to make those jerks go away."

"C'mon, Bobby. It's the best sea story of the war. We'll laugh about this later."

"*Someone* will, anyway."

Epilogue: Distinguished Gallantry and Valor

24 March 2039, CSF Headquarters, Norfolk, Virginia

"Did Captain McCoy get back to you?" Freddie asked the next morning, nursing her second cup of tea between meetings. She had a senator next, and then it was onto the Bureau of Personnel telling her how they were going to not be able to man the next nine *Ceroes* planned to commission next year. They were already behind on the eight for 2039.

When everyone talked about American industry or self-sufficiency before the war, they always assumed that manufacturing parts and building ships or submarines would be the bottleneck. Not people.

"Funny you should ask." Maria laughed bitterly. "She emailed me last night. Much faster than I expected her to."

"Oh?" A shiver ran down Freddie's spine.

"There's a warehouse in Pearl with seven hundred forty Mark 84 torpedoes inside. None have been sent to boats on patrol."

Freddie threw her tablet at the wall, shattering the screen irreparably. Neither she nor Maria cared.

Naval Base Perth, Perth, Australia

There were no bodies to bury. There never were.

But there was always a memorial. Submariners always gathered out at Cliff Point, just outside the navy base, to mourn their own. HMAS Stirling—or Perth Naval Station—was located on Garden Island, which was seventy-seven percent nature preserve. That meant there were a lot of quiet places to meet.

Alex stepped out of his Jeep and straightened his dress whites. George, riding with him, did the same, and they walked in silence to where the other senior submariners were gathered near the shore. Dozens joined him; every captain and XO in port always came to every memorial.

It wasn't required, but it was the right thing to do. And your peers would never forgive you if you skipped one.

The wind whipped around them, almost knocking a few covers off. Despite that, Commodore Amanda Madison stood straight-backed and regal in her dress whites; one might have thought her at a parade if not for her ashen-white face. She commanded Submarine Squadron Thirty-One and was Alex's new boss. To her left stood Commodore Adel Karimi, commander of SUBRON Twenty-Seven. But there was no sign of the third squadron commander based in Perth...and from what Alex had heard, Commodore Banks rarely attended the memorials.

Even when his boats went down, like *Skate* had.

"We're here to mourn our brothers and sisters on eternal patrol," Madison said, her voice hoarse. "In the last two months, we have lost *Darter, Skate, Pacu, Florida, Gato, and Grunion*. Only *Skate* and *Grunion* had any survivors. Together, these five boats represent five hundred thirteen sailors lost to the deep."

Everyone was silent. Alex swallowed, thinking of the hollowed-out eyes of *Skate's* survivors. Then a slight scuffing came from his right, and he snuck a glance over. Commander Wade Peterson, from *Bluefish*, was tracing impatient circles in the sand with one toe.

"Admiral Hamilton has decided to make *Darter's* video data recorder logs available to all officers in command—or in the command track—for training purposes." Madison's glare swept the crowd. "Needless to say, if these logs are released to the media or make rounds in the fleet for *entertainment* purposes, there will be consequences."

Alex swallowed. Did he want to watch *Darter* die? He wasn't sure. Yet Kurt Kins had become a legend in his short time in command for taking the fight to the enemy every chance he had. There had to be something to learn from that.

"Is there a reason for releasing them?" Commander Brenda Vicar from *Narwhal* asked. "It seems...macabre."

"No one's requiring you to view them, but I recommend it," Madison replied, her gray eyes steely. "We all know that our approach in this war has not been ideal. Our weapons are inferior. We have lost many friends. And few captains have found a balance between recklessness and valor. Commander Kins demonstrated great courage on *all* his patrols, and we can all learn from his successes."

And his failures, no one said. No one needed to.

Alex wished John were here. John Dalton was the one man who seemed to have found that balance Commodore Madison spoke of...but he was underway again.

"I'll watch them," he said without thinking. "We should learn what we can, every time we can."

Madison gave him a small smile. "Thank you, Commander."

Several others agreed, their voices quiet. No one really wanted to watch a friend or colleague die—the thought sent Alex's gut twisting with nerves—but they had an obligation to their crews, and their nation, to use every tool at their disposal.

"I have one last announcement before the chaplain takes over," Madison said. "I received confirmation this morning that Commander Kurt Kins will be posthumously awarded the Congressional Medal of Honor."

A hush ran through the crowd. No submariner had been awarded the Medal of Honor since World War II. Only eight submariners had *ever* won the nation's highest award for military valor, and the last had been Commander George Street in 1945.

Now Kurt Kins would be the ninth.

Alex's eyes flicked over his fellow submarine commanders. Would any of them be next? Would the U.S. Navy figure out how to fight this new war of the submarine without losing boat after boat? Sooner or later, they had to find a way to take the war to the enemy without losing their best.

Or was the next Medal of Honor winner doomed to be posthumous as well?

...to be continued in *Fire When Ready*, available for pre-order now!

Thank you so much for reading *The War No One Wanted!* I hope you enjoyed (and if you did, you wouldn't mind leaving a review). As an indie author, reviews mean the world to me – every single one is like getting a fresh baked cookie (and who doesn't like fresh baked cookies?). The story of Alex Coleman, *Jimmy Carter*, her crew, and all of our other favorite characters will return soon in *Fire When Ready*.

If you want another peek into the depths of World War III – specifically, the story of Medal of Honor winner Commander Kurt Kins and USS *Darter*, they are featured in the short story *Pedal to the Medal*. You can get it on Amazon OR you can get it for free by joining my mailing listat bit.ly/PTTMfree.

Also By

War of the Submarine
Before the Storm
Cardinal Virtues
The War No One Wanted
Fire When Ready (September 2023)
I Will Try (Coming Soon)

Read the serial version of *War of the Submarine* on Kindle Vella and get to start *I Will Try* (book 4) before anyone else!

War of the Submarine Shorts
Never Take a Recon Marine to a Casino Robbery (subscriber exclusive)
Pedal to the Medal

Age of the Legacy
Shade
Night Rider

Legacy Shorts:
Prelude to Conquest (subscriber exclusive)
The First Ride (subscriber exclusive)
City of Light (coming soon)

Alternate History
Against the Wind
Caesar's Command

Other Works
Agent of Change (Portal Sci-Fi with an Alternate History Twist)
Fido (Cozy Fantasy Serial, high on humor)

About R.G. Roberts

R.G. Roberts is a veteran of the U.S. Navy, currently living in Connecticut and working as a Manufacturing Manager for a major medical device manufacturer. While an officer in the Navy, R.G. Roberts served on three ships, taught at the Surface Warfare Officer's School, and graduated from the U.S. Naval War College with a masters degree in Strategic Studies & National Security, with a concentration in leadership.

She is a multi-genre author, and has published in military thrillers, science fiction, epic fantasy, and alternate history. She rode horses until she joined the Navy (ships aren't very compatible with high-strung jumpers) and fenced (with swords!) in college. Add in the military experience and history degree, and you get A+ anatomy for a fantasy author. However, since she also enjoyed her time in the Navy and loves history, you'll find her in those genres as well.

You can find R.G. Roberts' website at www.rgrobertswriter.com or find all her links at linktr.ee/rgroberts. From there, you can join her newsletters! Joining the newsletter will get you a free short story or novella, set in either the War of the Submarine or Age of the Legacy universes (or both, if you like both genres). Newsletters are a twice-a-month affair, so there won't be a ton of spam in your inbox, but you'll be the first to hear about sales, get sneak peeks of new writing, and get to read a few subscriber-only short stories, too!

Printed in Great Britain
by Amazon